"A wholly engrossing behind-the-scenes look at real life behind the pomp, power, and prestige of a high-powered law firm that wants to still play by a 1950s rule book."

—Emma McLaughlin and Nicola Kraus,
coauthors of *Citizen Girl* and *The Nanny Diaries*

"Smart, incisive, and fast-paced, *The Partner Track* is a sparklingly readable look at the inner workings of a Wall Street law firm—from the vantage point of a brainy, beautiful, and self-doubting Asian American associate. Wan has the remarkable ability to make you feel as if 'you are there'— inside the law firm, inside protagonist Ingrid Yung's head. I did not want to put this book down."

—Susan Cain, *New York Times* bestselling author of
Quiet: The Power of Introverts in a World That Can't Stop Talking

"Hell hath no fury like Helen Wan's savvy heroine in this terrific debut. We all know women like Ingrid Yung: the well-educated overachiever who does everything right to ensure a long, productive journey on a lucrative career path. But what happens when someone blows up the path? *The Partner Track* is a delicious, satisfying read for anyone who has fantasized about getting the better of the boss, the ex-lover, the corporate powers that be—or all three. Ingrid Yung has done it for all of us." —Kristin van Ogtrop, author of *Just Let Me Lie Down* and editor of *Real Simple*

Praise for *The Partner Track*

"Ms. Wan's prose is straightforward and unfussy. . . . But law firms don't lend themselves to lyricism; the pleasures of this novel lie in character and plot. Ingrid is plucky and appealing, likable but imperfect, with a rich backstory that explains her sensitivity to race- and gender-based slights. What is especially impressive is how few liberties Ms. Wan takes with her setting, the large corporate law firm. . . . She dissects the tokens of status in this world in a manner that's reminiscent of Tom Wolfe."
—*The Wall Street Journal*

"Wan succeeds in exploring and fictionalizing the timely topics of sexism and racism in workplace politics in a fluent, thought-provoking, and compelling tale."
—*Booklist*

"Wan has written a sensitive story of discrimination faced in 'old boy' law firms in particular but also in the world in general. . . . intriguing and entertaining. This reviewer is looking to Wan's next novel."
—*Library Journal*

"From lawyer-turned-author Helen Wan comes an illuminating look at the social and racial politics at a prestigious New York law firm."
—*Audrey Magazine*

"Ingrid is way ahead of the game and after a reversal that would have had most taking a nasty tumble, she triumphs in a conclusion that is unexpected and exciting. The author, Helen Wan, with a background in corporate law, has created realistic characters and an involving, suspenseful story set around the racial and sexual politics that exist in corporations. Whether you've a mind to climb a corporate ladder or not, *The Partner Track* is a great read."
—*BookPleasures.com*

"*The Partner Track* romances us with power, all the while revealing the betrayal, bigotry, and illusion congealed inside of it."

—*Amherst Magazine*

"Provides the reader with valuable and nuanced insights into life at a large New York City firm. *The Partner Track* will resonate with anyone who has ever confronted the challenge of trying to calibrate the right mixture of worthy pursuits, happiness, accomplishment, and retained integrity into a workable and personalized formula for success."

—*New York Law Journal*

"The snappy pace and tone of this read belies the fact that it tackles serious subjects: career ambition, sexism, racism in the workplace. A fresh, engaging debut."

—*Real Simple*

"What a terrific debut novel. Ingrid Yung is a fresh, funny, and fearless heroine. Her razor-sharp wit and keen observations of gender, race, and class politics in corporate America make *The Partner Track* an entertaining, engrossing, and ultimately deeply compelling read."

—Cristina Alger, author of *The Darlings*

"*The Partner Track* is a marvelous story about female ambition and power, about betrayal, identity, and the conflict between self-interest and desire. In short: all the big, human stuff. Read it."

—Alison Clement, author of *Twenty Questions*

"Behind Helen Wan's wit and sparkling prose is a poignant and, at times, painfully honest tale of loyalty, ambition, and sacrifice. Funny, fragile, sometimes bold, often unsure, Ingrid Yung is one of those unforgettable heroines that you actually miss, like a dear friend, when the story's over."

—Ann Leary, *New York Times* bestselling author of *The Good House*

THE PARTNER TRACK

HELEN WAN

ST. MARTIN'S GRIFFIN

New York

For my family
and in loving memory of my grandmother
An Ching-Chun

THE PARTNER TRACK. Copyright © 2013 by Helen Wan. All rights reserved. Printed in the United States of America. For information address St. Martin's Press, 175 Fifth Avenue, New York, N.Y. 10010.

www.stmartins.com

Designed by Kathryn Parise

The Library of Congress has cataloged the hardcover edition as follows:

Wan, Helen.
   The partner track : a novel / Helen Wan. — First edition.
     p. cm.
   ISBN 978-1-250-01957-8 (hardcover)
   ISBN 978-1-250-01958-5 (e-book)
   1. Women lawyers—Fiction. 2. Chinese American women—Fiction. 3. Office politics—Fiction. 4. Diversity in the workplace—Fiction. 5. Discrimination in employment—Fiction. 6. New York (N.Y.)—Fiction. I. Title.
   PS3623.A4557P37 2013
   813'.6—dc23

2013025226

ISBN 978-1-250-05649-8 (trade paperback)

St. Martin's Griffin books may be purchased for educational, business, or promotional use. For information on bulk purchases, please contact Macmillan Corporate and Premium Sales Department at 1-800-221-7945, extension 5442, or write specialmarkets@macmillan.com.

First St. Martin's Griffin Edition: September 2014

10 9 8 7 6 5 4 3 2

I would not like to be the only woman on the court.

—*Ruth Bader Ginsburg*

ONE

୬

The Parsons Valentine dining room—affectionately known as the Jury Box—resembled nothing so much as a high school cafeteria, writ large. We were all older, sure, with expensive haircuts and finely tailored suits. The food was a lot better, and it was served on fine china, classic white with a platinum border. And then there was the view. Instead of a track or a football field, our windows overlooked the grand expanse of Fifth Avenue and Central Park. No trophy cases or spirit banners, either, just a vast Ellsworth Kelly painting and a few signed Chuck Close prints adorning the otherwise stark white walls. But these were just trophies of a different sort.

At Parsons Valentine & Hunt LLP, every step you took was a carefully calibrated decision, right down to where you sat at lunch—especially the year you were up for partner. The powers-that-be took meticulous note of who was allied with whom. If you regularly sat at a table to gossip and gab with other associates, it telegraphed *lazy* and *unambitious*. If you sat only with partners, it screamed *brownnoser*. Sitting off by yourself, not surprisingly, was the worst kind of professional suicide—you might as well walk around wearing a big SOCIAL LIABILITY sign around your neck. And the worst thing you could be at Parsons Valentine was *unpresentable*.

At lunch in the Jury Box, we were spoiled for choice. I navigated my way around the freshly stocked salad bar, past the sushi chef, deli counter, brick-oven pizza and teppanyaki lines, and stopped at the hot entrée station. Mason, the firm's executive director of Dining Services—he'd apprenticed at Le Bernardin—was standing behind the sneeze guard, wearing his chef's hat and a crisp white apron. Mason was one of my favorite people at the firm. He'd once sent a steak sandwich to my office when I was stuck on a late-night conference call. I'd never forgotten it.

"Hey, Mason, what are you pushing today?" I asked.

"Well, well. Ingrid Yung. My favorite customer." He gestured with a flourish at the row of silver chafing dishes. "Today we've got some beautiful seared ahi tuna steaks with avocado tartare."

"Hm. Sounds healthy."

"And over here I've got my famous spicy three-cheese lasagna."

"Sold."

I walked my lasagna and a Perrier over to the cashier line. The guy in front of me, some fourth-year Litigation associate I'd never spoken to, was busily scratching a client matter number onto a checkout form with a stubby yellow golf pencil.

Parsons Valentine attorneys had the option of paying for our Jury Box meals in one of two ways: cash from our own pockets, or charging it to the client whose matter we were working on. We were supposed to do this only when working late and bringing dinner to our desks, but a lot of lawyers just charged their meals whenever they felt like it. This meant that Microsoft might be springing for your breakfast bagel, while Time Warner picked up your turkey club at lunch. I always just paid cash. It was faster, not to mention more honest.

I picked up my tray, entered the dining room, and surveyed my options.

Jeff Murphy half-stood from his table, waving me over to where he sat with Hunter Russell, another associate in our class. Good old Murph. He was one of my best friends at the firm. We'd shared an office as summer associates, exactly nine years ago this month. Frankly, I hadn't expected to like him much at first. I'd taken one look and assumed he'd be too entitled for my taste, the worst kind of irritating, backslapping, how-the-hell-are-you frat boy. But he'd grown on me. Murph was a smart guy, despite the rich jock pedigree.

I set my tray down next to his on the starched white tablecloth and pulled out a chair. I nodded at Hunter, who barely glanced my way, thumbs frantically working the keys of his BlackBerry. Hunter loved his BlackBerry. It gave him the appearance of responding to urgent client messages while he checked his Fantasy League Baseball stats.

"What's up, Yung?" said Murph, jostling my elbow. He grinned at me, and I looked sidelong back at him.

Murph was a good-looking guy, and he knew it. I was reminded of this once again, seeing him in his crisp white dress shirt, open at the throat, sleeves rolled up, his tanned, muscular forearms lying easily on the table. His wavy, dark blond hair just brushed the top of his collar, and his new tan set off his eyes to brilliant effect, making them look even greener than usual. Murph's family had a house on the Cape, and he spent a week there every Memorial Day. He'd just gotten back, and he practically glowed with privilege and well-being.

Murph and I had once had something of a moment, you might say, years ago. When you hire ninety-five young, smart, attractive, ambitious people every fall, who've all just graduated from the same five law schools and landed in Manhattan, and then make them work twenty hours a day together in close quarters, there's obviously going to be sexual tension. Back when we were first-years, Murph had thrown a huge Halloween party at the loft he shared in Tribeca with one of his college buddies. I hadn't really wanted to go, and I didn't have a costume, but all the other associates in our class were going, and there was nothing I hated more than feeling left out.

So at the last minute, I rushed from work to my apartment and threw on my high school prom dress—the one I'd worn the night I'd been crowned Potomac Valley High's first-ever Asian American prom queen. (Oh my! Mrs. Saltzstein, the guidance counselor, had gushed. She'd heard of Oriental valedictorians before, but never a Chinese prom queen!) The dress was a strapless pink taffeta number. The zipper took some coaxing, and I was mushrooming a little out the top, but damn if I didn't still look pretty good in that thing.

By the time I cabbed downtown to Murph's loft, the party was in full swing.

"Yung!" said a very drunk Murph upon greeting me at the door. He was dressed as Pope John Paul II. We air-kissed—funny how being at a party makes it okay to air-kiss your co-workers—and he led me to the drinks in the kitchen. Many hours and margaritas later, Murph, Hunter, Hunter's wife, and I were huddled around his CD collection (this being before the iPod age) and someone put on "Son of a Preacher Man." Murph looked at me, bleary-eyed, and said, "Yung. What *are* you wearing?" I batted my lashes and purred, "My prom dress." Hunter's wife threw back her head and laughed. "What about some fake hickeys? You can't be a prom queen without the hickeys!"

Without missing a beat, Murph volunteered to provide the real thing, and before I could think better of it, Murph bent over my bare neck and shoulder and did the honors while I leaned back against his Sharper Image CD tower. I remember being surprised at the warmth of him, and how good the burr of his late-night stubble felt against my skin. It tickled, and I was laughing, and Dusty Springfield was singing that being good isn't always easy, but when Murph stood back up and gazed at me with a deadly serious, intensely hopeful look on his face, I realized I'd made a grave mistake. Sure enough, later that night, as Murph helped me look for my coat among the huge pile on his bed, he fixed me with a solemn if drunken gaze and leaned in toward me at a deliberate angle. I gently disentangled myself and pretended to laugh it off. "If only you weren't dressed as the pope," I'd said, the easiest way I could think of to let him down lightly. This was *Murph,* after all; he was like my brother. Furthermore, everyone at work knew he was an incorrigible flirt. Monday morning we both acted like it had just been the tequila talking. That had been eight years ago. We'd never spoken of it since.

"Health food?" Murph asked now, nodding toward my plate.

"Shut up, it's delicious," I told him, and took a huge bite of lasagna.

I did not appreciate Murph or anyone else scrutinizing what I was eating. It always felt, just a tiny bit, like I was back in my fourth-grade cafeteria, shyly unwrapping the scallion pancake or shrimp toast my mother would pack in aluminum foil in my lunchbox. "What's *that?*" Becky Noble would wrinkle up her nose, her own tidy baloney-and-cheese sandwich raised halfway to her mouth, causing all of the other girls to giggle. Years later, on a blind date at the Campbell Apartment, my twenty-dollar martini had arrived alongside an appetizer of those same scallion pancakes, cut into dainty bite-size triangles and served with a ginger-soy dipping sauce. My blind date—an anesthesiologist named Ethan—pushed them toward me. "Try one. These things are amazing," he enthused, popping one into his mouth. "They *are* good, aren't they," I replied, smiling vaguely and wondering what had ever happened to Becky Noble.

Murph shook his head at me. "I swear I've never seen a woman eat so much and still be a size two, Yung."

I shrugged.

Here was another thing about all the male attorneys I worked with. They all called me by my last name, Yung, instead of by my first name,

Ingrid. I wondered if some of them even knew what my first name was. But I didn't mind this. I'd been in the corporate world long enough to know that it was a good sign. When they felt comfortable enough to swear like sailors around me, I knew I was finally in.

I looked over at Hunter. He was hunched over a piece of paper, scribbling on some sort of cryptic sketch that looked like a tree.

"What's that?" I asked.

"Huh?" Hunter looked up. "Oh. I'm doing our softball brackets. See?" He slid the paper toward me. "This is how the season's shaping up. Wachtell's out. All we have to do now is beat Simpson Thacher in two weeks. And trust me, we will. They suck this year. So if Davis Polk takes down Skadden next week, and then they knock out the DA's office after that, we'll face them in the finals." He beamed.

Murph looked at me. "Glad you asked?"

Hunter was captain of our firm's softball team, the Parsons Valentine Prosecutors, and he was obsessed with winning the Central Park Lawyers League championship trophy. He spent twice as much time on softball captain duties as he did on legal work, but Hunter could afford to. He was pretty much unfireable. Nine years ago, during his final year of law school, he'd had the good fortune to knock up the daughter of a longtime Parsons Valentine client. This bank CFO had promptly forwarded Hunter's résumé to the head partner in our Corporate Department with a lunch invitation and a handwritten note, gently suggesting that his new son-in-law was sure to be an asset to any firm. Hunter was hired the following week. He'd been here ever since, billing about two-thirds of the hours the rest of us did. We grudgingly accepted him in our midst. We knew they'd never actually make him a partner—the firm was too worried about malpractice for that—but he was assured a cushy job as a senior associate or Of Counsel for as long as his father-in-law's bank kept paying its bills.

"A word to the wise," Murph said in a lowered voice. "I hear Adler's looking to staff some monster deal. If you see him around, look busy."

We usually got assigned to deals at the Corporate Department meetings, so the process could appear fair and transparent, but sometimes partners just randomly trolled the halls looking for help. If you had too clean a desk or were blatantly surfing the Web when a partner poked his head in your office, you'd be slapped with a new deal. This was known, resentfully, as drive-by assigning.

"That's not Adler's MO," I said. Marty Adler was the top rainmaking partner at Parsons Valentine, the real deal. He didn't need to troll the halls. Associates wanted to work with him. If he liked you, he could make your whole career.

Murph shrugged. "Look, believe what you want. I'm just the messenger."

"Speak of the devil." I nodded toward the other side of the room. Marty Adler, Harold Rubinstein, Sid Cantrell, and Jack Hanover—heavy hitters, all of them members of the firm's Management Committee— were rising from a table and pocketing their BlackBerrys. (Partners left their trays on the table for the dining room staff to clean up. Associates bused our own.) We all watched as this gang of four exited the Jury Box through the glass doors and stood talking in front of the elevators. Adler was gesticulating wildly about something. The others were nodding in agreement, apparently unaware that all of the associates were looking on.

I took another bite of lasagna. This brand of naked, unabashed partner worship amused me. We were senior associates, on the verge of our own partnership votes, and yet we still accorded the partners a distant, irreverent kind of celebrity—sort of like the way kids talked about their teachers in junior high. Partners walked among us. We worked alongside them. We talked to them every day. But despite this charade of equal footing, they remained shrouded in mystery. They were beings to be scrutinized and revered, hated and loved—and gossiped about. We were all expected to call them by their first names to their faces, but in private, we bandied about their last names only, as if they were baseball trading cards.

We watched as the four partners disappeared into an elevator.

"Well, back to the grind," said Murph, balling up his napkin and tossing it onto his tray. "I've got a ton of shit to do today."

Hunter pushed his chair back from the table and stood. "Yeah, I guess I should get going, too."

Murph glanced at me. "Hey, you don't mind, do you? You want us to sit with you til you're done?" Actually, I did mind. Eating alone in the Jury Box made me feel like my cover had been blown. But I couldn't tell them that. "Go, go, I don't mind," I said, shooing them away. "See you guys later."

I took two more bites of Mason's spicy three-cheese lasagna and stood to bus my tray.

My office was on the thirty-first floor, along with those of the other senior M&A associates. Hunter's office was the first I passed on my way from the elevator bank. HUNTER F. RUSSELL, read the polished brass nameplate. Next to Hunter was Murph, and next to Murph was a seventh-year named Todd Ames, who'd had his name legally changed from Abramowicz while still in law school. For ease of spelling, I'd once heard him explain.

Hunter's, Murph's, and Todd's offices were all clustered together on the good side of the building, in a stretch of hallway known as Fraternity Row. They had scored these sweet offices with their panoramic views by flirting shamelessly with the firm's office logistics coordinator,

Liz Borkofsky. It was rumored that Liz had taken this job in hopes of snagging a male attorney, any male attorney, on track for partner. Finally, last winter, she'd gotten engaged to the firm's slightly shy, balding director of IT. The joke went around the office that Liz had slept her way to the middle.

I rounded the corner and got to my own office. It was nice enough, but it faced Madison Avenue, not the park. I'd tried to make it a comfortable place to spend my waking hours, since we did spend almost all of them here. I'd brought in a cheerful vase that I kept filled with fresh flowers. Vintage travel posters for the walls. And a framed photograph of the Manhattan skyline that I'd once taken from the Brooklyn Bridge.

Margo was just getting back from her lunch break. Ridiculously, secretaries were not allowed to eat in the attorney dining room. Margo brought sandwiches from home and ate them in the park.

"Hey, Margo," I said. "How is it outside?"

"Hot and crowded," she said, sighing. "All those European tourists, you know. They get the whole damn summer off."

I loved Margo. She was one of the best secretaries at Parsons Valentine, and I was lucky to have her. (I'd lobbied to call her my "assistant" instead of "secretary," but this had been roundly vetoed by the partners, for setting "the wrong kind of precedent.") As a young associate, I'd had a few rocky starts with secretaries who hadn't worked out, like chain-smoking Dolores, who had complimented my "very good English" the first time I'd dictated a letter. Explaining that I'd been born in Maryland didn't help. After a few more choice comments—*I've never been a big fan of sushi, no offense*—I finally mentioned it to Human Resources, and Dolores had been swiftly reassigned to another practice group. The firm knew a walking liability when it saw one.

"Any messages?"

"No messages, but here's your afternoon mail." Margo handed me a stack of interoffice envelopes, the library routing copies of *The Wall*

Street Journal, the *Financial Times,* and the *New York Law Journal,* along with a dues notice from the City Bar Association.

The phone on her desk rang. Margo glanced at it and signaled to me that it was my line. I leaned one hip against the ledge in front of her desk and waited, rifling through my mail.

"Good afternoon. Ms. Yung's office," Margo said into the receiver. "Hold on, please, I'll check." She clicked on the mute button and blinked up at me. "Are you here for Marty Adler?"

Everyone was here for Marty Adler. "I'll take it in my office."

"She'll be right with him," said Margo to Marty Adler's secretary.

I walked into my office, nudged the door closed with my heel, and tossed my mail onto the credenza. A tingly adolescent glee bubbled up inside me. *He called!*

I sat down in my black swivel chair and grapevined my legs around so that I was facing out the window. I took a moment to compose myself. Never mind Murph's warning at lunch about a "monster deal." I was very pleased that Adler was calling me. I had worked on a few small projects with him, but they hadn't been any of his really high-profile deals. I'd dealt mainly with his senior associate and not Adler himself. Now, in my eighth year, I *was* the senior associate on my deals.

Associates were rarely called personally by Marty Adler to work on anything. This was news.

I cleared my throat and said in the mellifluous voice I reserved for partners and clients, "Hi, Marty, how are you?"

"Hold on," said a woman's gravelly smoker voice. "I'll get him."

Shit.

What an amateur mistake. Of course Adler was the type of man who waited until his secretary got me on the line before getting on himself. At $1,125 an hour, his time was valuable.

There was a beep, followed by Marty Adler himself. "Ingrid, hello," he said. His voice was deep and growly, yet I had always thought there was something kind about it, too. I rather liked it.

"So," he continued without preamble, "I'm wondering about your availability this month. Do you have any time coming up?"

"Well, Marty, I—"

"I'll tell you why I ask," he continued, as if I hadn't spoken. "There's a high-worth, highly confidential acquisition that's just come into the office. Their usual M&A counsel got conflicted out, so this is a big win for us. It's going to require a great deal of time and attention, and I'd be very grateful if you would be on my team." This was a funny quirk about partners in law firms: When telling you to do something, they often said "I'd be very grateful," as if you had a choice in the matter.

"Of course," Adler went on, "the client wants it done yesterday. This deal's on a rush timetable, so I'd need you to focus on it as your top priority. That is, if you're able to take it on." He paused a moment to let this sink in. He knew exactly what kind of opportunity he was dangling in front of me.

Chances to shine in front of Marty Adler didn't come along every day, especially not mere weeks before your partnership vote. "I'd love to be on your team, Marty."

"Wonderful," he said, completely unsurprised. "Why don't you come on up to my office, then, and I'll fill you in on the deal."

"I'll be right there," I said, and hung up.

Eeeeeee!

I did a happy dance in my swivel chair, spinning three full revolutions. I stopped and tilted my chair all the way back, feeling dizzy but exhilarated. Taking a few deep breaths to calm myself down, I gazed at the smooth cherry bookcases that lined an entire wall of my office.

I loved these shelves. They were home to the stacks and stacks of deal books I'd accumulated from every transaction I'd ever worked: mergers, asset purchases, asset sales, stock purchases, stock sales, all-cash deals, all-stock deals, stock swaps, recaps, roll-ups, reverse triangular mergers, forward backhanded mergers, around-the-ankle, behind-the-back, over-the-shoulder mergers. You could easily lose track of the names and hundreds of ways these deals could be structured. Half of this job was simply learning how to lob these terms around as casually as tennis balls.

I loved the closing of every deal. I could feel the power and influence that coursed through these conference rooms like electrical currents high atop the city. I loved listening to closing dinner toasts at Jean Georges or La Grenouille at the very moment that gazillions of dollars, or yen, or euros, were originating from somewhere and landing, through the miracle of wire transfer, in our clients' bank accounts halfway around the globe. It was thrilling, the promise of such a world.

I walked over to my cedar wardrobe, opening the side with the full-length mirror. I checked my mascara and lip gloss and carefully retied the silk sash at the waist of my Audrey Hepburn–style sheath. Then, grabbing a pen and legal pad from my credenza, I fairly floated out to the elevator bank.

Marty Adler had a huge corner office on the thirty-seventh floor. I stopped at his secretary's desk, expecting to have to give my name, but she glanced up and flashed me a familiar smile. "Hi, Ingrid. I'm Sharon. Nice to meet you. Mr. Adler's expecting you. Go on in."

"Thanks."

I should have realized. Secretaries knew everything around here.

I rapped on the door once and pushed it open. Adler was sitting all the way across the room, in a green leather swivel chair, behind a massive antique mahogany desk piled high with stacks of paper and Redwelds. On the other side of the room, a high-backed couch and two antique chairs were nestled around a beautiful teak table with a conference phone resting on it. Enormous picture windows ran along two sides of his office and all the way to the ceiling, flooding the room with midday sunlight that glinted off the top of Adler's shiny bald head. The long, low windowsills were cluttered with framed awards, plaques, photographs, and deal toys. Deal toys were the souvenirs—little trophies, really—given to mark the successful closing of a merger or acquisition. I loved collecting these. And wow, Adler had a lot of them.

"Come in, come in, Ingrid." He came around the side of his desk, gesturing with his bifocals toward his couch. He was not a tall man, but he had heft. "Please sit."

It seemed a long walk just to get there. I perched on the edge of the couch and positioned my legal pad demurely over my knees.

Adler lowered himself into a chair opposite me. "First off, I know I don't need to tell you this, but this deal is still highly confidential."

"Of course, Marty. No problem," I said.

He leaned back, raised his arms, and clasped both hands behind his head, closing his eyes. Pale yellow pit stains tarnished his white dress shirt. I willed myself not to look directly at them. I did not like to be disillusioned.

"So," said Adler, eyes still closed, "as you've probably heard through the grapevine, we've just been retained by SunCorp, the energy conglomerate based in Houston."

I nodded as though I had.

"They're about to acquire a clean energy upstart, Binney Enterprises, for nine hundred million and change," Adler went on. "They've been after them for a year and a half, and finally shook hands with the Binney people last week."

I scribbled furiously on my legal pad. Adler talked very fast.

"SunCorp is a huge opportunity for us. It could lead to a lot more work in the energy sector."

He looked at me to make sure I understood this deal's significance; I nodded brightly.

"Now, Ted Lassiter—SunCorp's CEO—expects this to be top priority," Adler continued. "He's coming in Thursday to meet with us. Whatever else is on your calendar, move it. They want to sign a binding term sheet ASAP so they can announce publicly at the close of the quarter."

I raised my eyebrows. "But that's less than five weeks away."

"I know." Adler blinked. "That's why I'm counting on you to focus on this as your top priority, Ingrid."

It would require Herculean efforts from a team of lawyers working around the clock to bring an almost-billion-dollar acquisition from square one to a signed term sheet on that timetable. "Absolutely," I said. "I'll give it a hundred percent."

"Good. That's what I wanted to hear." Adler clapped both hands onto his knees and stood. This seemed to be my cue to stand, too. "Now, I told Ted Lassiter that after we meet with him Thursday, we'd get a preliminary draft term sheet to the other side by end of next week. Does that timing work for you?"

This was a rhetorical question.

"Of course," I said.

"Great." Adler smiled. "Oh, and Ingrid," he added in a low voice, almost as an afterthought, "I want you to understand . . ." He paused conspiratorially.

Yes? Yes?? I realized I was actually holding my breath.

"I hope you understand that I wouldn't trust a deal of this magnitude to just *any* associate. You've impressed a lot of the right people around here, and we knew you'd be able to run with this."

My heart gave a little leap. "I really appreciate that, Marty. Thank you."

He fluttered his hand at me—*de nada*. As I turned to go, barely able to suppress the huge smile forming on my face, he added casually, "Oh, just one more thing, Ingrid. There's a particular Corporate paralegal

I've asked to assist on this deal. He just started here at the firm. Name's Justin Keating."

I'd never heard of him. "Oh, a newbie?" I said. "Wouldn't it be better to get one of the senior M&A paralegals for this? I usually work with either Evelyn Griffiths or Joseph Cruz, and they're both terrific. Really smart, and on top of everything."

Adler looked up. Annoyance briefly crossed his face. "Justin Keating will be the paralegal on this deal," he repeated. Then, just as suddenly, the grin was back. "From what I understand, he's a very bright young man, eager to work hard and prove himself. In fact, Ingrid, I'd consider it a personal favor to me if you could show the kid the ropes. His father's an old friend of mine, and a very good friend of the firm's." He looked at me significantly. "I'd love for you to take Justin under your wing. Really integrate him onto the deal team. I'd do it myself, of course, but, well, I'm looking incredibly busy this month."

And *I* had just been tasked with taking a brand-new deal to announcement stage in less than five weeks' time. No pressure, really.

"No problem, Marty," I said. "It would be my pleasure."

"Thanks, Ingrid. I knew the firm could count on you." Adler sat back down behind his massive mahogany desk, signaling the end to our conversation.

TWO

❧

"Margo, call Marty Adler and tell him I booked room 3201-A for the SunCorp meeting. And would you see if Justin's around?"

Justin Keating had just graduated from college. Hardly the kind of paralegal usually assigned to work on a billion-dollar deal. But when Donald Keating—a Wall Street executive with a lot of pull—had casually mentioned to Adler that he hoped his son's brief paralegal gig might turn into an interest in law school, Justin Keating became my problem.

I was dusting bronzing powder onto the bridge of my nose when Justin appeared. His tall frame in my doorway startled me.

"You rang?" He'd shaved and put on a suit today for our client meeting. I noticed without surprise that the suit looked expensive—a better cut and drape than you saw on many men twice his age. His hands were shoved in his pockets, and he leaned against my doorjamb, grinning. It was an amused, deliberate smile. Almost a smirk.

"Hi, Justin. Yes, I rang," I said. "Our friends are going to be here in forty-five minutes."

Justin didn't blink. "And?" He made a lazy rolling motion at me with one hand, as if to say, *Your point is?*

"And," I said evenly, "how does the conference room look?"

"All set up. I put everything in there yesterday."

"Copies of the working group list?"

"In the room."

"Coffee order?"

"Done."

"Legal pads?"

"Yup."

"Pens?"

"Yeah."

"Both highlighter and ballpoint?"

He shot me a look.

"Okay, thanks," I said. "Why don't you just hang out in your office, then. I'll call you when the oil barons get here. And tell Dining Services we might order up sandwiches later, unless the clients want to go out for lunch."

"No problem." Justin pushed himself off the doorjamb and sauntered off in the direction of his cubicle.

He'd only been here a few weeks, but I'd already overheard a bunch of female paralegals giggling in the coffee room over Justin Keating's bedroom eyes. I didn't see it. For one thing, he was only twenty-three, and I had a low tolerance for twenty-three-year-old boys, even when I was twenty-three.

Margo buzzed my intercom.

"Hi, Margo."

"Your mother's on line one."

"Thanks."

I hit the blinking red light for line one. "Hey, Mom."

"Ingrid?" Her voice was tentative.

"Yeah, it's me. Hi, Mom."

My mother had a love-hate thing with calling me at the office. On the one hand, she loved that I had a secretary. On the other hand, Margo intimidated her. Even after living in the States for over thirty years, my mother still preferred to speak in Mandarin.

When I'd graduated from law school and started working at Parsons Valentine, my mother had called up every friend and relative she had and given them my new office number, so that if anyone tried to call, they'd hear my secretary pick up and say, "Ms. Yung's office. May I help you?" For a few months at the start of my career I'd gotten a rash of anonymous calls, where someone would dial my office number, listen to my secretary answer, then hang up. My mother had never owned up to this.

"Ingrid-ah, are you busy now? Is this a good time?"

I sighed. "Not really, Mom, I have a meeting in a few minutes. With some *new clients*. I can't talk long." This was a good strategy to use with her. I'd cultivated it back in grade school. Whenever my mother wanted me to clean my room or practice the piano, I'd just peer at her over the top of a book and say, "Mom, I'm *reading*. For *school*."

Even now, my mother remained terrified that I'd lose my job. My parents believed that Chinese American kids, especially girls, were better off in quiet, stable careers that relied on technical expertise instead of killer instinct. Doctor, yes. CPA, okay. Corporate shark, no. They knew I was up for partnership, and they were extremely proud of me. But sometimes my mother still asked if it was too late for me to apply to medical school.

"Okay, I'll make it quick." She began chattering in Mandarin. "I was just calling to remind you about Jenny Chang's wedding invitation. Did you tell Auntie Chang yet if you can go?"

"Not yet, Mom. I've been really busy. *Hen mang.*" I repeated "really busy" in Mandarin, for emphasis. I spoke to my parents in a hybrid Mandarin and English mix, my own personal dialect of Chinglish.

"Two months from now."

Two months! I couldn't even predict what my schedule would look likc in two *days,* much less two months. "Mom, I'll try, but you know I can't promise."

She sighed. "I know, I know, you never can promise. But Ingrid-ah, you should come! Auntie and Uncle Chang invited over two hundred and fifty guests! Twenty-eight tables! I told you it was at the Potomac River Country Club, right?"

Only a dozen times. "Yes, you'd mentioned."

I heard a low beep, and then the indicator light for my second line came on. I could hear Margo outside my door, saying pleasantly, "I'm sorry, she's on another call at the moment."

"The Fongs' sons were invited, too," my mother was saying. "Eddie Fong just bought a brand-new condo in D.C.! Not to live in, to rent out to *tenants*! He's going to be—how you say—a slumlord!"

I laughed. "I think you mean a *landlord,* Mom."

She ignored this. "Auntie Fong said that Eddie is a doctor, specializing in endo . . . endo-something."

"Endocrinology," I supplied.

"Yes, that," my mother confirmed. She paused for a small, soft sigh. "And Vincent Lu is going to be there. Such a nice boy. You remember Vincent?"

"Of course," I replied, and found myself smiling. My mother had been trying to interest me in Vincent Lu for as long as I could remember. From what I knew of him back when we'd been at Potomac Valley High School together, he was a nice enough guy, but precisely the kind of stereotypical Asian kid I had worked so hard *not* to be—Coke-bottle glasses, first-chair violin, Westinghouse science competition, tiger-mommed to within an inch of his life. Our senior year, I sat next to him at a dinner at the Washington Hilton honoring local National Merit Semifinalists, and I remembered how embarrassed I'd been when the mayor's wife automatically assumed we were boyfriend and girlfriend.

"Oh, Cindy Bai and Susan Wu are going to be Jenny's bridesmaids."

My mother paused and sighed again. "Ingrid-ah, Cindy and Susan are such *good* girls. So sweet, so nice. You could really learn something from them. They're not like you, always working, working, no time to meet anyone, wasting your beautiful years."

I'd grown up with Cindy Bai and Susan Wu in the suburbs of D.C. We'd gone to the same Chinese language school every Sunday afternoon from kindergarten through senior year. Cindy was an orthodontist with her own practice in a local strip mall, and Susan was a computer analyst at the Treasury Department. They were both married—not to each other, although that would have made them infinitely more interesting—and lived less than fifteen minutes from our old high school. My mother was right. Cindy and Susan probably *were* both sweeter and nicer than I was. But you didn't make partner at one of the most powerful firms in the country by being sweet and nice. My parents did not understand this.

"Mom, I have to go. The clients will be here any minute."

"And how's your friend Rachel?" my mother continued, as if I hadn't spoken. My mother adored Rachel Freedman, my best friend and former law school roommate from Columbia. Back in the day, when Rach and I had shared a small apartment in Morningside Heights, I'd been surprised when she and my mother had bonded over, of all things, my mother's fiery *ma po tofu* recipe—which my mom showed Rachel how to make in our tiny law student kitchen. Rachel cooked. I didn't.

After graduation, Rach and I had both started off as associates at large corporate law firms—me at Parsons Valentine, Rachel at Cleary Gottlieb. But Rachel had quit after just three years, when she married a hedge fund manager named Josh and moved to a charming house in the suburbs. Rachel had given up her prestigious law job to stay home with their two adorable kids. My mother approved. *Rachel* wasn't wasting her beautiful years.

"Rachel's doing just fine, as always," I sighed. "Anything else, Mom?"

After a few beats of silence she said in a small voice, "Auntie Chang and Auntie Fong always asking how you're doing up there in New York. Daddy tells them, 'Doing very well!' But I tell them you're still working too hard, like always. They ask me, 'Still no boyfriend, ah?' I tell them no. Still no boyfriend."

My mother really knew how to pick her times. "Okay!" I chirped. "Gotta go. I'll call you later, okay?"

"Okay," she said. She didn't sound happy.

At ten twenty-five, Margo buzzed my intercom. "The SunCorp people are waiting in reception. Mr. Adler is finishing up a call and wants you to start without him. Shall I go down and get them?"

"Yes, please. Just bring them to conference room 3201-A. I'll meet them up there."

I smoothed my pencil skirt over my knees, retrieved a few business cards from the silver cardholder on my desk, and strolled down the corridor to the drab interior room where the paralegals lived.

Justin was in his cubicle, staring at an eBay bidding screen. "2 TIX, SPRINGSTEEN AT MADISON SQUARE GARDEN, 14th ROW!!!!!!" The current bid was $689.

I watched as he typed "$780" next to YOUR MAXIMUM BID.

I cleared my throat. "Justin, the oil barons are here. Let's go."

"Hold on. In a sec." He absently held up one finger as if to shush me.

Seriously?

"Actually, no. Not in a sec," I said, with a little edge to my voice. "We don't keep clients waiting."

Justin looked up at me, one eyebrow slightly cocked in surprise. He let out a heavy sigh and then clicked the SUBMIT button. "You're the boss," he added sarcastically.

I had booked my favorite conference room, the one I used for all of my closings, meetings, and late-night work sessions, the one that afforded the best view of Manhattan, including all of Central Park. I could even make out the top of my apartment building if I looked hard enough. Sometimes, alone, poring over agreements and financial statements in the wee hours of the morning, I would stand against the windows, press the full length of my body up against the glass, and look down. The cool hardness on my forehead and the dizzying vertical effect left me breathless and exhilarated.

Justin had placed a legal pad with PARSONS VALENTINE & HUNT LLP printed in crisp block lettering, along with two new sharpened pencils, at every place. Sleek black trays containing paper clips, binder clips, and pens, sorted out by color—black, blue, and red—were evenly spaced along the length of the polished mahogany conference table. The room looked good, and I told him so. Justin shrugged, not bothering to look at me.

I could hear Margo's voice floating down the hall, something about the unusually cool month of May we'd had. "Here we are," she said, opening the door to the conference room. The oil barons stepped inside, and Margo retreated, quietly closing the door behind her.

They didn't look so bad. Both men were tall and broad-shouldered and wore conservative navy business suits with just-off-the-plane wrinkles. One of them was in his late sixties, with a shock of snow white hair, laughing blue eyes, and a reddish complexion. He looked like Santa in cowboy boots. I suppressed a smile. All that was missing was a big old Stetson on his head. The other one was taller and a bit younger-looking than I'd expected. He even bordered on handsome, in a predictable all-American, aging-quarterback kind of way.

I'd purposely chosen the most conservative suit in my closet that morning. Now I realized I could have worn something a little slinkier.

"Welcome," I said, directing my comments to them both. "Marty's just on his way. He'll be along in a moment."

"Thank you," Santa said politely, then crossed the room and offered his hand to Justin. "Ted Lassiter," he introduced himself. Justin shook the client's hand with a kind of bewildered expression, half-looking over at me. Ted Lassiter then turned back to me. "When you get a sec," he said, "could we get some orange juice ordered up to the room?"

When you're the only woman, with the darkest skin, the weirdest name, and the softest voice, in a roomful of Big Swaggering Suits, you have to learn to pick your battles. This barely registered on my comparative sliding scale of slights. It was the racial-bias equivalent of finding a hair floating in your soup—annoying, but not worth making a big fuss.

"Of course," I said smoothly, turning to a slightly reddened Justin Keating. "Justin, would you please call Dining Services and let them know?"

Justin scurried over to the phone to call in our order. For his part, Ted Lassiter didn't look the least bit embarrassed by his mistake.

"Hello, Ted," I said as I held out my hand. "I'm Ingrid Yung. It's great to meet you." I smiled warmly and looked directly into his eyes.

This was a habit I'd developed my first year at the firm, when the partners had made all of us attend a one-hour seminar entitled "Effective Networking Strategies for Lawyers." "Always, *always* repeat the person's name aloud after you've been introduced," urged Valerie, our effective networking expert. "And always look *directly* into the person's eyes when shaking his or her hand. Remember to look *directly* into their eyes."

Murph and Hunter, who'd sat next to me at the seminar, had found both Valerie and her advice hilarious. They'd sniggered through her entire presentation. For days afterward, if I ran into one of them in the hall, they'd giddily pump my hand up and down and whisper menacingly, "Nice to meet you, *Ingrid Yung*," boring into my eyes with a serial-killer death stare. I agreed there was something cheesy about a class on how to network; still, I'd gone straight into my office right after Valerie's seminar, closed the door, and scribbled down as much of her advice as I could remember.

"So *you're* Ingrid Yung," repeated the cowboy Santa, looking me up and down with a mildly bemused expression. His voice somehow exuded both gruffness and warmth. "I'm Ted Lassiter." He shook my hand, then gestured toward his companion. "This is our general counsel, Mark Traynor."

The quarterback's handshake was pleasantly warm. "Nice to meet you, Ingrid," he said. He smelled lightly of a good aftershave.

Justin had reappeared by my side, and I gestured toward him. "This is Justin Keating, one of our Corporate paralegals, who'll be helping out with the acquisition," I said. Justin quickly stepped in front of me. "Pleased to meet you," he said, with a toothpaste-commercial smile, and shook hands with both men.

"Keating, eh?" said Lassiter. "Where'd you go to school, son?"

"Colby, sir," said Justin, grinning from ear to ear.

"Fine school," said Lassiter. "Fiiine school. My son almost went there himself. Finally got off the wait list at Dartmouth, though."

I suppressed a small smile. It amused me how certain men were able to turn every conversation into a pissing match. This was especially true when it came to billable hours. At Parsons Valentine, it was a twisted form of bragging right to say you'd spent all night in the office. It was an even better badge of honor to miss a scheduled vacation due to work. The firm paid out thousands of dollars each year to reimburse its attorneys for missed flights and lost deposits on hotels, spas, and rented villas. One guy up for partner in Litigation had recently upped the ante for all of us by skipping the birth of his first child in order to take a deposition.

There was a swift knock at the door, and Marty Adler, without waiting for an answer, strode in. You always knew when and where Adler was in the room. Though short in stature, he had an unmistakably commanding presence. Some associates—especially the ones Adler routinely passed over when staffing his deals—called it his Napoleonic complex. I thought of it as genuine leadership quality.

"Morning, gentlemen," Adler said. Ted Lassiter shook his hand and clapped him on the shoulder familiarly. "I'm Marty Adler. Good to see you here. I believe you've already met Ingrid Yung, my associate?"

"We have, and I've gotta ask you one question," said Lassiter in a mock-stern voice. "What the hell kind of show are you running here? You promised to put your best associate on this deal and then you trot out this little lady who can't be a day older than eighteen!" Lassiter gave a short, barking laugh.

Okay, now this guy was testing my patience. I pressed my lips together.

Adler shot me a warning look that said, *Don't worry. I've got this.*

"Listen, Ted, I told you we put together our A-team for this deal. Ingrid's one of the best associates this firm has ever had, and she's been running the show on some of our biggest transactions for a while now. Personally, I wouldn't trust your deal to anyone else."

"Of course!" Lassiter chortled. "I'm just pulling your leg, Marty. Relax."

Adler threw an appraising glance in my direction, with a lift of the eyebrows. *Are we good?*

I gave him a nod and half-shrug. *We're fine. Let's get on with this.* In fact, even though my heart was pounding and I kind of hated Lassiter already, I felt genuinely touched by what Adler had said, defending me so passionately to the client.

Mark Traynor cleared his throat. "Why don't we get started? We've got a lot of ground to cover."

"Yes." Adler nodded at Traynor. "Yes, that's an excellent idea. Gentlemen?" He gestured toward the conference table.

Lassiter pulled out the leather swivel chair closest to him, which was at the head of the table. Traynor quickly settled into a chair to Lassiter's right, and Adler sat directly across from Traynor, angling his chair so that he could face both of the clients at the same time.

I drew up my shoulders, took a deep, calming breath, and squeezed into a chair to Adler's left, leaving me off to the side. Avoiding eye contact, I reached across to the supply tray closest to me and pretended to give careful consideration to the selection of ballpoint pens as I struggled to regain my emotional bearings.

Justin hesitated a moment, then took a seat at my left elbow. At this Adler looked annoyed, but it only registered on his face for a moment. Paralegals were expected to sit in one of the chairs lining the perimeter of the room during client conferences, for ease of getting out if something needed to be fetched, faxed, or copied. No career paralegal would have made this kind of gaffe. Typical, though, for Justin to assume he should have a *literal* place at the table.

Ted Lassiter didn't seem to notice. He tented his fingers and rested his elbows on the dark gleaming wood of the conference table.

"Now, let me preface this meeting by saying that this deal is still highly confidential."

Adler cleared his throat. "That goes without saying, Ted."

Lassiter nodded approvingly. "There's already been some media speculation, of course, and our PR office keeps fending off calls, but no one's gotten anything specific. We only shook hands with Binney on this about a week ago. We don't even have a preliminary deal sheet yet."

"But the purchase price is settled at nine ninety in cash and stock?" asked Adler.

"That's right. And we're anxious to seal this deal. That's bargain-basement pricing."

I jotted on the legal pad in front of me: *$990MM. Cash/stock.*

Justin looked over my shoulder as I did this. I resisted the urge to shield the notepad with my arm.

"Now, I'm sure I don't have to tell you that the purchase price has to be kept under wraps til we can get this binding term sheet signed," Lassiter continued, talking only to Adler.

"Of course." Adler nodded and turned quickly to me. "Make a note to send Ted a quick-and-dirty NDA to look at. Let's get that signed up before we even get to a draft of the term sheet."

I scribbled rapidly on my notepad.

"What's happening to the top executives over there?" Adler asked. "Anyone staying on, or are they all parachuting out?"

"A bunch of top guys are going out on parachutes," Lassiter replied, "but we're mainly interested in keeping Jack Barstow on." He leaned toward Adler conspiratorially. "That's Fred Binney's right-hand man. Youngest COO in the history of the company."

The name rang a bell. "Barstow," I repeated. "That's the guy who gets credit for bringing Binney's revenues up forty percent over the last four years, isn't he?"

You could practically hear every head in the room swiveling in my direction. From the corner of my eye I was aware of Marty Adler blinking furiously at me.

"That's right," Lassiter said slowly. He was looking straight at me now, as if seeing me for the first time.

I pressed on. "Word on the street is he's pissed that he spent four years slaving away to get their offshore drilling operations up and running, only to learn old man Binney's looking to sell. He's probably talking to a bunch of headhunters already. We'll definitely want a key-man provision in the term sheet."

No one spoke for a few seconds. Then Lassiter cleared his throat. "That's very impressive," he said, grinning. "Now how'd you know that about Barstow?"

"*Oil and Gas Investor,*" I shot back, with my first real smile since this meeting had started.

"You read *Oil and Gas Investor*?" He sat back in his chair, folding his hands across the formidable expanse of his belly.

"I read a lot of things," I said sweetly. My chin was up. I met Lassiter's gaze directly and held it. *I'm glad we finally understand each other.*

Lassiter turned toward Adler. "Very impressive, Marty. I gotta hand it to you."

Adler's expression changed back from alarm to casual confidence. "What did I tell you?" Then, clearing his throat, "Now, getting back to the term sheet—"

"That's terrific," Lassiter continued. He laughed and cocked his head back toward Adler. "Beautiful, with brains, too. Now, Marty, when you told me on the phone that *Ingrid Yung* would be handling our deal, I expected some sour-faced old fräulein. Believe me, I'd rather work with a pretty little Asian gal any day."

"He said *what*?"

Murph sat crossways in one of the armchairs opposite my desk, his long legs dangling over the side. We'd just gone to Starbucks for our morning coffee run. I was spreading cream cheese onto my whole-wheat everything bagel, and Murph was balancing a tiny paper football on his knee, aiming it at me.

"I swear, that's a direct quote," I said. "You should have seen Adler's face."

Murph burst out laughing.

Jeff Murphy had a distinctive laugh. It was sort of halfway between a hyena and a rooster. On anyone else, it would be obnoxious. On Murph, it was endearing.

"And *then*," I continued, "as Lassiter's leaving, he turns to me and says, 'I'm glad my wife won't be meeting you. She'd never believe you were our *lawyer!*' "

Murph hooted. We were both laughing now. I somehow felt reassured by his reaction.

"Actually, though, he kind of has a point," said Murph. "How *did* two Chinese immigrants decide to name their kid Ingrid?"

I got this question a lot.

Asian parents often name their American kids in a complete cultural vacuum. That's why you see so many hapless Normans and Eugenes, why there'd been a Eunice Kim, a Florence Liu, *and* an Elvis Chang in my graduating class at Yale. As a kid, I'd longed to be a Jennifer. I'd gotten off lucky, though. It could have been worse. Much worse.

"My parents went to see *Casablanca* when they were dating back in Taipei," I explained. "I was named after Ingrid Bergman."

"Nice." Murph nodded. "Well, think of it this way, Yung. The CEO of a Fortune 500 company thinks you're hot. You *are* hot. What's so bad about that?"

I rolled my eyes. But a tiny, agreeable thrill went through me.

"Anyway, did Adler have anything to say about it?"

"He came into my office after the meeting to go over some points for the term sheet. On his way out, he apologized for Lassiter's 'politically incorrect' remarks."

Murph turned up his palms. "See that? Even Adler recognizes the guy's an asshole."

"Yeah, but he's a paying asshole," I shot back. "What if Lassiter does something even worse, and I end up having to beg off the deal? What's that going to look like at my partnership review?"

Murph shook his head. "You're being dramatic. Trust me, you're going to do just fine at your partnership review. For fuck's sake, Marty Adler just handpicked you to run the biggest deal in the office! I'd quit worrying if I were you."

He had a point.

For a moment neither of us spoke. Murph drained the last of his Frappuccino.

"So, anyway, what's going on with you?" I said quickly, dabbing at a dollop of cream cheese at the corner of my mouth. "What are you up to this week?"

He looked at me and grinned. "Anna Jergensen."

I raised my eyebrows. "Who's Anna Jergensen?"

"Paralegal at Debevoise."

I shook my head.

I had a theory about why every reasonably well-groomed thirty-something male in New York with an apartment and a college degree appeared to have his pick of women, while so many successful, intelligent single women couldn't find a date to save our lives. It was this: For better or worse, women in this town only wanted to date up, or at least laterally. Men, however, were free to date up and down and over and under the age, education, and career gradients with reckless abandon and no one ever batted an eye. This was why twenty-four-year-old Debevoise paralegals, forty-eight-year-old MILFs, cute belly-pierced bartenders, Croatian au pairs, Hooters waitresses, and NYU undergrads were all fair game for guys like Murph. Yet my single women friends—doctors, lawyers, professors, consultants—always seemed to limit themselves to men who matched or exceeded their own age, education, and income level. It was a completely self-defeating strategy.

"And? What's she like?" I asked.

He shrugged. "We'll see. I think she was a gorgeous girl, but there was something that kept her from being a complete ten. You know, like when a pretty girl can't walk in heels or something."

"What a shame." I shook my head mournfully.

"Plus," Murph continued, "it was pretty dark in the bar where I met her. She may be kind of a bakkushan."

A moment passed as I chewed my bagel. "Okay," I said. "I give up. What's a bakkushan?"

Murph grinned. "It's the Japanese word for a chick who looks hot from behind, but from the front, not so much."

I shook my head. Poor Anna Jergensen, whoever she was.

As the only senior female M&A associate left at the firm, I was used to this. While Murph could come to work and recount all the gory details of his dating exploits—and did, ad nauseam, to the great amusement of Hunter, me, and all of our colleagues—I never talked to any of the guys in the office about my romantic life. Granted, there'd been nothing to tell for the last two and a half years, but that was beside the point. Gloria Steinem notwithstanding, there was still a clear double standard for men and women when it came to talking about our sex lives in the office.

In Murph's case, it was almost expected, the bawdier, the better. In my case, it would seem unprofessional at best—and at worst, slutty.

"You gonna make it to the outing this year?" asked Murph.

Parsons Valentine was about to hold its annual firm outing at a Westchester country club. It always took place on a Friday, and the firm gave secretaries and paralegals the day off—which sounds like a magnanimous gesture until you stop to consider that they were not invited to the outing itself. It was strictly for the lawyers and summer associates. As with all firm events, attendance was surreptitiously taken.

"Do I have a choice?" I said.

Murph shrugged. "Not really."

"Then I guess I'll be at the outing, won't I?"

He waggled his eyebrows at me. "Bringing your bikini this year, Yung?"

"Keep dreaming, Murph."

He laughed. "Oh, I will, Yung. I will."

My phone rang, and we both glanced at the display:

MARTIN J. ADLER x3736

Murph gave me a crisp military salute. "Guess you need to get that," he said, unfolding his limbs from my chair and rising. At the door he turned back around. "Not to say I told you so, but I knew you should have looked busy that day Adler came calling. Now you've ruined your whole summer!" He shook his head in mock pity.

"Bite me, Murph," I called after him. But I was smiling.

Murph was jealous, and we both knew it.

THREE

I was running late for lunch with Ted Lassiter. Even if I sprinted from my office to the restaurant, I'd still be late. Five minutes at least. Maybe ten. Fuck. Ted Lassiter was not the sort of client you kept waiting. I cursed the stiletto pumps I'd selected that morning, even as a little voice in my head assured me they had been the right choice. Ted Lassiter was clearly the kind of man who felt that if he absolutely had to work with a woman lawyer, at least she should show him the courtesy of wearing a skirt and high heels.

I stepped out of the elevator and hurried across the marble lobby.

"Where's the fire?" yelled Ricardo, who worked Building Security. He and I had been friends ever since he'd rescued me from a stalled elevator eight years ago. It was my second month at the firm, and I'd just worked my first all-nighter when, in my sheer exhaustion, I'd stumbled into an elevator car that was disabled for the night, then stupidly pressed DOORS CLOSE. It had been Ricardo who found me at 5:00 A.M., crumpled in a corner, panicked and crying. He had never mentioned the incident to another soul, and I was eternally grateful.

"Late for a meeting, RC," I threw back over my shoulder as I headed toward the doors. "See you on the way back."

I careened down Madison, hung a left at Fifty-first, and waited at the corner to cross Park Avenue. I took in a long breath. This particular section of the city always had a calming effect on me, especially on a day like this, with the sky a vivid blue against the endless crawl of bright yellow cabs as they made their way up and down the canyon of hotels and investment banks. A handful of tourists were stranded on the little concrete island that divides Park Avenue and I felt a little pang of sympathy. I remembered how much it used to bother me, as a young graduate who'd just arrived in New York, to misjudge the timing of those Park Avenue traffic lights and get stranded on that little slab of concrete, as the taxicabs and town cars whizzed past. I'd felt exposed, an amateur. Now I felt completely at home. I loved this feeling. Why not? I'd earned it.

The light changed, and the crowd surged across Park.

I looked at my watch again. If Lassiter was on time, he'd have been waiting for seven minutes now. Shit. I quickened my pace. I half-walked, half-jogged past the soup kitchen line at St. Bart's, past office workers eating their lunches outside, past carts and trucks dishing out kebabs, gyros, arepas, empanadas, dumplings, buns, jerk chicken, lobster rolls, Indian curries, and Southern barbecue. Everything smelled delicious to me. I would have much preferred something out of one of those shiny metal carts to the Cobb salad I always ordered at these client lunches.

The restaurant was up ahead, just on the other side of Lex. As I approached the corner, I noticed a jowly middle-aged man seated beside an array of framed watercolors and charcoal sketches. The man's head was turned about ninety degrees to follow the backside of a young female office worker as she crossed the street. Ugh. There are few things more galling than having to walk directly toward a man you know for sure will be watching your ass as you walk by. Especially when it's so clearly not a man (a) who you particularly want checking out your ass, or (b) whose ass you would want to check out in return. From time to time, depending on my mood, I found it amusing to surprise these guys—to turn around abruptly and actually catch them in the act. Four times out of five, they blushed. Sometimes we'd even laugh, the man and me.

I took a breath, squared my shoulders, and clicked past the sidewalk artist. But the light had just changed, and as the wave of traffic nosed forward, I was forced to step back and wait by his corner.

"Ni how!" he called out to me.

I sighed.

"Konnichiwa!" he tried again, louder. "Hey, you! *Konnichiwaaaaa!"*

I rolled my eyes. This was going to be a long light.

I did not understand why more men could not grasp the subtle yet important distinction between overtures toward women that carried a snowball's chance versus those that didn't. For example: *Nice hair,* okay. *Nice pair,* no. Was it really so difficult to master?

As the light finally changed and I stepped off the curb, the man hissed at me in a loud stage whisper, "Fucking chink."

I froze. There it was. That familiar churning, centered deep in the pit of my stomach. An acute flash of anger. Then rage.

The voice inside my head screamed, *Hey, you really don't have time for this!* even as I felt myself pivoting, hard, on my right stiletto heel. I walked up to the man. I planted myself directly in front of him, forcing him to look at me. I was standing close enough to one of his crappy little watercolors to drive my Jimmy Choo pump right through it. It would be so easy. I'd played women's soccer for three seasons at Yale.

The sidewalk artist blinked up in surprise, then pretended to be fascinated by a fixed point ten yards behind me.

"Excuse me," I said, very loudly and very clearly. "What did you just say?"

I could see him clench and unclench his jaw muscles, could see the deep flush of red spreading out from beneath his collar.

I cocked my head to one side and waited. I fought back the urge to check my watch. Let him think I could stand here all day.

This asshole wasn't going to win just because I was running late.

I was very well aware that I was wasting the time of a very important man, a Fortune 500 CEO who was not accustomed to being stood up. Especially not by some *girl lawyer* whom he hadn't even wanted running his deal in the first place. I could already hear him sputtering this, red-faced and furious, to Adler. Oh yes, I knew there would be hell to pay once I got to the restaurant, and certainly once I got back to the office. But at the moment, I really didn't care.

Because this jerk could have called me *anything* else. He could have followed me across the street hollering *you bitch* into my ear, and I wouldn't have flinched. Wouldn't even have remembered him by the time I was handing my wrap to the coat-check girl in the cool interior of the restaurant, smoothing my hands down over my skirt, and following the maître d' to Lassiter's table, a sweet smile and some rehearsed apology on my lips.

But *that* word—the one the sidewalk artist had so carelessly hurled in my direction—that word, I could not let go. It didn't matter who I kept waiting.

I edged closer to his dirty canvas chair and asked him again. "Something you wanted to say to me?" I crossed my arms over my chest and waited. "Well?"

He let out an ugly, dismissive snort. He glared at me, threw his hands up in the air, and shrugged. "Look, lady, I don't know what the fuck you're talking about. So just get out of my face."

"I'm talking about when you called me a chink back there, you fuck. That's what I'm fucking talking about."

He paused for a second, then put his hairy hands on his knees and laughed. "You're crazy." And then he stood up. He was much bigger than he'd looked sitting down. I felt a hot rush of panic, but I stared him down until he turned his back on me and pretended to busy himself with a row of postcard-size prints.

For the first time I got a real look at what he was selling. They were amateurish, cartoonishly bad pictures—portraits, I suppose—of dogs and women. Sometimes alone, sometimes together in the same scene. The dogs were all cast with human characteristics: dogs driving taxis, dogs selling newspapers, dogs drinking beer, dogs playing football. Ironically, none playing poker. I almost laughed.

The women in his paintings were all nude and large-breasted. What a surprise. I glanced down at the biggest watercolor, the one closest to me. It showed a voluptuous blond woman, naked and spread-eagled on a motel bed. A dog was lying next to her, smoking a cigarette.

He saw me eyeing it. "Oh, you like that one, eh? Yeah, it's one of my personal favorites. Five hundred dollars," he said, his lips twisted into a mocking smile. He was enjoying himself. He looked me languidly up and down, his eyes lingering on my breasts. "But for you—eh, I'll let you have it for an even twenty," he said with an exaggerated wink. "I got a special discount today for the pretty Chinese girls." He jerked his chin roughly at me. "You're Chinese, right?"

I didn't answer.

"Or is it Japanese? Or Korean?" He smirked and waved dismissively. "Ah, well, it doesn't matter. You people all look the same."

BAM!!!!

I'd plunged the pointy tip of my alligator pump all the way through the painting. Reflexively, I'd bent my knee and drawn my foot all the way back, then snapped my leg sharply out and forward, making contact at the precise angle I'd perfected so many soccer practices ago. I still had damn good aim. Pretty decent form, too. Coach would have been proud. I'd landed my kick in the dead center of the canvas, leaving a large, ragged hole. I'd taken out the cigarette-smoking dog completely, and half of the naked woman, too.

The man dropped to his knees in front of his painting, waving his arms and yelling. "What the fuck? *What the fuck!*"

I was dazedly inspecting my right shoe, which, impressively, wasn't damaged—see, *that's* why you pay for top quality—when the guy threw his ruined canvas onto the ground and came toward me. His face was red and shiny.

I tried to back away, but my legs refused to obey me, and I remained rooted to the spot.

The sidewalk artist took two lurching steps toward me.

"Easy, buddy," I heard a gruff male voice say.

I whirled around to see Ted Lassiter standing directly behind me. He pulled a money clip from the pocket of his perfectly draped gray suit. The sidewalk artist suddenly looked unsure of what to do, and Lassiter took advantage of his momentary arrest to peel a single twenty from a thick wad of bills. He crumpled it into the other man's palm. "I believe this was your going rate."

The sidewalk artist looked too bewildered to respond.

Lassiter turned to me with a broad grin. I grinned right back at him.

As we crossed Lexington Avenue, Lassiter clapped me on the shoulder, in exactly the same way he'd greeted Marty Adler at our first meeting.

"Come on, Slugger. We're late."

FOUR

❦

I padded into my kitchen and opened the stainless-steel fridge. The immaculate shelves stared back at me, empty save for a carton of orange juice, a takeout container of chicken tikka masala, an ancient Chobani yogurt, and—*bingo!*—a bottle of Pinot Grigio. The kitchen spoils of a woman who had eaten dinner at home exactly three times in the last month.

Although I'd bought the place two years ago, my apartment still wasn't lived in—no pictures on the stark white walls, no rugs on the bare hardwood floors. "But it doesn't look like anyone *lives* here!" my mother had exclaimed on her last visit to New York. My father just murmured approvingly about the state-of-the-art security system.

I poured myself a glass of Pinot Grigio and returned to the living room to contemplate the events of my day in peace and quiet. I sank down onto the couch—the one splurge I'd allowed myself, a little gift to celebrate my closing on this place. Plush, low-backed, celery-colored, and horribly, impractically, expensive, it was the sort of couch meant to be looked at, more than sat on. Having grown up in a house where every piece of furniture was purchased on sale and remained neatly covered until the precise moment company walked in the door, I was not accustomed to making impulse buys. Still, I'd allowed myself this one luxury.

I took a swallow of wine, settled back against the cushions, and closed my eyes, finally letting myself think about the thing that had been bothering me all afternoon—had nagged at me, even as I sailed through a productive lunch meeting with Ted Lassiter, followed by a successful strategy conference with Marty Adler back at the office.

By all objective measures, it should have been a great day.

But it was an extremely unwelcome realization, to a grown woman of thirty-three who was about to make partner at one of the most powerful law firms in the world, that a single stupid, careless word tossed underhand on the street could still slice right through me as if I were nothing and no one at all.

I felt like I was six years old all over again, and the other kids at Ravenwood Elementary were pushing up the corners of their eyes at me on the blacktop at recess, chanting,

> *Chinese,*
> *Japanese,*
> *Dirty knees,*
> *Look at these!*

This was not still supposed to be happening, was it?

Get a grip, Ingrid, I admonished myself. *What is wrong with you? Why do you even care what some random jerk on the street says? Everything's going just the way you always wanted.* I took another big swallow of wine, put the glass down on the end table, and curled up on my impractically expensive couch, trying to sleep.

I could remember with perfect clarity the first time I saw the gorgeous spirals and peaks of my beloved Manhattan skyline.

It was summer, and I was nine years old. That June weekend, my parents and I drove from our suburban house in Maryland to visit New York City for the first time. I had chattered for weeks about nothing else.

We were going to visit an old colleague of my father's, a well-respected Princeton economist named Roger Giles. Dr. Giles had been a visiting American scholar at my father's university many years ago in Taipei, Taiwan, and he and my father had managed to remain in touch all this time. Every Christmas, my mother would carefully copy a single English sentence that I had written down for her—*Season's greetings to you and yours, and best wishes for the coming new year!*—into a set of boxed Hallmark cards purchased for half-price the previous December 26 and stored for eleven months in our basement. Each year, my parents dutifully sent these cards to the handful of non-Chinese acquaintances they had acquired in the two decades since immigrating to America: a few co-workers; my piano teacher, Mrs. Johnston; two or three neighbors who had invited us to the occasional barbecue or block party (not all our neighbors did); and Dr. Giles.

After retiring from Princeton, Dr. Giles and his wife lived full-time in New York and for years invited my family to come visit them in Manhattan. *After all,* they scrawled in cheerful script across the bottom of their annual holiday letter, *New York is only three hours from Washington by train! We'd love to see how little Ingrid has grown. It sounds like she's turning into quite a good student!*

My father finally accepted their invitation after I came home from school one day and announced that I was one of the few kids in my class who had never seen the top of the Empire State Building.

I loved going on long car trips with my parents. I had no siblings to squabble with in the backseat, so it was always peaceful, sitting with the two people I loved and admired most in our own enclosed, private vessel. I felt safe and comfortable and cocooned from the outside world. Sailing by the factories and old houses and storefronts, my father told funny made-up stories about every point of interest that we passed. My mother hummed along to tapes of old Connie Francis and Elvis songs she and my father liked—the very songs, she said, that my father had used to *woo* her back when they were both college students in Taiwan. There had always been certain oddball English words my mother could surprise me with by actually using in their proper context, and "woo" was one of them.

I loved having their complete and unhurried company for hours. From the front passenger seat, my mother twisted all the way around to explain to me how my father had been Dr. Giles's star economics grad student at Tai Da, the best university in Taiwan, especially because he spoke English far better than most of his peers. My heart swelled with pride and affection. His eyes on the road, my father murmured that she was exaggerating, but I could tell from his voice that he was smiling. As we hurtled along the interstate at seventy miles an hour, I remember feeling as perfect a happiness as I'd ever felt, either before or since. Our little family was completely content and at ease in that car, on our way to see someplace new.

We got to New York around noon. As my father drove around and around midtown, swearing under his breath as he looked for street parking, my mother pointed out the Chrysler Building and Grand Central Terminal and Carnegie Hall and Rockefeller Center.

I couldn't take my eyes away from the window. I had never seen any city like it, and I had never felt so small, but small in such a wonderful way. Small in a way that didn't feel bad, or lonely. Everything felt vital and important here. Bigger, better, faster, more. As if everyone were essential and functioning in a great big machine with lots of moving parts, and it really mattered that they were all here and going about their business exactly as they were doing. That was the moment I vowed that I'd move here one day, the moment New York wooed me.

First, because it was what I wanted, we went to the very top of the

Empire State Building, where a lady greeted all the kids coming out of the elevator with big red lollipops wrapped to look like candy apples, tied with ribbons that said I ♥ NY. My parents hoisted me up to the railing so that I could see all the way down, each of them maintaining a firm grip on my elbows. There was so much to look at from up there. I could even see the line where the blue sky ended and the gray matter that made up the city began.

There was another kid right next to me, about my age, whose dad lifted him up and pointed intently at something. "See that building over there, Max? The big one with the greenish pointy top next to the one with the gold round top?"

"Yeah," the boy replied, bored. I strained to see the one the man was talking about.

"That's where your dad goes to work every day," said the man proudly. "What do you think of that?"

"I know. Can we go now?" said the boy.

As his father let him down from the railing and they walked away, I remember being fiercely jealous of both of them, although I couldn't really have said why.

My ears popped in the elevator down. When we were back on the street, my dad stepped off the curb, raised his arm with a flourish, and gave a merry little wave at the end, showing me how to hail a cab. But the light was red, so no cars were moving. Then my dad looked over at me, winked, and asked, "Want a try?" I nodded. He scooped me up and took a step closer to the street. I raised my arm and waved at the traffic. The light changed, the cars surged forward, and like magic, a yellow taxicab pulled up right next to us. I was enchanted.

The cab dropped us off in front of an enormous, fancy toy store near the entrance to Central Park. We stayed there for hours, but I wasn't allowed to buy anything. I was, however, allowed to get an ice cream cone from one of the vendors in the park, even though my mother said it was getting close to dinner. As I sat there on a green park bench between my parents, with chocolate ice cream dripping onto my knees, watching the horses and carriages going by, I decided that New York City was absolutely the best place in the world.

When long tentacles of afternoon shadow stretched across the park, my father glanced at his watch and said we should make our way to the neighborhood where Dr. and Mrs. Giles lived. We didn't want to be late for dinner. We walked out of the park and paused on the flagstones. My mother suggested stopping for a nice bottle of wine to bring as a gift, and a kind elderly lady out walking the smallest dog I had ever seen pointed us in the direction of a wine store.

After purchasing a bottle of red wine, we hopped into another cab. My father quickly murmured directions to the driver, and he took off. I was proud that my father knew his way around the city and didn't need a map. I was still young enough to believe that my parents knew everything.

We shot up Madison Avenue, turned left onto a block of tall, stately buildings, then took a left again down another wide avenue, where we stopped at a red light. Across the street to my right, the sidewalk had opened onto a large flat plaza, with fountains and benches. "Look." My mother pointed out the window. I peered up at the Metropolitan Museum of Art, the impossibly grand reach of it, the endless tiers of neat white steps, its thick round columns flanking two gigantic, colorful banners. THE OLMEC ART OF ANCIENT MEXICO, I read. REALISM REVISITED: THE AMERICAN MASTERWORKS.

"Can we go in?" I asked.

My father shook his head. "Not today, Ingrid. We don't want to keep Dr. Giles and his wife waiting." He saw the crestfallen look on my face and added, "Next time, okay? New York will always be here. I promise."

The cab stopped in front of an enormous white building with a polished gold plaque at its entrance. My father looked up at the numbers on the green and white awning and said, "This is the one. Right here's fine, thanks."

We pushed through the revolving doors and walked into a gleaming marble lobby with a separate area off to the right that actually looked like someone's living room. Someone rich. I remember thinking suddenly that my mother's shoes made a lot of noise. For the first time that day, I wondered whether we were properly dressed. My mother had wanted to bring a fresh change of clothes for dinner after tromping around the city all day, but Dr. Giles had said to just come as we were, we weren't going anywhere fancy.

A rotund, rosy-cheeked man in a forest green uniform with gold piping at the cuffs and hem stood behind a tall wooden desk a few yards from us. He was busy signing a clipboard held by a skinny man in a brown uniform, who was balancing a large parcel against his hip.

"Forgot the wine!" my father exclaimed under his breath, and dashed back out through the glass doors toward our cab, which was just pulling away from the curb. He took off after it.

My mother approached the doorman and said politely, "We're the Yungs. We're here to see Dr. and Mrs. Giles?"

He looked my mother and me up and down. "How do you spell that?"

"Y-U-N-G," she said, enunciating each letter clearly.

"One moment." He picked up a green phone and dialed a number he seemed to know by heart. He announced us, listened for a moment, then hung up and said, "Yes, they're expecting you. The elevators are around the corner, down the hall, and to your right. Twenty-E." Then he turned back to the newspaper half-hidden in front of him.

"Let's wait over here for your dad," my mother said in Mandarin, herding me away from the doorman. A moment later, my father burst through the doors and came puffing up, holding the black plastic bag that contained the bottle of wine.

The doorman glanced up, jerked his head to the left, and said, "Delivery entrance is around the corner."

My father paused a second, then started past the doorman. "No, I'm here to—"

The doorman stepped out from behind his desk and planted himself in front of my father, blocking his path. "I said, deliveries are around the corner. Can't you understand English?"

My mother made a small noise I hadn't heard her make before, a kind of startled choke.

My father didn't speak for a moment. Then he said evenly, "We are here to have dinner with Dr. Roger Giles. You can tell him it's Dr. Le-Wen Yung and his family."

The doorman looked over at my mother and me now, more carefully this time. My mother raised her chin a little as she returned his stare. I thought for a moment that he might apologize—he *had* to, didn't he? But he just stepped back behind his desk and picked up his paper again. "Yeah, okay," he said. "Twenty-E."

My father had turned a dark shade of red. He and my mother were both silent as the three of us made our way down a long carpeted hall to the elevators. I knew from the set of their faces not to say a word.

I remember wanting to cry, but not a sad kind of crying. An angry kind. I was angry at the man in the dark green uniform, and angry at myself, for feeling embarrassed for my father.

Finally we reached a dark-wood-paneled elevator with a shiny brass handrail. I was surprised to see that another man in green sat inside. He smiled at us and asked, "Which floor?" My parents looked startled by the appearance of another uniformed man, but I piped up, "Twenty, please."

"Right away, young lady."

The doors closed and whisked us the twenty floors up. The elevator traveled so fast that my ears popped, and I thought what a strange and wonderful thing that must be—to live so high above the ground that your ears popped every time you got home!

I snuck a glance at my father. He still had a dark look on his face and stared resolutely at the lit numbers as they counted up to twenty. My mother straightened her skirt and inspected her reflection in a compact from her purse. She reached over and smoothed down my hair, and I squirmed away from her, embarrassed and annoyed, before the elevator stopped at the twentieth floor.

After we sat stiffly through a delicious dinner of roast beef and whipped potatoes, during which neither my mother nor my father had said much, for which I'd compensated by keeping up a constant chatter with the Gileses about what I was learning in the third grade, Dr. Giles suggested retiring to the living room for something he called a cordial. It had been light out when we sat down to dinner, so when we stepped back into the living room, with its wide picture window open to the city, I was not prepared for the view that greeted us.

My mother, father, and I stood together in front of that picture window, gazing out over the dark tops of the trees in Central Park and the majestic spires and towers of Manhattan, glinting silver and pink in the deepening dusk. It was the most beautiful thing I'd ever seen.

"It's quite something, isn't it?" Dr. Giles remarked cheerfully, as he poured four drinks into ornate crystal glasses. "That view's what finally sold Nancy and me on this place."

I could not stop looking and looking out that window, at the deep violet hue spreading across the sky. It felt as if the day's humiliations were draining from my body, and I was waking up fresh. I had never wanted to belong to anything more than to that shimmering landscape of office towers lit up against the dark New York sky. Each individual glittering box of light—like gems strung along a necklace—seemed to me to be a tiny oblong window onto success, acceptance, respect, that is to say, *a place in the world*. Everything that must be good and great and worth striving for. I thought about how each glimmering box of light came with a telephone, a computer, a keyboard, a desk, diplomas on a wall, shelves full of books. I thought to myself that these must be the kinds of things anyone would want. I resolved at that moment to come back here and look at this city skyline someday after I was grown, and know that one of those millions of tiny, far-off, glittering boxes of light in the sky was mine.

I wasn't big. I wasn't strong. I wasn't tall. I wasn't even a boy. But people said I was smart. So I simply willed myself to *succeed*—over and over and over again—because I had to. It was the only way I could think of to protect my parents and myself. It was how I would justify what my family was doing here. I didn't see any other way.

FIVE

The morning of the firm outing dawned bright and beautiful. Of course it did. It was as if Parsons Valentine had ordered up the weather. I wouldn't have been surprised. If anyone could do it, they could.

At nine o'clock on the dot, while the rest of the midtown commuters scrambled to clock in and get to their desks, I boarded one of the luxury charter coaches lined up on Fifty-first Street.

Tyler Robinson, another Corporate associate who worked in the Securities group, waved his arms above his head. "Seats back here, Ingrid."

People were laughing and talking excitedly; golf bags were strewn across seats. The air was charged with the buzzy anticipation of a busload of kids going to summer camp. I made my way down the aisle toward Tyler, nodding to various partners and associates along the way.

Tyler Robinson was six foot four and gorgeous. The only African American associate in Corporate who'd stuck around past his third or fourth year, he was also one of a handful of openly gay attorneys at Parsons Valentine. In private, Tyler and I joked that together we made up the firm's Diversity Dream Team. Between the two of us, the firm got to tick off four boxes on its National Association of Law Placement diversity questionnaire: black, gay, Asian, female. Four exotic birds with just two stones.

And we were, by far, the two most-photographed attorneys in the firm's glossy recruiting brochure. *Look, here's Tyler in a boardroom! There's Ingrid in the law library! Here they both are interacting meaningfully with senior partners!* It was as hilarious as it was sad.

Tyler half-stood. "Window or aisle?" he asked.

"I'll take the window."

He stood up obligingly so I could slide in.

I sank into the seat and, glancing out the tinted window, spotted Murph looking for a bus to board. He was wearing a white golf shirt and khaki shorts, with a tennis racquet bag slung over his shoulder. I rapped once on the glass, and Murph looked up.

I waved.

Murph gave me a thumbs-up. In another second he was striding down the aisle.

Tyler shot me a look. "Really?"

"Come on, it's just for an hour," I said.

Murph and Tyler Robinson were *not* buddies. I wouldn't say that they disliked each other, exactly; just that they were two extremely different kinds of men. Tyler wasn't a "joiner" in firm activities, but if Murph ever left the firm, well, you got the feeling that social life at Parsons Valentine would simply grind to a halt. Not surprisingly, Tyler avoided Murph, Hunter, and the rest of the firm jocks whenever possible. For their part, Murph and Hunter thought that Tyler was "aloof" and "standoffish."

But I had always been a pleaser. I wanted people to get along—with me and with each other. It was exhausting having friends who weren't friends themselves.

"Hey," Murph said breathlessly, flopping into the seat in front of me. "Did you have to find seats *all* the way in back?"

"The cool kids sit in the back of the bus," I told him.

"Yeah, yeah." He stowed his tennis racquet under the seat and then settled himself comfortably against the window, one tanned arm resting along the back of the seat in front of me. He glanced over at Tyler and nodded.

Tyler nodded back without a word.

"So," I said, a little too loudly. "I see you're signed up for tennis today, Murph?"

"Definitely. Hunter and I put in for some doubles. Who knows who we'll get paired up with, though. Hopefully no losers."

"Hopefully not," said Tyler mildly.

Now I gave him a look. *Try harder.*

Tyler rolled his eyes and turned away.

Murph looked at me and mouthed, *What's with him?*

I decided to change the subject. "Why doubles?"

Murph shrugged. "Easier to get court time. Ever since Trask took over."

The Management Committee had discreetly asked Ann Trask, the firm's director of special events, to take over the assigning of teams for golf and tennis. In recent years, the most jocklike male partners had excluded the less athletic lawyers from their golf carts, a practice the firm had deemed *unsporting.*

For the rest of the ride, Murph and I placed bets on which partners would get the most shit-faced while Tyler pretended to nap.

An hour later, the coach turned onto Country Club Drive. We rolled past tall green hedges and a set of massive stone gates at the entrance, bearing a sign that read:

OAK HOLLOW COUNTRY CLUB
EST. 1883
MEMBER AND GUEST ENTRANCE ONLY

The coach pulled up to the clubhouse, a once gracious manor that was now home to corporate events and political fund-raisers. Everybody stood up at once, gathering their stuff and crowding into the aisle. A boisterous clique of summer associates huddled at the front of the bus, joking and talking. "Let me at those pancakes," said one, rubbing his hands together. "Forget the pancakes—let me at that open bar!" said another. "Not til noon, Steinberg," said a third. "Remember, we've got to pace ourselves."

"Oh my God, you guys aren't going to start drinking before noon, are you?" shrieked one of the young women, zipping up a Louis Vuitton squash bag.

The other girls in the group laughed and tossed their long, straight hair as we filed off the bus and into the clubhouse.

Once inside, we walked down a long hallway, our footsteps echoing on the impeccably polished floors, passing a library and a large empty sitting room, until we reached a set of French doors that led out onto the vast stone terrace. Along one edge of the terrace stood a white-tablecloth buffet breakfast, complete with an outdoor grilling station staffed by men in white chef's hats, flipping made-to-order omelets. The air smelled of sizzling bacon and freshly mown grass.

We stood for a moment and surveyed the Parsons Valentine crowd: men decked out in tennis whites or golf shirts and khakis; women wearing crisp sleeveless shirts and tailored shorts, or light-colored tennis skirts. And you've never seen so many people wearing visors.

"Let's go sit over there," suggested Murph, tilting his head toward a table where Marty Adler and Harold Rubinstein sat chatting with a group of summer associates.

"Sure," I said. Tyler just shrugged. We threaded our way through the crowd, only to find Justin Keating sitting at the table, looking bored and complacent. I felt a flash of annoyance. No other paralegals had been invited to the outing. Then again, no other paralegals had Justin's connections.

Adler looked up and half-stood, holding on to the napkin in his lap. "Well, well! The party can begin. Make yourselves at home."

Murph, Tyler, and I pulled out chairs and sat down.

Adler introduced us to the summer associates at the table. Then he asked, "And you all of course know Justin?"

Tyler shook his head. "We haven't met. Hi, Justin, I'm Tyler Robinson."

Justin barely looked at him. "Hi."

Then Murph leaned over, and he and Justin greeted each other with the white male fist-bump. "Hey, Keating."

"Hey."

Just when had *they* gotten so friendly? As far as I knew, I was the only Corporate associate who had the misfortune to have Justin assisting on a deal. Adler leaned toward me and said, "So what's new, Slugger?"

I tried not to look too pleased.

Murph grinned. "Slugger? Who's Slugger?"

"Ingrid. Ever since last week." Adler winked at me, then turned to Harold Rubinstein. "Seems that Ted Lassiter witnessed our very own Ms. Yung here dressing down some jerk on the street. He called me personally to tell me how impressed he was with Ingrid's 'gumption.' Now he's taken to calling her Slugger." Adler looked absolutely delighted.

Harold Rubinstein grinned at me and raised his coffee mug in a little toast. "Here's to you, Slugger."

Tyler and Murph seemed amused.

"Speaking of our friend Ted Lassiter," said Adler, "what's the latest on SunCorp?"

The three summer associates all turned to look at me.

"Well," I began, "I served up the binding term sheet to Binney's lawyers last week and just got a redline back. I'll have my markup to you on Monday, which keeps us on track for an on-time announcement," I said.

In unison, the three summers swiveled their heads back toward Adler, as if they were at a tennis match.

"Any red flags I should know about?" he asked.

"None so far. They marked up the seller's reps and MAC clause pretty heavily, but I'll let you know if I see any showstoppers."

"Impeccable, as always, Ingrid," said Adler. "Keep up the great work."

One of the summers spoke up. "What's a MAC clause?"

"I'll let Ingrid take that." Adler nodded at me.

"Sure." I turned to the guy who'd asked the question. He'd impressed me. Back when I was a summer associate, I would have been too scared to ask a question like that in front of a partner. I would have been terrified to admit that there was so much I didn't know. "So, a MAC is a material adverse change," I told him. "It just means a change in circumstance that affects a bargain after the deal is signed but before it gets closed. If a MAC clause gets triggered, a party might be able to back out of a deal."

"So, for example?" prompted Adler.

"For example," I continued, "if an embargo suddenly went into effect that cut off a main import supply, or a new tax law passed that substantially impacted an industry's bottom line, you could pay your breakup fee—and it might be hefty—but you could walk away from the deal."

The three summers nodded in actual or feigned understanding.

"And there you have it," said Adler.

Murph cleared his throat. "So anyway, Marty, you getting in any golf this year?"

Adler looked at his watch. "As a matter of fact, Justin and I have a ten-thirty tee time. We better get going." He clapped his hands to his knees. "Enjoy the day, everybody. Have fun."

With that, he and Justin stood up, placed their napkins on the table, and walked off into the clubhouse. Murph excused himself to join Hunter at the tennis courts. Tyler peeled off for his squash court reservation.

It was hard not to feel a little lonely as I headed to the deserted women's locker room, stowed my duffel bag, and then wandered down to the pool by myself.

The scene by the pool was in full swing by the time I got down there. No one was swimming, but a line had already formed at the bar. Coolers packed with ice, Perrier, Gatorade, and bottled beer were positioned at convenient intervals across the spotless pool deck. I did what I always did—got a club soda with a wedge of lime and then stretched out on a green-and-white-striped lounge chair, crossing my ankles demurely, pasting a smile on my face, and trying to look like I was having a fantastic time.

The sun reflected off the glittering surface of the pool like tiny gemstones. It felt good on my face and shoulders. I leaned back and closed my eyes, relaxing a little.

Before long, I heard two loud splashes and some high-pitched giggles. I opened my eyes. It was the same group of chatty summer associates I'd seen on the bus. Two of the guys had cannonballed into the deep end of the pool. A third was making a beeline for the open bar— Steinberg, I presumed. The rest of the group were picking out deck chairs and moving them out of the shade, arranging them in a sprawling semicircle a few yards from me.

I put my sunglasses on so I could watch more carefully. I was curious, and more than a little nostalgic. There had been ninety-five of us in my class when we'd first started out, and over a third of us were women. Now, eight years later in Corporate, it was just me, Murph, Hunter, Tyler, and a handful of other guys left standing.

I was still friends with a lot of the women lawyers who'd left Parsons Valentine over the years. I knew they all rooted for me. Every Christmas, I received an enthusiastic chorus of messages: *Keep up the good fight! Looking forward to toasting the firm's first female Corporate partner!!!! Go Ingrid!!*

These messages typically came scrawled on the back of a holiday photo card featuring some impossibly cute two-year-old in a reindeer costume, or one of my former colleagues and her husband, both wearing elf hats and hugging an affable-looking Labrador retriever between them.

As I watched this latest crop of summer associates, shrieking and splashing each other in the pool, I thought about how much I missed that easy camaraderie—the freedom you felt when you were nowhere near up for partner, that blissful safety in numbers. It was so much harder to blend in when there was only one of you.

The one called Steinberg was back with a large tropical drink served in a hollowed-out pineapple. "Hey," he yelled to one of the girls. "Why aren't you in the pool yet?"

This particular girl—the prettiest girl in the group—was a tall, willowy blonde with high cheekbones, fair skin, and a faint spray of freckles across the bridge of her nose. Her hair was swept back into an unfussy chignon and secured with a tiny tortoiseshell pin. She was wearing a chic black cover-up; the white spaghetti straps of a swimsuit top were visibly knotted together behind her neck.

I knew her name—Cameron Alexander—because Murph and Hunter had pointed her out in the Summer Associate Directory, also known among the male attorneys at the firm as The Menu. Cameron had been to Exeter and was a double-Harvard—both college and law school—and, according to her firm bio, did some modeling in her spare time. Runway, not catalog. Rumor had it she was also dating a client, the manager of an exclusive hedge fund the firm represented.

"Come on, Cameron," said the one called Steinberg. "You said you'd be going in."

"I don't see anyone stopping *you* from swimming, Jason," Cameron said with a toss of her head. "Why does it always have to be follow-the-leader with you?"

This seemed to shut Steinberg up for a moment. The other men in the group sniggered.

Good for you, Cameron, I thought.

"Hey, Ingrid, mind if I join you?"

I looked up. It was Tim Hollister, a youngish Corporate partner in our Emerging Markets group. A glint was coming off of his Clark Kent glasses where the sunlight hit them just so.

"Of course not," I said, sitting up and pushing my sunglasses up onto the crown of my head. "Pull up a chair."

I liked Tim. He'd been in the associate class three years above me and Murph, and seemed a little surprised to have woken up one day to discover himself occupying a huge corner office. Even after he'd made partner, Tim still managed to seem like one of us. He was the type of young partner who rarely asked associates to work on weekends if he wasn't also coming in himself. Once, I'd even stood behind him in line in the Jury Box and heard him greet the cashier by name.

Tim swung the nearest deck chair around, parked it next to mine, and sat down, stretching out his long legs. He opened the bottled water he was holding and took a swallow.

"No tropical slushy for you today, Tim?" I asked, inclining my head toward Jason Steinberg and his hollowed-out pineapple.

He looked over and grinned. "Wow. It's only ten fifty. I try to wait til at least noon." Then he looked at me and said, "This is always such a *long* day, you know?"

I nodded, and felt grateful to him for having said it.

We sat in comfortable silence for a moment. I slid my huge Audrey Hepburn–style sunglasses back on my face and studied Tim Hollister in profile. Rumor had it that he actually had a Ph.D. in political theory in addition to his law degree, which made him rather noteworthy to the women at the firm. Tim had salt-and-pepper hair and kind gray eyes. He was the type of guy whose appeal, I guessed, was obvious to most but not all. Intelligent women might disagree as to whether or not he was handsome.

As I was busy thinking all this, he opened his mouth and said to me, "So, Ingrid, the buzz is that you've impressed the hell out of the Sun-Corp CEO."

I nearly fell out of my chair. Tim Hollister and I didn't know each other very well. We barely talked. The fact that this had made its way to him was news.

I tried not to sound giddy. "I'm surprised you heard about that, Tim. But thanks," I said, and meant it.

"Are you kidding?" Tim looked genuinely happy for me. "There are no secrets around this place, believe me. Marty Adler's been crowing about you all week. Just wanted to say I think it's really well deserved. And the timing couldn't be better for you, obviously."

I felt my face flush with pleasure. I was trying to think of something both witty and sincere to say back, but Tim had already turned away and was looking toward the entrance to the pool. Gavin Dunlop, another young Corporate partner, was gesturing impatiently at Tim, pointing at his watch and making exaggerated swinging motions with his arms.

Tim stood. "Gotta run. Eleven o'clock tee time. I'll see you around."

"See you. And thanks. I really appreciate what you said."

"Anytime." He raised both arms and made a graceful free throw with his empty water bottle. I watched it arc smoothly into a nearby bin. Then Tim jogged over toward Gavin Dunlop, and the two of them headed up the grassy slope toward the clubhouse.

I took in a long, deep breath and stretched out my arms and legs as far as they would reach, feeling the pleasant pull in each muscle, the sheer joy of being young and appreciated and good at what you did. I draped one arm lazily above my head and closed my eyes, luxuriating in the warmth of the sun and Tim's words. *I think it's really well deserved.*

My eyes were still closed when suddenly I thought, *It's really quiet. It's too quiet.* A reverent hush had fallen over the pool deck. When I opened my eyes, I saw why.

Cameron Alexander had peeled off her cover-up and was sauntering toward the shallow end of the pool, wearing only a white string bikini. She moved with an unhurried grace, as if she were aware of so many eyes on her and really didn't mind. Steinberg was obediently loping along behind her, still clasping the ridiculous pineapple beverage. He looked like a kid on Christmas morning.

For women lawyers at a firm outing, the swimsuit question presented a conundrum. Just what should a young career woman wear to what was essentially a pool party thrown by her employer? On the one hand—let's be honest—law firms valued good looks and sex appeal as much as anyone. So if you were an attractive young woman, you didn't exactly want to be the class prude, huddled poolside in a parka. On the other hand, showing too much skin wasn't a good idea, either. Not if you ever expected to be taken seriously again. I watched the male attorneys on line at the bar surreptitiously smirk and nudge each other. People pretended to return to their momentarily abandoned conversations but continued to stare in her direction.

Unflustered, Cameron stood alone at the water's edge. She raised one perfect, Pilates-toned leg and dipped a pointed toe into the water.

"Still pretty cold," she announced, loud enough for all of us to hear. "I think I'll wait a bit."

Steinberg didn't seem disappointed to hear this. His objective had been achieved.

"Fine with me," he said, shaking his pineapple drink at her. "I'm out. Let's go get something else to drink."

Cameron shrugged and walked with Steinberg to the back of the drinks line, where they were joined by—I should say *she* was joined by—two male partners who were suddenly extremely interested in striking up a conversation with the summer associates. Before long, Cameron and Steinberg's group of friends had joined them, too, forming a large gaggle in front of the bar.

All the summers were trying to schmooze the partners, but none succeeded like Cameron Alexander. She looked almost queenly, wearing a beneficent smile and occasionally throwing her head back with laughter, as if it were the most natural thing in the world to be standing around barefoot with the Corporate Tax partners, chatting animatedly about the latest summer action flick, while wearing a white string bikini and gesturing with your mojito for emphasis.

I was, if I'm being honest, jealous. Of course I was—but not of the way Cameron looked in her white string bikini. Instead, I was jealous of her confidence and her utter *unself-consciousness*. What would it be like, I marveled, to go through life so utterly unwary? So wholly certain of your belonging to a place that it was never necessary to consider how your next move would be perceived?

Making partner at Parsons Valentine felt like a big final exam to which a select few held the answer key. While the rest of us schmucks had to study.

But you're getting there, too, Ingrid! I quickly reminded myself. Hadn't Tim Hollister just personally congratulated me on the great work I'd been doing? Hadn't Marty Adler called me Slugger? Today was not the day for a pity party. I decided to treat myself to a celebratory margarita or two. I stood up and walked over to join the drinks line.

cy.

Just before dusk, having passed a pleasant afternoon of schmoozing and socializing, watching a little tennis and strolling around the grounds, I made my way over to the clubhouse to get ready for dinner. I slipped into the dress I'd brought—a slim white linen sheath with a simple scalloped neckline—along with a pair of strappy alligator slingbacks. I brushed my hair into place, stepped back, and surveyed the effect in the mirror. Elegant, yet effortless. This was what we were expected to channel all the time. If only it were as easy as Cameron Alexander made it look.

I had a pleasant buzz as I crossed the lawns to the area where dinner would be served. The tent looked lovely, like an oasis. It was a perfect summer evening, the sun had just dipped below the treeline, and the first stars would soon be visible in the night sky. Across the lawn, the stone path near the clubhouse had been lit up with hundreds of tiny tea lights, and the tent itself was adorned with little paper lanterns. Everything felt cozy and festive.

This had been the best firm-outing day I could remember from my eight years at Parsons Valentine. With the buzz from the tequila, and the high from Tim's compliment, I was the happiest, most relaxed I'd been in a very long time.

Under the canopy, the dinner was set up like a stylish wedding reception—twenty round tables set with china and crystal, floral centerpieces glowing in the candlelight. Elegant ivory name cards directed us to our seats. I was pleased to see that Murph and I were assigned to the same table. In fact, it was a good table overall, with Corporate partners Harold Rubinstein and Gavin Dunlop; Pamela Karnow, a no-bullshit, fortysomething partner in Litigation whom I admired; two senior Litigation associates I'd never worked with; and three random summer associates.

Gavin and the three summers were already at the table, discussing the Broadway show the firm had taken them to the previous evening. Then Murph appeared, freshly showered and shaved after his tennis game. His dark blond hair was still damp, and he'd put on a clean white dress shirt and freshly pressed khakis. He looked handsome, and I thought about telling him so.

I sat down between Murph and Gavin Dunlop. Since Gavin was in the Securities group I'd never worked with him, but Tyler had, and thought he was a good guy—a little stodgy, perhaps (Gavin wore bow ties and seersucker without irony), but a straight shooter.

"Hey, Ingrid," Gavin greeted me. Then he introduced me to the three summers.

I scanned the name cards arranged in front of their plates. *Caleb Sweeney, UNC–Chapel Hill. Nate McArdle, Duke. Andrea Carr, Yale.*

Caleb and Nate seemed to know each other well already—I guessed they'd bonded over the North Carolina thing. Nate McArdle had an athletic build and a good tan, and was handsome in an unoriginal way. Caleb Sweeney looked like a nice kid, earnest and scrubbed. I noticed with a sympathetic pang that his hair was neatly parted on the side, unironically, while most other guys were wearing that mussed-up, no-part style. Andrea Carr was a pretty, petite blonde wearing tortoise-shell glasses, a tasteful black dress, and a single strand of freshwater pearls at her throat.

Murph immediately introduced himself to Andrea, grinning his most dazzling grin. How predictable. I'd have to tease him about this later.

Andrea replied in a practiced voice that was faultlessly polite but utterly neutral. I knew that voice. I'd used it myself many times. "Hi, Jeff, it's very nice to meet you." No hair toss, no giggling, no flirtation whatsoever. This surprised and impressed me. Women were not usually this resistant to Murph's charms. On a hunch, I snuck a glance at

Andrea's left hand. Sure enough, there it was: a gigantic engagement ring, winking at me in the candlelight.

After we were joined by Harold Rubinstein, Pamela Karnow, and the two senior associates from Litigation, the waiters came around to fill our wine goblets, and we all tucked into our salads.

I was still enjoying a pleasant buzz and a general, comfortable feeling of all being right with the world. The margaritas hadn't quite worn off yet, and the red wine I was drinking was keeping the glow going.

The waiters came around to take our orders for either steak or salmon. Everyone got the steak except for Andrea Carr. When our entrées arrived, the steak was melt-in-your-mouth delicious—center-cut filet, cooked to rare perfection, served with the chef's award-winning Béarnaise sauce. Appreciative murmurs were making their way around the table when, across from me, Caleb Sweeney raised his hand to flag down a retreating waiter. "Yes, sir?"

Harold Rubinstein, Gavin Dunlop, and Murph, who were busily arguing about the Yankees' abysmal record this season, glanced over at Caleb.

"When you get a chance, could I get some A.1. sauce over here?" Caleb said.

"Excuse me?" asked the waiter.

Gavin Dunlop was staring at Caleb, his fork stilled halfway to his mouth.

"A.1. sauce. For my steak?" Caleb repeated, gesturing toward his plate.

"Sir," began the waiter in a patient voice, "perhaps, if you don't care for Béarnaise, we could offer you the black peppercorn sauce instead? The black peppercorn is also superb."

Harold Rubinstein cleared his throat and waded in. "Yes, Caleb, I'd highly recommend that—I've had it myself, and it's excellent."

"No, I'd really just like some A.1.," Caleb continued, oblivious.

Right then, though, in the split second after, you could see the corners of his mouth go slack, as the realization slowly dawned on him that somehow, without his even noticing it, something had gone terribly, terribly wrong. And it was too late to turn back. The peppercorn life raft had been thrown out and cruelly reeled back in.

The waiter sighed softly. "Very well. We'll see what we can do." He turned on his heel and walked away.

Harold and Gavin exchanged a brief, pointed glance.

Andrea, Nate, and everyone else at the table pretended to concentrate on their dinners. For several moments the only sound was the delicate clinking of forks on china dinner plates.

My heart was breaking for Caleb Sweeney. I realized that I was actually holding my breath. I wanted to reach out, give him a hug, and march him out of that tent and back to the safety of the NYU Law dorm where he was living that summer. *I know,* I wanted to tell him. *It's not fair, and it's not easy. But you'll learn. You just practice until it looks natural, that's all. Fake it til you make it.*

After a few minutes our waiter bustled back to our table clutching something in a neatly folded white cloth. He made a big show of setting the single bottle of A-1 sauce down on our table with a flourish. Then he hurried away without a word.

Caleb Sweeney looked shell-shocked. He sat staring at that bottle of A.1. sauce. I could see him actually turning over and over in his mind what he'd done, how he was going to recover from this later, how hard he'd have to work to make people forget. That is, if he ended up getting an offer from the firm at all.

Murph was engaged in a lively conversation with Harold and Gavin about the Yankees' pitching so far this season. "Yeah, yeah, I know, they never should have traded DeSoto, but they're making up for it with Sanchez. Seriously, look out for him later this season . . ." Still talking, without breaking stride, Murph reached out to the middle of the table, grabbed the A.1. sauce, uncapped it—still making his point about the Yankees' latest trade—and, as if it were the most natural thing in the world, proceeded to pour a glob of the salty brown stuff onto his beautiful, perfect center-cut filet.

After a moment, Caleb Sweeney—the redness already beginning to recede, just a little, from his face—reached out for the bottle and poured a river of the stuff onto his own plate. He polished off his steak in three minutes flat. He even managed to look cheerful again by dessert.

I took another sip of my wine and looked at Murph. Really looked at him. He was still talking baseball with Harold and Gavin, but now they'd moved on to the Mets. My head felt a bit light, and I let myself sink back in my chair and enjoy the warm buzz of the room and the soft candlelight that made everyone look like they were glowing, like old-fashioned movie stars in a black-and-white movie. I was happy.

There was something else I was feeling, something I couldn't quite name at that moment if you were to ask me. When I looked back at Murph, he was looking at me. I was so full of appreciation for him just then. I suddenly wanted him to know that I *loved* what he'd just done for that kid. I flashed him a big warm smile. Murph glanced away from me, replying to something Harold Rubinstein had just said, but underneath the table, I felt him reach over and lightly pat my knee. It was a reassuring, brotherly pat. Just an *I see you, too.*

Then came a loud squawk at the opposite end of the tent. Dave Cavender, a tall, affable partner in Corporate Tax, was standing on a narrow raised platform, adjusting the mike stand. I'd heard that Dave Cavender was friends with Conan O'Brien from back when they'd been on the *Harvard Lampoon* together, and had never quite gotten over the fact that Conan hosted his own TV show while Dave had wound up a goddamn tax attorney.

Across from me, Pamela Karnow pushed back her chair and stood.

"Excuse me, folks," she said genially. "It's showtime!" She threaded her way through the tables to join Dave Cavender up on the stage.

An expectant hush fell over the crowd. People angled their chairs toward the stage. Whistles and catcalls sprang from the tables down in front.

The annual Parsons Valentine Law Revue—a hallowed firm tradition—was a rare chance to laugh, let loose, and see your buttoned-up, straitlaced colleagues make fools of themselves in a way that was not only spectacularly public but also ordained by the firm.

Dave Cavender had been the official emcee of the Law Revue for the last three years, ever since the summer he'd unveiled a spectacularly hysterical short film he'd written, directed, and shot himself that spoofed *The Godfather*. He'd even managed to get Marty Adler to swivel slowly around toward the camera in his massive green leather chair, holding a cigar and a Scotch, and say in a low, gravelly voice: *Never go against the firm, Dave. The firm is family.*

"We've got a great show for you this year, folks! Great show!" Dave was up at the mike, wearing a top hat at a jaunty angle, holding both palms up in the air. He seemed to be enjoying himself.

Pamela Karnow stood next to Dave, beaming. She had donned a matching top hat and was holding a set of index cards and a PowerPoint clicker.

Offstage, Ann Trask was sitting at a small table with a sound system and speakers. I liked Ann Trask—even before I'd found out that she'd once nixed the Management Committee's idea of making the cafeteria staff dress in traditional ethnic costume for "International Food Day."

The lights dimmed. Pamela looked over at Ann and nodded, and she cued the music at full blast. I laughed, recognizing the first few notes of a cheesy pop song I hadn't heard in years, something about a guy on a catwalk and being too sexy for—what? His pants? His shirt? I looked over at Murph. Too sexy, indeed. He laughed, too, and nudged my arm.

A video began to play. Pamela Karnow shouted into the mike, "And now, ladies, for your viewing pleasure, may I present—the men of Parsons Valentine!"

We whooped and applauded.

It was a Chippendales-style video calendar. The first image announced MR. JANUARY! followed by a beefcake photo of Lincoln Forster, a popular, lanky, redheaded Tax associate in his sixth year, whom everybody called Link. In the shot, Link was standing outside by the bronze corporate sculpture in front of the Parsons Valentine building, turning to the camera with a shy smile, fully dressed in a crisp shirt and tie, with his gray suit jacket hooked over one shoulder. He was adorable. The pose sort of made him look like England's Prince Harry, and this was not exactly a bad thing.

The room erupted in laughter, whistles, and applause. Everyone was in hysterics. I glanced around, looking for Link Forster. He was sitting a few tables away, at a table crowded with tax partners and summer associates. His male colleagues were convulsing with laughter and clapping him on the back as Link grinned and blushed profusely.

The images on screen shifted. Phil Calabrese, a new lateral partner in Private Equity, was Mr. February. Phil had been photographed in his corner office, standing by the windows in a kind of power stance, feet planted widely apart, arms crossed over his chest, eyes boring into the camera lens with a challenging, *I mean business* expression. Actually, it was distinctly sexy.

Mr. March was some third-year Litigation associate I didn't know, but Mr. April turned out to be none other than Murph.

I fell over laughing.

Beside me, Murph pretended to be insulted. "Come on, Yung, it's not *that* funny." But he was nearly doubled over in hysterics himself.

In a classic Murph move, he'd decided to camp it up for his photo, actually allowing himself to be photographed shirtless, emerging from a glassed-in shower, with damp hair and a white towel wrapped loosely around his waist. You could tell he was trying for a steamy, *fuck me* expression in the eyes, an effect that was spoiled by the huge goofy grin on his face.

I recognized the setting. Murph's shower photo had been taken in the firm's infamous "R&R suite" up on the fortieth floor—a pair of cool, dark rooms with cots and pillows, like in a school nurse's office, and an adjoining bathroom with real bathing facilities. These rooms were provided for the "convenience" of Parsons Valentine attorneys pulling all-nighters in the office, to catch a wink of sleep or freshen up before a morning closing. But the suite had all the ambience of a prison cell, so being there felt less like R&R and more like detention. Luckily, I'd never had to avail myself of the Parsons Valentine shower facilities—I lived close enough to cab home in those silent, wee hours of the morning, take a fast shower in my own bathroom, blow-dry my hair, and change into a fresh suit and clean underwear before turning around and cabbing straight back to the office.

To the crowd's disappointment, the slides stopped abruptly after Mr. October. As the end credits rolled and the lights came back up, Pamela Karnow returned to the mike.

"Hey, what gives?" a male Litigation partner heckled from the front row. "What about Mr. November and December?"

Pamela deadpanned, "Well, the plan was to have a different photograph for all twelve months, but unfortunately we were not able to locate twelve hot guys who actually work at our firm."

At this, every single woman in the audience burst out laughing, cheering, and clapping. I let out an appreciative whoop.

"Amen, Pam!" somebody else hollered.

Murph leaned over to me, grinning, and stage-whispered, "Um, isn't this, like, sexual harassment or something? There's no way we could talk about any *female* attorneys like that!"

I shouted happily above the din, "Come on, Murph, can't you take a joke?"

Pamela Karnow bowed dramatically and exited the stage. Dave Cavender returned to the mike, clapping.

"Thanks, Pam! I'll try not to take it personally that I wasn't asked to pose. I must have been away that week."

The audience tittered appreciatively.

"Next, ladies and gentlemen, for your entertainment, the musical stylings of Matt McCallum, Kyle Latham, and Hunter Russell!"

Murph and I hooted in delight.

"Oh, now *this* I've got to see!" he laughed.

"*Hunter?* Can *sing?*" I leaned over and elbowed Murph happily.

Harold Rubinstein glanced at us with a mock horrified expression. "Musical stylings of Hunter Russell?" he shouted over the noise of the crowd. "I think we should all be very, very afraid."

Murph grinned, cupped both hands around his mouth, and chanted "Russ-*ell!*" at the stage.

The lights dimmed.

I was taking another sip of wine when I sort of *felt,* rather than heard, a low, excited murmuring, followed by a few barks of raucous laughter coming from a few tables behind ours. Beside me, Murph had a mildly shocked look on his face. "Oh, shit. Oh, no, they did not."

I looked toward the stage.

I didn't actually understand what I was seeing at first. Well, I mean I *knew* what I was seeing, but I didn't really *believe* it. Hunter, along with Kyle and Matt, both fifth-year associates in the Securities Litigation group, were standing in a row onstage, next to a huge, old-school boombox stereo. Kyle and Hunter, arms crossed defiantly across their chests, their lips curled into insolent snarls, were both wearing dark, baggy tracksuits, ropes and ropes of gold chains around their necks, and dark glasses. Hunter wore a Lakers baseball cap turned to the side. Kyle had put on a do-rag and two ostentatiously fake gold-capped teeth, and he was holding something that looked suspiciously like—*No! They wouldn't, would they?*—a crack pipe.

Matt McCallum was dressed in a black T-shirt and extremely baggy jeans, which he had pulled halfway down his ass, so that his abs and the top of his briefs were showing. He, too, wore tons of heavy gold jewelry and had given himself huge fake tattoos of Chinese characters up and down both arms. Like Hunter and Kyle, Matt was wearing dark sunglasses, but—unlike the other two—he had added a wig.

Matt McCallum had given himself fake cornrows.

"Yeeeeah, yeeeeah!" Matt screamed into the mike. "A'ight, fools! Me and my homies are *in the house!*"

Oh my God. This could only end badly.

I craned my neck and scanned the surrounding tables, looking for Tyler. It was too dark with the dimmed lights. I couldn't see him. I turned back around and screwed my eyes shut tight for a second. *Please, please don't.* I sent up a fierce, desperate prayer.

Onstage, Hunter knelt down and pressed a button on the boombox. In the next instant, a thick, pulsing beat shook the entire tent. We could feel the earth beneath us throb along with the deep, steady bass. Then a familiar swelling of orchestral strings began to sing up top, and I recognized the song immediately. It was a popular hip-hop song from years ago, the soundtrack to a Hollywood movie. It had been one of the earliest rap songs to cross genres and hit the top of the mainstream pop charts.

It was, in other words, a rap song that rich white people had heard of.

Hunter, Kyle, and Matt swayed their bodies to the beat of the low, steady bass, their palms open and swinging in front of them, swiping at the air in random arcs. Both Hunter and Kyle were comically awkward dancers, but then I realized that they were doing this deliberately, poking fun at themselves, purposely stepping on the offbeat, playing directly to the stereotype of clueless white guys attempting to rap.

But Matt McCallum seemed really into it. Matt was pumping his fists in the air and violently jerking his body in time to the music. He had a steely, pissed-off death glare in his blue eyes and a convincing sneer on his face. Matt McCallum was not going for comic effect. He was in character.

I strained to focus on the spoof lyrics they were belting out:

> *As I walk through the valley of the shadow of death*
> *I take a look at my life and see there's not much left*
> *'Cuz I've been working at this firm for so damn long,*
> *Even my mama thinks my mind is gone*
> *But we keep billing and billing, we can't ever stop*
> *If one of these days we want to wind up on top*
> *You better watch how you're talking, and watch how you're walking*
> *Or you and your homies might never get made*
> *Now I'm the kinda guy the little homies wanna be like*
> *Dinner at Luger's, weekend house at the seaside*
> *But ninety-hour weeks they go down kind of hard*
> *They never told us any of this back in Harvard Yard!*

Now Matt took a step backward to join Hunter and Kyle and, still swaying in unison and waving their arms in the air, the three of them launched into the chorus, singing at the top of their lungs:

> *Been spending most our lives, working in a partner's paradise*
> *Been spending most our lives, working in a partner's paradise*

Been spending most our lives, working in a partner's paradise
We'll keep spending most our lives, working in a partner's paradise

Oh my God.

The tent felt like it was closing in on itself; the air around me was still and very close. Slowly, taking care to have a neutral expression on my face—as neutral as possible—I glanced around the table. Gavin Dunlop was grinning and nodding his head in time to the beat. Andrea Carr's forehead was furrowed. She looked grim. I knew I liked that Andrea Carr. Caleb and Nate, meanwhile, just looked bored.

I snuck a look at Murph. His arms were crossed over his chest, and he had a quiet, thoughtful look on his face, but it was impossible to read. I couldn't tell if Murph looked thoughtful because—like me—he was contemplating the idiocy of three incredibly privileged lawyers spoofing a song that was a lament to the destructive cycle of gangster violence in the inner city, or because he was thinking that he could have come up with way funnier lyrics.

As casually as I could, I looked around at the neighboring tables. Many of the senior partners were laughing and actually tapping their toes and slapping their thighs in time to the throbbing bass beat. Most of them didn't seem aware that anything unusual was happening. A few younger lawyers did look uncomfortable, though, and just offstage, Pam Karnow looked downright pissed.

I finally spotted Tyler. He was seated a couple of tables behind me, with his arms hanging limply at his sides, making no eye contact with anyone at his table. The summer associate sitting next to him looked mortified. Tyler looked both sad and utterly unsurprised. I willed him to look over at me, but he didn't.

I turned back toward the stage. I watched helplessly as Hunter, Kyle, and Matt anchored their arms about each other's shoulders and belted out the next verse:

Power and the money, money and the power

Minute after minute, hour after hour

You accumulate your riches

Grab your hos and your bitches

Now that me and my homies got made

And so our wives get younger

Our cars get bigger

Gotta run a lot faster

To catch up with this n———!

Except they didn't say "N———." I couldn't believe it. They actually sang the word that rhymes with "bigger."

I gasped. And I was not alone. There was a collective sucking in of breath from the tables near us.

Murph glanced over, caught my eye, and shot me a look. *Holy shit.*

I twisted around just in time to see Tyler Robinson walk out of the tent. I pushed back my chair, murmured, "Excuse me," to no one in particular, and hurried after him.

"Tyler?" I ran out into the deepening dusk, peering across the shadowy, gently sloping lawn. "Tyler?" The evening had turned cool, and I rubbed my bare arms, shivering, not sure which way to go. He was nowhere to be seen.

"Tyler! Where are you?"

"Hey," he said, much closer than I'd expected.

I whirled around. He was a few yards away from me, leaning against the thick gnarled trunk of an old oak tree.

I walked over to him.

"Hey." I stood beside him, against the oak, which smelled mossy and damp. We were silent for several long moments.

I slid down along the base of the tree and settled onto one of its ancient, twisted roots, surprised at how solid and steady it felt beneath my weight. I tilted my face up, staring up through the wizened old branches at the stars, which stood out in sharp relief against the clear night sky. You never saw stars like this in the city, and I thought about how incongruous all this beauty was with everything that was going on underneath the tent.

I felt like I should say something to let Tyler know he wasn't the only one in the world who ever felt like this. As long as I lived, I would not learn to leave a quiet moment alone.

"Tyler, I don't know what those guys were thinking—" I began.

"Stop." He held a hand up like a traffic cop. "Don't. You don't have to. Let's not talk about it."

"Okay," I practically whispered.

"Damn." Tyler pounded his fist against the tree. I jumped. "Nothing surprises me around here anymore. You know that?" He broke away and started striding up the hill toward the clubhouse.

I followed him. "Wait, where are you going? The first buses back to the city don't leave for at least another hour."

"You stay if you want. I'm calling a fucking cab."

I sped up after him, struggling to keep up as the heels of my strappy sandals sank into the soft, moist sod. "But Tyler, what if someone asks where you went?"

He stopped. He laughed once and spun around. I realized I'd just asked an incredibly stupid question.

"Ingrid," he said, and both his hands were clenched in fists, "I'm done. I've already spent an entire day faking conversation with people I can't stand, and I'll be damned if I let myself just sit here and smile through another second of their fucking *dinner entertainment*."

"Listen, Tyler, what if we just—"

"No. I'm not doing this anymore." He shook his head. "I've stayed too long as it is." And he wasn't just talking about the outing.

"Tyler, wait." I reached out and touched his arm.

"No." He shook me off. Then he looked pointedly at me. "You stay, then."

His words stung me.

He broke into a fast run, up the hill. In another moment, he rounded the corner of the clubhouse and disappeared entirely.

I felt completely and utterly alone, more alone than I had ever felt in the nearly ten years since I'd been at Parsons Valentine. Because Tyler had just planted a nagging, bitter little seed of doubt. About what we were both still doing here.

I shivered, noticing again the chill in the evening air. I wished I'd brought a wrap. Slowly, carefully, trying not to slip on the grass moist with evening dew, I made my way back across the lawn to the tent and slipped back inside.

As I slid back into my seat, Gavin Dunlop leaned over and whispered, "Everything okay?"

I nodded.

Everything was *not* okay. I felt sick. Incredibly, the crazy skit was still going on. Onstage, Matt McCallum was still "rapping." Hunter and Kyle were rhythmically bending their knees and arcing their arms around wildly.

> *Been spending most our lives, working in a partner's paradise*
> *We'll keep spending most our lives, working in a partner's paradise*

I couldn't stand to look at them. I tried staring down at the table instead, but the streaks of raspberry ganache left on my dessert plate suddenly looked garish and obscene—pornographic, even—and made me feel more nauseous. Everything seemed to be happening in slow motion. Across from me, Harold Rubinstein shifted uneasily in his seat. Just outside the tent, Pamela Karnow and Dave Cavender appeared to be arguing, she gesticulating at the three men on the stage, Dave's shoulders up in a permanent shrug, as if to say, *I know, but what exactly do you want me to do?*

The space around me was spinning, and a stifling hush fell over the crowd; I had the weird sensation that we were all underwater. It felt almost like I was drowning. And every other sound underneath that tent was muffled to my ears except for those three clear voices—bright, drunk, gleeful, a little off-key—coming from the stage.

The song went on for another two verses. No one made a move to stop the performance.

When they had finished, and the throbbing bass beat finally faded out, I could still feel a hammering in my throat and in my chest and, seemingly, in the ground beneath our table. An edgy silence fell over the tent, followed by some uneven applause. About half the audience was clapping. How was that even happening? A few partners actually seemed amused by the skit. Most people looked baffled and uncomfortable. Some were absolutely livid and were whispering and gesturing toward the stage.

I looked back around toward Tyler's empty seat. *I don't blame you,* I thought.

"Jesus H. Christ, doesn't anyone ever vet these things before the outing?" I heard Harold Rubinstein grumble in a low voice, more to Gavin Dunlop than to anyone else at the table. "We're gonna hear about *that* again, believe me."

Gavin shrugged. "Come on, it's called satire! No harm, no foul. Just a bunch of drunk guys having some fun. Tasteless, maybe, but no one'll even remember this by Monday."

Harold gave Gavin a disbelieving look. "I'm not so sure about that, Gavin."

Gavin ignored this.

"Well," he said brightly to the rest of us. It seemed like he was look-ing directly at me. "*That* was certainly—interesting, huh?"

"Interesting's not quite the word," said Murph.

I could not will myself to say anything. I didn't trust myself to sound as breezy and blasé as I felt I needed to at that moment. I looked away and noticed a uniformed waiter calmly clearing dessert plates from a nearby table. He was the only African American man underneath the whole tent, and, aside from me, the only person of color in sight. He was older than my father.

I picked up my wineglass, which had just been refilled, and downed the whole thing in a couple of swallows.

Murph leaned over and whispered, "Hey, whoa. Take it easy. What's wrong with you?"

What was wrong with me? My head was swimming, my ears were pounding, and I just wanted the night to be over so I could get away from this crowd, as quickly as possible.

A few tables away, Marty Adler gestured toward Harold Rubinstein. "Excuse me," Harold said, pushing his chair away from the table. He and Adler walked out of the tent and conferred quietly in the darkness. Rubinstein was nodding his head and rubbing his temples while Adler appeared to be telling him something very serious.

Pam Karnow was back up onstage. She looked flustered and angry, but she grabbed the mike and said, "Okay, folks, we're gonna keep things rolling here. Next up, we have . . ."

But the air had been sucked out of the place, the mood had irrevo-cably changed, and a few more senior partners from the Management Committee were walking over to join the huddle of partners talking quietly just outside the light of the tent.

"I don't feel so good," I suddenly leaned over and whispered to Murph. "It feels like the room's kind of, um, spinning."

Murph looked at me and quickly handed me his glass. "Here, have some water." I took great big thirsty gulps. The water felt good and cool going down.

"Jesus, how many margaritas did you have by the pool today?" Murph said, in a low voice only I was close enough to hear.

"I don't know." I held up three fingers. "Four? Five? I feel like I'm going to be sick."

"We need to get you home," Murph said. He glanced at his watch. "Listen, the first buses back should be boarding pretty soon. I'll walk you out of here. Do you think you can stand?"

I nodded, but my head felt light.

Murph and I quickly bade good night to the rest of the table. He discreetly kept a firm steadying hand on the small of my back as we made our way back up the terraced path to the clubhouse.

As soon as we got inside the cool, darkened hallway of the old stone building, our footsteps echoing on the polished floors, I started to feel better. It felt so good to be away from the din of the tent and that incredibly stupid song, and Hunter, Kyle, and Matt seemed very far away from here.

Also, it felt good to be alone with Murph.

As we walked down the corridor, Murph glanced out a window toward the long, winding driveway. "See? Looks like two of the coaches are already boarding. Come on, let's go. You'll feel better after you've gotten some sleep on the ride home."

But I wasn't ready to leave the cool stillness of the clubhouse, not yet.

"Can't we just sit somewhere for a minute?" I said. "Please. Just for a minute." I reached down and took hold of Murph's hand.

Murph looked at my hand, then back up at me. "You okay, Yung? Do you still feel sick?"

"I'll feel better if I just sit here for a minute." I led him a few tentative steps out of the corridor and into an empty parlor room.

He didn't argue.

I peered around in the semidarkness, spotted a plush, inviting divan in the corner, and steered us both toward it.

We sat.

Then—because it felt natural, and before I realized I was going to do it—I leaned my head against Murph's shoulder, nestled myself against him, and closed my eyes. He smelled nice—he had that scrubbed young bachelor smell of shaving cream and deodorant soap and laundry dryer sheets—and I took in a long, deep breath, trying to fill my lungs with it.

The room had stopped spinning, and I felt very close to sleep.

"This is nice," I heard myself murmur.

Murph said nothing. But I could hear his calm, measured breathing, could feel the reassuring rise and fall of his chest beside me. When I raised my head slightly to look at him, he had tilted his head back along the top of the couch, and his eyes were closed. He had extremely long, sandy eyelashes. I had never noticed that before.

"Murph," I said sleepily.

Pause.

"Huh."

"Why were you so nice to that Caleb kid tonight?"

Murph didn't answer, and for a moment I thought it was because he didn't know what I was talking about, or maybe he'd fallen asleep. But then he said in a low voice, "Because I would hope that someone would do something like that for me."

I thought about that for a moment. Then I looked up and said, "I don't understand. Why would anyone need to do something like that for *you*?"

His eyes fluttered open. He looked at me. "What are you talking about?"

"It's just that—well, you're Murph."

"What's that supposed to mean?"

"You know. You just fit in so perfectly."

Murph laughed. "You think you know everything, don't you?" he said softly. His eyes were closed again.

"No." I shook my head and sat up. It suddenly seemed extremely important that I set the record straight. "That's just it, Murph. I *don't* think I know everything. When I first got here I didn't think I knew *any*thing! I just mean that you know how to play the game so well, that's all. It doesn't come naturally to me the way it does for you."

I couldn't believe I was actually saying all of these things to Murph. I'd never said anything like this to anyone before except Tyler. And I knew Tyler would not approve of my telling all this to someone like Murph. One of them.

"And what makes you think it comes naturally to me?" Murph asked.

"Are you kidding? It's obvious. It's all about what you're used to."

"What I'm used to?"

"Yeah. I just mean that when you come from a place of privilege, this place is a lot easier to navigate."

Now he turned his head and looked at me sideways. "A place of privilege?" he asked. I could hear his quotes around the phrase. "And what would *I* know about coming from a place of privilege?"

Murph was confusing me. I knew that rich white people didn't like to talk about their money, but as long as I was being this honest with him, I felt he should be so with me. It seemed only fair.

"Huh?" he nudged. His voice was gentle. I could tell he wasn't mad, just curious.

"Well, your family's house on the Cape, for one," I blurted. It was the first thing I could think of.

He laughed again.

"What?" I said.

"You've got a vivid imagination, Yung. It's not *my* family's summer house—it's my college roommate's. I've just been invited up to Chatham every summer since sophomore year. They let me tag along."

"So that's when you learned to sail?"

"Well, there wasn't exactly a sailing club at West Tilden Regional High School," Murph said.

"You went to a public high school?"

Murph leaned in close, like he was letting me in on something. "I just finished paying off all my student loans last year, Yung. I had tons to pay off, college *and* law school."

I felt like an idiot. All these years I had somehow managed to make up a whole life, an elite prepster history for Jeff Murphy that simply didn't exist. As much as it bothered me when people assumed things about me, well, seems I was just as guilty.

"Wow," I said finally. "I'm sorry I—"

"Look," Murph cut in. "We all make assumptions about each other. It's what people do."

"I guess." I still felt sheepish.

Murph leaned his head back and closed his eyes again. "And for the record, I think about that stuff sometimes, too."

I think I said, "Then you and I have more in common than I thought." But maybe I just thought this.

We sat there, peacefully, in the stillness of the darkened clubhouse, with my head resting on Murph's shoulder, for what seemed like a long time. At some point I dozed off. I don't know how long we sat there in the darkness—maybe ten minutes, maybe an hour—before a large, clamorous group of summer associates made their way down the corridor toward the buses, talking loudly.

"I couldn't fucking *believe* those guys!" shrieked one.

"Yeah, this'll be up on YouTube in about two seconds," giggled another.

"Good luck explaining *this* at on-campus recruiting this fall," someone else said, laughing.

Murph gently jostled my shoulder. "Okay, Yung, we should go." He stood up, grabbed both my wrists, and pulled me to my feet. He had to work at this, because I was resisting. I never wanted to leave the comfort and safety of that room, and I wanted Murph to stay there, too.

When we were both on our feet, he gave me a brief, awkward little hug. "Come on, we still need to get our stuff from the locker rooms. The sooner we get back to the city, the sooner we can get you home."

I dozed nearly the entire bus ride back to Manhattan—my head against the window, Murph feeling solid and warm beside me, eyes closed. Having him there made me feel so protected, so safe. Even more than that, I was beginning to feel *understood*.

Murph was right. I did feel better by the time we stepped off the bus in front of the Parsons Valentine building, although I was still a little woozy and the silhouette of midtown looked a hazy blur. I stood obediently on the sidewalk while Murph flagged down a cab to take me the ten blocks uptown to my apartment. He waited until I'd folded myself into the backseat before leaning into the cab and telling the driver, "Make sure you see her get safely into the building, right?" and handing him a twenty.

Get in, I wanted to say to Murph. *Don't leave me yet.* It had felt so nice to be so close to him, in the safety of the clubhouse and on the bus, and to be talking, really *talking,* but now it felt like some precious window was abruptly closing, and I wasn't going to get a chance to say what I really wanted. *Get in, Murph. Come home with me.*

"Get in," I actually mumbled, but if Murph heard this, he chose to ignore it.

He gently shut the door of the cab, leaned his head in the window, and said, "You'll be all right, Yung. Sleep it off. I'll see you Monday."

As my taxi pulled away from the curb, I watched Murph's figure get smaller and smaller in the rearview mirror.

The driver let me out in the horseshoe drive of my building. True to his promise, he waited until I reached the lobby doors before speeding off. Safely ensconced inside the soothing, tomblike privacy of the elevator, I closed my eyes and slumped against the brass handrail as it hurtled the nineteen floors up.

Once inside my apartment, I kicked off my shoes, tossed my bag toward the couch, and noticed the message light blinking on the phone on my hall table.

"Ingrid-ah," my mother's voice came through in Mandarin. "It's Friday, after ten o'clock, you're still not home? I heard it's a little cool in New York today—make sure you bring a sweater when you go out. Daddy and I worry about you, up there all by yourself, always working so hard. Call home when you can. Love, Mom."

Hearing her voice made me inexplicably sad. I didn't want my parents to worry about me all the time. Wasn't I doing just fine as it was? Wasn't I getting everything they came here for in the first place?

I went into my bedroom and stepped out of my white cocktail dress, leaving it in a little pool on the floor. As I climbed into bed, exhausted, tipsy, a little sad, wrapping myself tightly in my duvet, my final thought before my head hit the pillow was that I should have kissed Jeff Murphy as we sat there alone in the darkness of that clubhouse, and now the moment was irretrievable.

SIX

❦

"Parsons Valentine Summer Outing Marred by Racist Parody."
That was the headline of Monday's *New York Law Journal.* The
New York Post was more creative—"Ghetto, Fabulous? White-Shoe Law
Firm Gets Black Eye." All the legal blogs and chat rooms were abuzz
over the "racist scandal over at Parsons Valentine." Ninety-three seconds of grainy cell phone footage had been posted over the weekend
to both YouTube and Above the Law before the firm had finally gotten
them to take it down. In the video, you couldn't really make out what
was happening onstage, but you could hear the song's refrain clear as
you please. A scathing post on Gawker was titled simply "Parsons: Paradise?" It had already gotten 477 comments, and still counting.

It was nine fifteen when Rachel called. "So were you there for the
skit?" she asked breathlessly. "Did you actually *see* it?"

"Oh, I saw it, Rach," I sighed.

"And? Was it as bad as all the blogs are saying?"

"It was worse."

"Wow," she breathed. "So what do you think they're going to do
about it?"

"What do you mean?"

"I mean, they've got to be in full damage control mode by now."

"I'm not sure there's much they *can* do," I said. They sure as hell weren't going to fire Hunter Russell, that much I knew.

"But they've got to do some kind of CYA," Rachel shot back. "Don't you remember what happened at Foster Cowan?"

Of course I did. Foster Cowan & Mays LLP had been one of the dozen or so firms in the city that considered itself Top Five—until a few years ago, when six female associates reported being groped by two inebriated male partners during the firm's annual summer booze cruise around Manhattan. After weeks of stubborn silence, Foster Cowan had finally issued a single tepid statement: *We are regretful if anyone in attendance felt in any way aggrieved by any of our attorneys' actions.*

Basically, we're sorry you're so sensitive.

In an even more stunningly boneheaded move, each female lawyer at the firm had received a ceramic mug and a hoodie.

The nation's top law schools had responded swiftly, some even going so far as to ban Foster Cowan from recruiting on campus. All of the SAs—WLSA (Women Law Student Association), AFALSA (African American Law Student Association), APALSA (Asian Pacific American Law Student Association); LALSA (Latino American Law Student Association); and LGBTLSA (Lesbian Gay Bisexual Transgendered Law Student Association)—mobilized their troops, firing off thousands of e-mails urging recipients to PLS FORWARD!!!!!! Sure enough, fewer *Harvard Law Review* résumés came in to Foster Cowan that year than at any previous time in the firm's hundred-year history. A small but conspicuous cluster of Fortune 100 clients began publicly taking their business to other law firms—news that rated a brief item in the business section of the *Times*. The firm's Top Ten ranking plummeted.

Foster Cowan had been, as it were, *blacklisted*.

Two years later, however, Foster Cowan had recruited a high-profile African American female senior partner and inaugurated the Foster Cowan Women in Law Fellowship at Columbia Law School. Many of its top clients returned, and Foster Cowan was allowed back to recruit at Harvard and Yale.

It was back to business as usual.

By midweek, Pamela Karnow, along with a dozen or so other Parsons Valentine partners and associates outraged by the skit, had formed a group called FLARE—Firm Lawyers Against Racism Everywhere. I'd heard that even a few summer associates had joined up, including none other than Cameron Alexander (along with, I was sure, a couple of members of her fan club). FLARE was demanding an emergency meeting with the firm's Management Committee to discuss an appropriate response and possible disciplinary action.

To my knowledge, no one on the Management Committee had said a single word to Matt, Kyle, or Hunter about any disciplinary action. In fact, the three of them were looking quite chipper when I spotted them together at lunch in the Jury Box. There'd even been a flattering note in the firm newsletter—the *Daily Brief*—on our recent Lawyers League softball victory over Simpson Thacher, in a squeaker, thanks to a double late in the final inning, hit by Hunter himself.

In the days since the outing, I'd been trying hard to avoid running into Hunter. Personally, I didn't think he was an actual racist, just an idiot. Anyway, I resolved not to get in the middle of it. Let FLARE do its thing, if it wanted to. I had enough on my plate to worry about.

"Knock, knock."

I looked up from the SunCorp purchase agreement I was reviewing to see Marty Adler leaning into my office, a big Cheshire Cat grin on his face. "Hi, Ingrid. You coming up to the meeting?"

"Of course."

"The meeting" was the Corporate Department lunch scheduled for twelve thirty. We held these department luncheons the second Friday of every month, ostensibly to "bond" as a department. The real purpose, however, was for the rainmakers to beat their chests and let the associates know what new deals we should expect to be slaving over in the weeks ahead.

"Care for an escort?" Adler held out an arm as if asking me to dance.

I laughed. "Thanks, but I have to respond to an e-mail from Ted Lassiter first. See you in a minute?"

"Okay. But don't be late, now."

Something was up. Marty Adler did not come to associates' offices merely to round us up for a routine department meeting. "What's going on, Marty?" I asked, smiling a little, looking at him sideways. "Why are you so worried about me being there?"

"Well, let's just say we have something a little special on the agenda today. I think you'll be very pleased, Ingrid." He winked. "See you up there." Then he was gone.

I stared at the empty doorway for a full minute, trying to suppress my jubilance. The e-mail could wait. Adler was clearly planning to mention to the entire department what an amazing job I'd been doing on SunCorp. How I'd won Ted Lassiter over after our rocky first meeting, and how he would now only phone Adler with a question when he couldn't reach me first.

I arched my back, took a deep breath, and sauntered over to my wardrobe mirror. I freshened up my lip gloss and mascara before heading up to the conference room.

People were still trickling in, even though it was already ten minutes past our start time. This was common practice. Parsons Valentine lawyers did not show up for internal meetings on the dot; it would suggest you didn't have enough to do at your desk.

A lectern had been set up at the front of the room. The tables were arranged in a wide U. Water pitchers were set up at four-seat intervals along the length of the starched white tablecloths, and a buffet lunch was laid out in silver chafing dishes along one wall. The aromas of roasted potatoes and some kind of fish wafted toward me. As I got in the buffet line, Hunter came up behind me and said, a little too close to my ear, "God, I hope this doesn't take all day. I've got so much shit to do."

I wasn't thrilled to see him, but I was in too good a mood to really mind. "Yeah, tell me about it."

Murph came into the room, spotted me, and smiled. I smiled back at him, and my face grew warm as he walked toward us.

"Hey, guys."

"Hi," I said, trying to sound casual.

Murph studied me. "You look happy. What's the occasion?"

"Oh, nothing," I said demurely. I picked up a starched napkin and silverware and used a pair of silver tongs to convey a dinner roll onto my plate.

Murph had gotten a haircut. There was a faint tan line by his ears where his dark blond hair used to be a little longer. He had just shaved. And oh, he smelled good.

The Monday morning after the outing, I'd gotten to work, turned on my computer, and saw an e-mail waiting from *jdmurphy,* no subject. I purposely made myself go through the normal motions of any other morning—getting my coffee, playing my voice mails, reading the *Journal* and the *Times* business section—before I couldn't stand it any longer and opened his e-mail.

Hey. So how was your hangover on Saturday? Must have been rough.

My heart filled. I leapt out of my swivel chair and practically floated over to the window, looking the thirty-one stories down at the tiny yellow rectangles moving up and down Madison. *Here we go! Our office romance commences!*

I stood there at my window mentally auditioning a dozen clever, breezy, flirty replies before finally flopping back down at my desk and typing.

Yeah, pretty brutal. Thanks for putting me in the cab, btw. My hero. How was the rest of your weekend?

The answer came back in two minutes.

Eh. Jury still out on Anna Jergensen. Anyway. Jury Box at 12:30?

Just like that, I deflated. Just like that, Murph had told me that, as far as he was concerned, the old equilibrium had been restored between us. Here was the old kidding-around, paper-football, a-girl-a-month Murph. I wanted the Jeff Murphy from the clubhouse, but he was letting me know gently that I wasn't getting him back.

Murph and I didn't talk about what had happened between us. Which I now realized was, actually, nothing. It's not like Murph and I had hooked up. He hadn't come back to my place. We hadn't even kissed. So why was I so nervous? Why was I so worried over how we would act or what we would say to each other once we were back at the office? Well, Murph had done the humane thing by quickly putting any ambiguity to rest. Besides, guys like Murph weren't interested in someone like me. By rights, the firm's golden boy should be with someone like Cameron Alexander. So whatever there'd been the potential for last Friday, or however many signals I'd misread, it was over now, and there was nothing to do but follow his cue and pretend that everything felt completely normal to me, too.

But it didn't.

I knew I was being ridiculous. Here I was, a grown woman, working on a billion-dollar acquisition for the firm's biggest new client, about to make history at one of the most powerful firms in the world. Yet for over a week now, I had been lying awake at night wondering why Jeff Murphy hadn't kissed me that night when he'd had the chance, and realizing with a surprising and sobering clarity that I had really, really wanted him to.

Marty Adler got in line behind us. He gave me a quick smile—almost conspiratorial. I felt a little better.

Adler surveyed the buffet table. "Anything good on the menu?"

At this, Hunter perked up and sidled around Murph and me, installing himself directly in front of Marty Adler. "Hey, Marty," said Hunter, "I saw your great golf game last week."

Murph shot me a look. Generally, it was considered uncouth to try to schmooze a partner in front of your friends. Yet Murph and I didn't really mind when Hunter did it, because—let's face it—Hunter's employment here was kind of a joke.

"When he's done giving Adler his tongue bath, ask Hunter if he's in for bingo," Murph said in a stage whisper.

We'd started playing Conference Room Bingo back when we were all first-year associates. The object of the game was simple. Before a meeting began, each player would choose a "phrase that pays"—lines of MBA-speak or sports metaphors worked best—and someone would write them down. Whoever's phrase got spoken aloud first during the course of the meeting was the winner. We played for twenty-buck stakes.

We sat down. Murph whipped out his Montblanc and took a business card from his wallet. He flipped it over and paused, pen in air, like a waiter taking an order.

"So? Yung? Ladies first."

"I'm going with 'kick the tires,'" I said.

Murph nodded approvingly. "Good one." He scribbled this down. "Okay, I'm down for 'circling the wagons.'"

"I'm in for 'slippery slope,'" said Hunter. Murph and I both looked at him. Not a bad entry, especially for Hunter.

Tyler Robinson walked in. I waved at him. He quickly nodded a greeting, then, after seeing Hunter and Murph sitting beside me, chose a seat by himself on the far side of the conference table.

Tyler and I had not spoken about the "Partner's Paradise" skit. When I'd tried calling him on Monday, he'd simply said, "I don't want to talk about it." I had to respect that.

Adler stood up and clapped his hands together to get our attention. "All right, people. Let's get started. We've got a lot on the agenda today."

The room quieted. Stragglers got their cod filet and roasted potatoes and filled in the empty spots around the conference table. I sat with perfect posture, my hands clasped neatly in front of me, ignoring my lunch. I didn't want to be caught with a mouthful of cod filet when Adler began his big pitch about me.

"I'm passing around the meeting agenda," said Adler, "and you'll see that after our usual order of business, I'm going to introduce a very special guest."

Huh? Heads swiveled toward a stranger seated in the back: a trim, bespectacled man, maybe fifty years old, with a neat salt-and-pepper beard and thinning hair on top. He wore a tweed blazer, white shirt, corduroy slacks, and no tie. More professorial than lawyerly. I twisted in my seat to look at him, and he nodded at me, as if we knew each other. I looked away, embarrassed. *He* was the "something special" on the agenda, not me. I leaned forward and stuffed a forkful of salad into my mouth.

Adler raced through the deals that had been brought into the firm since last month—four high-tech IPOs, two leveraged buyouts, a hostile takeover defense. When he got to SunCorp, Adler said, "Everything's moving at a fast clip. The term sheet's nearly signed up, and

Ingrid and I are working on the purchase agreement." As he paused, I drew myself up, expecting him to acknowledge me. "It goes without saying, of course"—he looked meaningfully around the room—"that the terms of this deal are still highly confidential."

No acknowledgment. I should have known better.

Harold Rubinstein nodded. "How much time are you looking at, Marty, to get the purchase agreement put to bed? I mean, assuming everything's kosher after we've gone down there and kicked the tires?"

Ha. I shot Murph a victorious smile and mouthed, *Bingo.*

Murph mock-scowled and narrowed his eyes at me. Hunter twitched in his seat and pounded his fist lightly on the table.

Easiest forty bucks I ever made. I did dearly love to win.

Tim Hollister strode to the podium. He was looking adorable today in an earnest, Ivory-soap kind of way. I wished that Tyler had sat next to me. He was the only person at the firm with whom I could share this kind of observation.

This year, Tim was in charge of Continuing Legal Education options for the attorneys—one of the grunt jobs the senior partners farmed out to the younger ones. He rattled off a list of upcoming CLE seminars.

"In addition to the in-house lunch on the Foreign Corrupt Practices Act on the twenty-eighth, there's a breakfast program at the Princeton Club next Tuesday addressing director and officer liability. It's called 'The Evolution of Dodd-Frank: The Current Rules of Financial Oversight and What They Mean for You!'" He looked up at us. "Now don't all run out and register at once."

A couple of people laughed. Murph tapped quietly on his Black-Berry, then nudged me in the ribs. I looked down at his message: *Kill me now.*

Adler reappeared at the podium. "Thanks, Tim." He remained silent for a moment. "And *now,*" he said, beaming beatifically around the room, "I am pleased to introduce our very special guest. Dr. Rossi, would you join me up here, please?"

The bespectacled Dr. Rossi walked through the room with a determined stride. He stood slightly to the left of and behind Marty Adler, gazing out at us with a benign expression, like a vice presidential candidate.

"As all of you are aware, there is a growing imperative at the nation's top law firms to ensure diversity and sensitivity in the workplace," Adler began.

I knew exactly where this was going. I sank a few degrees down in my seat, hoping to blend into the furniture.

"Obviously," Adler continued, "this has recently become a hot-button issue for us because of certain unfortunate events that occurred at last week's outing."

More than a few heads swiveled in Hunter's direction. His cheeks were bright red. Amazing. I had never seen Hunter Russell embarrassed before. So the bad press had gotten even to him.

"Which brings me to our special guest, Dr. Stephen Rossi." The professor stepped forward and acknowledged us with a curt nod as Adler read in a monotone. "Dr. Rossi is founder and president of the consulting firm Diversity Scorecard LLC. Before that, he was the director of diversity and inclusion at a number of top national law firms, most recently Foster Cowan and Mays."

I raised my eyebrows.

Adler looked around the room and beamed at us. "I'm thrilled to announce that we have engaged Dr. Rossi to examine how well we are doing as a firm to increase diversity and inclusion among our ranks, and to recalibrate our business to better leverage our diverse talent pool. We will also be hosting a large-scale diversity-themed event later this summer, to which clients and friends of the firm will be invited. I expect all of you to welcome Dr. Rossi warmly, and cooperate with him in any way you can as he tackles this very important task. Stephen?"

A smattering of applause followed Dr. Rossi to the podium. Many attorneys' eyes had already glazed over. A few partners, including Gavin Dunlop, looked annoyed or skeptical, but not Harold Rubinstein, who stared attentively at Dr. Rossi. This made sense. Rubinstein and Adler were the Corporate partners who sat on the firm's Diversity and Inclusion Committee.

"Thank you, Marty." Dr. Rossi smiled. "For the next two months, I will be studying the unique corporate culture at Parsons Valentine, and formulating new strategies to better attract, retain, and develop diverse talent, particularly at the very top levels of management. Toward this end, I will conduct a series of confidential interviews of our partners and associates, particularly minorities, women, and our LGBT colleagues."

Someone to my left gave an audible snort.

If Dr. Rossi heard this, he ignored it. "This information will be thoroughly analyzed and collected in a comprehensive report, with prescriptive recommendations, that I will present to the firm's Management Committee at the conclusion of my engagement." He paused, and when he spoke again, he sounded serious and deliberate. "I cannot emphasize enough that anything you tell me will remain strictly confidential. No statement will be attributed to any particular lawyer, and all responses will be kept anonymous."

I snorted then. It wouldn't exactly take a genius to figure out where any statements from a female, Chinese American senior M&A attorney had come from. Tyler Robinson was going to have the same problem.

"I look forward to meeting as many of you individually as I can in the coming weeks. Thank you."

I might have imagined it, but it seemed that Dr. Rossi was looking directly at me as he finished his statement. Well, he could forget it. I wasn't about to contribute an interview for his little report, "confidential" or not. I wasn't about to rock the boat. Not this close to shore.

As Dr. Rossi walked back to his seat, the din of voices and clink of silverware rose again around the conference table. People ambled over to inspect the desserts.

"I'm going to get a brownie or something," I told Hunter and Murph. "You guys want anything?"

Hunter shook his head. "I gotta take off," he mumbled. He was out of the room like a shot.

I wandered over and made myself a little plate with some fruit salad and a chocolate chip cookie. When I returned to the table, Murph and Gavin Dunlop were talking and laughing quietly. A waiter was clearing plates and blocking my path to my chair, so I stood behind him, waiting for him to finish.

"I can't believe we're wasting so much time and money on this," Gavin sighed.

Murph laughed and said in a low voice, "Well, no one told those idiots to get drunk and carried away at the summer outing."

I stopped short. *Carried away?*

"Seriously," Gavin said. "What do *we* need diversity training for? Why the hell are we even still talking about this? Didn't we just name *two women* in a row to the Supreme Court?"

Yep. And three white men in a row before that. But who's counting?

Gavin shook his head. "I mean, for Chrissakes, look who's sitting in the freaking White House! What more do they want? What's next, maybe a wise Latina?" Gavin cracked himself up.

I coughed loudly, and they both looked up at me. Murph seemed startled.

"Oh, hey, no brownies today?" he said, shooting Gavin a warning look.

Gavin didn't catch it. "It was a harmless skit. In bad taste, yes, but just a joke. Don't these people have any sense of humor? I mean, can you imagine the uproar if *I* decided to start a White Male Eating Club at the firm?"

I couldn't help letting out a quiet snort.

Gavin looked at me. "What?"

"Nothing."

"No, what?"

I looked squarely at him. "Seriously, Gavin? The firm already *is* a white male eating club."

Murph laughed.

"Well, what I don't get," Gavin continued, "is how they always keep talking about 'equality.'"

I wondered who Gavin meant by *they.* And whether he would include me as part of *them* or *us.*

Now Gavin was making mock quotation marks in the air. "I mean, if they're after *equality,* seems like it would make more sense to *ignore* race and gender instead of constantly drawing *more* attention to it, right?"

"This country isn't ready yet to ignore race or gender," I snapped, regretting it the instant it was out of my mouth.

Silence. My words hung there in the air.

"I didn't know you felt that strongly about it one way or another, Yung," Murph said softly.

"Yeah," Gavin finally said. "I mean"—and he said this gently, in a conciliatory tone—"I wasn't even talking about Asians."

Murph shot him a *you are fucking hopeless* look.

Gavin went on, "Seems to me like Asian Americans have done all right."

"Gee, thanks," I said. "I'm really glad it seems that way to you, Gavin."

"Come on. I'm just saying that by any objective economic measure, Asians are right up there with whites."

"Gee willikers, Gavin, do you mean it? Really and truly?" I widened my eyes, made my voice high and earnest, and laced my hands together underneath my chin. "You mean we're really *right up there*? And if we promise to work really really hard and practice our English *every day*, would we even rate as honorary whites?"

Now Gavin and Murph both stared at me.

If I were them, I'd be staring at me, too. I had never spoken to anyone like this at the office, least of all them. I had never even thought about saying these words before they came tumbling out of my mouth. Like they'd been trapped there for a long time.

I snuck a glance at Murph. In all the years we'd known each other, I'd never seen such utter bewilderment on his face. But I thought I was seeing something else, too; it looked like Murph was trying hard to keep the corners of his mouth from tugging upward.

"Anyway, can't stay and chat." I turned abruptly from the table.

Murph leaned over and reached for my elbow. "Hey, we didn't—"

I cut him off. "I have to get that draft out to SunCorp today. See you guys later."

Murph and Gavin exchanged glances. Avoiding eye contact with them, I walked out of the conference room and headed down the hall. I could imagine their conversation as soon as I was out of earshot.

Jesus. What's her problem?

Beats me. Maybe that time of the month.

Heh. Yeah.

My hands were shaking. My face burned. I needed to get to my office—fast. I very rarely lost my cool at work. And I was furious with myself. I had just broken my own cardinal rule—to avoid discussing race with my colleagues. These were conversations doomed to turn out badly.

I was so painfully, tantalizingly close. All I had to do now was stay on track for a couple more weeks—*just a couple more weeks!*—and then I'd be one of them. I'd be in.

"Hey, Ingrid, wait up."

Now what.

It was Marty Adler.

I'd made it as far as the elevator bank. I rearranged my face into as neutral an expression as I could manage.

"Ingrid," he said, puffing a little from his brief jog down the hall. "Glad I caught you." He reached over and pressed the down button for the elevator.

"Marty. What's up?"

"You left so abruptly, I didn't get a chance to personally introduce you to Dr. Rossi."

"Oh? And why were you hoping to do that?"

He coughed. "Well, Ingrid, actually, the Management Committee met about this a couple of days ago, and, well, there seemed to be a prevailing consensus that, ah . . ."

"Yes?"

"We think you'd make a terrific associate liaison for our Diversity Initiative." He beamed, as if this were very good news.

No, I thought. No, no, no, no, *no.*

When I didn't answer right away, Adler tried grinning sheepishly. But sheepishness looked disingenuous on Marty Adler.

I stalled for time. "Associate . . . liaison?" I faked a perplexed, apologetic smile. "Sorry, what exactly is that?"

Adler was studying me carefully. He was about to call my bluff.

"Well, we'd really appreciate your help promoting this initiative, Ingrid. You're such a role model for our junior associates. We could use your leadership. You know, work with Dr. Rossi, brainstorm ideas for the diversity and inclusion event we're hosting. Most of all, we need you to talk it up, get the major stakeholders on board, put the word out, yada, yada."

I felt exposed. Helpless. Like I was standing outside myself just watching this train wreck happen. And there was nothing I could do to stop it. They were officially crowning me the Parsons Valentine Diversity Poster Girl, because, as usual, I was running unopposed.

"Listen, Marty." I kept my voice level. "You know how busy I'm going to be with SunCorp heating up. I need to give that deal one hundred percent."

Adler turned his head a little to the side and rubbed his chin. The warmth drained from his expression. He said slowly, in a voice I'd only heard him use once or twice before and never with me, "Well, perhaps you'll just have to find it in yourself to give one hundred and ten percent then, Ingrid."

I hesitated, and he saw me hesitate. Adler had nothing if not that killer instinct, and now he pounced. "I think you know how grateful the firm would be if you were to help us out in this capacity. I don't have to tell you how much we value an associate's nonlegal contributions to the firm when we're making our partnership decisions."

This was almost out of bounds—a dirty, underhanded move—and we both knew it.

"I'd be glad to help with the Diversity Initiative in any way possible," I said, with a steel smile. "I'll speak with Dr. Rossi first thing."

Adler brightened. He smiled and half-shrugged in mock relief. "Thank you, Ingrid." He pressed his hand lightly against my back. "I knew we could count on you."

The doors to one of the elevators opened, and he gestured inside. "After you."

I shook my head. "No, I'll take the next one." I added, "I'm going up."

Adler stepped into the elevator. "Suit yourself," he said.

As if that were really an option.

SEVEN

❦

I hated being singled out for reasons I'd had nothing to do with. As long as I could remember, higher-ups—not just bosses but teachers, professors, deans, recruiters, and HR directors—were forever asking me to serve on this committee, come to that reception, be a mentor, speak on a panel. I didn't flatter myself by thinking that because I was possessed of such wit and charm, such keen legal acumen, my absence was unthinkable. I knew the rule: When you find an attractive, articulate minority woman in your midst, who's neither too strident nor too soft-spoken, who speaks English without accent or attitude, who makes friends easily and photographs well—you want *her*.

Being singled out was bad enough, but I resented even more the sense of burden, of unsolicited responsibility, of having constituents when I hadn't run for office. When you're the only one around of a particular race and gender combination, people feel wildly free to suggest how you should be utilizing your time and abilities. I noticed the disapproving looks on people's faces when I politely turned them down. *No, sorry, but I don't have time to take the foreign-exchange lawyers to lunch today; why don't you try someone who actually works in our International Group? Sorry, I really can't mentor any more summer associates this year. You've already given me Christine Han, Danny Rodriguez, Victor Cho, Meera Patel, and Herman Lim. I really need some time to get my own work done.*

Even though I'd felt like something of an outsider all my life—the firstborn child of first-generation Chinese American immigrants, the first in my family to be educated in America, the first to go to law school—I had never been made to feel more keenly aware of my Specialness than when I'd stepped through the gleaming glass doors at Parsons Valentine. If I got voted in this year I wouldn't just be making partner, I'd be making history. I would be the first woman of color ever elected to the partnership at the prestigious law firm of Parsons Valentine & Hunt LLP. That was the term they used for me at the firm. "Woman of color."

It was such a peculiar term, "woman of color." The first time I'd heard it, I'd thought about my favorite moment in *The Wizard of Oz,* when Dorothy's farmhouse lands with a tremendous jolt and she opens the door and steps out into a beautiful new Technicolor world, winning instant friends and enemies. That was how I felt here, sometimes. I had opened the door to Oz. Where everything was shiny and grand and beautiful and looked tantalizingly within reach. I knew what it felt like to be embraced as an exotic new stranger, even as I roused the suspicions of some. I knew how it felt to try to winnow out the good sorts from the bad, and to be urged on by a pack of persuasive new companions to keep marching toward everything I always said I was looking for. I was sticking fast to the partner track like it was my very own yellow brick road.

The day after Adler cornered me at the elevators, I called Dr. Stephen Rossi and introduced myself. He'd been expecting my call and suggested we speak that afternoon.

At four o'clock, I trudged down to the makeshift office that the firm had set up for Dr. Rossi. It was in the shadowy reaches of the twenty-ninth floor, an unfrequented section of the building where the firm shunted off much of its nonlegal staff: Payroll, Travel, IT, Petty Cash, and the diversity consultant.

I found him dipping a fresh teabag into a blue Parsons Valentine mug. "Dr. Rossi?"

He looked up. "Ingrid, come in, come in. I appreciate how busy you must be. We can get started right away."

He strode briskly around his desk and pushed the door shut. I was a little alarmed by this. People rarely closed their office doors at the firm. It was considered rude, as if going against the atmosphere of "collegiality" that Parsons Valentine was forever touting in its glossy brochures. It was also a good way to get the firm's rumor mill in gear.

I waited until he was seated behind his desk again before speaking. First, I needed to make it clear I was not here of my own free will.

"Dr. Rossi," I said, "I hope you won't mind my being totally honest here."

He smiled. "Well, I certainly hope you will be, Ingrid. And please call me Stephen."

"Fine. Stephen." I spoke in a rush. "I just want you to know that I've really got a lot on my plate right now. I'm closing a particularly high-worth acquisition in a few weeks, so I'm hoping this won't take up too much time today. My understanding is that I'm just here to help you encourage participation from other associates and brainstorm ideas for the diversity event the firm will be organizing."

Confusion flickered across Dr. Rossi's face, but only for a second. He folded his hands neatly on his desk. "Well, Ingrid, I'd be grateful for any help you might provide in getting the other attorneys to participate. But now let *me* be totally honest. I was specifically instructed by the partners on the Diversity and Inclusion Committee that *you* would be a particularly good associate to interview, so I was hoping that we might have our first session today."

Our *first* session?

From the moment this guy was introduced I knew he'd be a pain in my ass, but I had promised Adler I'd cooperate. *In any way possible,* I'd even said.

I crossed my legs, leaned back in the armchair opposite his desk, and sighed. "Fine. I'll be happy to answer some questions, though I can't imagine what I could say that would be all that helpful. What do you want to know?"

"Thank you, Ingrid. I appreciate that." He took a small tape recorder and a yellow legal pad out of a desk drawer.

I sat up. "You're taping our conversation?"

Again he looked puzzled. "Well, I often find it helpful to tape these sessions, but I certainly won't do so if it makes you uncomfortable."

I wished he would stop calling this a session. He wasn't my shrink.

"It makes me uncomfortable," I said.

"No problem." He slid the tape recorder back into his desk.

I sat back again and glanced at my watch. "Now, what is it you need to ask me?"

"Well, to begin with, let me ask you why you think the firm gave me your name first as someone I should interview for the report."

The answer to this was so obvious I laughed out loud. "Well, you're reporting on *diversity* at this law firm, right?"

He tilted his head slightly. "And?"

"*And,*" I said, with a ferocity that surprised me, "how many other non-white nonmales do you see around here who've stuck it out for eight years?"

I pressed my lips together. I'd already said more than I'd planned. *Watch it.*

"That's an excellent place to start," said Dr. Rossi, producing a pen from his shirt pocket. "So you feel that you've been singled out by virtue of being"—he paused and looked at me searchingly—"a woman? Or an Asian American?"

As if one could be disentangled from the other. "Well, both," I said. "Corporate firms *love* a twofer like me."

He looked up. "Come again?"

"A twofer," I said. "You know, like landing on a double-word square in Scrabble."

Dr. Rossi laughed quietly, jotting this down. "I like that, Ingrid. Do you mind if I use it?"

"Be my guest."

"So, to start off, let me ask you this. How many, as you describe them, 'nonwhite nonmales' are there at the firm who you believe are actually on the partner track?"

The directness of his question took me by surprise. Immediately, I thought about Tyler. He'd confided to me that he had gotten a couple of second- and third-round interviews to go in-house, and would probably be giving notice in a matter of weeks. I pretended to smile and said lightly, "I feel a little weird naming names. I mean, this isn't the McCarthy Commission, right?"

Dr. Rossi didn't smile back. Instead he took off his glasses and began kneading the bridge of his nose. "Ingrid," he said, "believe it or not, I'm on *your* side here. The reason I'm here is so that the firm can improve the quality of life for all of its associates. But I can't do my job if people aren't willing to be forthcoming with me."

He blinked up at me. If he had whipped out a guitar and burst into a rousing rendition of "Kumbaya," I would not have been surprised.

He let out a breath. "Okay, tell you what. Let's get at this another way." He made a big show of pushing away his legal pad. "What made you decide to become a lawyer in the first place?"

I pretended to consider this. Actually, I knew exactly when the idea had been planted in my head.

When I was in elementary school my mother had started a tradition in our house called Library Night. Every Wednesday, after my mother got home from work, no matter how tired she was, or what shape dinner was in, she would drive me to the library, where she would upend the canvas tote bag filled with last week's books onto the counter to be checked in, and then help me carry the canvas tote bag filled with new books I checked out. I was allowed to check out as many books as I wanted, even ones from the adult section. My mom and dad didn't know what any of these American books were, so by the fourth grade, I was reading *Lady Chatterley's Lover* and *Clan of the Cave Bear* and *Wifey*. I'd sit on the couch in our family room—in plain sight—and my parents were none the wiser. As far as they knew, I was just reading for school.

"You're our best customer," the frosted-blond lady would say each week as she beamed down at me from behind the checkout counter.

That year, the year I was ten, our washing machine had broken down one night. My mother called Sears and, after being on hold for the better part of an hour, explained in her halting, accented English what had happened and when she had purchased the machine. I was sitting at the kitchen table, doing my fraction problems, half-listening to my mother's end of the conversation. The customer service representative curtly replied that Sears was not obligated to repair anything, then hung up on my mother.

My mother saved everything. She found the original sales receipt for the washing machine we'd gotten at Sears and asked me to read the warranty language. The warranty was good for a whole year, and it had only been ten months since we'd gotten it.

That week when my mother took me to the library, she asked at the desk for a book on how to write an official business letter. The librarian seemed overjoyed to have been asked a question. She led my mother over to the stacks and removed a shiny yellow paperback, dusted off the cover, and handed it to her: *Business Letters That Work!*

I studied and studied that book. I carefully read the explanations of each component of a formal letter. Many of them were new words to me, but they seemed so grown-up and important. I loved the sound of them. *Salutation. Greeting. Body. Closing. Signature.*

With this book and the crumpled, yellowing Sears receipt lying on the table, I prepared to type on my father's Smith-Corona typewriter. I used a jar of Skippy peanut butter to hold open the book's pages.

First, I typed the date. Next, the recipient's name and address. "Sears Customer Service Center." I carefully copied the address from the warranty slip. Then came the *salutation*. "To Whom It May Concern," I typed, following the example in the library book. Finally, I reread the directions for composing the body of the letter.

"Step One: Clearly state the purpose of your letter. Your tone should be courteous but firm. Step Two: Give the supporting information the recipient will need to evaluate your request. Step Three: Restate your request, and thank the recipient for his or her time and consideration."

Carefully, I typed:

> *The purpose of this letter is to inform you that my washing machine from your store is broken and to ask you to please fix it for free.*
>
> *The machine was purchased at your store in Rockville, Maryland, on December 4. The warranty stapled to my receipt says that "Repairs and*

*service are guaranteed until one year from date of purchase," and the year is
not up yet. (I still have the receipt because I save everything.)*

*I will now restate my request. Please send someone to fix my washing
machine, because the year is not up yet. Thank you for your time and
consideration.*

Fondly,

Mrs. Elinor Yan-Mei Yung

My mother read it, smiled at me, and pronounced that it was perfect. She signed her name at the bottom in careful script and mailed it. Three and a half weeks later, a man in a Sears van pulled into our driveway and repaired our washing machine at no charge.

My parents had never been prouder of me. Beaming, my mother hugged me and said that I was her very smart girl. And that I should grow up and become a lawyer, and that way my mother and father would always be sure that no one could push them around just because they looked or talked differently from anyone else.

Nobody bosses my Ingrid around, my mother had said, in Chinese. I thought about that quite a lot, even now. Especially now.

I looked across the desk and shrugged at Dr. Rossi. "I don't know, it beats flipping burgers," I said.

Dr. Rossi was looking carefully at me. He leaned way back in his chair, placed his right foot on his left knee, and crossed his arms. "Ingrid," he said.

I blinked at him.

"I can't help you if you won't help me," he said.

"I hope you won't take this the wrong way, but I don't remember asking anyone for any help."

Dr. Rossi leaned forward again in his chair. "Look," he said in a lowered voice. "This may surprise you, but I completely appreciate the position you're in. I realize you're up for partner in a few short weeks, and I've heard the scuttlebutt that your chances are thought to be excellent."

I perked up a little. Scuttlebutt? There was *scuttlebutt*? I cleared my throat. "Where have you heard this?"

Dr. Rossi gave me a sidelong look. "You forget that I've been having lunch with various groups of partners here all week. People talk."

This was good. This was very good. I looked down at my lap so he wouldn't see the broad grin spreading across my face.

"So you see," he continued, "I appreciate why you might have very little incentive to speak candidly with me about diversity and inclusion at this firm. I mean, so what if the system's broken, it's working all right for you, is that it?"

I didn't nod, but I didn't correct him, either.

"You've obviously been very successful in your career here, and that's terrific. But could I invite you to speculate on why there's only one of you who's made it this far? That is to say, why there aren't more women of color up for partnership?"

While I tried to think of a diplomatic response, Dr. Rossi held up an Excel spreadsheet. "For example, I see that in your entering class, there was another Asian American woman, but she quit within the first year and a half. I'm curious to hear your thoughts about why she might have left. Why do you feel the firm was unable to retain her?"

I remembered this woman—Zhang Liu—very clearly, though I'd tried to forget. For the first few months after our new associate orientation, a lot of the partners and secretaries had had trouble telling us apart, even though we looked nothing alike. Zhang wore her hair short with bangs. Mine was long and layered. She also stood a head taller than me. But a year later, we still got each other's interoffice mail.

Zhang Liu was from Beijing and had come to the States at the age of eighteen to attend MIT. She had aced the bar exam and every other standardized test known to civilization. Rumor had it she was brilliant,

but it was hard to tell, since she spoke English that was technically correct but strongly accented. Her blunt-cut hair always looked like it
needed shampooing, and she wore shapeless, ill-fitting suits that ob-
scured what was actually a pretty decent figure. She was extremely shy,
and almost never joined in when a group of us went out to grab lunch
or drinks. On the rare occasions she did come out, Zhang hovered silently on the outer fringes of our group, nursing a 7-Up, while the rest
of us tossed back martinis and traded dirty jokes and gossip. And when
she did speak, her voice was so soft and low it barely rose above a whisper. Once, at a Corporate Department meeting, I'd seen Marty Adler
lose his patience and snap, "Speak *up*, Zhang, for God's sake." I'd never
heard Adler speak to an associate like that before or since; it had stuck
with me.

Another time, Harold Rubinstein had actually praised her for an
excellent research memo she had prepared on some new securities dis-
closure regs. "It was extremely well done, Zhang," he had said, in front
of all of us. "Great job." Zhang had blushed, and murmured something
in protest about how it had really been a group effort and that, really,
two summer associates had done most of the research. I shook my
head. She just wasn't getting it. Everyone knew that on the rare occasion when a partner publicly praised your work, the only right answer
was *Thank you*.

About a year after we started, Zhang ventured to my office late one
night. She knocked tentatively on my door, and I looked up, startled,
from the stack of corporate minutes I'd been reviewing and marking
with a yellow highlighter. Apropos of nothing, she asked me if I knew
how to speak Chinese.

"No," I lied.

I knew how much courage this must have taken on her part; I knew
just how much it must have cost her. And yet, to my embarrassment, I
could not summon the courage in myself to do the kind thing.

It had only been my first year. My own position at the firm was not yet so secure that I could afford to be associated with Zhang Liu any more than I already was. I was terrified she'd drag me down.

I was passing, and she was not.

Zhang stuck it out at Parsons Valentine a few more months, collected her December bonus, and quit. I had no idea where she'd gone.

I thought about Zhang Liu from time to time, especially last winter, when I'd reread one of my favorite books from college—*The Woman Warrior,* by Maxine Hong Kingston. I got stuck on one scene in which the tough, rebellious heroine terrorizes a Chinese American classmate in the girls' bathroom, pulling on her pigtails and pinching her cheeks to force her to speak English. *I looked into her face so I could hate it close up,* she wrote. I realized, with a sharp stab of guilt, that that was exactly what I had done—looked into Zhang Liu's lost, lonely face and hated it close up.

"All right, look," I sighed. "Let's just say that, in my experience, most white men are still a lot more comfortable working with guys who look, talk, and act just like them."

"But what about the various initiatives of the Diversity and Inclusion Committee?" prodded Dr. Rossi.

I snorted. As far as I could tell, until the incident at the firm outing, the Diversity and Inclusion Committee had been all but defunct. Their "initiatives" had consisted of taking the associates to see *The Lion King* on Broadway, throwing a margarita happy hour on Cinco de Mayo, and serving spring rolls and dumplings in the Jury Box during Asian Pacific American Heritage Month.

Well, we didn't need fucking Dumpling Day in the firm cafeteria. We needed decoder rings for all of the unwritten rules of survival here.

Dr. Rossi was rubbing his chin. "Do you think it's possible for young women of color to find mentors at a place like this?"

"Possible, yes. Easy, no," I said.

"Have you, personally, made attempts to find mentors during your career here?"

I smiled ruefully.

"Did I say something funny?" Dr. Rossi asked.

I shrugged. "Well, they're always giving advice to young associates to 'find a mentor early on.' Oh, sure. Like it's just that easy."

"Isn't it?" he prompted.

"No."

When we'd first arrived at Parsons Valentine, we were cheerfully given name tags and ushered into a first-year orientation session in a midtown ballroom, where we were plied with Perrier and sushi as a chorus of shiny young partners trumpeted advice. *Seek out mentors and sponsors! Walk right up and introduce yourself to the partners you want to learn from! Don't be shy about asking for work!*

I took their advice. Or tried to. I carefully planned how I would approach Ellen Chu Sanderson, the only Chinese American woman at the firm, who had been named Of Counsel (a rung that was a step below partner, *just not quite there*). I'd already read her profile in the *New York Law Journal,* where she had once been featured as one of the Top Ten Women Lawyers of Color to Watch. (The joke went that it hadn't been hard to make the list when there were only fifty or so practicing.)

Ellen was in her midforties, married with no kids—her husband was a managing director at Goldman—and she'd been named Of Counsel when she was thirty-nine, in the firm's Intellectual Property group. I knew all of this because I had done my research. She'd gone to Yale, too—both college and law school—and had even played on the Yale women's tennis team. With all that in common, how could she not take me under her wing? She'd tell me which partners to work with, the ones to avoid. The screamers, the nice guys. Perhaps she'd take me to lunch. It would start out as an occasional thing, but soon we'd have a monthly lunch date where we'd dish about everything from who was making partner to where she got her hair done. Eventually she'd invite me to her house in the Hamptons, where we'd giggle over lemonade and tea cookies and I would let her beat me at tennis. (I knew she and her husband had such a house; they'd once offered it as a summer rental in the Parsons Valentine newsletter. Fifteen thousand for the month.)

So one morning soon after arriving at the firm, I'd looked up Ellen Chu Sanderson in the firm's online directory and mustered up the courage to stop by her office. I walked past the unfamiliar names on the brass nameplates—I hadn't been up to the thirty-third floor yet, nor had I met many lawyers from the IP group—and paused in front of the one that read ELLEN CHU SANDERSON. The door was partially closed, and I could hear her on the phone inside. I hesitated.

"Help you with something, sweetie?" asked Ellen Chu Sanderson's secretary, a young, pretty, heavily eyeshadowed woman sitting behind the counter across from me.

"Oh!" I whirled around. "I'm a new associate here, and I just wanted to say hello to Ellen." Then I thought that might sound weird, so I said by way of explanation, "We—we both played tennis on the same college team."

She smiled. "Well, I'm sure Ellen'd love to meet you." She winked and lowered her voice. "Ellen's a real sweetie. I lucked out, you know? You should have seen the guy they gave me when I first got here."

I smiled and nodded. "Yeah." And I welled up with pride that my future mentor was someone whom secretaries spoke kindly about.

"Oh, looks like she's off the phone," said Ellen's secretary. "Quick. Better catch her before she gets on another call. Just knock and go on in."

"Even though she has her door closed?"

"Oh yeah, she just does that when she's having her breakfast or lunch in there." Again she lowered her voice and whispered. "She doesn't like it when people see her eat," she informed me.

"Oh," I said, stepping up to the door and giving it a firm knock.

"Come in," said a sweet voice, lilting and warm.

I opened the door and walked into Ellen Chu Sanderson's office. She looked younger than she did in her photo. She wore her hair in a short shiny bob and had cat's-eye glasses and very white teeth.

She blinked up at me, and I swear her smile disappeared in about a split second.

"Can I help you?" she asked. Her tone wasn't unfriendly (not quite), but it wasn't welcoming, either. Undaunted, sort of, I put on my best interview smile and walked forward to her desk. "Hi," I said brightly. "I'm Ingrid Yung."

She remained where she was. "Ohh-kay. And I'm supposed to know you *how*?"

She might as well have slapped me. I wanted to turn and run, but I stood my ground. "Uh, you don't know me, actually," I heard myself say. "I'm a new associate in Corporate, and I just wanted to come and introduce myself. I understand you also played Yale Tennis when you were there."

"And how would you know that?" She narrowed her eyes at me.

I suddenly felt incredibly stupid. This had been a very poor idea. How could I have been so presumptuous? Ellen Chu Sanderson had more important things to do than adopt some first-year as the little sister she'd never had.

"Oh, I, uh—"

"Listen," she said with a fake half-smile. "I'm swamped. Now's really not a good time."

I looked at the half-eaten English muffin and the copy of *The Wall Street Journal* open on her desk.

"Okay. I—I'm sorry," I said, backing out of her office.

"It was good of you to stop by," she said, closing the door in my face.

That was the first and last time I ever spoke to Ellen Chu Sanderson.

For years afterward, whenever we spotted each other at firm cocktail parties, we'd duck our heads and avoid each other. She seemed as reluctant to cross paths with me as I was to run into her. Maybe she figured there was only room for one Asian American, female, Yale Tennis alumna at the firm, and that was just fine with her. She left Parsons Valentine last year after being appointed to a high-ranking counsel position at the U.S. Patent and Trademark Office. I suspect we were both relieved.

Dr. Rossi was looking at me gravely. "And how does it make you feel, Ingrid, to know that it isn't as easy for women to find willing mentors as it is for men?"

I flinched. Dr. Rossi was making my head hurt. I had neither the time nor the desire to help him perform his dramatic overhaul of the gender and race hierarchy in corporate America. If he thought he'd found his little Norma Rae, he was sorely mistaken.

"Sorry," I said. I'd had enough. "I have a conference call in five minutes. Can we continue this conversation another time?"

He looked thoughtfully at me. "I look forward to it."

EIGHT

❧

"Come on, Yung, hurry it up." Hunter poked his head inside my office. "Murph and the rest of the guys are all waiting downstairs. If we don't show by seven fifteen, we forfeit the game!"

"I don't know how you talked me into this," I said from the other side of my office door. "Lawyers League softball isn't exactly how I planned to spend my night."

Hunter was wearing a blue and white Parsons Valentine baseball cap with the brim pulled down low. His left shoulder was weighted down with a huge duffel bag bearing the firm logo, and in his arms he carried three bats plus a catcher's mitt. He lumbered around to the other side of my door, knocking over my neat piles of Lexis printouts, SEC filings, and Redwelds as he went.

"Hey, hey, hey. Careful with the wide load there." I transferred sneakers, clean socks, and yoga pants from my cedar wardrobe into my gym bag. "Uh-oh. I don't have a clean T-shirt."

Hunter shook his head. "Nice try. But everyone has to wear the team jersey." He jerked his chin toward the duffel. "We have tons. I'll give you one when we get there. Let's just *go*."

"All right, all right, just give me a second to change. I'll meet you guys down in the lobby."

"Make it fast." Hunter looked at his watch. "I really hate forfeiting to that Davis Polk guy, competitive prick."

Hi, pot, meet kettle.

Hunter was absurdly competitive about Lawyers League softball. For someone who'd married into this job, knew no law, and regularly padded his hours, he played strictly by the book when it came to softball. The official rules of the Central Park Lawyers League required each law firm to field a team of at least eight players, of which at least one must be a woman. Otherwise, you had to forfeit. That morning, Hunter had panicked after finding out that Melissa McCabe from Trusts and Estates, the only woman on the team, was being sent to Boston to deal with a client emergency and wouldn't be able to play. That had inspired his ridiculous e-mail plea.

TO: PARSONS_NY_OFFICE_ALL_ATTYS
FROM: Russell, Hunter F. <hrussell@parsonslaw.com>
SUBJECT: DESPERATELY SEEKING FEMALE...

...TO PLAY IN TONIGHT'S SOFTBALL CHAMPIONSHIP MATCH
VS. DAVIS POLK, THAT IS. CENTRAL PARK, EAST MEADOW, 7:00
PM SHARP!!!!!! IF INTERESTED, CONTACT HUNTER RUSSELL, x3146,
ASAP!!!! FREE JERSEY!!!!!!!

I'd laughed out loud and said, "Yeah, right, good luck with that," before hitting DELETE.

Three hours later, Hunter showed up at my office.

"*Please.* I'm *begging* here." Hunter—in his custom-tailored Paul Smith suit—dropped to the floor in the doorway of my office and, hands clasped as if in prayer, shuffled toward me on his knees. "Seriously, Yung, I can't find *any* other female associate to play tonight. It's the *championship* game! If we can't field a regulation team we automatically forfeit! Please, Yung. *Please.*" He shuffled over to my swivel chair and clung to my leg.

"Hunter," I said, looking down at him calmly.

He blinked up at me from the floor.

"Have some dignity, Hunter. You're embarrassing us both."

"*Please,* Yung!" he wailed.

"I'm not much of an athlete these days."

He released his grip on my leg but remained on his knees. "Come on. You played women's soccer in college, right? And tennis?"

I wondered how Hunter knew all this. "Those aren't the same," I said. "I don't know the first thing about baseball."

"Softball, Ingrid. *Softball.* And we don't even use a regulation ball! Lawyers League uses a ball that's even softer than regulation. It's really easy to hit." Hunter flashed me a hopeful smile.

I pretended to tap thoughtfully at my chin. "Okay, hmm, let's see. How do you think this would look to the partners—I'm supposed to be running this billion-dollar megadeal for Adler's client, yet I'm leaving the office at six forty-five to go play softball in Central Park?"

Hunter smiled smugly. "Actually," he said, "Adler usually shows up to watch all our games. And Tim Hollister's playing tonight."

I frowned. "I didn't know any of those guys came to your games."

"Yeah, they do," Hunter continued proudly. "We all go out for beers afterward at Paddy Maguire's, and Adler picks up the tab at the end of the night. It's great. You should totally come. Murph started up this tradition a while ago."

"Huh." Murph had never mentioned anything to me about going drinking with the partners. I thought about how Marty Adler had cornered me at the elevators about the Diversity Initiative, the impatient, vaguely hostile way he'd said, *I don't have to tell you how much we value an associate's nonlegal contributions to the firm.* I wondered if Murph organizing private little drinking outings with the senior partners counted as his *nonlegal contribution.*

"Come on, Yung. Be my hero."

I looked at Hunter, still groveling on the floor beside my desk. Something about the way he'd said "hero" appealed to me—especially if Marty Adler was going to be there to see it. *You want nonlegal contributions? I'll show you nonlegal contributions.*

"All right, all right. I'm in. Jesus. I can't stand to see a grown man beg."

Hunter sprang out of the car as soon as we got to the Central Park playing fields. He bolted up the path, bag full of jerseys, three bats, and mitt in tow. Murph and I followed behind.

The Davis Polk team had already arrived. Their team captain was waiting by the bleachers, arms crossed over his chest, hands tucked into his armpits. "Nice of you guys to show," he called over to us.

"Asshole," Murph said under his breath. The rest of our team had also just arrived and were standing around stretching and doing warm-ups. Tim Hollister was indeed among them, and he smiled and waved when he saw me. I waved back. Tim had shed his glasses for the game; tonight he was looking a little less Clark Kent and more Superman. The other player I recognized right away was Link Forster—Mr. January from the firm outing. The team was rounded out by three first-year guys from Litigation whose names I didn't know, who all had that arrogant, freshly shaven, self-congratulatory look about them, belonging singularly to young graduates dazzled to find themselves twenty-five years old, living in Manhattan, and suddenly making six figures a year.

I was surprised by the number of people who'd showed up to cheer us on. The crowd from Parsons Valentine was mostly nonlegal staff— even Margo said she'd attended one or two of the games—but I also recognized quite a few associates, and not just first-years, either. I spotted Tyler among a group of assorted Corporate associates. He was waving both arms over his head so I'd see him. *Bless you, Tyler.* I'd convinced him to come tonight for moral support. It was probably the first and only time Tyler Robinson would ever attend a firm softball game. I was touched.

I waved enthusiastically back at him, widening my eyes and giving him a sheepish *what did I get myself into* shrug. He smirked back at me. *No idea how you got talked into this, darling.*

I scanned the rest of the crowd; no Marty Adler.

Now Murph was walking over to me with the bag full of jerseys. "All right, so you're supposed to put this on," he said, reaching in and tossing one to me.

I held up the white heavyweight cotton jersey with three-quarter-length navy blue sleeves. The firm logo was discreetly embossed in the upper left corner, like an alligator or a polo pony, and across the chest it read, in blue script slanting slightly upward, THE PROSECUTORS. It wasn't the most creative name, but it was better than their original choice: the Well-Hung Jury. Fortunately, the firm's Management Committee had intervened.

Legal humor was so lame. Back in law school, when I'd go out to dinner with a bunch of classmates, somebody would invariably say something like "Guess I'll have the chocolate *torte,*" and everyone would crack up. It was painful.

I held the jersey up to my chest. On me, it was a dress. I checked the tag. "Murph, this is a size L. Isn't there anything smaller?"

"Oh." He looked taken aback. "Even smaller than *that*? Uh, yeah, let me look." He pawed through the bag and finally came up with another jersey. "No smalls, but here's the last medium," he said, tossing it at me.

I pulled the jersey on over my camisole, and still I was swimming in it.

I went to a lot of firm outings and client retreats, and for some reason, no law firm, investment bank, or corporation ever ordered its company T-shirts in enough size smalls.

Hunter and the Davis Polk captain were busily conferring over by the stands, their heads bent over two clipboards. Then Hunter turned and pointed in my direction. The Davis Polk captain looked my way, nodded briefly at Hunter, and crossed something out on his clipboard.

After a few minutes Hunter jogged back over to us. "Okay, so here's the deal," he said. Tim Hollister, Link Forster, and the three first-year Litigation guys came over, and together we all huddled around Hunter's clipboard. Link lifted his chin at me and said, "Hey, thanks for filling in for Melissa." Man, he *was* adorable.

The three first-years looked me up and down but said nothing.

"Okay, guys, this is the lineup," said Hunter. "Forster, you're up first." Everyone nodded quickly, unsurprised, and I looked over at Link's athletic frame and realized he must be considered something of a powerhouse, at least for Lawyers League.

Hunter proceeded to rattle off six more names. Finally, he said, "Uh, so that means—Yung, you're up last."

I was suspicious.

"Does Melissa normally go last?" I asked.

Hunter glanced up from his clipboard. "Uh, no. Why?"

"No reason, just curious," I said. I knew Melissa was a very good player, from hearing Hunter and Murph's game recaps over lunch in the Jury Box. Apparently she'd co-captained an intramural softball team while at UVA Law. I'd never actually worked with her, but Melissa seemed cool. She was tall—taller even than a lot of the men she worked with—with lots of freckles and a loud, jokey personality. Hunter, Murph, and all those guys spoke fondly of her, but I could tell from their tone she was the type of girl they'd never try to sleep with. Or they would, but they wouldn't be falling all over themselves to tell their buddies about it the next day.

Hunter shifted the clipboard to his hip. "You got a problem with going last?" he asked, not unkindly.

Everyone turned to look at me.

"No, no, it's fine. I'll go last, that's cool." I smiled to say, no hard feelings. But I knew now that I was definitely the weak link in tonight's lineup. They were shifting me to the position where I could do the least damage. I'd probably have one less turn at bat than everyone else. Even so, Link Forster would be up right after me, to execute any necessary damage control.

"Okay, then," Hunter said, clapping his hands. "Let's go."

Davis Polk was in the field. We were batting first. Hunter instructed us to line up in order and wait our turn behind the chain-link fence that backed up the catcher and home plate. Link Forster rubbed his hands together briskly and then picked up a bat.

"Okay, Forster, let's do this," said Hunter, clapping Link on the shoulder as he approached the plate. I could see that Hunter took his team captain duties very seriously.

Some scattered catcalls and screams of "Liiiiink!" erupted from the crowd behind us. The chorus was distinctly female.

Link was a lefty. He stood to the right of the plate, holding the bat at a careful angle above his shoulder, cap down low over his eyes, knees bent, butt stuck out. The Davis Polk pitcher, a beefy bald guy, scrunched up his face, scrutinizing Link. Then he wound his arm up three times and fired the ball at Link at an alarming speed. It was a well-placed pitch. I watched Link swing at it and miss.

"Fuck." Beside me, Hunter let out a loud, disgusted sigh, cupped his hands around his mouth, and yelled, "Come *on*! You're phoning it in, Forster!"

Link turned around toward Hunter, rolled his eyes, and made a casual jacking-off gesture. Then he turned back to the plate. Hunter laughed and made a catcall back.

I was charmed. I thought about how much easier conflict resolution was when you were male. Maybe that was why I'd always gotten along better with men than with women. They didn't pretend to like you when they didn't, and they didn't feel the need to please everyone all of the time. I admired this. It was just so efficient, so clean. Sure, they weren't going to win any congeniality awards, but imagine how much time and emotional energy they saved.

The next time Marty Adler came knocking about another *nonlegal contribution,* I should simply roll my eyes and flash him a casual jacking-off gesture.

The pitcher fired at Link again. This time, bat and ball connected with a loud *pop.* As the Davis Polk outfielders ran, cursing, past the far reaches of the marked-off playing field, Link shot Hunter a lopsided grin, and shrugged—like *happy now?*—before setting off at a slow, loping jog around the bases. The crowd went wild, and for a moment I was reminded why people adored athletes. Even I was a little bit in love with Link Forster by the time he made it all the way home and stamped on the plate for emphasis.

When I finally went up for my first turn at bat, I saw all of the Davis Polk outfielders grin at each other and then jog all the way in toward the pitching mound, leaving the outfield wide open. I felt my cheeks burn and thought, *Just watch, you bastards.* But I swung and missed, then swung and missed again, the wind whistling in my ears as my bat whirled vainly through the air, completely missing the ball's graceful downward arc.

I expected Hunter to yell at me, to give me shit for how poorly I was batting, the way he'd dished it out to Link. Instead, Hunter just shouted encouragingly from behind the dugout, "That's all right, that's okay, Ingrid, don't worry about it. Remember, just wait for your pitch. Really try to keep your eye on the ball!"

Oh, just shut up, *Hunter,* I thought, before swinging and missing again. His kindness was killing me.

123

Finally, late in the fifth inning, I landed a single to first base—I know, it was only a single, but it sounds easier than it is—that brought Tim Hollister home for his third run. *"Nice hustle, Yung!"* I heard Hunter hollering from somewhere behind me, and this time it sounded sincere. Right after Tim had tagged home base, as he walked by me in the dugout, he casually reached out his hand to brush my fingers in that male-coded, mutually congratulatory way, which was something I'd just seen him do with Hunter and Link Forster. Murph punched me—surprisingly hard, actually—in the arm. "Nice work, Yung," he said, looking genuinely impressed. "Thanks," I said, grinning, resisting the urge to rub my arm where he'd punched it. And I was even prouder of that particular moment than I was of having gotten the damn base hit in the first place.

We won the game, seven runs to four. Not through any spectacularly dramatic feat by me, but—thankfully—not in spite of me, either.

When the game ended, the Davis Polk team was gracious enough to come over and congratulate us, and then the fans poured onto the field. Tyler came up and put his arm around me. "So I see why they call you Slugger," he said. "You were great."

I smiled. "Thanks."

"Surprised you're not chained to the office. Aren't you buried with the SunCorp thing?"

"Just sent a new round to the other side. Buys me a free night," I said. Tyler nodded.

At the mention of SunCorp I looked around again for Marty Adler, but realized that he hadn't shown up. I couldn't help feeling let down. I'd come out tonight for nothing.

Even without Adler, though, the celebratory beers were still a go. About fifteen or sixteen of us, including all eight of us who had played, along with Tyler and three bubbly young women I recognized as new Litigation paralegals, headed off to the nearest Irish pub.

Paddy Maguire's was a great dive with sawdust on the floor, a good jukebox, and a midtown mix of suits and neighborhood regulars. We elbowed our way past the boisterous after-work crowd and wedged ourselves around the bar. Tim Hollister was buying and passed the bartender his Corporate AmEx card. There was only one bar stool free, and Tim offered it to me. Chivalry was alive. I perched there with my Amstel Light, wishing I'd ordered something a little less girly.

We raised a toast to the Prosecutors, but as the crowd got progressively larger and pushier, some of the team scattered to the back of the room, where there was more space. Soon it was only me, Hunter, Murph, and Tyler still hanging out by the bar. Hunter and Murph were each on their second Guinness, and even Tyler was having a black and tan. This surprised me. Tyler and I occasionally went out after work by ourselves to the Royalton or the Peninsula, and I'd never seen him drink anything but a martini.

"What, no martini tonight?" I joked, nudging him in the elbow.

"No martini," Tyler replied quietly. He looked annoyed.

After a minute Hunter and Murph came over to us.

"Glad you came out, Robinson," Murph said to Tyler. (At this, I thought I heard Hunter chuckle, just a little.) "Haven't seen you at a game all season. What changed your mind tonight?"

"You're kidding, right?" said Tyler, pasting on a grin. "Ingrid Yung, out in the dirt, playing *softball*? This I had to see."

They all laughed.

Now *I* was annoyed. I took a sip of my Amstel and looked sideways at the three of them. *Et tu, Tyler?*

Hunter cast his eyes around the bar until he spotted Tim Hollister, talking with Link and two of the first-years, over by the jukebox. The third first-year guy had already struck up a very private-looking conversation in the corner with a petite blond girl with heavy eye makeup and a rose tattoo just above her belly button.

"This song sucks," Hunter announced. "I'm going to go put on some decent music." And with that he pushed his way through the crowd toward Tim Hollister and the associates encircling him.

"I'll go with you," Murph said.

I stayed where I was and watched as Hunter and Murph pressed their way through the crowded bar and approached the Tim Hollister semicircle. I wasn't surprised when none of the other associates opened up to let them in. This was common practice for associates trying to schmooze a partner. It was especially predictable at the firm's weekly conference room happy hour, Fridays at Five, where you were supposed to show up and grab a cocktail wiener and a seltzer for about fifteen minutes before loudly announcing that you were swamped and absolutely *had* to go back up to your office or you'd be there all night. At Fridays at Five, there was about a one-to-six partner-to-associate ratio, and each partner who bothered to show up was quickly surrounded by a semicircle of eager young associates hanging on his every word, so that the room became filled not with the convivial fluidity of a crowd but with tightly guarded circles of conversation, each led by a single partner. *Literal* spheres of influence.

Hunter and Murph insinuated themselves into the Tim Hollister semicircle until it was forced to widen. Link Forster looked annoyed. Of course, during all of this associate jockeying for conversational position, Tim Hollister himself remained oblivious, just talking. I was sure none of the associates surrounding Tim had the slightest interest in *what* he was saying; the important thing was that he was saying it to *them.*

When I swiveled back around, Tyler and I exchanged a loaded look.

"Okay," he said quietly. "Basic rule of thumb. Never ask a gay man why he's not having a martini in front of two jocks, *especially* not at a dive bar with sawdust on the floor."

"Sorry," I said, and meant it. He had a point, and it hadn't occurred to me. And it bothered me that it hadn't occurred to me. It seemed like the kind of thing that should have.

But then I narrowed my eyes at him and said, "Well, what about you?"

Tyler blinked. "What *about* me?"

I rolled my eyes. "What was all that 'A girl playing *ball*? This I have to *see*!' crap? I half-expected you and Hunter to start licking Jell-O shots off of some sorority girls and then go play beer pong."

Tyler burst out laughing, and I could tell I was forgiven.

"Touché," he said, bringing his mug up to my beer bottle and giving it a conciliatory clink.

We sat in companionable silence for a while, sipping our drinks and taking in the crowd, and I was basking in the glow of my base hit and the way I hadn't played *that* much like a girl when Tyler said, "So, I got my subpoena from Dr. Rossi today."

"What?"

"I got a personal handwritten note from Dr. Rossi through interoffice mail, telling me he would like to have a 'friendly chat' with me at my earliest convenience."

I was quiet. I had already had several meetings with Dr. Rossi—but I'd drawn the line at trying to draft anyone else. Predictably, most of the associates were treating Dr. Rossi and the Diversity Initiative as a big company joke. No one ever came to see Rossi in his office except for the few partners on the Diversity Committee, me, and the occasional hapless first- or second-year he'd succeeded in corralling for a mute, unhelpful, ten-minute noninterview. He was still hidden away in his dark, untrafficked corner of the twenty-ninth floor, which, owing to Rossi's argyle sweaters and mild manner, had been nicknamed Mister Rogers' Neighborhood, courtesy of some fourth-year wit in Tax.

"And?" I said encouragingly. "Are you going to go talk to him?"

Tyler sighed. "I don't want to be interviewed for the firm's little diversity report, Ingrid. You know that." He paused, then added, "Especially not now, when I've already got one foot out the door."

"I know," I said. "But, I mean, Dr. Rossi's really not that bad."

He looked skeptical.

"Like when I'm telling him about some of the stuff that goes on around here? Like the Corporate guys' weekly squash court reservation at Chelsea Piers? And how no women are ever invited to play? I mean, I don't even think I'm supposed to *know* about that. And Rossi was totally not surprised to hear this. He gets it."

Now Tyler looked alarmed. "You told Rossi about the Corporate guys' standing court reservation? You don't think that's a little too much information?"

"Maybe," I admitted. "But, I mean, I've talked with the guy a couple of times now, and I actually think he believes in what he's doing. He's just so *earnest*. He genuinely thinks he can level the playing field a little. I figure, least I can do is give him the benefit of the doubt."

Tyler gave a short, bitter laugh. "Sounds like you've been drinking the Kool-Aid. You think they're going to level the playing field just by interviewing a couple of us lawyers with melanin and having us spill our guts? Come on, Ingrid. You're too smart for that."

"Well, I've hardly been spilling my guts, Tyler," I said mildly.

"Okay, maybe that wasn't fair." Tyler looked serious. Concerned. "Look, I just don't want to see you get played, that's all. Make sure you protect yourself."

"Thanks, Dad," I said, punching him lightly in the arm.

He shook his head. "I mean it, Ingrid. Don't get yourself too closely tied up in this whole 'diversity' bullshit, you know? You were doing just fine on your own. SunCorp loves you. Adler loves you. You're golden."

I paused. "One thing has nothing to do with the other."

He laughed. "Oh, sweetie. You have a lot to learn."

Fuck you, Tyler.

Tyler Robinson did not have a monopoly on being a Minority Darling. I'd lived it for thirty-odd years, too. And I was sick of all this cynicism. What was wrong with trying a different tack?

"So this is just the way things are, huh? It's not worth sticking our necks out to change anything, because no one cares?"

Tyler flashed me an angry stare. "Oh, you're wondering if the firm really cares? Just take a good look at Hunter and Matt and those other pricks. They go onstage and sing the freaking *N-word* and the firm doesn't do a damn thing about it."

I was incredulous. "So why do you think they hired Rossi?"

He shrugged. "Damage control. Just covering their asses."

"Okay, so if Rossi's such a joke, you got a better idea?"

"Yeah," he snorted. "How about we just wait around for the old white guys in charge to die off."

"Oh, *that's* really helpful, thanks. I think I'll suggest that at our next committee meeting."

He pushed his empty glass away and crossed his arms in front of him. "Hate to break it to you, but bringing in an expensive consultant isn't going to change a damn thing around here."

"Well, especially not if people like us refuse to tell him anything," I said.

We glared at each other.

I was reeling. This was the first disagreement Tyler and I had ever had. Not counting the moment he'd stormed off at the firm outing, we weren't used to any sort of tension between us. Tyler Robinson was the one person I depended on to *get* it, my only friend at the firm who'd laugh with me at egregious instances of white hetero male cluelessness behind his closed office door. And I knew I was the only one he confided in, too. Being on opposite sides of an issue—especially this one—made me sad and uneasy. I'd already lost Murph. I couldn't afford to lose Tyler, too.

Tyler seemed to be reading my mind. His voice softened. "Look. It would be different if I believed anything was ever really going to change."

I grinned. "Wow. That's the first time I've ever been accused of being an optimist."

He didn't crack a smile. "Just pick your battles carefully, that's all. I don't want to see you get hurt."

Murph reappeared next to me, which Tyler took as a cue to look at his BlackBerry and slide off his bar stool. "It's getting late," he said. "I should get going."

Murph didn't protest. "Okay, later, man."

"Later."

Tyler gave me a meaningful look and left us alone.

I took a slow sip from my Amstel, still thinking about Tyler's parting shot. When I set my beer back down, Murph was looking thoughtfully at me. I spoke first.

"So," I said brightly. "Getting anywhere with the new Litigation paralegals? The brunette one's really pretty." I was trying as hard as I could to sound natural, to get back to that easy, carefree banter that had once come so easily—but had eluded us ever since the outing.

"Nah," Murph said, grinning in the direction of the jukebox. "Forster's doing just fine, though. Figured I should get out of there, stop cockblocking him." He hopped up onto the bar stool next to mine and lightly brushed against my arm. "I wasn't interested anyway, if you want to know the truth."

"Really. Why not?" I asked. I kept my tone light and noncommittal.

"It's just—you'd be really proud of me, Yung—I think I'm finally reformed," said Murph, and he sounded like he might be kidding, a little, but only just.

"Well, *this* is news. Reformed, you say. How so?"

"The way I see it," said Murph, and his tone was jocular again, "I'm already thirty-five years old. That's halfway to seventy."

"You're ancient," I agreed.

Murph grinned. "Exactly. And so, at some point, I have to get serious. I mean, I can't be chasing twentysomethings around the rest of my life, can I?"

"Well, if anyone can, it'd be you."

"You know what I mean. I don't want to be That Guy who's forty, never been married, trolling his nephew's wedding reception for bridesmaids, you know?"

I nodded. "Nobody wants to be That Guy."

"So, then." Murph swiveled his bar stool around so that his knee was unmistakably touching mine. "You see my dilemma."

I smiled. And, newly minted optimist that I was, I decided to seize the moment.

Lowering my voice conspiratorially, so that Murph had to lean in very close, I fixed him with my most inviting smile. "I *think* I do, but the question is—what are you going to do about it?"

I expected Murph to grin and say something flip, but his expression changed. He looked at me for a long solemn moment, then pressed his mouth right next to my ear and whispered, "What I should have had the guts to do at the outing."

His breath was warm and close against my neck, and I flushed with pleasure. I tried to contain the tingling that started in the base of my stomach and was radiating through the rest of me. I cast about for something witty to say, but all I could manage was "So why didn't you say anything to me that night?"

He paused a beat and put one of his hands over mine, looking straight into my eyes. "You're not my usual type, Yung. I don't normally date women who are smarter than I am. I really don't want to screw this up."

It was the best thing anyone had said to me in a very long time.

"So, don't screw it up, then."

He grinned, and suddenly something about the old Murph was back. "Well, I've been a complete gentleman so far, don't you think? I didn't even come home with you when I could have."

I blushed. "What are you talking about?"

"The night of the outing. When I put you in the cab. You told me to get in."

I was mortified.

"You heard that?"

He nodded. "But I didn't think I should take advantage of you in that state."

I tried, unsuccessfully, to stop blushing.

Murph tilted his head toward my empty Amstel bottle. "Another drink?"

I looked around. Murph and I were the last ones standing.

"No." I smiled at him and slid off my bar stool. "Let's get out of here."

NINE

❧

Murph still lived in the same Tribeca loft I remembered from that long-ago Halloween party, except now he had the whole gorgeous place to himself. As a thirty-five-year-old bachelor with no kids (that he knew of) and no obligations except to the international law firm of Parsons Valentine & Hunt LLP, this was doable on his salary of three hundred and twenty thousand dollars a year. *Before* bonus.

Murph opened the front door and stood aside to let me in. I took a few tentative steps into his apartment. When I turned around to say "Nice place," he was leaning down and coming in toward my face at an angle that made me think he was going for my cheek. But as I tilted my face to the side, I realized I'd guessed wrong, and his lips landed half on my mouth and then skidded wetly off to the left.

"Whoops." He laughed.

I laughed, too. We broke apart awkwardly. I took a deep breath in and said, "It's been a while."

Murph gave me an odd look, so I clarified quickly, "Since I've been here, I mean."

"Not since that Halloween party I threw back when we were first-years," Murph said. So he remembered. "Not to brag, but I've got to say that party was pretty legendary."

I smiled. "It was."

"So," said Murph, gesturing around the living room. "Want the grand tour?" he asked me.

"Sure."

He remained in one spot and pointed around the enormous space. "Office, kitchen, living room. Bathroom's over there, bedroom's through there."

I nodded. "Very nice."

It *was* nice. I could easily imagine Murph living his life here. I noticed his bookshelves first. They were hard to miss. They reached from the floor to the ceiling—crammed to overflowing, with books jammed spine in, spine out, lying facedown, any way they would fit. Had Murph actually read all these? Personally, I didn't like to display any books in my living room that I hadn't actually read. It seemed, somehow, dishonest.

In the center of the living room sat a battered and fraying beige sofa that would have been at home in a frat house. On the opposite wall was mounted a brand-new, state-of-the-art, jumbo-screen plasma TV. I smiled. This was the kind of contrast common to thirtysomething bachelor apartments in Manhattan.

"Sit down, make yourself at home." Murph walked backward to the stainless-steel kitchen. It looked a lot like the one in my own apartment. Spotless. "You want something to drink?"

What I wanted was a gin and tonic, light on the tonic. But I had to pace myself. My face sometimes flushed a deep red after about two drinks, especially when I was nervous, and I didn't want to spend my evening worrying about the dreaded Asian Blush.

"Just some water would be good right now," I said.

He filled a tall drinking glass with water and ice, and walked it over to me.

"Thanks," I said.

"No problem." As he walked back to the kitchen, I looked down at my hands. They were shaking a little. *Get a grip! Don't blow it!* I held the glass firmly between my knees to silence the ice cubes.

Now that I was actually—finally—here in Murph's apartment, I was beginning to second-guess myself. We had been friends and colleagues for so long that this felt incredibly surreal, a little dangerous.

I perched on the very edge of Murph's sofa and glanced down at the ancient fabric as casually as I could, looking for beer stains—or worse. Finding nothing too alarming, I settled back against the cushions. The couch was surprisingly comfortable.

Something soft and warm rubbed against my leg. Startled, I looked down and saw a small gray cat with four white paws staring intently at me.

I froze. Murph had a *cat*? I was a dog person myself.

Murph was rummaging in the freezer for more ice.

The cat was still regarding me.

"Oh, you have a cat?" I asked, keeping my voice as neutral as possible.

"What?" Murph spun around. "Oh, yeah, him. He's my sister's cat. I'm pet-sitting for her while she and her boyfriend are in Costa Rica."

"Oh. *Pet*-sitting," I said. I reached out and gave the cat a tentative stroke. "What's its name?"

"Steve Buscemi."

"Steve Buscemi?" I repeated. "That's his name?"

He laughed. "Well, my sister calls him Mittens. But, I mean, I wasn't going to live with a cat named freaking Mittens for a month. So I temporarily renamed him."

"Why Steve Buscemi?"

Murph shrugged. "He's small, but he's really tough. And my sister found him in the alley next to her local firehouse. Did you know Steve Buscemi used to be a fireman before he got into acting?"

"Yeah," I said. This fact had always impressed me, too.

I stroked Steve Buscemi, and he purred beneath my hand.

Murph was making himself a drink. Then he switched off the kitchen light and made his way toward me. Most of the light in his apartment had been coming from the kitchen, so the room was now noticeably dimmer. Yet it wasn't quite dark enough to remark upon. I smiled.

Murph knew *exactly* what he was doing.

Now he lowered himself down next to me on the couch. My stomach tensed, and I suddenly felt very warm. I glanced at his drink and envied him. *He* was having what looked like a gin and tonic.

"So," he began, turning to me.

"So," I repeated.

"I'm glad you're here," he said quietly.

"So am I." I took a tiny sip of water, not because I was thirsty, but to buy myself a few seconds. Now that we'd been delivered from the noisiness of the bar into the utter privacy of his apartment, I was lost. I was so pathetically out of practice at this.

For the first time in a long time, I was actually at a loss for words. I was just very, very conscious of Jeffrey Devon Murphy sitting an inch away from me on his couch.

Steve Buscemi leapt onto the sofa and padded across my thigh and into my lap, his tiny paws sliding a little on the slippery plane of my leggings. I scratched behind his ears, grateful for the distraction.

Murph laughed and said, "He likes you."

He likes you. For some reason this made me think of the childhood game *he loves me, he loves me not* that my friends and I used to play at recess. We'd rid countless daisies of their petals, one by one. We'd also played a similar game with an apple, where you twisted the stem around and around as you recited the alphabet, and whichever letter you were on when the stem came off was your future husband's initial. First initial or last? I'd asked the older girl who taught me the game, but she didn't know, either. Even now, at thirty-three, I couldn't eat an apple without reciting the alphabet and twisting off its stem.

Murph set his gin and tonic on the table. I snapped to attention. *Here we go.* I smiled to myself, tucking a stray strand of hair behind my ear, wetting my lips, trying subtly to push Steve Buscemi out of my lap and onto the floor.

But Murph stood up and walked away.

"Anything special you want to listen to?" he asked, his face bathed in the glow from his laptop.

I shrugged. "Surprise me."

After a couple of quick clicks of the mouse he sat back down next to me on the couch, almost imperceptibly closer this time.

I smiled in recognition as the first few unmistakable cool bass notes from "Son of a Preacher Man" filled the room.

"You remembered," I sighed, and then immediately wished I hadn't. It was a naked admission of how well I remembered that long-ago night here at Murph's apartment, when I'd felt his warm breath on my neck and shoulders, his lips and late-night stubble on my bare skin. I wondered with a shudder if Murph had any idea how many times I'd recently replayed that memory in my head.

I waited a beat. But Murph surprised me by not gloating, not pointing this out at all, as if it had been the most natural thing in the world for me to say.

I began to relax a little, resting my head back against the cushions. I was aware of my long shiny hair fanning out gently along the top of the couch the way I knew it would. I murmured, "This is a great song."

"The best," he agreed.

We sat there together in the semidarkness and listened without speaking to the perfection that was Dusty Springfield—the husky notes hanging thick and low in the air, the high notes curling upward into the stratosphere.

I was still petrified about what would happen next. It had been such a long time since I'd been in this situation, with *anyone,* let alone with Murph himself, the most dazzling of all of the golden boys I knew, the heir most apparent, who'd been the source of all my consternation, who'd been keeping me up at night.

I closed my eyes. *Please, please don't screw this up.*

I finally worked up the resolve to turn my head toward Murph. When I did, he was already looking at me. He reached over and stroked my cheek very gently with his fingertip, and it felt so good that my eyes nearly filled.

Oh, sweetie, you are *in trouble,* I thought to myself.

And then he flashed me a smile, and it was such a specific smile, so perfectly disarming, so well calculated, that I couldn't help it, I actually *giggled*—because I was nervous, because I needed to break the tension of the moment, and also because it struck me as sort of funny, this very particular, sideways smile that I knew must have closed the deal for him on many a previous occasion.

Murph's expression grew solemn again. He looked at me for a long moment, and I thought happily that there was absolutely nothing else like it—this moment when you know for sure he's going to kiss you.

I tilted my face toward him at the same second he bent down toward me, and his kiss was so soft and so gentle that I would have been hard-pressed to pinpoint the precise instant when our lips actually touched. Then we were kissing in earnest. Murph pressed one hand against the small of my back and with the other gently traced the curve of my shoulder. I felt a delicious shudder. Goose pimples rose on my arms. It had been a very long time since I'd felt like *this.*

It struck me as ridiculous that after eight years of banter and flirtation delivered in sleek boardrooms high atop Manhattan, and at cocktail parties and formal dinners in elegant dress attire, Murph and I were finally getting together while wearing disgusting dirt-stained Parsons Valentine Prosecutors T-shirts. It was absurd. It was absurd, and it was perfect.

I let out a soft laugh.

He looked up. "What?"

I shook my head, smiling. "Nothing."

I stood up. Grabbing both of his hands, I backed slowly toward the hallway leading to his bedroom.

"Come here," I said.

He did.

I lay on my side with my head resting on Murph's chest, listening to his breathing slow down and even out, and then I flipped onto my back, exhausted and happy and close to sleep.

Murph raised himself up on an elbow and asked quietly, "Do you want some water?"

"Sure," I said, and my voice came out scratchy. I cleared my throat and tried again. "Water. Yes."

"Okay. I'll be right back." He kissed my cheek, disentangled himself from me, and rolled deftly to the side.

I sat up in Murph's platform bed, my back resting against the low angled headboard, the covers drawn self-consciously up over my chest, and watched as, unself-consciously, he shoved into gray boxer briefs before crossing in front of the floor-to-ceiling windows on his way out to the hall. In another moment, I heard him opening and closing kitchen cabinets, as he belted out an old Aerosmith song at the top of his lungs.

He was singing it off-key, Broadway showstopper style, and I knew he was trying to be funny for my benefit. I hugged my knees to my chest and grinned to myself. I had gotten my old Murph back, only better. And I really, *really* liked him.

I felt around underneath the covers for my clothes. They weren't there. I experienced a fleeting panic before noticing that my softball jersey, underwear, and leggings had been neatly folded and draped across the back of a chair—and I found it oddly touching that he had taken the time to do this.

I retrieved my underwear and lay down to tug it back on, grateful that I'd had the random luck yesterday to have been wearing a pretty pair of robin's egg blue panties.

Feeling less vulnerable now, I sat back up and peered more closely around Murph's bedroom. *So this is where Jeff Murphy lays his head at night,* I mused happily. *And probably where he's laid a whole lot else, too.* But I quickly banished this thought.

On Murph's nightstand sat a Bose SoundDock, his iPhone, and two snapshots in simple black frames. I waited a moment, then, when I was sure Murph was still busy banging around his kitchen, picked up both photographs and examined them.

One showed a tanned, unshaven Murph with his arms slung lazily around the shoulders of a couple of other grinning college-age men. They were all good-looking guys, wearing windbreakers and baseball caps, holding beers and standing on the deck of a beach house, with hillocks of sandy dunes and scrubby yellow grass visible behind them. The roommate's fabled house on the Cape, I presumed. It was a charming house, shingled and gabled and weathered gray and white in the solid old New England style. It was handsome and tasteful, and looked completely assured of its place in the world, not unlike Murph and his friends did themselves. So *unlike* the suburban McMansions that my parents and their friends all lived in back home, with faux marble columns and yawning two-story foyers, houses with something to prove.

I set the photo back down on Murph's nightstand and peered closely at the second one, an old-fashioned snapshot of a young family. An earnest-looking mother and father posed next to a fire truck with two kids—a beaming ponytailed girl and an adorable towheaded boy easily recognizable as a four- or five-year-old Murph. Murph was hauled up onto his dad's shoulders, high in the air, and he was wearing a red fireman's hat that was too big for him. Murph's father, I was not at all surprised to see, was himself a handsome man, striking and well made, and quite dashing in a black dress uniform of some sort with fancy epaulets and big brass buttons. Murph had an astonishingly beautiful and happy-looking family—the sort you would expect to see pictured on the front of a catalog, wearing linen and seersucker and dungarees, running along a beach, or cheerfully knotting a necktie onto a Labrador retriever.

I heard Murph's footsteps just outside the door and quickly arranged both picture frames exactly the way I'd found them.

Murph strode back into the bedroom and handed me a glass of water. He stood next to the bed, raised his own glass to his lips, and took three or four long swallows.

"Is this your family?" I asked, nodding toward his nightstand.

"What?" He glanced at the photograph. "Oh. Yeah. Those would be my folks."

"It's a nice picture. Your parents make a really handsome couple."

"Thanks. They try."

"Is that a fire chief uniform your dad's wearing?" I asked.

"Captain."

"Oh."

"He never made chief."

"It must have been fun as a kid having a dad who was a fireman," I said.

Murph didn't respond, draining the rest of his water. Then he asked, "What does your old man do?"

"He's a college professor. Of economics."

He smiled as if I'd said something funny.

Then he said suddenly, "Hey, you hungry?"

I glanced at his phone. It was after one in the morning. Neither of us had had anything to eat since lunch the day before. I hadn't felt hungry at all, but as soon as he asked the question I realized I was starving.

Murph retrieved a stack of delivery menus from his kitchen and splayed them out in accordion fashion on his bed. We ordered from the all-night sushi place down the block. Then we slurped miso soup and gorged ourselves on shrimp tempura and spicy tuna rolls while sitting across from each other on his mattress, Murph in navy blue pajama bottoms and me wearing an ancient Williams College Baseball T-shirt of his that smelled of sweat and deodorant and reached nearly to my knees.

In faded letters it read, WILLIAMS MEN DON'T STOP AT THIRD BASE, which made both of us laugh.

TEN

❧

"Tell me *everything!*" Rachel commanded, stirring a cube of brown sugar into her chamomile tea.

Rachel and her little daughter, Isabel, were in the city running weekend errands. We were having brunch at our favorite Upper West Side café—a bright, bustling place where delicious crepes and quiches were served on large communal tables. Rach and I used to come here a lot back when we lived together in Morningside Heights. The preppy Saturday morning brunch crowd here was equal parts earnest new couples on the Morning After and their counterparts five years later, now parents with kids in tow.

"I mean, why *now*? After eight years?" Rachel pressed. "What finally *happened?*"

"I'm not really sure why now," I tried to explain to Rachel—and to myself. "It just finally felt right, I guess."

Rachel raised one perfectly sculpted eyebrow. "And even *more* importantly," she smirked with barely restrained glee, darting a look over at four-year-old Isabel, who sat coloring quietly at the table, *"how was it?"*

Ah. The Question. I'd been wondering how long it would take Rachel to get around to asking it. My married friends were *much* more interested in hearing about their single friends' sexual exploits now that they themselves had, in front of God and everyone, committed to a single penis forever after. These happily married women thought it downright rude *not* to ask after my love life, when of course the opposite was true. Single career women did not like to feel that we were out here getting our hearts trampled on for our married friends' entertainment. Revealing our romantic humiliations and our most vulnerable selves for the sake of a funny anecdote or two at someone's next book club.

Rachel often liked to say that she lived vicariously through me—still single in the city, still keeping crazy hours, still chasing the brass ring after she'd given it up for a wedding ring. To which I often apologized that she wasn't having more vicarious fun.

But this time felt different. This time, it was Murph we were talking about.

"Well, it was—kind of great," I murmured vaguely.

"Elaborate."

"It was really nice, actually," I said, noticing a pleasant pull in my stomach as I thought again about Murph, the gentle way he'd kissed me good-bye at the door, the message he'd texted me during my short cab ride home: *You were worth the wait.* I thought once again about our sweet, half-remembered conversation in the Oak Hollow clubhouse. And I realized with a slight stab of guilt and surprise that some moments were too perfect, too private to share, even with Rachel.

"Isn't he the one you said was a *huge player*?" she shrieked. An older couple at a neighboring table glanced over at us.

I felt a ping of annoyance. I took a big swallow of coffee and decided to change the subject. "I just don't know how we're supposed to act around each other at the office. I mean, is he going to act like my boyfriend now? Does *he* think he's my boyfriend? Do we tell people at work we're together? What?"

"Well, let's not get ahead of ourselves. I think you should just play it close to the vest for a while," Rachel said.

"Mommy?" piped up Isabel, next to me. "What does 'play close to the vest' mean?"

Rachel leaned across and bent down, speaking softly into her daughter's hair. "It means to keep some things to yourself. Now, Isabel, remember you promised you would let Mommy and Auntie Ingrid have our grown-up time this morning. Okay?"

Isabel nodded, turning back to her coloring book. I looked down at the page. She was studiously giving a fairy princess a pretty fringe of curly brown hair like her own. Like Rachel's. My heart melted.

No one would ever describe me as oozing maternal instinct, but Isabel completely disarmed me. I remembered babysitting her when she was still very tiny, and sitting there by her side in the semidarkness for a long while after she fell asleep, just staring, marveling at her ten perfect little fingers and ten perfect toes and the gorgeously long eyelashes she already had. A few months ago, when Rachel and Josh had a black-tie benefit to attend, I'd gone up to Westchester to stay with Isabel and her baby brother, Jacob. While eleven-month-old Jacob slumbered upstairs, Isabel and I had entertained ourselves by drawing movie posters and designing jewelry for each other. I showed Isabel how to make a chain-link construction-paper bracelet with the letters of her name drawn onto each link in bright rainbow colors, and she'd insisted on making one for me. Isabel had been delighted to discover that our names not only both started with the letter I but were also each six letters long. She'd worn her I-S-A-B-E-L bracelet and I'd worn my I-N-G-R-I-D one the whole evening. When Josh and Rachel came home and she woke briefly, Isabel murmured sleepily, "Auntie Ingrid, don't take off your bracelet until you get home, okay?" "Oh, I won't, honey." And I didn't. I'd kept it on all that weekend and only took it off, reluctantly, when it was time to go back to the office. I still had it, in a cloisonné jewelry tray on top of my bedroom dresser.

"Don't worry, I wasn't exactly planning to broadcast our hookup in the firm newsletter, Rach."

"No, I know. I just mean, okay, so you guys have hooked up once. It's exciting and everything, but that could be it. You don't know if this is actually going to *go* anywhere, right? There are all kinds of issues with dating someone at work, obviously. *Especially* for you, this year."

"Rach, I know. Dating a colleague in my own department. It's in the bad-idea handbook, right?"

"It's not just *in* the book, sweetie," Rachel said gently. "It's on the cover."

I sighed.

I knew she meant well. But sometimes I felt that Rachel—beautiful, happily married, stay-at-home Rachel, who had never been without a man for longer than a month (and that was during finals)—had married dependable Josh and left the corporate world so long ago that she'd simply forgotten what it was like for us single professional women still flailing around out here, trying to make it on our own.

When in the world would I *ever* have time to meet someone outside of Parsons Valentine? Even if I did, I had been on enough blind dates and setups in my lifetime to know that whenever a man starts off a conversation with *Yeah, so I'm already practically heading up my group over at Weil, and I'm up for partner next year*—trust me, they did *not* want to hear you say, *Me, too.*

With Murph, I didn't need to worry about any of that. He was someone who understood and empathized with my crazy hours and erratic work schedule, who never took it personally when I had to cancel plans at the last second because a deal was heating up, who wasn't the least bit threatened by my job or how much money I made because he did it, too, and who understood exactly what I was talking about when I described the headlong adrenaline rush of closing a billion-dollar acquisition and seeing the headline the next day in the paper. Murph and I had sort of grown up together, side by side, at the firm. We trusted each other.

Still, I knew that Rachel cared about me. She was only trying to help.

"I'll be careful, Rach. I'll play it close to the vest, okay?"

"There are some things you should keep to yourself," said Isabel sagely.

"You are absolutely right, honey." I leaned over and tousled her hair, then gave her a big kiss on the top of her head.

Rachel looked a little sheepish. "Look, I don't mean to be a downer. It's just—God, you're *so* close, Ingrid. Why do anything that could jeopardize your chances now? All you have to do is stick it out a few more months. Think of all the women who'd kill to have made it this far. You're this close to being the first *ever,* Ingrid! You have a responsibility!"

A responsibility to whom? To me, or to Rachel?

I thought of Dr. Rossi, and the fight I'd just had with Tyler over speaking out. *You have a responsibility.*

Once again, I wondered why so many people felt entitled to project their own particular choices onto everyone else. It ended up making things much more confusing for us all.

Back in law school, I'd had a professor named George Tanaka. He was an extremely good, extremely popular professor, and his classes were always full. I'd taken his Civil Rights Law survey course and seminar on Critical Race Theory and gotten A's in both. My third year, after the school published an alphabetized list naming each 3L student's employer after graduation, I received a scrawled note from Professor Tanaka, saying he'd like to speak with me at my earliest convenience. I assumed he wanted to wish me luck in my future endeavors. But when I dropped by his office, Professor Tanaka gave me a tight-lipped smile before saying, "I'll be frank. I was surprised to learn that you'll be heading to Parsons Valentine this fall."

I was stunned. And he could see it, because he smiled hastily and shook his head. "Don't misunderstand me. Parsons Valentine is one of the best firms in the country. It's just that I was curious whether you'd considered other avenues. Like public interest law. A federal clerkship, or the Justice Department. Perhaps, eventually, academia."

He looked at me hopefully.

"Well, I—I'm . . ." I was speechless. He was being presumptuous. He was putting me on the defensive, and he had no right. "I appreciate your thinking of me, Professor Tanaka, and of course I was aware of the clerkship process and the Justice Department, but I—I really enjoyed my summer at Parsons Valentine, and for now I think I want to try the law firm route."

"I see." He sighed a drawn-out, world-weary sigh that seemed to signal the end of our conversation. As I was turning to go, Professor Tanaka murmured, "Sometimes, Ingrid, in the grander scheme, it behooves us to do certain things not because we *want* to, but because we are among the very few who *can*."

Rachel's fervent wish—that I make partner on behalf of all the women lawyers who'd gotten mommy-tracked over the years—was Professor Tanaka's grave disappointment that I was selling out. There really was no pleasing everybody. Maybe there was no pleasing *any*body.

I looked at Rachel now, sitting across from me, trying to interest Isabel in her oatmeal and strawberries. Rachel, who professed to live vicariously through me, who claimed to be jealous of everything I was about to achieve at Parsons Valentine, the very things she had once dreamed of achieving herself, back when we were both bright-eyed, idealistic young law students. We'd been so brash, so full of ambition.

We had not come to law school to get our MRS degrees. No, we were there to kick some ass.

Rachel and I had both grown up in that fortunate class of American women who had been taught that, at last, we could truly have It All. For years, a cheerful chorus of Ivy League professors had insistently painted us glowing pictures of our futures as one great big, fat, glistening, juicy oyster. But, one by one, as all the women I knew dropped out of their high-powered careers, or let their last few childbearing years slip away with resignation, or married men they didn't love simply because they felt they were *running out of time*—I was realizing that we had not quite been told the truth. It wasn't that we had been lied to, exactly. Rachel and I *were* extremely privileged women in many ways. We could definitely have A Lot. Many of us even managed to have Quite A Good Deal of It. But we were all finding out that, no, actually, regrettably, painfully, we had not quite figured out how to have It All. At least not All at the Same Time.

For the moment, at least, you still really did have to choose.

I thought about the handful of precious Saturdays I'd taken Metro-North up to Westchester to babysit at Rachel and Josh's house. These were evenings I enjoyed, not just for the sheer pleasure of seeing those two beautiful, tousle-headed kids, but for the chance to get away from the hustle and relentlessly expectant pulse of Manhattan, the modern starkness of my immaculate, brand-new condo, to sit in somebody's real live living room, with a deep, fluffy sectional couch and a wood-burning fireplace and stuff scattered everywhere and family pictures cluttering the mantel and actual *sconces* on the walls. This felt like a place where *lives* actually happened.

After I tucked Isabel and Jacob into their beds, I would creep quietly about the warm, comfortable family room, feeling a little like an intruder, carefully examining each framed photograph in turn—a laughing Rachel and Josh feeding each other pieces of wedding cake;

Josh relaxing on a porch swing with Jacob sleeping on his chest; Isabel and Rachel hugging each other and beaming in front of a Cinderella castle—and I would wonder to myself about which one of us was luckier.

ELEVEN

❧

I pulled the fresh pages off the printer and walked them back into my office, closing the door. I'd been working balls-out—so to speak—on the SunCorp acquisition, and everything was clicking. For weeks, I'd been practically living in the office, making sure we stuck to Lassiter's accelerated timetable. Now we were ready to send a last round of the term sheet and pre-close documents over to Binney's lawyers at Stratton and Thornwell—right on schedule. I just needed Adler's final okay and then I'd pitch them over to the other side. Next week, Ted Lassiter would be coming into the office, and Adler and I would walk him through the pre-close documents in person.

I glanced at my phone display. 5:09 P.M.

I'd been up for thirty-four hours straight. My silk tank was clammy and stuck to my back. I was sure I must stink, but I felt terrific. There was nothing like getting a document out to the other side late on a Friday afternoon. This bought me a free weekend and a blessedly quiet week ahead, although it ruined the same weekend and upcoming week for our counterpart lawyers at the opposing firm.

I felt kind of sorry for the unsuspecting sap over at Stratton and Thornwell who was no doubt getting ready to call it a week. I imagined him lazily surfing the Internet in these golden late Friday afternoon hours, on his cell phone to a wife or girlfriend, negotiating where to have dinner and what movie to see. I knew exactly what would happen tonight and how it would all go down—the phone on his desk ringing just as he was walking out the door, the guy glancing at his caller ID, seeing the partner's name flash across the screen, his heart sinking, his weekend dreams dashed, the wife or girlfriend throwing a fit. *Fuuuuck.*

"Just got the revised draft in from Parsons Valentine. Would you stop by my office, please? I'd be very grateful if you could review it over the weekend and get your preliminary markup to me by Monday."

It was vaguely ridiculous, this *I'd be very grateful* aspect of the partner-associate relationship. I always preferred it when people spoke their subtext. And the law firm subtext for *I'd be very grateful* was *You will lose your job unless.*

The cruel beauty of this system was that the other guy's loss was my gain. Now I actually had a whole weekend off, to do with what I pleased. Even better, Murph and I were planning to spend the entire weekend together. I didn't really think of Murph as my boyfriend yet, but I certainly did think of him. All the time.

I picked up the phone and dialed Justin Keating's extension. I needed him to stick around until Marty Adler had had a chance to approve the pre-close documents and help me send the distribution to the client and the lawyers on the other side.

Justin picked up the phone at the end of the fifth ring. *No, please, don't trouble yourself, Justin, no need to rush.*

"Yeah?"

"Justin, can you come to my office, please?"

He sighed. "Yeah." And hung up.

In another minute he was standing just outside my door.

I cleared my throat. "Okay, listen," I said briskly. "I'm going to head up to Adler's office and make sure he signs off on this. Then I'm going to need you to help me proofread the revised docs one last time and send them to the other side."

"Um, it's Friday night. Isn't that, like, what a secretary's for?"

"Um," I said, "it's actually, like, *your* job to assist me on any aspect of this deal that might require your help."

Justin's lips parted in a small *O* of surprise. He looked at me for a long moment. Then he rolled his eyes. "Fine. You know where to find me." He slouched off down the hall.

My phone rang. It was Adler.

I grabbed up the receiver before the first ring had finished. "Hi, Marty."

"Ingrid!" said Adler. He chuckled. "Should have known I'd find you on the first ring. Hard at work, as always."

Good of you to notice.

"Were you still going to show me the SunCorp docs tonight? I thought I'd call to check, since I'll be heading out pretty soon. My wife and I have opera tickets."

Of course you do.

"Yes, actually, I was just on my way up when you called. I'll be there in a second. If you could take a look and make sure all looks good to you, then Justin and I will be sure to get this out to Stratton tonight."

Marty Adler paused.

"Justin? You mean the *Keating* kid?" he said. "Don't tell me you asked *him* to stay late on a Friday just to send out some FedEx for you."

I frowned at the receiver. "Well, yes, Marty, actually I did ask him to help proof the documents with me before they go out," I said slowly. "Didn't you tell me to show him the ropes?"

"Hell, I meant be *nice* to the kid, not make him work all hours of the night. Couldn't you have gotten some random floater secretary or paralegal instead? Give Justin a break?"

I took a deep, calming breath. Marty Adler was getting on my last nerve. It was lovely that he was so concerned about ruining Justin Keating's weekend when I was the one who'd been up for thirty-four hours straight, who'd been working late nights all week and all day Sundays and ordering greasy takeout at 3:00 A.M. to sit here in my office, exhausted and haggard and bleary-eyed, to review draft after draft marked up with endless comments and questions from seller's counsel at Stratton, and Mark Traynor at SunCorp, and even Ted Lassiter himself. I was the one single-handedly bringing this deal in for an on-time close. Not Marty Adler, and certainly not Justin.

I couldn't help thinking about the countless times, as a junior associate, that I'd been forced to wait around til midnight or one on a random weeknight only to have the partner or senior associate call—as an afterthought—from home to say, "Sorry, I thought someone else had already let you know. You can go home. We won't be sending anything out tonight after all." So many weekend mornings, I'd been called in at 8:00 A.M. just to fetch things or correct typos for the clients and senior partners—*Casual Saturday,* went the office joke—and I'd never heard anyone complain on my behalf.

"Marty," I said evenly, "just so you know, I never ask anyone to come in or work overtime if I don't really need their help. Since this draft's gone through so many revisions, I thought I could use the extra pair of eyes before it went out. I'm not sure you realize, but I've been here since eight in the morning—"

"Well—"

"*Yesterday* morning," I said.

This shut Adler up for a moment. "I see." Then he said, "Look, Ingrid, I know you've been working flat out on this SunCorp deal. And your efforts certainly aren't going unnoticed. My point is, let's not make a habit of these late nights for Justin Keating. It would be best for all concerned not to let him start hating his job quite so soon."

"Of course."

"Thanks. I knew you'd understand. See you up here in a minute."

I put the phone down harder than I'd meant to. I opened up my wardrobe to the side with the mirror and peered into it. I looked like a woman unhinged. I reached up and shook my hair out from the messy ponytail it had been in since about ten o'clock last night. The elastic left a funny indentation so that, now loose over my shoulders, my hair bore an odd and unintentionally angular shape, sticking up on one side. Not a flattering look. I thought about putting my hair back in a ponytail, but that made me look about twelve, so I just left it loose and tried to smooth down the flyaway ends with my hands.

I sighed. I looked exhausted. I *was* exhausted. My complexion was sallow and washed out, and my mascara—last applied at home the morning of the *previous* day—had created a lovely raccoon effect that would not budge. I hadn't even had time to go shower in the fortieth-floor R&R suite, and besides, I didn't have a fresh change of clothes. Well, it couldn't be helped. I'd promised Marty Adler that I would bring this deal in for an on-time close, and that was exactly what I was going to do.

I did what I could, reapplying lipstick, retucking my crumpled tank as neatly as possible into my pencil skirt, trying to smooth out the wrinkles bunched across my lap, and slipping on the black silk suit jacket I'd abandoned the night before when I'd gotten down to work.

I gathered up my copy of the revised term sheet and took the elevators up to the thirty-seventh floor.

Adler stood from behind his massive desk and looked me over a beat longer than usual. I knew he was taking in my disheveled appearance. I felt self-conscious—but also annoyed. *I've been up for thirty-four hours straight. What do you want from me?*

He gestured with his glasses toward his teak conference table.

We sat down, and I handed the redlined term sheet to him. He pulled a silver fountain pen from his shirt pocket, uncapped it, and began to review the document. His lips moved as he read. I'd never noticed this before, and felt slightly embarrassed for him. I never knew where to look when people were evaluating your work right in front of you. It seemed rude, somehow, to watch them read. I looked discreetly out the window. Outside the sky was turning pink and purple over the spires of Manhattan.

When I looked back at Adler, he was underlining things and scribbling little notes in the margin. That he had notes to scribble at all made me nervous. I hoped I hadn't missed anything. I'd been very careful.

He took off his reading glasses and handed the draft back to me. "Looks good, Ingrid. I just marked a couple of tiny nits."

I had always hated this word "nits." In my public elementary school, I had found it extremely undignified to be subjected to our mandatory annual screening for head lice, which took place in our school cafeteria, with brown paper carefully laid out over the linoleum floor. "Nits" was what the school nurse had called them, as she took a barber's comb over each of our bowed heads, searching for signs of chaos or incompetence at home. I'd had a distaste for the word ever since.

Marty Adler stood, signaling that we were through. I cleared my throat.

"Actually, Marty, I just wanted to run a couple of things by you."

He looked over at me. "Shoot."

"As I mentioned the other day, Stratton's last markup focused heavily on the seller's reps and MAC clause, and I have a feeling those are still going to be big sticking points when they see this draft."

"What are they trying to take out?"

"It's not what they're trying to take *out;* it's what they're trying to get *in.* They want all kinds of new contingencies that shift the burden of risk to SunCorp if anything happens between now and closing."

"What kind of contingencies?" Adler folded one arm across his chest and held the stem of his reading glasses to his lips.

"Well, they've been very insistent that they're not responsible for any changes in general market conditions occurring before closing. More insistent than we usually see."

Adler nodded. "That doesn't surprise me, though. Ever since the credit mess, seller's counsel would be idiots not to try to carve out general market conditions."

"Fair enough, but they also want to carve out changes in *law,* and shift *that* risk over to the buyer, too. Who knows what Congress might do between now and then."

Adler looked at me. He was smiling as if I had just fetched him the paper. "Very interesting, Ingrid. Let's try to stick to our guns on that. But I'm not that concerned. We agreed on exclusive jurisdiction in Delaware, didn't we?"

"We did," I replied.

"Well, no buyer has ever—"

"No buyer has ever successfully invoked a MAC clause in Delaware court, I know. But there was that recent *Gilder* decision in Delaware Chancery Court that seems to say that might not hold forever. We could have a fighting chance with a MAC clause, as long as it's drafted properly in the first place," I finished.

Adler was still smiling. And he was sizing me up. "I admire your spirit, Ingrid. I knew I'd put the right associate on this deal. But can I give you a little piece of advice?"

"Please."

He leaned forward. So did I.

"Don't take it all so fucking seriously."

What?

I couldn't have been more surprised if he'd actually reached over and slapped me. I felt both confused and humiliated. Here I was, killing myself to bring *his* deal to announcement stage on his crazy breakneck schedule, and Adler—Mr. 110%—was telling me not to take it all so fucking *seriously*?

He grinned. "Listen. If you really think there's anything to *Gilder,* I'd suggest you ask Jack Hanover to weigh in. He's the expert. Show him the term sheet so he gets the context. But just between you and me, I wouldn't lose much more sleep over how many commas are in the MAC clause. Let's close this thing." He glanced at his watch. "Now if you'll excuse me. Those opera tickets."

I wondered if Ted Lassiter would appreciate how cavalier Marty Adler was being with SunCorp's billion bucks.

"It just seems like Binney's being kind of cagey here about something," I tried again. "They've also asked to take up the breakup fee by another percent. It just strikes me as a little odd." The breakup fee is the amount one party has to pay the other if it backs out of the deal before closing.

This made Adler pause. "Seems kind of late in the game for them to be screwing around with the breakup fee."

I nodded. "That's what I thought, too."

Adler tapped his glasses against his chin, then stood back up again. "These are all excellent points, Ingrid. Check with Jack offline about the *Gilder* implications, but you can send the document out tonight. Let's stick to our guns, and see what Stratton comes back with. And be sure to take Lassiter through all of this point by point at our pre-close meeting next Thursday."

"Got it." I unfolded myself from his wingback chair and stood.

"By the way," Adler said, striding back to his desk. "No one knows better than I do how hard you've been working on this deal. And we do value your truly excellent work and dedication."

"Thanks, Marty."

Here was the thing about law firm partners. They knew exactly how to dole out enough praise at exactly the right moment to make an associate feel just appreciated enough to stay. We weren't colleagues; we were more like pets.

As soon as I got back downstairs to my office, I flipped through my draft to see what recommendations Marty Adler had for me. But he had barely made any comments at all. He had changed two of my commas to semicolons and capitalized a defined term. Where I'd defined the formula for "net profits," Marty had crossed out "profits" and written in his reckless, expansive scrawl, "earnings."

I sighed and tossed the draft onto my desk. I was suddenly reminded of an evening years ago, when I was still a summer associate, and Tyler and I had been sent to the printers late one night. As we waited in a plush room for the next round of offering memoranda to come off the presses, Tyler and I watched Letterman on the jumbo flat-screen TV and feasted on shrimp cocktail, stone crab claws, and buffalo wings. These were the perks provided by our corporate printers to make our interminable nights of waiting a little easier to bear. Tyler and I were sitting next to two second-year gunners from Cravath, heads bent over a draft offering circular. Suddenly, one of them jumped up and slapped his colleague on the arm. "Hey! This comma right here. *Shouldn't it be a semicolon?*" "You're right! Great catch!" The two of them exchanged excited high fives before bending over the document again. Tyler looked at me with wide eyes and we busted up, laughing silently. For weeks afterward, all I had to do was mouth *Great catch* to Tyler across a conference room or cocktail reception, and we'd both crack up.

Now it didn't seem so funny. That night at the printers, little had we known that we would soon *be* those guys from Cravath we'd skewered so mercilessly. That those tiny adjustments of commas and semicolons would soon be the little things we came to believe in.

"Burning the midnight oil again, huh?"

I looked up to find Ricardo, who was making his evening rounds, leaning his head into my office.

I gave him a wan smile. "You know it, RC."

He paused a beat, taking in my exhausted appearance. "I do know it. I see you here all the time." He shook his head and grinned. "I sure hope it's worth it."

There was a scratchy clamor from his walkie-talkie. "I gotta run," said Ricardo, turning to go. He made a shooing motion at me. "Go home, young lady. It's a Friday night."

For a moment I stared at the space in the doorway where he'd been.

Then I picked up the phone and dialed Justin's extension. No answer. *Of course,* I thought irritably. Wouldn't be surprised if the kid had taken off for the weekend without telling me. No chance of Justin Keating being reprimanded so long as Adler had anything to say about it.

I waited for the beep. "Justin, it's Ingrid. I just got Marty's sign-off, so I'm making a couple of final changes and then we'll be ready to send this out. So could you just swing by my office whenever you get this? Thanks."

I rolled my cursor over the online firm directory and clicked on Jack Hanover's name. His steely blue eyes and aquiline nose stared back at me, along with his firm bio, extension, and office number. This picture must have been taken three decades ago. He looked not quite fifty.

Jack Hanover was the lone surviving granddaddy of the firm, a pioneering corporate litigator who'd been one of the most influential men in town back in the day. Now nearly eighty, he still held a lot of sway in courtroom circles. He'd kept an honorary spot on the Management Committee and an office at the firm, where he stopped in three days a week to read the *New York Law Journal,* return professional correspondence, and compose op-ed pieces for the *Times.* He was as old-school as they came. Rumor had it that Jack Hanover still kept cigars and a fine bottle of Scotch on the bottommost shelf of his credenza, and was not shy about partaking in the office.

I glanced at the clock again. 5:45. I doubted that Jack Hanover would still be here, but I dialed his extension anyway. His secretary picked up on the first ring. "Good evening. Mr. Hanover's office."

"Hello, this is Ingrid Yung," I said. "Is—ah, is . . ."

I hesitated. Jack Hanover was such a legendary figure that it felt flat-out *wrong*—both disrespectful and disingenuous—for me to call him Jack. Yet that was the very charade the firm expected us all to perpetuate—that everybody was on equal footing, that we were all on a first-name basis, that we were all just one big, happy, functional family. But it still secretly shocked me whenever Hunter or Murph casually referred to Jack Hanover, to his face, as Jack. Somehow, even now, even as I was about to make partner at his firm, I still felt weird calling him anything but Mr. Hanover, thereby underscoring exactly how unlike him I felt.

"Is Jack available?" I made myself say. "Marty Adler suggested that I run a quick question by him, if he has a chance."

"Hold on a moment, please, I'll see."

A second later, she said, "Yes, Mr. Hanover says he can see you now. His office is thirty-nine-oh-one, first corner office after Reception."

By the time I got off the elevator, buzzed myself in through the glass doors, and found Jack Hanover's corner office, his secretary had already left for the evening. But there was a sliver of light coming through beneath his office door, which was slightly ajar. He was expecting me.

I smoothed my hands over my hair and skirt in a final attempt to pull myself together. Then I gave a tentative knock.

"Come in," boomed a voice.

I pushed open the door.

The office was shadowy and dim, the only light coming from a green-shaded banker's lamp on the credenza. I took a few tentative steps into the room. Jack Hanover was seated behind an antique walnut desk with ornately carved legs and claw feet. Directly across from Jack Hanover, each seated in a wide leather club chair, were none other than Hunter and Justin Keating. They looked as startled to see me as I was to see them.

All three of the men were cradling highball glasses, with an inch and a half of amber liquid sloshing around in the bottoms.

Jack Hanover's famous Scotch. So that part was true.

"Hello, hello," Hanover boomed at me, beckoning me forward. His voice was not unkind. "You called with the quick question, yes?" I knew he didn't know my name, but at least he seemed aware that I was an associate.

I was at a complete loss. Bleary-eyed, looking every bit as disheveled as I felt, I opened my mouth but no words came out. I stood there, stupefied. I looked from Jack Hanover to Justin Keating to Hunter, one by one by one.

Justin had straightened abruptly when I entered the room. Even *he* seemed aware that there was something slightly indecorous—something *unseemly*—about the whole situation.

Hunter, for his part, looked completely unsurprised. I wanted to reach over and wipe the complacency right off his face.

"Don't mind my friends here," Hanover said jovially, waving a hand in the direction of his *friends*. "We're just having a little visit. Hunter's father-in-law and I go back a long time. Justin's dad, too, of course."

Of course.

I nodded, unsure what to say. Not even sure an answer was expected. Jack Hanover was not being unkind. To him, it must seem perfectly normal that we should all be gathered here in this room in this precise configuration.

Upon seeing the older man's nonchalance, Justin settled himself back into his chair. He may even have sipped his Scotch a little more deliberately, but maybe not. Turning away from me, he pretended to study the crowded collage of framed awards and photographs on Jack Hanover's walls and bookshelves, but I saw a telltale flush spread across the back of his neck.

Good. I *hoped* I was making him uncomfortable.

I bent down in an awkward sort of crouch next to Hanover's desk chair, showing him the SunCorp acquisition document and pointing out the clause in question.

Jack Hanover sat back, crossed his arms behind his head, and began to lecture me on the profundities of the *Gilder* decision and their potential impact on the Delaware Chancery Court. I was mortified. Humiliated. I couldn't absorb a word he was saying.

I felt like a child stumbling onto a grown-up dinner party.

So I just stood there, a reluctant maid-in-waiting before Jack Hanover and his royal court. And I grew angrier and angrier. Until I was roiling.

Now Justin was staring directly at me. His expression was neither mocking nor pitying, just watchful. He appeared to be waiting for my reaction. Justin Keating—the paralegal who was supposed to be assisting *me* on this all-important deal—had been up here shooting the shit and sharing a fine tumbler of Scotch with the firm patriarch while I'd been running around the office like a chicken with its head cut off.

I felt humiliated and sweaty, unkempt and unwashed. I was a mess. And what a perfect little triumvirate to be a mess in front of! As I stood doubled over in my little awkward crouch by Jack's chair, hoping my underarms didn't stink and that my hair didn't stick up too much, that my mascara wasn't running *all* the way down my face, I could feel Justin Keating's prying eyes sticking to me, and I hated him.

When Jack Hanover finally finished holding forth on the precedential value of *Gilder,* I gathered up the pages of my term sheet without looking at him, without looking at any of them. My face was burning, and I could feel the sting of little pinpricks behind my eyes.

"Thanks for your time, Jack," I bleated—hating myself, hating my weak little voice—before hurtling out of the room.

Back in the safety of my office, with the door closed, I sank into my desk chair, closed my eyes, and began to cry quietly. I could hear more lawyers and secretaries leaving for the night. *Have a good weekend. See you Monday.* Then silence. After a time, I heard the cleaning ladies make their way down the hallway, vacuums roaring.

Why don't we start our conversation another way, Ingrid. What made you want to become a lawyer in the first place?

I swiveled over to the window and looked out at the wide expanse of evening sky. Lights were coming on all up and down Madison Avenue. I stared for a long time at my beloved Manhattan skyline, its jagged silhouette so familiar to me now that I could sketch it by memory. I thought about the long-ago dinner party my parents had taken me to in Dr. Giles's Fifth Avenue apartment, with its view of the world that I wanted.

It was the very reason I had willed myself to stay at Parsons Valentine all these years, the reason it had now become absolutely crucial—completely nonnegotiable—that I make partner. It was what would make all of these little humiliations and exclusions *amount* to something. It had to. More than anything, I wanted, once and for all, to shake that haunting suspicion that, while my record impressed and my work made the grade, I was ultimately *not valued.*

Oh yes, at a place like Parsons Valentine, I felt liked, but I did not feel *well* liked.

And yet, to become the first woman of color ever voted into the partnership at the prestigious law firm of Parsons Valentine & Hunt

LLP would make things better for everyone in the long run. Wouldn't it? *Sometimes, in the grander scheme, it behooves us to do certain things not because we want to, but because we are among the very few who* can.

Because I was one of the very few who *could*, I had long ago decided that I must.

TWELVE

〰

With the next draft of the acquisition term sheet safely pitched to the other side, Murph and I spent Saturday night in the city together—a Hitchcock revival at the Film Forum, a three-hour, two-bottle-of-wine dinner at my favorite little bistro on Cornelia Street, and then, finally, my apartment.

It felt like a real date.

Murph felt like a real boyfriend.

When I opened my eyes the next morning, the first thing I did was to look over at Murph's sleeping form. I half expected him not to be there. But sure enough, there he was, snoring lightly beside me, one of my eggshell, eight-hundred-thread-count sheets twisted half underneath his body. I rolled onto my side as quietly as I could, propped myself up on an elbow, and studied his face. I'd never noticed before the tiny rivulets forming in the crepe-paper skin around his eyes.

Few things are more disarming than a man asleep. No matter who he is or what he does in his waking hours, a man sleeping just looks so winningly vulnerable—so innocent and blameless. They all do. This is my favorite way to pass the time on long business flights. After the evening meal is cleared away, after everyone clicks off their overhead lights and tries to get comfortable with the airline-issue pillow and blanket, I entertain myself by studying the men around me in the Business Class cabin as they sleep. And make no mistake: The majority of these passengers are still men. I draw an odd and comforting sort of pleasure in seeing such men—these potent, chest-beating captains of industry, these Masters of the Universe—felled by something as natural as sleep.

I lay there happily for a moment longer, watching the rhythmic rise and fall of Murph's smooth chest, when it suddenly occurred to me that I had nothing at all in the apartment to offer him for breakfast—no eggs, no bread, no cereal. I couldn't even remember if I had any coffee. I crept out of bed and shivered, goosebumps rising on my bare skin.

The hardwood floors were cold beneath my feet. I'd always meant to get a rug for my bedroom but had never gotten around to it. Quietly, I opened my top dresser drawer, slipped on some underwear and a ribbed cotton tank top, and wandered out into the hall.

I looked critically around my apartment. My living room was a total mess. Starbucks cups and a half-empty pizza box littered the floor around my sofa, next to my laptop and three legal pads containing my SunCorp notes. I closed my laptop, gathered up all the papers, and stacked them neatly on my coffee table.

In the kitchen, I quickly confirmed what I already knew: nothing to eat. I wondered what that said about me and my priorities. Who bought an apartment with a Viking range and a Sub-Zero refrigerator and never used them? I thought about Anna Jergensen and all the other twenty-something girls whose cramped, homey Williamsburg shares Murph regularly went back to. What did a girl like that serve guys like Murph for breakfast? She'd probably breeze into the kitchen and whip up a batch of pancakes while he was in the shower. Whereas I was someone who actually had to Google how many minutes it took to boil an egg. I remembered Rachel telling me once that she'd made blueberry pancakes for Josh the first time he'd slept over at her place and that later he'd told her it was one of the first things that had made him fall in love with her. I'd never made pancakes in my life. What was even the name of that stuff you were supposed to use for them? Bisquick? I had no idea.

I slipped back into my bedroom and checked on Murph. Still asleep. I threw on some yoga pants and running shoes. As I pulled my hair through an elastic band, I tripped on one of my high-heeled sandals that had been kicked onto the floor late last night.

Murph stirred, sitting halfway up.

"Sorry," I said softly. "Go back to sleep. I'm running out to pick us up some bagels or something. Be right back."

"Mmn-kay." He flipped over onto his stomach. In a second his snoring resumed.

I lingered a moment. This was nice, I thought, leaving my bedroom with someone still in it.

By the time I'd returned from the bagel shop with coffee and half a dozen plain and everything, Murph was wide awake and reading my Sunday *Times*. He'd parted the curtains so that sunlight flooded in through the picture window. The duvet was bunched up near his crossed ankles at the foot of my bed.

He looked up at me over the top of the business section and flashed me that big, winning Jeff Murphy grin that I loved. "Hey."

"Hey, yourself." I set our bagels and coffee on the dresser, stripped back down to my tank top and underwear, and flopped dramatically onto the mattress next to him, entwining my legs with his.

"Hold your arm out," he said.

"What?"

"Just close your eyes and hold out your arm."

I did as I was told.

Murph gently placed something on my wrist. I opened my eyes. It was the construction-paper bracelet that Isabel had made for me.

"Oh, this." I smiled. "This is my favorite piece in my jewelry collection. My friend's four-year-old daughter made it for me last time I babysat."

He raised his eyebrows. "You? *Babysit?*"

"Thanks for sounding so surprised. I'll have you know I'm actually really good with kids."

He smiled. "I'm not so surprised," he said softly, into my ear. Goose pimples rose on my arms, and I shivered in happy anticipation.

But when I looked back at Murph, he had gone back to reading the *Times.*

"Really?" I said. "This is what you do when you wake up in a beautiful woman's bed on a lazy Sunday morning? You read the business section?"

"I'm one paragraph from the end of this article. Did you see this? About that pipeline project in Nigeria that went under at the last second? Good cautionary tale for Rubinstein's São Paulo clients, eh?"

I disentangled my legs from his, landing them on my side of the bed with a thud of protest.

Murph looked over at me. "You know, it wouldn't be a bad idea for you to read this stuff, either. I shouldn't have to tell you this, Yung—you should always be thinking about business development."

"Wow. Could you try to sound a little less like a *lawyer?*" I asked.

He ignored this.

I was getting nowhere. I reached down and pulled the duvet up to our waists. I sidled over toward Murph until my body was aligned against his. I looked up at him. He was frowning at the *Times* business page. Slowly I brought one leg upward to his groin, then moved my thigh very gently back and forth against the partially open fly of his boxers—one stroke, two strokes, three—until I felt him make an appearance.

The business section landed on the floor.

HELEN WAN

I smiled up at Murph with my eyelids at half-mast, a look I'd learned from a babysitter when I was twelve and later perfected in college.

Murph leaned over me. Just as I was about to close my eyes, I saw him glance at the clock on my dresser.

I laughed.

"What?" he said.

"Um, did you just look over at the *clock?*"

"No," he lied.

"I saw you."

He grinned. "So? I like to know what time it is."

"Jesus, Murph. You make love like it's billable."

"Ouch." He clutched at his heart. "That really hurts, Yung."

He leaned in to kiss me. I shut up after that.

Later, I lay happily on my side, with my head resting on Murph's outstretched arm.

"Murph?"

"Hmm." He'd drifted half to sleep.

"Do you think anyone at work knows about us?"

"No." He opened his eyes and rolled over on his side to look at me. "At least, I haven't said anything to anyone. Why?"

"Just curious."

"Would you care if they knew?"

I hesitated. "No."

But I did care. I cared deeply. I knew that I had more, *much* more, to lose than Murph did in this particular respect. It was one thing for him—loud, boisterous, ladies' man, frat boy Murph—to have slept with one of his fellow senior associates in the group. It was quite another for me—the only senior woman attorney left standing—to have slept with him. I didn't want this getting around, especially not now, when

170

we were both less than a month away from partnership. Oh God. If only Murph and I had just gotten all of this out of our systems back when we were first-years, things would be so much simpler now.

Timing was everything.

I knew very well, from having been around them for eight years, the way my male colleagues bragged about their conquests—professional and sexual. They'd stopped censoring their conversations around me many years ago. I was just one of the guys by now. And while I liked to imagine that out of professional respect for me, their only female colleague, they might stop themselves from talking about me like they did their other female conquests . . . well, in reality there were probably more than a handful of male colleagues who would be slapping Murph on the back if they knew. Boys will be boys and all that.

I pressed the heels of my palms hard against my eyes, thinking.

The conventional wisdom around the firm was that Murph and I were both shoo-ins for partner in M&A this year. Murph knew it, and so did I. There was a certain romantic symmetry in that idea that I liked. Mr. and Ms. Partner & Partner. It had a nice ring.

But knowing that our upcoming partnership vote was only a couple of weeks away also led me to a new and unpleasant concern.

Would Murph and I have to remain a secret after we officially became partners? There was no official antifraternization policy at the firm, and everyone knew there were plenty of random hookups at the annual holiday party at the Plaza, but this was different. This was an *us*. I'd never heard of two partners dating each other before. Maybe, after we both became members of the firm, Parsons Valentine would actually have to institute a new rule to govern our relationship. Now, that would be an embarrassing policy for Murph and me to have to vote on at a partners' meeting. *All in favor of allowing new members of the firm Ingrid and Murph to continue sleeping together? . . . Say aye. All opposed?* I could just picture it. Marty, Harold Rubinstein, Jack Hanover, and the rest all convening discussion on the pros and cons. Oh God.

The thought of Jack Hanover made me groan. I flopped back onto my pillow, wincing at the memory of Friday afternoon.

Murph looked at me, concerned. "What's wrong?"

I told him everything. It came out in a jumbled, bitter rush. I told Murph all about the horrible late night I'd had, about Adler's seeming indifference to the SunCorp deal and how he was letting me do it all myself, without guidance from him *or* the assistance I should have been getting from Justin Keating, about stumbling into Jack Hanover's office and finding Hunter and Justin in there, having a nice after-hours drink with their good friend Jack.

Murph stroked my hair and held me quietly. "I'm sorry about that," he said after a few minutes.

"Thanks." I smiled up at him, genuinely touched. "I mean, I know I'm sensitive. You probably think I'm *too* sensitive."

He shook his head. "No. I don't. I totally get it. I've been on the receiving end of some of that shit myself."

I twisted around in bed so I could look straight at him. "What do you mean? *You?*"

He looked at me. "Yeah, me."

"But what in the world could they ever say about *you?*"

Murph laughed softly. He reached over and touched my cheek. "Forget it."

"No, I don't want to forget it." I sat up in bed, cross-legged, and leaned toward him, like a kid asking for one more bedtime story. "I really want to know, Murph."

He paused, not saying anything right away.

I waited.

"You're not the only one who feels on the outside of things, Yung."

"Go on."

Murph sighed. He rolled onto his back and clasped his hands behind his head, staring up at my ceiling.

"Okay, well, once after softball, at Paddy Maguire's, I was feeling great that night, right? 'Cause I'd scored two runs. Then some first-year douche who's really hammered starts asking about my family. So I tell him I have a sister. He asks if she's older or younger, so I tell him she's thirteen months older than me. And you know what the fucker says?"

I shook my head.

" 'Oh, so you're Irish twins.' "

Murph looked at me, waiting for a reaction.

"Wow," I said.

"Right?" Murph said to the ceiling. "And don't even get me started on all the Irish drunk jokes."

Seriously? *That* was the best he had? Sure, it was stupid, and insulting, and it wasn't a line of conversation I'd ever pursue myself, but if Murph thought that it compared to some of the shit Tyler and I had to deal with, well, I was unimpressed.

Murph turned back toward me. He reached over and covered my hand with his. "So, all I'm saying is, I get how annoying Hunter and all those guys can be sometimes."

Ah, *now* I understood. Murph was simply trying to make me feel better. I felt suddenly tipsy with a feeling I recognized as happiness. I looked down at his hand and grinned up at him again. What had I ever done in my life to deserve a guy like Murph? Whatever it was, I was grateful I'd done it.

I leaned over, closed my eyes, and kissed him. We wrapped our arms around each other and lay there, not speaking, not needing to speak, for a few moments.

Then Murph raised himself on an elbow, turned to me with a sly look, and said, "Okay. You want to hear something that'll really make you feel better? Something truly hilarious?"

I was intrigued. "Obviously, yes."

Murph laughed a little himself, unable to contain his own glee at what he was about to tell me.

"Okay. You know who Hunter's father-in-law *is*, right?"

"Vaguely."

"He's only the CFO of Great American Bank and Trust, that's all. Apparently Great American's got a huge new financing deal, and they're doing a little lawyer-shopping for it."

I frowned. "But we're already their lawyers."

He shook his head, grinning. "No. More precisely, *Marty Adler's* already their lawyer. Hunter's father-in-law is pushing for Hunter to be Great American's new relationship attorney with the firm. He wants Hunter to get origination credit for the new deal."

"But that's usually a relationship *partner*, not an associate."

"Right," said Murph. "That's exactly where Hunter's father-in-law is going with this, don't you see? He's hoping if he can toss this new business his way, then Hunter will finally make good on partnership, and his little princess will be set."

"That's crazy. Hunter can't handle a beauty pageant. He doesn't know any law! He spends half his time updating his Lawyers League softball brackets, and the other half brownnosing."

Murph nodded. "Exactly. I know it. You know it. Adler knows it. Hell, I bet even Hunter knows it. But apparently dear old dad-in-law doesn't know it. So he wants Parsons Valentine to come in for a brand-new beauty pageant, and guess what? *Hunter's* going to be running the show!" Murph hooted with undisguised glee. "This time, Adler can't help. Can you imagine *Hunter* trying to wow a bunch of senior executives, none of whom are any relation to his wife? It's going to be a complete clusterfuck!" He was really laughing now. If it were anyone but Murph, I would even have described it as a sort of demented giggle. I was kind of surprised that Murph was enjoying himself this much. I mean, Hunter *was* his friend, after all.

Still, I understood Murph's point. Putting Hunter Russell in charge of winning over the chief executives of Great American Bank and Trust was a doomed strategy. They would eat him alive. In spite of everything, I almost felt a little sorry for Hunter. He was being set up for a train wreck.

"So now, if Hunter loses this beauty pageant—and obviously he will—the firm loses Great American as a client altogether. No more Adler, or any other competent partner, for that matter. Apparently the new rules are, it's Hunter as the relationship partner or nobody."

"Wow," I said. "Adler's got to be beside himself."

"Well," said Murph, his eyes glittering, "I guess he should have thought of that when he hired Hunter in the first place. Now the chickens are finally coming home to roost."

THIRTEEN

❦

Cocktails began at six, the seated dinner at seven. The Diversity Dinner could not be happening at a less convenient time. Sun-Corp and Binney were supposed to sign in a few short days, and we were still far apart on a handful of issues. But Marty Adler had already impressed upon me that my attendance at tonight's event was *not* optional. Neither was the black-tie attire.

I had decided on one of my tried-and-true Corporate Function Cocktail Dresses—shimmery and black with spaghetti straps, so no one at the firm could accuse me of not looking festive, but with a demure matching wrap that also made it work appropriate. I closed the door to my office and changed in there, not wanting to run into anyone in the ladies' room down the hall. Harold Rubinstein had sent around an e-mail to the firm's delegation to tonight's event—Marty Adler, Tim Hollister, the other partners on the Diversity Committee, Dr. Rossi, and me—telling us all to meet at five forty-five at thirtieth-floor Reception.

At five forty exactly, I poked my head out my office door and looked around. Margo and the other secretaries in her cluster had already left for the night. The hall was quiet.

Even though it was not uncommon to see an attorney racing through the halls of the firm in a tuxedo, late to some client reception or a Bar Association awards dinner, I felt exposed and wary as I grabbed my beaded clutch purse and slipped into the hallway. I walked as quickly and quietly as possible, heading for the internal stairs instead of the elevators, which would be in heavy use at this time of the evening.

Rounding the corner by the men's room, I collided with Murph. "Hey, hey," he laughed, disentangling himself from me. He looked effortlessly adorable, as usual. He'd slightly loosened his tie around his collar, and his sleeves were rolled up, revealing his tanned, muscular forearms.

"Hey, stranger," I said in a low voice, not wanting anyone to overhear us.

Murph looked me up and down admiringly. "What's all this?" He grabbed my hand, put his other arm around my waist, and twirled me around in a sort of bastardized mambo. I spun down the hall with him a few tentative steps, laughing, but also keeping an eye out in case someone was coming.

When we stopped he let out a low whistle. "You clean up nice. Hot date? Should I be jealous?"

"Sadly, no. I've got that Diversity Dinner thing tonight, remember? I can't wait to get this over with."

"What Diversity Dinner?" he asked.

"You know," I said, "that networking thing at the Rainbow Room. Marty Adler practically put a gun to my head."

A funny look flickered across Murph's face. "No, I *don't* know, Yung. *What* networking thing at the Rainbow Room?"

"Oh, come on, Murph," I said, lightly hitting him on the arm. But I was starting to feel uneasy. "I know I mentioned this to you." Why was he making this into a thing?

Invitations had been mailed weeks earlier to the firm's clients, selected alumni, and political and academic luminaries from around the city and up and down the East Coast. Now I tried to recall the fancy corporate rhetoric that had been printed on them.

"The firm's calling it 'A Celebration of Diversity in the Profession: Breaking Barriers, Bridging Gaps,'" I said, trying to sound breezy. "This is how it'll go down. We all go have white wine and shrimp cocktail, the partners swagger around the Rainbow Room, shake some hands, slap some backs. They show off their fancy new hired-gun consultant, make a few speeches about 'leveraging diversity' and 'celebrating difference,' and ask why we can't all just be friends. Then everyone goes home with their corporate goodie bag and forgets about it for another year. You know the drill."

"Ohhh, I see. So this is all still a result of that whole 'Partner's Paradise' thing." Murph was no longer smiling. "We're *still* talking about that." He folded his arms tightly across his chest. "So, who all's going to be there tonight?" He was eyeing me closely.

Resentment rose in my throat. It wasn't like any of this was *my* idea. Yet I was feeling defensive, and there was no reason on earth why I should. Hate the game, not the players. I hadn't created this world; I was just trying to play by its rules.

"Well," I said, "I think it'll be Adler, Rubinstein, and Hollister from Corporate, maybe a couple of others, and Pam Karnow, Sid Cantrell, and I think Mitch Lawrence from Litigation, and from Tax—"

"Adler? Rubinstein? Cantrell? Pretty heavy hitters," Murph observed. He raised an eyebrow and cocked his head to one side. "Not a bad chance to get in some prime schmoozing time for yourself." His tone was sharp.

I jerked back as if he'd hit me. This was bullshit. Especially coming from Murph. Just how long had he been organizing his private little drinking outings with the senior partners?

"Well, Murph, you know what? I don't suppose it's any better schmoozing time than when you go out for beers with Marty Adler after every softball game. Or maybe it's more like when Jack Hanover invites you to the Century Club every year for the live satellite feed of the Amherst-Williams game, huh? Maybe it's more like that."

Murph stared at me.

"Yeah, I know about that," I snapped. "Anyway, I'm late. Gotta go." I pushed past him.

"Hey, whoa, whoa, whoa," he said, placing his hands on my bare shoulders where my evening wrap had slipped loose. His grip was surprisingly strong.

"Don't be pissed, Yung," he said, looking contrite, smiling at me, and I could see that the old Murph—my familiar kidding-around, paper-football, affectionate Murph—was back. "I didn't mean to make a big deal of this. I just wanted to know where you were off to, looking so gorgeous, that's all. I'm sorry. I really am. Most of us weren't invited to this thing, you know."

"Of course you weren't," I said, shrugging myself free. "That would spoil the whole illusion, wouldn't it. Now if you'll excuse me. I'm late." I slid past him and hurried down the hall. I shook my head, trying to rid myself of the encounter. How had everything gotten so complicated?

On the carpeted landing between the twenty-ninth and thirtieth floors, I stopped and forced a practiced smile back on my face before hurrying up to Reception.

Marty Adler, Harold Rubinstein, and I shared a town car to the Rainbow Room. There was room for one more lawyer, but he would have had to sit in front, with the driver. Tsk. The firm ordered five cars to shuttle fourteen people the seven blocks to Rockefeller Center.

Rubinstein told our driver to let us off on Fifth Avenue, and we walked briskly the rest of the way to the entrance of 30 Rock. As always, I had to take two or three strides for each one of Adler's and Rubinstein's, and I had to do it in three-and-a-half-inch heels while swerving in an awkward, drunken pattern to avoid the slots of the damn sidewalk grates, all the while keeping up a cheerful patter about which kindergartens had just accepted their grandchildren, and the Yankees' latest trade, and what the word was on that new oyster bar in Union Square, and—oh, yeah, how the SunCorp deal was going.

"I spoke to Ted Lassiter two days ago," Adler said, "and he tells me he's very impressed with your work, and the way you've kept this deal on track and on time. *Very* impressed," he repeated, beaming.

I darted a glance at Harold Rubinstein. He was beaming, too. "Keep up the great work, Ingrid," he said. "Don't think it's going unnoticed."

Eat your heart out, Murph.

We stopped in front of the Forty-ninth Street entrance. "After you." Adler waved me through the revolving doors, and we proceeded across the gleaming marble lobby. A line had already formed at the elevator bank. Distinguished-looking gray-haired men in tuxedos escorted well-preserved women in tasteful evening dresses, a few of them holding silver-and-blue invitations embossed with the firm's logo.

"Arthur! Glad you could make it," Adler said to a dashing man with graying temples and a pronounced chin. "Where's Elizabeth? Don't tell me she couldn't be here tonight."

The elevator doors opened, and Adler and the man he called Arthur entered the car. I followed along with the rest of the crowd, but Harold Rubinstein placed a hand on my elbow and gently steered me away to wait for the next elevator. When one opened, we wedged ourselves in.

The doors opened on sixty-five, and the crowd spilled out into the reception suite.

Harold Rubinstein hurried forward and tapped a debonair-looking older gentleman on the shoulder. "George. I thought that was you." He smiled and held out his hand for the older man to shake. "Harold Rubinstein. Rick Fallon introduced us?"

"Oh, of course," said George.

"It's funny, I was just thinking I should give Rick a call," Rubinstein said. "How're things over at Time Warner these days? Didn't I read last week about your plans to . . ."

The two of them went on ahead, and I breathed a sigh of relief. I hated the brownnosing aspect of these things.

Rubinstein seemed to have forgotten I was there, and that was just fine with me. Taking my time, making sure to widen the distance between myself and Rubinstein, I walked into the Rainbow and Stars room, where an elaborate cocktail and hors d'oeuvre reception had been set up. The firm's staff was seated at a long table, greeting guests, checking names off on a printout listing the important friends and clients of the firm. Because of our tuxedos and evening gowns, we had been spared the usual plastic name tags worn on cords around our necks. Tonight we were supposed to be glamorous grown-ups at a ball, here of our own accord, enjoying ourselves.

"Hi there," I said to Ann Trask, who was sitting at the end of the reception table.

"Hey, Ingrid." She motioned me over. "C'mere a second."

I edged closer to her. "What's up?"

She jerked her head down the long conference table toward an arrangement of glittery midnight blue gift bags imprinted with the firm name and logo, and stuffed with silvery tissue paper peeking out the tops. "Make sure you pick up a swag bag on the way out. This one's to die for."

"Let me guess," I said. "A Parsons Valentine fleece and a ceramic 'We Love Diversity!' mug?"

She laughed. "Try a pair of Knicks tickets, an Apple Store giftcard, a free week at Equinox, a massage at Bliss, and a Bobbi Brown lipstick."

"Wow. Nice work."

"Thanks."

I looked around at the quickly filling room. "Well, guess I better go mingle, huh?"

She shooed me away. "Go. Schmooze, schmooze. That's what you're here for."

A waiter stopped in front of me with a heavily loaded tray. "Hors d'oeuvre, miss?" He was already perspiring through his shirt, and the cocktail hour had just started. I felt bad for him.

"Thank you." I smiled. I selected a skewer of grilled zucchini and shrimp and accepted the cocktail napkin he offered me, then wandered off to the far side of the room to look out over midtown and Central Park. I wanted to put off meeting and greeting people as long as possible. If I could just waste enough time until the seated dinner, I was home free.

These networking cocktail hours were pure torture for two reasons: I was a young single woman, and I was short. It was miserable to attempt to sidle into a conversation already under way between some CEO thirty years my senior, his wife who was about my age, and some hungry midlevel asshole trying to chat up the CEO. Add to this the fact that, even in three-and-a-half-inch heels, I still stood at eye level with most of the men's armpits, so they all had to twist down awkwardly in order to hear what I had to say. Either they didn't bother or, when they did, it was to look down my dress or check my hand for a wedding ring.

It was a perpetual challenge for young, non-wedding-banded female professionals to telegraph our intentions at these networking cocktail receptions. I remembered a conference for M&A practitioners that I'd attended in Tampa, where I'd spent forty minutes in a stuffy hotel ball-room nursing a single lime seltzer and talking up the firm's white-collar defense practice to the general counsel of some securities brokerage. He'd been on his third gin and tonic, but he was asking all the right questions and hanging on my every word. I'd already begun to imagine the glorious coup it was going to be back at the office, when I told the partners about this new client I'd just reeled in. Everything had gone swimmingly until the end of our chat, when he'd slipped me a business card with his hotel room number scrawled on the back.

As I stood now at the window with my back to the cocktail reception, gazing down at the view—the little yellow cabs tiny as LEGOs, the web of treetops in Central Park—I heard a low male voice behind me. "Ingrid? Ingrid Yung?"

I sighed softly, just once, before spinning around, preparing to paste a fake smile onto my face and make stilted conversation with some half-remembered client. I almost laughed in relief when I recognized who it was.

"Marcus!" I said.

"Hey, how've you been?" Marcus Reese, a classmate from law school, leaned down toward me. I reached up toward him with my half-eaten shrimp on a stick and we embraced awkwardly, laughing.

"Good, good. So, what are you up to these days?" I asked. "You went to White and Case, right?"

"Yeah, but I quit the law firm thing two years ago. I'm in-house at MTV now," he said.

"Oh yeah? That must be pretty exciting."

He smiled ruefully. "It's not any better or worse than a firm, just different. Politics as usual. *You* know what I mean," he said.

I nodded.

Popular and funny, Marcus Reese had been something of a star in our Columbia Law School class. He'd played football at Michigan before deciding on law school, then became notes editor of the *Law Review* and served as president of the African American Law Student Association for two years. Universally liked and affable as he was, a perfect diplomat with a winning smile and ready laugh, Marcus was another Minority Darling—a favorite of the law school administration. He was thoroughly and utterly *presentable*. Marcus Reese and I had this much in common.

I had always discerned a certain humbleness about Marcus Reese. Despite his popularity, he wasn't a showboating asshole. Many of our classmates from law school would have printed out flyers announcing their in-house counsel job at MTV. Often, when I bumped into law school classmates on the street or subway, they fell over themselves gushing about how fabulously everything was going for them, how wonderful their lives had been since our graduation. They'd go on for so long it was like they were trying to convince themselves, rather than trying to impress me. So I appreciated Marcus's honesty about "politics as usual." It was refreshing.

"Anyway, what about you? You're doing well at Parsons, I take it," he said, nodding toward the huge flat-screen monitor set up along one wall that read PARSONS VALENTINE & HUNT LLP WELCOMES YOU. "I mean, I'm sure they didn't invite *every* associate at the firm to come carry the flag here tonight, huh?"

I fixed him with a sober, penetrating gaze. "Oh, yes. Didn't you hear? They've determined that I possess the keenest legal mind of our generation, Marcus. That's the only reason I was asked to come out tonight and represent."

At this we both burst out laughing. Marcus gestured at his tuxedo. "Look, I'm just glad our CEO didn't make me put on a dashiki."

Right then we heard three cloying notes. "Attention, ladies and gentlemen," an announcer said, between chimes. "If you would please start making your way to your tables, the dinner program is about to begin. Thank you."

I watched as, slowly, about half of the crowd drifted into the ballroom while the other half chased down final hors d'oeuvres, lingered over half-finished conversations, and got in line at the open bars for last cocktails before dinner.

"Well," said Marcus, as he set his empty champagne flute down on a passing service tray, "I better go find the Viacom table. Great seeing you again, Ingrid. You got a business card on you?"

"Don't we get disbarred for coming to one of these things without them?" I unsnapped my evening clutch and handed him a card. I kept a stash in each of my handbags.

Marcus glanced at it. "Great. Hey, I'll e-mail or call you at the office sometime, we'll set up a lunch?"

"Definitely."

I gave Marcus a final wave before he disappeared into the crowd. As I watched his handsome figure retreating, I wondered exactly when Marcus Reese and I had turned into people who no longer simply met for lunch. Instead, we met for *a* lunch.

In this city, especially in my line of work, the casual business lunch invitation was issued so often, to so many people, and rarely did any of these proposed lunches actually take place. I knew with as much certainty as I knew my own name that Marcus would not be calling my office to schedule a lunch anytime soon. Not because we didn't genuinely like each other, and not because he hadn't truly meant the invitation. He simply wouldn't have the time, and neither would I.

Sighing, I moved away from the window and followed the crowd into the main ballroom. *Here we go,* I thought, looking around. I checked my watch once again. Where the hell was Tyler?

I paused at the threshold of the ballroom.

The Rainbow Room always took my breath away. New Yorkers were supposed to have perfected the art of looking perpetually unimpressed by places and things, but here, people's carefully disguised awe did not fool me. I noticed more than a few surreptitious glances at the exquisite candles and stunning floral centerpieces, the elaborate china and crystal settings, the spectacular glass chandelier lowered from the ceiling, and of course that billion-dollar view.

The round dining tables were set up on what was usually the sunken dance floor in the center of the room. A podium and a long VIP table had been set up on a raised dais in the front, underneath an enormous screen that, for now, displayed a simple blue background with the firm name and logo projected onto it.

Numbered black and white placards, printed with the names of corporate clients and friends of the firm, had been placed at the center of every table. *Citigroup. MetLife. Time Warner. American Express. General Electric. JPMorgan Chase. Google.* And so on. I was very aware of Marcus Reese standing across the ballroom with a bunch of older white men, laughing and talking loudly and finally pulling their chairs out from around the Viacom table. Marcus stood a head taller than most of his colleagues. *Well,* that *had to help,* I thought, with unmitigated envy.

Parsons Valentine had designated a separate table on the floor for those of us attending from the firm. But Marty Adler and Harold Rubinstein, as partners on the Diversity Committee and co-chairs of the planning committee for this event, were to be seated in special places of honor at the long table at the head of the room. Again, fine with me.

I finally located the firm's table, in a clearly visible and yet modestly off-center spot three rows in from the front. I was the first to arrive. I sat down, then immediately wished I hadn't; most people were still standing and chatting. Well, it was too late for me to get up now and stand—that would look foolish and indecisive, to anyone who might have been watching. No, better to remain seated. I whipped out my BlackBerry and pretended to be engrossed in important e-mail correspondence.

When I had taken as much time as a reasonable person could reasonably take reading through her messages, still no one had shown up at my table. I looked down and peered at the elegant appetizer plate already arranged in front of me—some sort of round, delicate, quichelike thing. I pretended to examine the ivory menu card propped artfully beside my plate.

Parsons Valentine & Hunt LLP
proudly presents

∾

"A Celebration of Diversity in the Profession:
Breaking Barriers, Bridging Gaps"

The Rainbow Room

Red & Yellow Tomato and Goat Cheese Tart
Drizzled with Parmesan Vinaigrette

Atlantic Salmon Stuffed with Spinach, White Beans, and Pinenuts
Roasted Fingerling Potatoes

Dark Chocolate Truffle Cake

∾

Well, the *meal* was certainly diverse. I glanced again at my watch, and looked again around the Rainbow Room. Still no Tyler, I observed, annoyed. And I continued to bristle over the fact that Murph begrudged me *this*—this dubious *honor* of being paraded around as the Diversity Poster Girl.

"Hey, Ingrid," said a voice, finally. I looked up. Tim Hollister was pulling out the chair next to mine. I was relieved to no longer be sitting alone. I was more than relieved to be sitting next to Tim.

"So how's our secret weapon on the softball team?"

I laughed. "Doing just fine, Tim. Thanks."

"Everything's still going well with SunCorp, I hear."

"So far, so good," I confirmed.

"I'm happy to hear it." He smiled at me. And I decided that intelligent women would not have to debate the matter, after all. Tim Hollister was handsome.

"Good evening, everyone," said another warm, familiar voice from behind us. Tim and I turned to see Dr. Rossi. He looked different tonight, handsome in his well-cut suit and freshly trimmed beard.

Dr. Rossi shook hands with Tim. Then he turned to me, nodded, and actually gave me a quick wink. It caught me by surprise. It was such an oddly intimate, oddly conspiratorial gesture that I was taken aback. *Let's not get carried away,* I thought. *I said I'd help, and I have. But let's not pretend for a moment that any of this is* my *show. I'll be thrilled when tonight is over with.*

"Plenty of seats," Tim said. "Join us."

Dr. Rossi shook his head. "Thanks, but Marty and Harold have asked that I join them up there." He tilted his head toward a long VIP table on a raised platform at the head of the room. I was relieved.

"Okay, then," I said brightly. "See you later."

"See you. Enjoy the evening," Dr. Rossi said, then turned and made his way over to the raised platform.

Adler and Harold Rubinstein were taking their seats on the stage. I saw Adler shuffle through a small sheaf of notes, adjust his bow tie, check his watch. Then he looked off to the side of the stage and nodded toward someone in the wings.

A frosted-blond woman, wearing a fastidious black dinner suit and bright red lipstick, picked up a microphone and tapped on it twice, producing a loud squawk of feedback. "Good evening, everyone." Her voice bounced above the noisy din of the crowd. "If I could invite all of you to kindly find your seats as quickly as possible, we'd like to get the evening's festivities under way."

There arose in the ballroom a convivial last wave of chatter and air-kisses, invitations to lunch and cocktails, a flurry of business cards changing hands, the clink of highball glasses being set down or sent away, and chairs being pulled out from tables, as this carefully handpicked assembly of the luminaries of New York—politicians and professors, prosecutors and judges, CEOs, CFOs, COOs—took their assigned places and then looked casually around for their first pours of wine.

I placed my tiny evening bag onto the seat next to me, saving it for Tyler, when he ever bothered to show up.

Two others puffed up to our table and sat down on either side of Tim Hollister. Pamela Karnow and Sid Cantrell. I hadn't seen Pam Karnow since the outing, and I'd never spoken to Sid Cantrell before. Sid was a powerful Litigation partner, a brilliant closer at trial, an infamous workaholic and screamer. He'd once created a small stir by making some poor associate spend a late night of billable time writing a memorandum comparing the relative merits and flaws of the eight pizza delivery joints near the office, complete with footnotes. The infamous "Pizza Memo" had, predictably, been forwarded to associates, partners, and paralegals at every major law firm in the country.

Pamela Karnow looked over at me and smiled. "Hi there. Ingrid, right? We met at the summer outing." As she shook my hand I felt a swell of pride. It was definitely a booster shot to my ego that Pam Karnow knew who I was. The firm was so big that most partners never bothered learning the names of the associates outside their own departments. No point. Most of us were gone by our third year.

Oh yes, there was definitely scuttlebutt about me, that was for sure. I smiled and took another sip of water.

Sid Cantrell leaned over and shook my hand, too. "Good to meet you. Mildred, is it?"

"Ingrid," I corrected.

Here was the thing about ego—easy come, easy go.

"And you practice in our . . . ah . . . Intellectual Property group?"

"Actually, no. I'm in M&A," I said. *Ellen Chu Sanderson had been the one in IP,* I wanted to tell him.

"Ah," said Sid Cantrell. "Very good. And you're"—he waved a hand at me questioningly—"what? A third-year? Fourth-year?"

This time my voice came out louder than I'd expected. "This is my eighth year with the firm, actually."

He nodded, not the least bit embarrassed by his mistake.

A tuxedoed waiter approached our table with an open bottle of Cabernet Sauvignon, a crisp white napkin collared around its neck, and deftly filled all of our red wine goblets.

After another authoritative screech from the microphone, we all directed our attention to the stage. Adler was at the podium, his hand on the mike.

I angled my chair to get a better view of the podium and accidentally bumped into the empty chair next to me. My evening bag slid onto the floor—beaded satin will do that—and as I leaned over to pick it up, someone tapped me gently on the shoulder.

"Is this seat taken, dear?" Jack Hanover asked in a stage whisper, pointing to the chair I'd been saving for Tyler.

"Uh, no," I blurted. "It's not taken." I had to swallow the word "sir."

I wondered if Jack Hanover even remembered me from that evening in his office, if he ever could have imagined how much humiliation and grief that single brief encounter had caused me, how much it had cost.

"Thank you, dear," he said, and sank into his chair just as Adler began to speak.

"Good evening, ladies and gentlemen," Adler boomed. The lingering din died down, and all eyes focused toward the front of the room. At the same time, almost imperceptibly, by slow, expert degrees, the ambient lighting in the room dimmed, and Marty Adler was bathed in a subtle spotlight up at the podium. It gave him an old and wizened look, and I thought again of the Wizard of Oz—this time, of the man behind the curtain.

"On behalf of everyone at Parsons Valentine and Hunt, I'd like to welcome you all to what promises to be a wonderful evening," Adler said proudly. He gazed out at the assembled crowd, beaming a confident smile, and I marveled at how he managed to look both arrogant and kind at once.

"We are very honored tonight to have all of you with us for our inaugural Diversity Dinner," Adler continued, "which we hope will become an annual tradition. I want you all to know that my colleagues on the firm's Diversity and Inclusion Committee and I thought long and hard about what to title tonight's event." Here he furrowed his brow and scrunched up his mouth a bit, as if to dramatize for us just how long and hard they had had to think about it. "Finally, we decided it was most appropriate to call it 'A Celebration of Diversity in the Profession.'" He paused to let this sink in.

I scanned the room. It was a pretty white crowd for a celebration of diversity.

"Now, some of you may ask, why call it a *celebration*? Don't we still have a long way to go to achieve true equality in the workplace? Isn't there much more hard work that lies ahead?"

Across the table, Pam Karnow tilted her head at a thoughtful angle, as if considering answers to Adler's rhetorical questions. Sid Cantrell was shredding a cocktail napkin into a thousand tiny pieces. Jack Hanover had crossed his arms lightly across his chest. His eyes were closed.

"The answer to each of these important questions is a resounding *yes*," Adler informed us. "However"—he slapped his palm onto the podium for emphasis—"we at Parsons Valentine feel strongly that it's important to celebrate all the gains we have made thus far, and all of the legal and cultural barriers that have already been broken, in *this*, our shared struggle toward achieving professional equality for *all* men and women, regardless of race, color, or sexual orientation."

The crowd burst into applause. I even heard a couple of catcalls and whistles thrown into the mix. For this crowd, on this night, Marty Adler was a rock star.

I fought the urge to laugh. Wasn't Adler being just a *wee* bit heavy-handed and self-congratulatory? I mean, we weren't exactly marching on Washington or refusing to give up our bus seats here. We were at the freaking Rainbow Room, eating tomato and goat cheese tarts drizzled with Parmesan vinaigrette, for God's sake. We were, quite literally, sitting on top of the world.

I glanced at my BlackBerry and noticed a new message in my inbox from "Reese, Marcus A." I looked over my shoulder and across the room at the Viacom table. Marcus was smirking at me. I looked back down and read his message:

I have a dream!!!!

I laughed out loud—softly, and just once, but out loud. Sid Cantrell shot me a fast disapproving glance.

I extinguished my smile and slid my BlackBerry into my lap.

Are we free at last? I wrote back.

Across the room, I saw Marcus laugh. Then, just as quickly, I watched him delete my message, put away his BlackBerry, and stare back up at the podium, calm and straightfaced. Oh, Marcus was good. He was very good.

Following Marcus's example, I turned primly back toward the stage, pasting a contemplative look onto my face.

There was nothing like one of these lavish corporate-style celebrations of ourselves to make me feel like I was just sitting on my hands, marking time. A willing pawn. Tyler had been smart not to come. I knew that now.

"So tonight," Adler boomed, "we pay tribute to those leading the charge. This evening, we are *thrilled* to have with us our keynote speaker, Professor Charlton James Randall from the Harvard Law School, who will be introduced by Dr. Marilyn DuBois, of the NAACP Legal Defense and Educational Fund. I look forward to hearing from them both later this evening. And now, please, eat, drink, and enjoy."

As if on cue, a squadron of waiters appeared from nowhere bearing salmon filet and wine.

The conversation at our table was restrained by the presence of Jack Hanover. That much was clear. Whole minutes would slink by with only the sounds of forks and knives scraping delicately against our plates, our water glasses clinking against our wine goblets as we raised them gently to our lips. Tim Hollister and Pam Karnow, both young, recent partners, seemed especially anxious not to say anything wrong in front of Hanover. So the politics of sucking up didn't end with partnership. Both Tim and Pam called him Jack but seemed to swallow the syllable a bit, as if still unsure of their right to use it.

Jack Hanover, for his part, seemed perfectly comfortable chewing in silence, with just his salmon for company. The only time he initiated any conversation was when he waved his empty wineglass, looked around for our waiter, and murmured, "Now where's one of those little guys when you want him?"

At the front of the ballroom, Professor Randall stood and made his way to the podium. I'd never seen the revered Charlton James Randall in person before, but I knew who he was, of course. We all did. In law school, I'd been assigned his Constitutional Law casebook and had done a preemption check on an article of his published in the *Columbia Law Review*. A tall, bespectacled, African American man in his sixties, with a very dignified mien, he withdrew a folded sheet of paper from his breast pocket and smoothed it out in front of him.

"Thank you, Marty, for inviting me to speak tonight at this wonderful gathering. First off, I must commend Parsons Valentine and Hunt for taking such a strong leadership role in the cause of diversity and inclusion in the corporate workplace. Let's have a round of applause for our gracious hosts."

The crowd complied with cheers and applause. Professor Randall took a sip of water and began.

"On an occasion such as this, and in such esteemed company, it may be hard to believe that it was only fifty-odd years ago that Chief Justice Earl Warren handed down the famous unanimous decision proclaiming that separate is *inherently* unequal, and that it was only some forty years ago that Thurgood Marshall became the first African American justice to serve on the United States Supreme Court . . ."

Jack Hanover was shoveling chocolate truffle cake into his mouth. Surely a black-and-white cookie would have been more appropriate, I thought, and smiled at my own joke. Twenty minutes later, Professor Randall wrapped up his keynote address to thunderous applause. My hands hurt from clapping. My face ached from holding a fake smile. I stifled a yawn and glanced at my BlackBerry. It was past ten. The waiters had cut off the wine supply ages ago. Now they'd stopped making rounds with the coffee and tea.

Adler, beaming and still applauding, walked to the podium, heartily clapping Professor Randall on the back. "Thank you so much for those inspiring words. And now, ladies and gentlemen, I'd like to say a few things in closing."

You could hear a collective sigh go up from the audience as people shifted impatiently in their seats, poised to flee, evening bags clutched in laps, programs dog-eared and discarded onto dessert plates. The attention span for celebrating diversity was apparently three hours, tops.

Adler cleared his throat. "On behalf of all my partners at Parsons Valentine and Hunt, let me just say how pleased we are that you have all joined us for tonight's celebration. By choosing to be here this evening, we are sending a message—loud and clear—that we cannot . . .

indeed, we *will not* tolerate exclusion of any kind in the courtrooms, the chambers, the legal boardrooms, and the hallowed halls of corporate America. Tonight we recognize this truth: that *all* of our institutions are only *enriched* by the inclusion of women and people of color. Racial and gender diversity is not just a trend, is not an albatross *thrust* upon us by political correctness. No, diversity is not merely an aspirational goal. It is one of our *strongest assets.* And I'll let you in on a little secret: It is the *only* way any of us can hope to stay competitive in the dynamic, global marketplace of the twenty-first century."

My mouth was dry, and my head was positively pounding. I noticed a single glittery black bead coming loose from my clutch purse and pulled at it.

"We at Parsons Valentine and Hunt have recognized this truth for years, and it is borne out in everything we do—from reaching out to deserving communities in need through our pro bono practice to our efforts in recruiting and hiring, and then developing, promoting, and mentoring our nontraditional attorneys at every single stage of their careers."

I picked absently at the loose bead. I glanced at my BlackBerry and scrolled through three new messages.

Adler continued, "And I am extremely proud that we have with us tonight one of the best examples of these efforts—truly a successful product of all of our recruiting, mentoring, and retention programs— Ingrid Yung, one of our most promising young attorneys in the Mergers and Acquisitions group. Ingrid, would you please stand?"

I snapped my head toward the stage. My BlackBerry banged onto the floor. *He did* not *just say that. Did he?*

"It's all right, Ingrid—don't be shy!" boomed Adler into the mike.

Everyone was staring at me. Marty Adler led the crowd in applause and smiled beatifically in my direction. Sid Cantrell and Jack Hanover were looking at me expectantly, clapping.

Pam Karnow and Tim Hollister looked on, appalled.

"That's you, kid. Stand *up*," Jack Hanover directed in a stage whisper.

I saw Tim's pleading look, shaking his head slightly, willing me not to. He opened his mouth and formed the word *No*.

The crazy thing about it was, I did it. I couldn't believe I was doing it, but on shaky legs I stood and smiled weakly at the crowd. I think, in my daze, I actually even gave a sheepish little wave. It couldn't have been more than a couple of seconds that I stood there in the spotlight, held up for the crowd's appraisal, but it felt like an eternity. It was the longest moment of my life, either before or since. *What the hell was wrong with me?* I was incapable of saying no to people. I was busy pleasing everyone else but myself.

When I finally sat back down, I felt faint. I could barely see.

My face was aflame. I felt a deep and burning shame, and regret. Regret that I'd been so, so stupid. That I'd been played, but even worse, that I had let it happen. I had seen it coming and just stood back and invited them in. They were only doing what came naturally—it was my job alone to protect myself and watch my own back. But I had failed spectacularly. I'd been a fool.

I looked back up at the stage and spotted Adler. I felt a profound and concentrated rage, a hatred so strong it scared me.

Adler grinned at the crowd. "Together, we can make a difference and level this playing field. Together, we truly *can* overcome!"

There was applause as Adler finished. As I looked out over the sea of tables, about half the audience was clapping and cheering enthusiastically. I glanced across the room at Marcus Reese, still sitting there with his Viacom colleagues. Marcus wasn't applauding. He looked grim. Sad. He felt sorry for me.

I was humiliated.

I remained at the table for a minute or two, more or less in shock. People at the other tables had fled almost as soon as Adler had finished his speech. Tim Hollister remained sitting. He looked concerned. He raised his eyebrows at me. *You okay?* I just shook my head. I couldn't speak to anyone right now.

Next to me, even Jack Hanover had turned a little in his seat and was also, finally, staring intently at me. He looked at me as though he were actually seeing me for the very first time. He probably was.

As the crowd filed out, and the din in the room slowly quieted down, I remained sitting at the table, still dizzy with shame and rage. I could barely see. I wanted to dig a little hole underneath the table and crawl into it. I looked up at the stage, and Marty Adler actually caught my eye and gave me a smile and a nod and a little thumbs-up sign.

That did it.

I stood up abruptly, picked up my purse, and stormed toward the illuminated red EXIT sign. As I threaded through the crowd, a number of distinguished elderly guests spotted me and nodded in recognition, smiling paternally. *Why, it's that Little Minority Lawyer they talked about tonight,* their smiles said. *Isn't she cute?*

I didn't smile back. I couldn't. Clutching my purse, I made my way toward the crowded elevator lobby. As I stood there, waiting, I could actually feel the embarrassment draining from me, and the fury— pure, unadulterated fury—forming in its place. It had started as a hard little knot somewhere in my stomach and was now welling up and spilling over.

Just as the crowd surged forward and I was about to fold myself into a waiting elevator, I felt a hand on my elbow. I looked up. Adler had me by the arm. He was beaming. "So what'd you think? Terrific turnout, huh?"

What did I think? My God, was he really that clueless? I jerked my arm away.

Adler looked puzzled. "Something the matter?"

"Everything's fine. But I really have to go. *Now.*"

"No, no, stick around, there are some people I want to introduce you to—"

"I don't think so, Marty," I snapped. "I think I've performed enough for one evening."

There was a moment of surprised silence, as my words seeped into the space between us, and then Marty Adler narrowed his eyes. "Excuse me?"

"I have to go. Now," I said. "And I mean, right this second."

Adler lowered his voice. "Ingrid, just what are we talking about here? Is there something that I need to be aware of?"

In other circumstances, his utter cluelessness would have been fucking hilarious. But not now, not this night.

My hands were shaking. I was dimly aware of a flashbulb going off as the official event photographer snapped a picture of Adler and me.

Adler placed his hand on my elbow again, as if to steady me, but when he spoke quietly into my ear, his tone was not entirely kind. "Look, Ingrid. I'm not sure exactly what this little outburst is all about, but I sincerely hope you'll be feeling more like your old self by Thursday's meeting with SunCorp. This is a very big deal for us, and I cannot—let me rephrase—I *will not* have my star player dealing with any sort of emotional craziness. So whatever it is you're dealing with on a personal level—and there's obviously *something*—deal with it. But I expect you to be back and in fine form by Thursday. I will need you to be one hundred and ten percent at this meeting. Am I making myself clear?"

"Oh, you've made yourself perfectly clear." I turned to go, then swiveled back around. "And Marty, when have I ever given anything *but* one hundred and ten percent?"

He looked at me angrily, then opened his mouth to say something.

Without waiting to hear it, I turned around and allowed myself to be swallowed up by the well-heeled, elegant wave of people already sweeping into the elevator, carrying me away.

∽

As I turned the key in my lock and slipped inside, the first thing I saw was the blinking light on my hall table. My mom. I knew it would be her.

"Ingrid-ah." Her familiar voice flooded into my dark and empty apartment, and my eyes filled with tears.

"It's after ten thirty." She sighed a soft, small sigh. "You're still at the office. But Daddy and I want to know if you're coming to Jenny Chang's wedding. Auntie Chang really needs to know. She says the country club is counting our heads! So call and let us know. Bye-bye. Love, Mom."

For some reason, my mom always signed off her phone messages like you would a letter. "Love, Mom," she said, to punctuate the end of her calls.

I wanted desperately to hear her voice. I wanted her to reassure me everything would be okay. That it would all be worth it. I looked at the clock. It was already past eleven. Far too late.

Nobody bosses my Ingrid around, my mother had once said to me.

Oh, but they do, Mom, I wanted to tell her. But couldn't.

They do.

FOURTEEN

❧

I didn't sleep at all after the Rainbow Room debacle. My eyes were puffy and bloodshot. My head felt too heavy to lift. Yet for the first time in a long time, I felt absolutely, resolutely calm.

I was calm because I'd spent all night figuring out exactly what I was going to do after tomorrow's big meeting with SunCorp.

I was going to walk into Adler's office and do what I should have done in the first place: I would inform him that I was off the Diversity Initiative, effective immediately. I would tell him that closing the Sun-Corp deal on time required all of my energy and that I intended to execute it as my number one priority. I would remind him that it was why I was at the firm in the first place, not to pose for pictures and be their trained seal. Tyler Robinson had been right. I never should have gotten mixed up with any of it to begin with. I was sick and tired of being the good little associate, doing everything—*everything!*—the firm ever asked and then getting punished for it. Well, no more.

Murph had been trying to text me all morning.

Sorry, his first message said.

I was an idiot, read his second.

Well, there's one thing we can agree on, I texted back.

Murph's reply came immediately.

Glad to hear it. Jury Box at 1?

Meet you there.

I wasn't mad at Murph. Not really. He had just been trying to find out what he was being left out of, that was all. I, of all people, should be able to relate to that.

One o'clock was prime attorney lunch time, and the Jury Box was crowded. I spotted Murph right away, chatting with Gavin Dunlop. They were in line at the hot entrée station. *Today's Specials: Miso black cod, wasabi shrimp dumplings, crispy kale.* I was in no mood to make small talk with Gavin Dunlop. Especially not when things were so weird with Murph. He and I needed a chance to feel things out, to see where we were with each other—without Gavin Dunlop or anyone else hanging around. I ducked behind a gaggle of summer associates waiting for their made-to-order brick oven pizzas.

"God, I'm so sick of the lunch options here," said one. "We should've gone out."

"Yeah, the Jury Box food sucks," said another.

"I don't think the food's that bad. Seriously, what sucks is that only attorneys are allowed to eat in here," said a third. I looked up. It was Cameron Alexander. Her statement seemed to shut up her companions, who meekly collected their pizzas and headed toward the cashiers. I smiled in spite of myself.

"Hey, Ingrid, there you are," I heard Murph call out.

Busted.

"Hey." I pasted what I hoped was a normal expression onto my face.

Murph waved me over to where he and Gavin were standing. I shook my head and gestured toward the salad bar. "I'll meet you at a table."

I took my sweet time assembling a salad and getting a Diet Coke, hoping that by the time I paid and made my way over to join Murph, Gavin would have made himself scarce. No such luck. When I rounded the corner into the dining room, Gavin and Murph were sitting together at a table over by the windows. They spotted me and beckoned.

I sighed, made my way over, and sat down.

"Hi, Ingrid," said Gavin.

"Hey, Gavin."

"So how was the thing at the Rainbow Room last night?" he asked. "At the partners' meeting this morning, people were saying it went off pretty well."

I hesitated, studying Gavin's face. I wondered if this was secret code of some sort, whether Gavin had already heard all about last night, and was being disingenuous. Then I decided that Marty Adler would not have deemed my behavior worthy of mention at the partners' meeting.

"It did," I said brightly, hearing the strain in my own voice. "I thought it did go well."

"Good, good," said Gavin. "And I hear you've been doing an amazing job with SunCorp, by the way. Bet you'll be glad when that deal's finally announced next week."

I shrugged. "It's been great experience. SunCorp's obviously a terrific client to work with."

Murph sat silently, looking from one to the other of us. He cleared his throat. "BOR-ing. Let's not talk shop. Hey, Gavin, you coming out to the last softball game tonight?"

"Can't. Too much work."

"What? It's the All-Stars game!"

Gavin shook his head. "I really can't. But hey, when you see Hunter, tell him congrats for me, will you?"

Murph laughed. "For what? Being such a brilliant coach?"

"Nah. I'm not talking about softball, for fuck's sake. You didn't hear the news?"

"What news?" Murph said.

"Hunter got the Great American Trust business. He actually *won* the damn beauty pageant. Beat out five other firms."

Murph hesitated before letting out a snort. "You're shitting me."

Gavin shook his head. "Nope. Listen, no one was more surprised or happy than Marty Adler. We all thought Hunter was going to fuck this up for sure. But he's smarter than he lets on." He winked at me, letting me know he wouldn't normally talk about other associates behind their backs, but this was Hunter, after all. Gavin looked at his BlackBerry. "Gotta run." He left his tray with his half-eaten lunch on the table.

Murph caught me staring at him and grinned. "That's pretty fucking unbelievable, isn't it? Who knew?"

I laughed. "What, you mean about Hunter? Not *that* surprising. Maybe Hunter's not as dumb as he looks. He did, after all, marry well."

"Heh. That's true."

"Anyway, at least we were able to hold on to the client. I'm sure that's got to be a relief. Even to Adler. Maybe especially to Adler."

"Yeah," said Murph.

I made sure no one was looking over at us. I lowered my voice and looked hard at Murph, forcing him to make eye contact with me. "So listen," I said. "I'm not mad about last night, you know. I was just irritated because——"

"Last night?" Murph asked. "Oh, yeah, right. Look, I'm sorry. I know I was being kind of a jerk."

I had to smile. "Forget it," I said, and meant it. Then I added, "Just be glad you never have to deal with any of this diversity stuff. I mean, the whole thing . . . it's just such a charade."

Murph smiled absently. "A charade. Right."

"Seriously. Take last night. So the evening starts with Adler making this big speech about how this firm embraces diversity, blah blah, and then he starts introducing all these big-deal speakers, right? Like Charlton James Randall, to give you an idea."

"Who's Charlton James Randall?"

I laughed and playfully nudged his arm. "Right. Who's Charlton James Randall. You're kidding, right?"

He frowned. "No, not kidding. Who is he?"

"Only one of the best constitutional scholars of our time. And if you ever read any critical race theory, his work's everywhere."

"Must be my public school education showing," Murph snapped. "Sorry."

"Whoa." It was as if he'd stung me. "Um, hello? Where did *that* come from?"

"Just forget it."

Murph was being very confusing.

"And by the way, *what* public school education?" I said. "Last time I checked, Williams College cost about fifty grand a year."

"Not when you're on financial aid, it doesn't," he muttered. "Anyway, I was talking about high school."

"I went to a public high school, too," I said, not really sure why I felt compelled to tell him this, why I was so defensive all of a sudden. How did I get into this pissing contest? Were we going to argue next about who walked farther to school? Uphill in the snow?

"Look, just forget I brought it up."

We were quiet for a moment, and then Murph said, "I'm sorry. I don't know what I'm blabbering about. I'm just really tired. I'm operating on, like, three hours of sleep. The partnership vote is coming up. It's a lot at once." He reached for my knee beneath the table and gave it a squeeze. "Sorry, okay?"

I brushed his hand away, looking around over my shoulder again. "Okay, okay." This felt like we were on a chaperoned junior high school trip, this furtive, sneaking-around-at-work thing.

We regarded each other silently. In that moment, I managed to convince myself that everything was normal between us. Murph was just in a mood. What we needed was to be able to really talk and be alone together again.

"Listen, Murph," I said gently. "We should make some plans away from the office. Just the two of us. What are you doing tomorrow night? Adler and I have the big pre-close meeting with SunCorp tomorrow, but after that, I'm going to be in the mood for some celebrating." I looked at him hopefully.

He seemed to be focusing somewhere else. "What? Oh. Tomorrow night. Sure. Okay."

I told myself we would straighten things out once we were in more intimate surroundings than the Jury Box. Murph and I were so good together—or *could* be—but we were best when we were one-on-one, away from the bullshit and corporate politics of the office. As soon as this SunCorp deal was over, as soon as I got off the Diversity Initiative, as soon as Murph and I were both officially invited into the partnership, we would simply take it from there. Everything would be just fine.

FIFTEEN

❧

J ustin yawned. "I think that's everything."

    We were sitting together at the long mahogany table in Conference Room 3201-A amid a sea of red, yellow, green, and blue tabbed folders. We'd just set them up into shiny metal accordion files and painstakingly arranged them two inches apart down the length of the conference table. Everything looked perfect. We were ready.

    As usual, I'd stayed late the night before, proofreading every pre-closing document to make sure it was flawless. To my surprise, Justin had stayed late with me. He didn't leave. He didn't even complain about not leaving. Even Justin had his moments.

    Justin and I had come in early this morning, printed off fresh sets of all the documents for review by the clients, and brought them up here to the conference room. Ted Lassiter and Mark Traynor would be here at eleven, and I would walk them through the closing agenda.

    As usual, Adler hadn't prepared anything himself. He seemed perfectly content to sit back and have me take the lead.

    Stratton and Thornwell had sent back their comments on our redline a day earlier. Basically, their response was no to everything. They were still asking for a reduction in the termination fee, and they were still asking for a number of inexplicable exclusions from our MAC clause. We were at a standstill. This was what Marty Adler wanted me to explain to Lassiter.

Lassiter, as always, greeted me like I was an old army buddy. "How're we doing, Slugger?" he asked, as he clapped me on the shoulder.

"Just fine, Ted. Good to see you."

Adler looked on, beaming like a proud father.

We all took our places around the conference table, Justin sitting in an outer chair to my right.

Adler began. "Okay, now Ingrid will take us through the term sheet page by page, Ted. She's pointed out some curious positions Binney's trying to take, and I want you to hear directly from the expert what we think the potential risks are here."

The expert was me. I felt my cheeks flush with pleasure.

"Thanks, Marty," I said. "Ted, Mark, if you'll turn to page eight of the draft term sheet, I can take you through the first of the exclusions that Binney—"

"Before we do that, Ingrid, what does it say here on the *first* page?" Ted Lassiter was peering closely at the document in front of him.

Marty Adler leaned forward quickly, scrambling to put on his reading glasses. "Where are you looking, Ted?"

"Right here, where it says 'Purchase Price.' There's a typo. It says '$990.5 *billion*.' That should say '*million*.'" He looked at Mark Traynor, who was looking puzzled, and kind of laughed. But you could tell he was taken aback. "That's a pretty damn big typo there."

"Heh. Yes, I'm sorry about that, Ted." Adler looked sharply at me. "Ingrid? Can you please make sure to fix that immediately?"

My mouth hung open, and I quickly closed it. There was *no way* this had been in the draft that Justin and I reviewed, together, last night. No way. I had meticulously proofed each line. I glanced over at Justin. He looked as dumbstruck as I did.

But it was a basic rule never to argue or make excuses in front of a client.

"Apologies, Ted, Mark. I honestly don't know how that got in there. But we'll correct that right away," I said.

"Yes, we'll make absolutely sure that gets fixed," Lassiter said, flipping the pages. "Now then, Ingrid, where'd you want us to look?"

"Ah, if you could please turn to . . ." I fumbled through the document, looking for the section I'd had my thumb on before. The mishap had thrown me. My game was all off.

"Page eight," Justin stage-whispered to my right.

"Right. Thanks. Page eight. Seller's reps."

There was the sound of pages rustling as we turned to that section.

"Ah, yes," I said. "Here we are. Now, you'll see that in the MAC clause, we'd wanted to say that—"

Mark Traynor cleared his throat. He looked at me almost apologetically. "I hate to interrupt, but I think I see another typo here at the top of the section."

Adler shot me a look. A very dark look.

"Oh, is there?" I chirped. My response to disaster like this was to be preternaturally cheerful. "Where?"

"Right here, under the breakup fee."

"Oh, we'll get to that. That was one of their asks. They want to increase it to five percent," I said.

"Five percent would be fine. But this says *fifty* percent," Traynor continued. "A breakup fee of *fifty percent* of the purchase price, Ingrid?"

Lassiter looked at me. "Ingrid, is this some sort of joke? What the hell's going on here?"

I felt like I was in a dream, standing apart from myself. I wanted to run, but my legs wouldn't work. I tried to take a deep, calming breath. *This is not happening.*

I looked at the page. Mark Traynor was right. Where it was supposed to say 5 percent—and where it *had* said 5 percent just last evening when I'd double-checked it—well, it now read 50 percent. Clear as day.

"Gentlemen, I'm very sorry. There's got to be something odd going on with our document retrieval system." Adler was pacifying them, but staring me down. "We'll get to the bottom of it right after the meeting. Again, I apologize."

Ted Lassiter was stony-faced. "Ingrid, this isn't the kind of work I've come to expect of you."

"I know it isn't, Ted. And I'm not quite sure what to tell you. I looked at these documents myself, proofed each page last night, and I can assure you, these numbers reflected the deal correctly."

"Let's not waste time pointing fingers," Traynor said. "Let's just make sure these all get corrected before the next round goes to Binney."

The rest of the meeting proceeded without incident, but I was stammering and flustered the whole time. Even Justin gave me a *holy shit, she's totally losing it* look before slinking around the corner and disappearing into his office.

As soon as we walked the clients to the elevators and saw them out, Adler turned to me and barked, "My office. Now."

I followed him down the corridor, my hands curled into sweaty little fists.

"What the hell was that?" he said, as soon as he'd closed the door.

"Marty, I don't know. All I can tell you is that I was here til midnight, and I proofread each and every line of that term sheet. Those mistakes weren't in the last version I saved."

"Are you sure you actually saved the last version?" he snapped.

"I back up my documents every thirty seconds."

He harrumphed.

"And besides, you know me." I struggled to keep my voice at a normal octave. "You know the quality of my work, Marty."

He glared at me. "I *thought* I did."

It was the worst thing he could have said to me. I felt just like a teenager, bringing home an F or a wrecked car, getting the *I'm terribly disappointed in you* speech from a revered parent. But Adler was not a revered parent. His love was conditional.

"You know I'd never let a mistake like that slip by me."

"Well, it would appear you just did, Ingrid."

I thought for a moment. "What if someone else accessed the document and was screwing around with it?" I said slowly. "That's possible, isn't it?"

Adler took off his glasses and pointed them at me. "What in the world are you talking about? Who could you mean?"

"I—I'm not sure. I mean, I just don't know how else this—"

Adler shook his head and walked around behind his desk. "There's no need to go making accusations, Ingrid. It's very simple. I never want to hear about this kind of error happening again."

"It won't. I'm sorry, Marty," I said, already forgetting that I had promised myself I would stop apologizing for things that weren't my fault.

I walked zombielike back to my office, my head buzzing. My chest felt tight, like it was going to burst. Margo was just putting on her coat. "Oh, there you are," she said. "Did you need anything else from me tonight?"

"No, nothing, thanks. Have a good night, Margo," I said, deflated.

She paused, her coat half on, elbows raised. "Are you okay?"

"I'm fine."

"Are you sure? You're white as a ghost."

"I'm fine, really. I'll see you tomorrow morning, Margo."

She turned around to stare at me as I disappeared inside my office and closed the door. I sat down, hard, at my desk. After a moment— after I heard Margo's footsteps going toward the elevator—I picked up the phone and dialed Justin's extension. No answer. Of course not! What a surprise. At the beep, I said, "Justin, Ingrid. Can you come to my office as soon as you get this? It's five forty. Thanks."

I sat there and stared blankly out the window.

I did not make these kinds of mistakes.

I'm not saying I wasn't capable of making mistakes—of course I was, I was only human. What I mean is that I physically did not allow myself the room to make mistakes of this sort. Not when I had come so far and worked so hard. Not when I was finally this close.

I reviewed the events of last evening. This just wasn't possible. It wasn't technically possible. Justin Keating and I had stayed til midnight working in my office. Together, we had personally proofread each and every line of those goddamn documents before leaving for the night. I had turned off my computer and locked my office door behind me. I had double- and *triple*-checked them to make absolutely sure. In my eight, almost nine years as a lawyer, I had never—never, not once—allowed a document to go out the door with a glaring error like that staring me in the face.

It's not that I thought I was perfect. It would simply never occur to me to allow myself the luxury of failing. When other people failed, they failed alone. When I failed, I let down everyone I had ever carried on my back. I failed all of them.

And I was sick with the burden. I was collapsing under its weight.

I was sick and tired of saying yes to everyone but me.

ENOUGH.

I swiveled back around to my desk. I clicked on the icon for the firm's internal document management database. Entering my username and password, I searched for "Project Solaris Draft Term Sheet." Project Solaris was the firm's internal code name for the SunCorp deal. This was Corporate Department protocol for every major transaction, for purposes of confidentiality.

The file appeared on my screen, and I clicked on "Document History." I looked up the last users' names, expectant, holding my breath. As if—what? What was I looking for? I didn't know, exactly. I was suddenly Nancy Drew and John Grisham rolled into one, waiting for an *aha!* moment—the breakthrough clue. The music would swell, the mystery would unravel. Once again, I would be the hero of my own tale. I was used to this. It was the starring role that had found me.

When you stuck around at a dysfunctional, gossipy workplace like Parsons Valentine for as long as I had, and when you stood to gain as much as I did, there were plenty of people who might hold a grudge. Maybe Justin really resented me for having bossed him around all summer. Maybe Hunter hated that I was on the Diversity Initiative and drawing attention to his crazy racist skit. I didn't know. But I wasn't really one for conspiracy theories.

I checked the electronic document history and found—with equal parts relief and dismay—that, sure enough, the document had last been opened by user *isyung* yesterday evening at 11:44 P.M.

No one had been screwing with the file. No one was out to get me. I had no one to blame but myself.

What I now had was cause to doubt myself . . . and whether I really wanted to be here, doing this.

I closed my eyes and leaned my head all the way back against the top of my swivel chair. A very unpleasant, very unnerving thought had begun to develop in my mind, like a Polaroid, and I had been trying to force it out, to keep the image from coming into focus. There it was, though, lumpy and misshapen, but still coming into view. Had I somehow done this to *myself*?

I was not going to allow my subconscious to sabotage myself, it was that plain and simple. It was of absolute importance—it was crucial—that nothing more go wrong on my watch between now and the announcement of partnership decisions next week. I was so, so close. And I did not have the luxury of giving up.

My phone rang. I glanced at the caller ID screen and saw that it was Murph.

I grabbed up the receiver before the first ring finished. "Hey."

"Hey. So. You celebrating yet? How about a drink? I can be ready to leave in five minutes."

Something about the juxtaposition of the SunCorp meeting disaster with Murph's breezy tone broke my heart a little.

"Not celebrating yet," I said quietly. I heard my own voice catch at the end. "Actually, things didn't go so well today."

"What do you mean? Are you okay?" Murph sounded concerned.

"I'm fine," I said, definitely not sounding fine.

"I'll be right there," he said.

A few moments later, Murph slipped inside my door and closed it behind him. "Hey. What's up? You sounded kind of—weird on the phone."

I was standing against the window, leaning my full body against it, pressing my forehead and fingertips to the cool surface of the glass.

Murph nudged my arm. "Don't do it," he whispered. "You've got so much to live for."

I pretended to smile, but this didn't make me feel better. For a few moments, Murph and I just stood there silently, looking down at the endless stream of yellow taxis moving up and down Madison Avenue. It seemed to me that a long time passed.

Gently, he touched my shoulder. "So what happened? Only if you want to talk about it, that is. We don't have to."

I sighed softly. "It was a complete fucking disaster, is what happened."

"Come on. I'm sure it wasn't as bad as you think."

"It was bad, Murph."

"I'm sure you're the only one who noticed anything was wrong."

I looked at him. "The purchase price was off by three zeroes."

"Holy shit," he said.

"Uh, yeah."

Murph let out a low whistle. "What the hell *happened*? You think it was that Keating kid? You always told me he was kind of useless, but I wouldn't have thought he could fuck up *that* badly."

I shrugged. "I don't know. I don't think so. Anyway, ultimately, it's my fault. The buck stops with the lawyer, not the paralegal."

Murph was shaking his head. "But that doesn't sound right. It's not like you."

"I don't want to talk about it anymore," I said. "It's done." I pressed my forehead against the window again and closed my eyes. When Murph moved next to me, I stood up on tiptoe and kissed him. Not a sweet *thank you for comforting me in my time of distress* kiss, but a real one, deep and unchaste and on the mouth. He seemed surprised at first, but then obligingly followed my lead, leaning into me, turning me around to face him, pressing my back up against the window. I just wanted Murph and me to go away somewhere, someplace far away from here, far, far away from Marty Adler and Jack Hanover and Justin Keating and Hunter Russell and Gavin Dunlop and partnership votes and firm outings and rap song parodies and softball quotas and diversity consultants and Corporate Department meetings and all the rest of it. All I wanted— all any of us here wanted—was to be able to work hard and succeed on my own terms. Was that so much to ask?

Murph pinned me against the window in my darkened office, kissing me. I guided one of his hands around my waist, and then farther down. I shivered. "Let's go somewhere," I whispered. "The R&R suite! You think anyone's up there?"

He didn't answer, pulling my wispy silk top loose from the waist of my skirt. Through the thin fabric of my blouse, I felt the cool, smooth hardness of the window glass pressed against the length of my back, and the warmth from Murph's body pressed against my front. It was thrilling. This was definitely the most fun I had ever had at the office. Why hadn't we ever done this before? I actually thought this, and then laughed. I was really laughing. This made Murph laugh, too, a little, before gently pressing me flat against the glass again and leaning down to kiss the hollow of my throat. I closed my eyes. We were making enough noise that neither of us heard the door open.

Murph tore away suddenly, slamming his leg hard against my desk.

Justin was staring at us with his mouth open. His body was frozen in midstep, one foot in front of the other. Justin looked stunned. If not for my own predicament, I knew I would have enjoyed the fact that I'd actually managed to shock him. For once, the smug know-it-all smirk had been knocked clean off his face.

Justin took a few awkward stumbles backward and banged into the door, hard. "Sorry, I—I just—I'll come back later," he mumbled.

And then he was gone.

SIXTEEN

❧

"I ngrid. Seriously. Just let it go."

"I can't. How long do you think he was standing there? What, exactly, do you think he *saw*?"

It was Sunday night, and I was sitting with my legs tucked up beneath me on the couch in Murph's living room. Steve Buscemi was curled up in my lap, asleep and purring. Murph was on the other end of his couch, head tilted back, eyes closed, listening to me. Takeout containers were strewn across Murph's coffee table, along with two glasses and a nearly empty bottle of Jameson's that Murph had basically killed by himself. It was one thirty in the morning, and I was anxious.

"Come on, Yung. It's late. Let's just go to bed. Tomorrow could be the big day. Don't you want to look all bright and shiny?"

The buzz around the office was that the firm might be announcing the new partners tomorrow. No one knew for sure, because Parsons Valentine never disclosed exactly when the Partnership Committee met to make its decisions. Unlike most other big firms in the city, Parsons Valentine held their vote in the summer, with membership becoming effective in the fall. This peculiar tradition was an idiosyncrasy that Parsons Valentine prided itself on—they liked to keep people guessing.

I shook my head. "Don't you get it? That's exactly why I need to know what Justin saw. Do you think he would tell Marty Adler or the other partners about us?"

Murph sighed wearily, his eyes still closed. "So Justin Keating saw us together. So what? Why would he care? Justin's not some gossipy little girl. We're not in high school anymore, Yung."

We might as well be. But I didn't say this to Murph.

"That's easy for you to say. We know *you're* in for sure" was what I murmured under my breath, more to myself than to him.

Murph opened his eyes and slowly turned his head toward me. "What did you just say?"

"Never mind."

"No. What did you say?" He pushed himself forward from his reclining position. He sounded wide-awake now. "I really want to know. 'Cause it sure sounded like you said, *that's easy for me to say.*"

I raised my eyebrows. "Calm down," I said. "I just—"

"Well, I've gotta tell you, it's *not* easy for me to say. Not easy at all. I have no fucking clue what's going to happen tomorrow. You know what? As long as I've known you, Yung, you've always seemed to carry around this idea that I don't have to work as hard as you do, that somehow I've got some sort of inside track. Well, here's a news flash for you. I don't."

His little speech floored me. I had no idea where this was coming from.

"Murph, I didn't—"

"Didn't what?" He leaned forward suddenly, and the remote control clattered off his lap onto the floor. "Huh? Didn't *what?*"

"I didn't mean anything by it. I'm not sure why you're getting all pissed off."

He laughed unpleasantly. "Oh, well, allow me to break it down for you, then. In case you hadn't noticed, I'm sort of the odd man out lately."

"What are you talking about?"

I was baffled.

The idea of Jeffrey Devon Murphy—he of the dazzling smile and amazing bachelor pad and endless one-liners and winning home runs and Cape Cod summers and model girlfriends and trail of broken hearts he'd left all over Manhattan . . . Mr. Fucking April himself, camping it up in his beefcake photo, the only guy I knew who managed to be *both* heartthrob and class wit at the same time and somehow made it all click, somehow just made the smart-jock charm and easy affability seem effortless—the very idea that this guy could be the *odd man out* of anything was, frankly, ridiculous.

"Everybody says you're a shoo-in, Murph," I told him.

"Oh, really, is that what they say? And just what the fuck do you think they say about *you,* Ingrid, huh?"

I was stunned. I had no idea what I'd done to provoke this, but I knew I didn't need this drama. "I don't know, Murph. And you know what? I really don't care. You've had way too much to drink. I should go."

"Wait," he said, reaching out and placing his hand on my arm.

I hesitated.

"You really don't have a clue what I'm talking about, do you?"

I knew what I should have done. I should have gently shaken off his hand, told him good night, and hopped in a cab home. Instead I said, "Enlighten me."

"Think about it. They only make two new Corporate partners every year. That was just fine for us, til Hunter's father-in-law came along and handed him Great American Trust on a platter. That pretty much seals the deal for him."

"Okay, fine. So Hunter's a special case. Maybe they make all three of us partners this year."

Murph laughed. "God, you're naive. Haven't you been paying attention? Business is down, Yung. M&A isn't moving. *Bankruptcy* is. This isn't the year to dole out *three* new slices of the pie."

"Even if that's true, they've always thought Hunter was a joke, and they've always loved you."

He snorted. "Love ain't the same thing as being the relationship attorney for Great American Trust, honey."

I had never heard him talk this way before. I had never imagined Murph could be so ugly.

"Well," I said, "what makes you so sure this screws *you* over, instead of me? If they're still only making two partners, they could just as easily take *my* spot and give it to Hunter."

He laughed again. "Jesus Christ. You're kidding me, right?"

Something in his tone, and the way he looked at me, made me brace myself.

"Do *you* see the firm hiring any expensive consultants to figure out how to make more white male partners, Yung? 'Cause I sure as hell don't."

"Careful," I said quietly.

He ignored me. "They've been dying to announce a female partner in Corporate for years! Problem was, all the women kept leaving. Then along comes Little Miss Goody-Goody here—the *impeccable* Ingrid Yung—and you came and you *stayed*. Hallelujah! Give her another gold star, folks! A woman *and* a minority! Are you fucking kidding me? Hell, you're a law firm recruiter's wet dream!"

I leapt off the couch. Steve Buscemi woke with a startled mew and bounded across the room.

"It's all right, cat. She was just leaving."

I stayed rooted to the spot. Murph and I stared at each other angrily.

219

He threw his head back and laughed. "You're really something, Yung, you know that? Really, really something." He shook his head, grinning, as if I had just played a very good joke on him. "Man, you've got everyone totally fooled, don't you. You've got us all just eating out of the palm of your little hand."

My face felt hot. "I don't know what the hell you're talking about."

"That night at the firm outing. In the clubhouse. All that stuff you told me about not knowing how to play the game. *Oh, but it all comes so easily to you, Murph.*" He made his voice high and affected in imitation of me.

I willed my arms and legs to move, but they would not.

"Well, I gotta tell you, Yung. Seems to me you know *exactly* how to play this game. Seems to me you're a fucking Jedi Master at it."

"Murph, I——"

"Please. All that *oh please feel so sorry for me* crap. You're so full of shit. You really have all the partners going, though. You should win a fucking Academy Award."

"Fuck you."

Trembling, I went down the hall to Murph's bedroom, snatched up my handbag, and slipped on my shoes. I looked wildly around the room, my eyes blurring with tears, and spotted a tank top and cardigan I'd left there a few nights ago. I stuffed them savagely into my bag, along with my toothbrush and hair dryer from the bathroom.

When I returned to the living room, Murph was blocking the front door with his body. I tensed up. This was no good. I wondered exactly how ugly Jeff Murphy could get. This seemed a very dumb way to find out.

"What are you doing?"

Murph folded his arms across his chest. "We're not finished with our conversation yet."

"Oh, yes we are." I made a reckless lunge for the door and—to my surprise—Murph made no move to stop me. I crashed my right shoulder hard against the metal door frame.

"Ow!" I winced, rubbing my shoulder.

He took a step toward me. "Here, let me see. Are you hurt?" he said, placing a hand gently on my injured arm.

"Get away from me, Murph!" I hissed. "Never touch me again."

His face darkened. "Oh, so now you're breaking up with me, is that it?"

"*Breaking up with you?*" I looked at him in disbelief. "Are you serious? I can't believe I never saw through you before! Now I know why none of the girls you date ever last very long. It's because they're onto you. You're a real asshole."

He looked at me and laughed.

"No, really, I get it now," I said. "The reason you've never dated any smart, successful women before is that you can't handle it. You can't stand the idea that a woman might be better at this than you."

Murph clutched his chest. "Oh, now that stings."

I had my bag slung over my shoulder. My shoes were on. My hand was on the doorknob. But something kept me from walking out of his apartment. It seemed like there was still something else in the air, something more that one of us wanted to say.

"I thought you said you were leaving," he said.

"I am."

He sauntered back over to his couch and lowered himself into it. Now that there were a few yards of distance between us again, I knew I should get the hell out of there, get home to the safety of my own apartment, and try to forget this had ever happened. But I couldn't.

Murph reclined on the couch and clasped his hands leisurely behind his head, flashing me a condescending smirk. "So, what are you waiting for?"

I knew I shouldn't do it. I really did, even in that moment. Yet I just couldn't help myself. I guess I just really wanted to know. I *did* care what people said and thought about me. Of course I did. I cared too much.

"So just tell me, then, Murph. What *do* they say about me behind my back?"

Murph grinned. "That you're a shoo-in for partner."

This was not what I had expected.

Then he continued.

"That you've got a nice rack. Smallish, 34B—some of the guys had a bet going, so I checked your lingerie drawer last time I was at your place—but really nicely formed. Really decent legs, too. Particularly in those pencil skirts you're always wearing around the office. Gavin Dunlop likes when you wear those, especially."

I stood frozen at the door, horrified.

"And let's see, what else." Murph cocked his head and looked thoughtfully at the ceiling. "That they're all glad they waited til they could find a *hot* minority chick to tap for partnership. If you've gotta have one around, might as well throw in some eye candy, right? Oh, and just so you know, I wouldn't worry about whether little Justin Keating blabbed about walking in on us. Because the whole firm's known about it for weeks. I told Hunter the very first day after I got into your pants."

"Fuck you, Murph," I whispered.

He clucked his tongue. "Is that any way to talk to a future law partner of yours? Can't we all just get along? If not, our weekly partnership meetings are going to be *really* uncomfortable for everyone. You and I are going to have to learn to play nicely together in the sandbox."

"I don't believe a word you're saying," I lied.

"Believe what you want." He shrugged. "I was there. You weren't."

"You're a pathetic excuse for a human being. I feel sorry for you."

"Oh-ho-*ho*. Don't shoot the messenger, Yung. Remember, you *asked*. Never ask a question if you're not prepared to hear the answer."

If there had been something large and heavy within reach I would have hurled it directly at his head. Instead, I drew up my shoulders, took two deep breaths, and said as calmly as I could manage, "Actually, Murph, in case you hadn't heard, I'm going to be bringing in the Sun-Corp acquisition for an on-time announcement. I've negotiated a pretty damn good deal in five weeks flat. The CEO loves me. And aside from a random computer glitch, Marty Adler seems pretty damn pleased with the way I run a deal. I think *that's* why I'm going to make partner, Murph. Not any of this disgusting bullshit you're spewing."

He narrowed his eyes at me.

"And by the way," I continued, "unlike you and Hunter, I didn't have to beg or schmooze or play softball with Marty Adler to get staffed on SunCorp. As you recall, he didn't pick either of you. Adler handpicked *me* to lead the biggest deal in the office."

Murph let out a big mean bark of a laugh. "Why don't you ask Adler sometime why that was, huh?"

I shook my head and turned around to go.

"Yeah, as a matter of fact, that I'd like to see. Why don't you just ask Adler sometime about SunCorp's vendor requirements, huh, Yung?"

I whirled around. "What are you talking about?"

Murph laughed. "Minority vendor requirements, Yung. Look it up. Turns out, a lot of Fortune 500 companies these days can't hire outside counsel unless they can bring at least one minority or woman lawyer to the beauty contest."

"And what the hell is that supposed to mean?"

"I'm just saying, if you think Marty Adler handpicked you to run the biggest deal in the office based on merit, keep kidding yourself.

SunCorp's board passed a rule that they can't hire a law firm unless it can staff the deal with a team that looks like a Benetton ad. And guess what, Yung? You're just what the client ordered."

"Good-bye, Murph." I walked out of his apartment, slamming the door behind me.

SEVENTEEN

I sat there in the calm morning stillness of my office, arms folded neatly on my desk. I felt so tired. So very tired, and incredibly sad. Directly across from me, as if accusing me of something, was the wall of polished cherry bookcases that housed all of the deal books and closing sets for every transaction I had ever worked on during my career here at Parsons Valentine. There was my prized collection of deal toys—a glittering menagerie of polished silver and glass figurines and trophies and cubes and globes. There was the tiny bronze soccer ball from the acquisition of a large sporting goods retailer, the first deal I'd ever closed at the firm. It was nestled next to a gleaming model jet plane—a souvenir of the merger of two commercial airlines I'd successfully handled the year before.

On the shelf below that stood a small framed snapshot of me and Rachel at the housewarming party we'd thrown in our first New York apartment, and another photograph of me with my parents the day I'd been sworn in to the New York Bar, almost nine years ago. My mother, father, and I were standing on the sidewalk outside the First Appellate Department building, down by Madison Square Park. I remembered that day as one of the happiest of my life. "We're so proud of you," my parents had kept saying, snapping photo after photo. "Attorney-at-law!" "Our daughter, Esquire!"

Alone that night, after I'd dropped my parents off at their hotel, I'd tried the words out in my mouth. *Ingrid S. Yung, Esquire.* I remember savoring it on my tongue. The corporate world—and the world in general—had seemed wide open to me then, full of hope and possibility. *You bright young women can accomplish anything you set out to accomplish!* Rachel and I had both been told this all our lives.

And we had believed it.

We had fallen for it completely.

I heard a light knock, and Margo poked her head in my office. She looked happy. "Mr. Adler's secretary just called. He wants to see you in his office. He said it's very important."

She leaned in my doorway, beaming. The reason Margo was beaming was that she had done the math and knew the news would be good. Early that morning, she had run into Hunter's secretary in the pantry. That was how we had learned that Hunter Russell had officially been voted into the partnership.

And Murph had not.

According to Hunter's secretary, after being called into Marty Adler's office at nine fifteen that morning, Murph had gone home sick for the rest of the day.

I would have thought I would be happier to hear this news. Avenged, or validated, or something. Murph had gotten exactly what he deserved. They'd taken Hunter over him. And Hunter would, of course, be infinitely easier for me to deal with at our future partnership meetings.

I knew I should have been jubilant on this morning, of all mornings. I should have been dancing a jig on my office floor, but I only felt tired and numb.

After all that Murph and I had gone through and all of the cruel and hurtful things he had spat at me last night, unbelievably, I still felt sorry for him. Regardless of how things had ended up between us, it was hard to forget that for eight long years he had been one of my only buddies at the firm. Ironically, it had been Murph who had often made me feel most included, like I belonged. Now, not only had I lost a boyfriend, I had lost a friend, too. Or at least the pretense of one.

Murph had worked hard. He was a smart lawyer, too. We'd both assumed for many years that Murph had it in the bag. I knew exactly how disappointed he must feel.

I wasn't happy that Murph was miserable. The truth was, I was sad that his theory had been right. I knew he had a point. And this bothered me. It did. Because I'd rather make it on my own merit. If it had been any other year except this one, the year they had all the Diversity Initiative efforts, there would have been no question. But now, since all this was happening when it was happening, I felt that my much-celebrated partnership announcement would be forever sullied. People would always wonder. *Well, hadn't that Jeff Murphy kind of had a point? Wasn't Ingrid lucky that the firm was paying attention to diversity when it did?*

"Shall I tell Mr. Adler you'll be right up?" Margo hinted.

I nodded. "Sure. Moment of truth, right?" I gave her a small smile.

"I'll tell him." She went back to her desk, closing the door to give me a little privacy.

I stood up, walked over to my wardrobe, and checked myself in the mirror. From looking at me, you wouldn't know that I was a woman who'd just broken up with her boyfriend, stumbled home to her apartment in the wee hours of the morning, and was operating on three hours of sleep. My makeup was tasteful and perfect. Every hair was in place. I looked, well, fucking *impeccable*.

I slipped off the right sleeve of my ivory silk crepe jacket and peered at my arm. A purple and yellow octopus-shaped bruise was spreading across my shoulder where I'd smashed it against Murph's front door.

How did things ever get so fucked up, I wondered.

I appraised the rest of my outfit—a slim black tank and ivory silk crepe trousers. I'd taken special care to avoid wearing a pencil skirt today. In fact, I wanted to throw out every single one I owned.

After tucking my hair behind my ears and taking one final look in the mirror, I walked past Margo—who flashed me a thumbs-up sign—and out into the hall. I reached the marble elevator bank and waited. When the doors in front of me opened, I entered the dark, gleaming, tomblike car—terrible if you were at all claustrophobic— pressed the button for the thirty-seventh floor, and leaned back against the wall. The car made its smooth, swift ascent, and I stepped out.

I clicked across the marble tile floor, slid my keycard into the security pad, opened the glass doors, and began the long walk down the carpeted interior corridor to Marty Adler's office. I felt absolutely calm, almost queenly. I could sense every secretary and paralegal I passed eyeing me closely as I glided serenely by. News—especially partnership news—spread like wildfire around this building. They all knew exactly whose office I was headed to. I consciously made myself hold my head a little higher and tried smiling a little. I should try to *look* happy today, after all.

It felt like a long walk.

When I finally got to Adler's corner office, Sharon smiled at me and said cheerfully, "Mr. Adler is expecting you. Go on in." She gestured at his closed door.

This was a good sign. Wasn't it? Secretaries knew everything around here. Sharon wouldn't look so friendly and cheerful if she knew the news was bad; that would just be cruel. Right?

Okay, get a grip, I told myself. *You are way overthinking this.*

I thought about the fortune-cookie fortune that had come with my Chinese takeout order one recent late night at the firm. *Confidence will lead you on.* If there was one thing I knew, after all this time at Parsons Valentine, it was how to fake that.

I approached Adler's closed door and knocked once, loudly.

"Come in," he boomed.

I tilted my chin up, took a deep breath, fixed a neutral smile on my face, and entered Adler's shadowy office. He hadn't switched on the overhead lights. I closed the door behind me with a quiet *click.*

Marty Adler was sitting four or five yards away from me, in his familiar massive green leather chair. "Good morning, Ingrid," he said. His tone gave nothing away—he sounded neither regretful nor jubilant. "Please. Have a seat." He gestured to one of the two wing chairs in front of his desk, instead of to the sitting area over by his teak conference table. This struck me as a bit odd. I'd always thought the other chairs in his office were much more comfortable.

And then I saw that Adler was looking somberly down at his hands.

"Ingrid," he began, "this is one of the hardest conversations I've ever had to have."

I blinked stupidly at Adler. Had I misheard? This was not the right way for him to preface this conversation, was it?

"I do wish I had better news for you."

Oh my God, I thought. *No, no, no no no.* Something had gone insanely, sinisterly, incredibly wrong. This was *me* they were talking to. Ingrid Yung. Who had done everything they had ever asked of me, and more, much more, than they had any right to expect.

I opened my mouth but no sound came out.

He sighed. "I do want you to know that the partners thought long

---

and hard about your candidacy, and that this was *not* a unanimous decision. You had—that is to say, you *continue* to have—a lot of support among the partners, a lot of strong enthusiasm for your candidacy, and we do think you are an extremely talented and hardworking lawyer . . ."

"But?" I said stupidly.

"But. We have decided not to invite you into the partnership. At least not this year, Ingrid. I'm sorry."

For one insane, blissful second, I actually expected him to burst out with *Just kidding! Of course you made partner! Welcome!*

Because the truth was, I was shocked. I could not have been more shocked if Marty Adler had opened his mouth and blown a big pink bubble, or stripped down to his boxers, black socks, and wingtips, climbed up onto his big antique desk, and danced the polka. Because *this* was unbelievable. This simply couldn't be happening. I wanted to pinch myself awake.

"Marty, I—"

"Please understand. We do hope to consider your candidacy again next year."

"But I—I'm sure I *don't* understand. All along, for all these years, I've been told that I was firmly on the partner track. That I was certain to be voted in this year. That as long as I kept on doing all my work exactly the way I was doing it, it was *a sure thing*."

Adler cleared his throat. "I understand your disappointment, Ingrid. Believe me, we did not come to this decision lightly. As I said, we will reconsider you for partnership next year. In fact, we strongly encourage you to continue your fine efforts, as we're very hopeful that next year, we might have better news for you."

I sat back in my chair, stunned. We regarded each other for several long moments.

Quietly I asked, "But what's happened between my last performance review and now, Marty? What's changed?"

Adler looked uncomfortable. "I don't like having to say this, but primarily, I was concerned that the level of attention to detail in your work may not be of partnership caliber."

I sucked in my breath, staring in disbelief at Marty Adler. I made no effort to hide my shock or anger. Adler glanced down at the floor. He looked somber, almost sad.

"Marty," I said, struggling not to scream. "I would like to know *what,* exactly, you feel about my work is not—as you say—partnership caliber. Because, as you know, I have been told, consistently, over and over, by every partner I've ever worked with at this firm, at every single performance review I've been given for the last four years running, that I have been leading and executing all of my deals at *partnership caliber.*"

Adler nodded. "I understand how frustrating this must be for you." He steepled his hands beneath his chin and sighed. "But, Ingrid, you must agree that the incident during our meeting with Ted Lassiter last week was quite embarrassing. That is not the kind of error we can simply overlook. As you know, Parsons Valentine and Hunt is one of the preeminent global law firms. Our M&A partners are highly sought after, and highly valued, and as a result we cannot afford to take any risks to our reputation."

"As I told you, I'd double-checked and triple-checked those documents the night before the meeting, and those errors weren't there when I last saved them. I can swear to that."

"I'm sorry, Ingrid."

"So that's it?" I could hear my voice getting higher and higher and made an effort to keep it low. "Because of a single *word-processing* foul-up, I'm going to be deferred another year?"

"Well," Adler said, and then he hesitated. And I could tell that that had not been the real reason, that there was something else.

"Well, what?"

He sighed again. "There was one other serious concern that was voiced by several of the other senior partners. Not by me, you understand, but several of the others."

"Which was?"

He seemed to be struggling for the right words. Finally he said, "Well, Ingrid, they questioned your ability to dedicate yourself to your legal work, because it has lately appeared that you have been heavily involved with other . . . *extracurricular* objectives."

My stomach twisted. *They knew!* About me and Murph! Of course they did. Oh, I was going to *kill* Murph. And that little brat Justin Keating. Absolutely kill them. Both of them.

I managed to say, "Just what *extracurricular objectives* are they referring to?"

Adler wouldn't meet my eyes. "Your work on the Diversity Initiative."

"My work on the *Diversity Initiative*?" I had never been punched out before, but I imagined that it felt much like this. The breath was quite literally knocked out of me.

Adler shifted in his chair, still looking anywhere but at me. "Yes." He cleared his throat. "It was commented upon that you've been devoting quite a lot of time and energy to our diversity and inclusion efforts, and a few of the partners questioned whether you would consistently be able to put the *legal* work of the firm first, ahead of your other, nonbillable priorities."

"But that wasn't *my* priority, Marty, it was yours! *You* forced me to carry that flag!" I said in a headlong rush. "I wanted nothing to do with your Diversity Initiative, but you practically made it a condition of partnership for me, Marty. I hope you told them that!"

"Whoa, whoa." Adler held up his palms, looking decidedly less apologetic now. "Careful. I think we should be extremely clear about what we're saying to each other. I never placed any conditions upon your partnership, Ingrid. Not a single one. Whatever you did or did not do was totally up to you. Let's be very clear."

"Actually, Marty, you made it *crystal* clear exactly what your expectations were of me, what the rules were, and now I'm getting punished for playing by those rules. For doing exactly what you said!"

He shook his head. "Ingrid, I'm very sorry you feel that way, and I'm even sorrier if you misunderstood."

We regarded each other. I cast about wildly to recall our exact conversation in the elevator bank—it seemed like so many years ago. What precisely had he said? Could Adler be right? Could I have completely misread what he was telling me to do? I replayed his words in my head. *I don't have to tell you how much we value an associate's nonlegal contributions to the firm when we're making our partnership decisions.* No. There had been no misunderstanding. My only mistake had been to trust him.

"I know exactly how you must feel," Adler said.

I looked at him, incredulous. "No. Please don't say that. You really don't."

He nodded. "I do. And I'm so sorry if you misunderstood."

That was it. What else could happen to me now?

"Go fuck yourself, Marty."

"Excuse me?" He blinked.

I took a deep breath. "Fuck. You."

"Ingrid, calm down." Adler glanced discreetly at his phone.

"I'm perfectly calm." I shook my head. "Eight years. Eight goddamn years. You say jump, I'd say, 'How high?' Take on SunCorp? Done. Close it in five weeks' time? No problem. Be your little trained seal at the Diversity Dinner? Of course! 'Take a bow, Ingrid. Ladies and gentlemen, for your entertainment, it's the Little Minority Who Could!'"

"Ingrid, I'm very sorry. But this conversation is over. I had no idea that you would react in this way. I must say, it's very unbecoming."

He picked up the phone and, keeping his eyes trained on me, spoke to Security. "Yes, this is Marty Adler. I'm going to need some assistance here escorting a young woman out of the building. Yes, right now. Thank you."

I was very surprised and a little bit pleased to see that I had finally managed to shock Marty Adler.

"Ingrid," he said, "I think you and I both understand that this is completely unacceptable behavior."

"Actually," I said, "I'm just following the best advice you ever gave me."

Adler lifted his eyebrows.

"You told me not to take it all so fucking seriously, remember?"

He hesitated for a moment, and I could tell he was actually trying to remember whether he had ever given me this piece of advice or not. But it didn't really matter.

"Ingrid, you're not giving me any choice. We're done here. I'm letting you go."

"Let me save you the trouble, Marty. I quit."

We stared at each other across the expanse of his desk. Finally Adler shook his head and said sadly, "You have no idea how sorry I am that this is how you are ending your relationship with the firm."

"And you have no idea how sorry I am that I wasted so much time."

I stood up and walked out.

Sharon and three other secretaries scattered back to their desks.

They all looked on as a uniformed security guard—a hefty, bald man I'd never seen before, and thankfully not Ricardo or one of the other guys I was friends with—fell in step next to me, without a word, and grimly followed me down the internal staircase to my floor. I held my head up, stared straight ahead, and took some small comfort in the fact that since it was before ten, not everyone was in their offices yet to see me go by.

When we got to my office, Margo stood from her desk and looked from me to the security guard in open surprise. "Ingrid, what—"

"It's okay, Margo," I croaked out, and the security guard followed me into my office. He informed me, not unkindly, that I was permitted to pack a box of my personal effects, but I left almost everything— even my law school diploma on the wall. I just grabbed my briefcase and handbag and the two framed photographs that I kept on my bookcase—of me, Rachel, and my parents. *Sorry, everyone,* I thought. *Sorry, Mom and Dad. Sorry, Rach. Sorry, Professor Tanaka. I blew it. For me, for you, and for everyone who was supposed to come after.* I choked back a sob as I stuffed them into my briefcase.

I took one last look at the mess in my office and my view of Madison Avenue. Then, as the security officer looked on, I swept my arm recklessly across the top shelf of my bookcase, knocking eight years' worth of deal toys and plaques and awards onto the floor with a satisfyingly loud crash. He made no move to stop me.

I walked out of my office with my head held high, the security officer following closely behind. He frog-marched me out to the elevator bank, where we ran into Cameron Alexander and her sidekick, that Steinberg kid from the outing, who both stared at me with open curiosity.

Down in the lobby, the security officer walked me out of the elevator, past the big granite receptionist desk emblazoned with PARSONS VALENTINE & HUNT LLP, past Ricardo, who was looking on openmouthed, and then out across the echoing marble floor to the revolving glass doors. Right before I exited Parsons Valentine & Hunt for the last time, the security officer held out his hand, into which I deposited my PV&H keycard, ID badge, and BlackBerry.

"Have a nice life, miss" was all he said.

EIGHTEEN

For three whole days I just stayed in bed.

I shut off my alarm when it started bleating at seven in the morning, crawled back under the covers, and slept like the dead til five in the afternoon. I got up only to stumble to the bathroom and get a glass of water. On my way back to bed, I glanced at my phone and saw four new messages from Rachel, three from Tyler, and two from Margo. And one blissfully ignorant one from my parents. I hadn't told them yet. I couldn't. This was going to kill them.

I shut off my phone, stuck it in a drawer, and went back to bed.

I fell into a feverish, anxious sleep, marked by so many vivid and unsettling nightmares—in one, I kept showing up late for a final exam being proctored by Marty Adler that everyone else had already finished the day before—that I only felt more exhausted and troubled upon waking.

When I couldn't sleep, I just lay there for hours, staring at the ceiling, or curled into a ball, feeling sweaty and itchy and fretful in the jumbled twist of warm and sour-smelling sheets, racked with worry, guilt, and anger, unable to imagine how I was ever going to get out of this. How exactly I would start all over.

What bothered me most—the single worst thought that I kept turning over and over in my mind—was that I was the one who'd *let* this happen. I had no one to blame but myself. I had allowed myself to be duped. *Me,* Ingrid Sabrina Yung. Valedictorian. Most Likely to Succeed. Phi Beta Kappa. *Law Review.* Well, turns out I hadn't been very smart after all. I had happily held out my hand and allowed myself to be led, like Hansel and Gretel, down the path, stupidly following the bread crumbs all these years, and now I had absolutely nothing to show for it.

I had completely bought into the myth of a meritocracy.

Somehow I'd actually been foolish enough to believe that if I simply kept my head down and worked hard, and did everything, *everything,* that was asked of me, I would be rewarded. What an idiot. Hadn't Tyler tried to warn me? Hadn't Rachel told me to watch my back? Hell, hadn't even *Isabel* cautioned me to keep some things to myself? Hadn't *everyone else* but me seen this coming?

I wondered what Mrs. Saltzstein, the high school guidance counselor, would say if she could see me now. Or my mother. Oh, God, my mother.

I was sure that I was already blackballed at all the other big firms in the city. I'd probably never work in this town again. Gossip of this kind spread fast, and I was certain I'd already been branded the Parsons Valentine Associate Who Had Made a Scene When She Didn't Make Partner. I didn't even need to flip open my laptop to know there was already some snarky, gossipy blog post about my firing up on Above the Law or Gawker, followed by a raft of gleeful comments, brimming with schadenfreude, shot through with vitriol, all written by a bunch of strangers who knew nothing about me or what had really gone down.

I knew that no one would question the integrity of Parsons Valentine's decision; at least, not anyone who could do anything about it. Hiring partners up and down the eastern seaboard, and all the way across from Boston to San Francisco, would have no choice but to assume I hadn't been able to hack it, that I simply Hadn't Been Partnership Material.

Isn't it a shame, people would cluck and tsk to each other. *These firms invest so many resources. We give these people so many chances; she just couldn't cut it.*

I awoke to a persistent buzzing at my front door. Raising myself up onto an elbow, I looked at the clock. 6:07 P.M. I didn't know what day it was. I didn't care.

The buzzing continued. I sat up, stumbled over to my mirror, and was not surprised to discover that I looked exactly as I felt, like hell. My eyes were red from crying, raw from lack of sleep. My skin was ashen. Sunken hollows shadowed my eyes, and my hair hung down around my face in lank strands. I was pitiful.

There was more insistent buzzing at the door, followed now by loud pounding.

"All right, all right. Coming." I was wearing a decrepit gray Radiohead T-shirt and underwear. I found a crumpled pair of running shorts in the hamper, shoved my legs into them, and went to the door.

Rachel muscled her way inside. "See? She's fine! I'll take it from here. Thanks for your help," she trilled to Dennis, the doorman, whom I could see peering curiously inside my apartment in the split second before Rachel shut the door firmly behind her.

Rachel dumped a large grocery bag and three old issues of the *Times* onto my hall table, pausing to glance at the double-digit tally of unlistened-to phone messages blinking on my machine. She did a double-take when she saw me up close. Her shoulders slumped so she could look me over. "Are you okay? I got your text, but then you didn't respond to any of my calls or e-mails. I've been really worried. Your *doorman* was worried, so I talked him into letting me up. He said he hadn't seen you in days and your *Times* was piling up at your door."

She took a step closer and touched my arm. "How are you holding up?" she asked.

"I'm really not ready to talk about it right now, Rach, okay?" I turned around, padded down the hall, and crawled gratefully back into bed, pulling the top sheet over my head.

Rachel followed me into my bedroom. "My God, Ingrid. It reeks in here."

I could hear her raising my window blinds partway, picking up and shaking out the duvet that I'd kicked into a heap on the floor. I felt her sit down at the foot of the bed. There was nowhere else to sit in my sparsely furnished bedroom.

"Look, Ingrid, you can't just hole yourself up in here and sleep all day. You've got to get up, get dressed, go outside, *do* something. Trust me. Living like the Unabomber is only going to make you feel worse." She was speaking patiently and gently, as she would to a scared little kid. I felt for a moment like I could be Isabel. I wished I *were* Isabel, with everything to look forward to and all of those happy decisions still ahead of me to make.

"I like living like the Unabomber," I mumbled through the top sheet.

She snorted. I heard her get up and open the window. A light breeze and some distant street noise wafted in. I had to admit that both were a relief.

Rachel came back and sat down again. She patted my ankle. "So," she said softly after a little while, "what do you think you're going to do now?"

I pulled the sheets off my head and sat upright, looking at her. "I really don't know," I said truthfully. "Start over, I guess."

Rachel studied me. "Wow. You look really horrible, Ingrid."

"Thanks, Rach. You always know just what to say."

"No, seriously. You're a mess. You look all pale. Have you been outside the apartment since last week? Have you even *showered*? When's the last time you had anything to eat?"

I considered this. "I think I had a Cup Noodles yesterday."

Rachel sighed and shook her head. I lay back down and rolled over.

A little while later, I awoke to the most delicious smell. Rachel stood over my bed, holding out a plate and wafting it under my nose like smelling salts. She had brought me a thick, golden brown grilled cheese sandwich and a glass of milk.

I sat up and gratefully accepted the grilled cheese. As I chewed and swallowed I realized I had been a lot hungrier than I'd thought. I would never find another friend like Rachel.

She settled next to me on the bed and effortlessly drew her legs up toward her into a perfect lotus position, exactly the way she used to sit in our shared apartment back in law school. I was impressed she could still do this, all these years later.

Rachel waited until I'd nearly polished off the sandwich before asking, "So, do you feel like telling me what happened? It's not clear from all the stuff on the blogs. What exactly did they tell you?"

I munched on the last crust of sandwich. "That my work was not quite up to 'partnership caliber.'" I made air quotes with my fingers.

Rachel shook her head angrily. "That's exactly the same bullshit every firm tells its female lawyers everywhere. After years of glowing performance reviews. You know, 'Just keep your head down and keep on doing exactly what you're doing! You're on track, don't worry!' Same old crap."

I nodded, not wanting to think too hard about this. Not yet. I reached down for my glass and took a big swallow of milk. I couldn't even remember the last time I'd actually drunk cold milk, as an actual beverage. It was delicious.

"It's always either that or the killer-instinct argument." Rachel was on a tear now. "You know, 'We worry you lack the killer instinct needed to bring in business. You need to be very aggressive in this line of work.' Killer instinct, my ass. What they mean is, 'We don't know if enough men will be comfortable hiring a lawyer without balls.'"

I polished off my milk and drew the back of my hand across my mouth. We sat there in silence for what felt like a long time.

Rachel was staring off toward the open window, not looking at me. A breeze wafted in and rattled the blinds. "It's always the same double standard," Rachel murmured. "If a *woman* has to leave early to pick up a sick kid or go to a soccer game, everybody tsks and wonders about her 'dedication.' But when a man does the same thing, everyone applauds and gives him a freaking medal."

I nodded. "I know." Even though I wasn't a parent, I'd seen this happen to other women at the firm many times.

"And what's happened to the deal you were working on? Do you know?" Rachel asked.

I nodded again. I knew that Murph had already been brought on to finish up the SunCorp deal. When I'd briefly logged on to my laptop, I'd spotted the brief *Wall Street Journal* report about SunCorp's announcement of the Binney acquisition, which occurred right on schedule, at the close of the quarter. And when I saw that, I couldn't help myself. I navigated to the firm website and clicked on the "Parsons Valentine in the News" tab. Sure enough, there was a link to the *Wall Street Journal* item, next to a "Meet Our Deal Team" box, with the attorney profiles and beaming firm photos of Martin J. Adler and Jeffrey D. Murphy displayed right next to each other. The sight of an affable, confident Murph grinning out at me from the screen was too much to bear. I switched off my laptop, and it had remained off since then.

So. Murph had gotten part of what he'd wanted after all. I guess he'd made out okay. I needn't have worried.

After I finished telling her this, Rachel did not once say *I told you so.* Again I was grateful.

"You know," she said, "I was always so crazily jealous of you, Ingrid. After I left Cleary."

I blinked up at her. I thought about beautiful, happily married Rachel, safely ensconced in her Westchester suburb, raising two beautiful kids, genuinely in love with the one living investment banker with the soul of a poet. "*You?* Jealous of *me?* Why?"

She shrugged. "I've always sort of wondered, what if I'd stayed on at the firm? What could I have accomplished? It always felt, somehow, like I'd sold myself short."

I didn't know why Rachel would be telling me any of this now. What was she trying to prove? Maybe back when I'd had a chance to do something about it, this would've been one thing. Now it just seemed beside the point. Like we were *both* utterly defeated. Like neither of us had anything to show for ourselves. I suddenly felt sorry for the idealistic younger self I'd been in college.

"Well, as it turns out, maybe I've sold myself short, too. I've wasted all this time."

"Don't say that." Rachel shook her head so fiercely she dislodged her hair from where it had been tucked behind her ear. "This hasn't been wasted time. You've *been* someone, out in the world. You were out there *doing* things, making things happen."

We were both quiet for a while, thinking.

I thought about the *New Yorker* cartoon I'd once cut out and taped to a corner of my computer monitor at work. It showed a plot of grass sitting on one side of a fence, looking at the other side, and musing to itself, *I'm greener, yes. But am I happier?*

Rachel and I both had a lot to learn.

She touched me on the shoulder. "There's one part I don't get. Is it true you had to get escorted out of the building? That part made no sense. What did they *say* to you?"

I looked at her, embarrassed. "It's not what they said to me. It's what *I* said to *them*."

"It can't be that bad. I mean, what did you say?"

"Told him to go fuck himself."

"You said that to . . . *Adler*?"

"To Adler."

Rachel's eyes got big. "You did not."

I nodded.

"Oh, Ingrid," she said. "Oh, honey." Rachel was trying hard not to laugh, but not hard enough. And as long as I'd known her, whenever Rachel started to laugh like that—her great, big, gaspy, *help me I am on the floor* laugh—it was difficult for me not to join her. Impossible in this case.

We laughed until we were both crying a little.

Late that night, as Rach was leaving my apartment and making me promise to take a shower and eat the turkey pot pie, frittata, and homemade gazpacho that she had left in Tupperware tubs in my fridge, she hugged me and said, "This isn't the end of the world, Ingrid. You'll figure something else out, eventually. Trust me. You will."

I was already starting to believe her.

NINETEEN

❦

R achel was right, of course. Living like the Unabomber was not the answer. I had to get up sometime.

The next morning, I forced myself into the shower; pulled on a favorite pair of jeans, a white V-neck tee, and flip-flops; slipped my hair into a low, loose knot; and took the elevator nineteen floors down to the lobby. Dennis was on duty. He grinned as soon as he saw me. "Well, look who it is!" He looked me up and down, taking in my ancient jeans, my flip-flops, my makeup-free face. "You got the day off or something?"

I smiled sadly. "Or something, Dennis."

I took a deep breath, then pushed through the revolving door and out into the sunshine.

The July day was hot but not sticky. It felt good to be outside and moving my arms and legs. But it felt odd, too—a little like sleepwalking. It was the most bizarre sensation, this idea that *I was not expected anywhere*. Margo wasn't waiting for me to respond to a thick sheaf of yellow "While You Were Out" slips. Marty Adler wasn't waiting on my revised, redlined draft of anything. Justin Keating wasn't waiting for me to show up and generally make his life miserable.

I had no conference calls. No meetings. No lunches. No appointments. No deadlines. No seminars. I had nothing.

I could actually put on the same old pair of jeans and flip-flops every day if I wanted to. I had a useless wardrobe full of expensive suits, Bergdorf tags still dangling from the sleeves. I tried to remember if I'd kept any of the receipts. Could I return everything? Or maybe I'd have a garage sale. A "going out of business" sale! FIRE SALE! FORMER CORPORATE ATTORNEY OUT ON HER ASS. EVERYTHING MUST GO!

I walked by a handsome young neighborhood dad wearing black Adidas track pants and a faded old Race for the Cure T-shirt, holding on to the hand of his son—his spitting image—as they crossed the street. The kid, about five, was toting a Wiffle bat. They were obviously headed to the park.

A trim older woman with close-cropped hair power-walked past me in the opposite direction, humming along to the song she was listening to on her headphones.

So *this* was what the city looked like during the workweek, during all those lost hours I'd spent at the firm. I marveled at these lucky people who were roaming the neighborhood in the middle of a random Tuesday morning. What was their secret? What did they do? They couldn't *all* be retired or have trust funds. Did they just work the night shift? Or maybe they were simply, as Dennis had assumed I was, taking a long-overdue day off.

As I continued down the sidewalk, it dawned on me that I was starving. Maybe it was the grilled cheese sandwich Rachel had fed me yesterday that had startled my appetite out of hibernation. Or maybe it was the fact that I was out in the relatively fresh New York air for the first time in four days. Whatever it was, my body was telling me that I hadn't been paying it enough attention. And my body was not happy about it.

I headed back in the opposite direction, to the bagel place three blocks down. I was practically running, I was suddenly so hungry. It felt good to have a sense of purpose and destination, even if the destination was the Bagel Boat.

"What can I get you?" asked the guy behind the counter, snapping on some plastic gloves. I'd never seen him before. I usually only came here amid the bustling weekend crowd, but this was a totally different staff and the place was quiet, nearly empty. So there really was this whole other Weekday Morning Nonoffice World that I knew nothing about.

"I'll have a toasted everything with cream cheese and lox, please."

"That be all?"

"And this, too," I said, picking up a copy of the *Wall Street Journal* from the wire rack. For old times' sake. For the want ads, too. Wait— did they even have want ads in newspapers anymore?

As the guy rang me up, the little bell above the door chimed, and three young women entered the store, chattering and laughing, each pushing a baby stroller. They were dressed alike, in T-shirts, jeans, and trainers or flip-flops. They parked the strollers and headed over to a little nook by the refrigerated drinks. Obviously, the bagel stop was part of their routine.

The women were all younger than I was, probably in their mid- to late twenties. The tallest had flawless caramel-colored skin, and when she spoke to her friends, I heard a Caribbean lilt to her voice. The other two women were Asian, with dark complexions and open, friendly expressions. Tibetan, I guessed, or maybe Thai.

And each of these three young women had in her care a fair-haired, blue-eyed child.

It was so striking, this parade of young brown women and their small white charges. I glanced at the big round clock above the cash register. 10:18. The apparent witching hour for the gathering of Manhattan nannies. The harried career moms who employed them would have dashed out of the apartment hours before, fingers flying on Black-Berrys and iPhones, en route to some hectic desk job or other—one that came with diplomas on the wall, files in the credenza, an assistant, a speakerphone, a window with a view to the streets below. The very same streets their nannies roamed every day of the week, until the career moms rushed home to relieve them, just after dark. Just in time for a single bedtime story.

I took my newspaper and sat down at one of the narrow little tables against the wall. "15 Killed in Kabul Bomb Attack." "Jobless Numbers Rise 2 Percent." "Congress in Partisan Standoff on Drilling Reform." "Councilman Steps Down amid Growing Bribery Probe." There was no good news anymore.

I glanced, for distraction, down into the stroller that was parked next to me. A pink-cheeked child was tucked inside, with blond curls and impossibly long blond eyelashes. She must have been four—really, a bit old to be pushed around in a stroller anywhere but New York—but there was no denying that she was adorable.

The bell jangled again, and in walked a woman who was obviously not a nanny. She was by herself, first of all. She had a perky, well-cared-for look about her. She was about my age, petite, ash blond, pretty. She wore gray yoga pants, a sleek black racerback tank, and cross-trainers. A fluorescent pink water bottle, a compact fanny pack, and an iPhone were strapped efficiently to her waist.

She walked up to the counter, ordered a whole-wheat bagel with one Egg Beater, and then turned around toward me. I could feel her taking me in—my messy hair, my jeans and flip-flops, the expensive stroller parked at my feet. She walked right up and looked inside the stroller. She sucked in her breath.

"Oh. My. *God*," the woman said to me. "That baby is just *gorgeous*."

I blinked at her. She had caught me off guard; in the workaday world of midtown, commuters usually didn't just walk right up and talk to each other. But maybe these were the unspoken rules in Weekday Morning Nonoffice World and people felt free to just start talking to strangers. I glanced over at the child's nanny, trying to catch her eye, but no luck.

I looked down at the little girl, then back up at the yoga woman. Not wanting to seem rude, I smiled.

Yoga Pants leaned down toward the stroller and waggled her fingers in the face of the clearly sleeping child. Then she bent *way* down—revealing impressive cleavage in the gentle V of her tank—before reaching into the stroller and actually tickling the girl's nose.

"Hey," I said, alarmed, rolling the stroller a couple of inches closer to me. "Um, I'm not actually—" I began, glancing over at the little girl's nanny, who, along with her friends, was now busy inspecting the available flavors of Vitaminwater.

Yoga Pants stood back up and smiled at me. "So how long have you been taking care of *this* little angel?" she asked.

I curled my fingers possessively around the handlebar of the stroller. "Uh, well . . ."

"And do you come into the city from Queens? Or from someplace else?" she asked, still smiling in a beneficent way.

"No, I'm—I actually live just around the corner," I said. What was I *doing*? Why didn't I simply explain her mistake to her? What was wrong with me?

Yoga Pants beamed at me. "You know, I just think it's so *smart* for parents to get an Asian-speaking nanny these days," she gushed.

Did I know how to speak *Asian*?

I smiled uncertainly.

"Listen, you seem really sweet. Let me give you my phone number." Yoga Pants fished a card out of her tiny fanny pack. She tilted her chin toward the stroller. "Once this one gets off to full-day kindergarten, which looks like it might be any day now, you might find yourself in need of another job. Rob and I have *plenty* of friends who'd just love a referral to an Asian nanny who's already familiar with the neighborhood."

She handed me her card.

"Thanks, that's nice of you," I said, almost meaning it.

She waved a hand gaily in the air. "Oh, it's nothing. That's just how I am. I love to help people!"

"Toasted everything, CC, and lox!" the guy behind the counter called out, brandishing a brown paper bag.

"That's me." I stood, picked up my paper, and retrieved my bagel.

I felt, somehow, that I should say something to Yoga Pants. She had, after all, in her own special way, just tried to find me a job.

"Well, it was very nice talking to you," I said, standing there a little awkwardly, with my bagel.

"Don't lose my number, now," she said with a magnanimous smile. "You just call if you ever need a referral to another family."

"Okay then," I said vaguely, taking a few backward steps toward the exit.

"Wait!" she yelled. *"You're forgetting the baby!"*

I smiled uncertainly, waved, turned my back, and scurried out the door.

Out on the street, for no reason at all, I started half-running, half-jogging, my flip-flops slapping noisily on the pavement. As I ran, I laughed hysterically. I was actually laughing. It made no sense, but suddenly I felt giddy and exhilarated. I felt oddly free.

I ran halfway up the block before I worked up the courage to look behind me. I paused, bent over slightly, with my hands on my thighs, trying to catch my breath. I half-expected to see Yoga Pants storming up the block, accompanied by an NYPD officer and an angry mob of

Upper East Side nannies, pointing me out. *There she is! That's the imp*
tor! Stop her!

I started running again, heading east. Up ahead, I spotted a bar
of anonymous, old-fashioned pay phones—one of the few that sti
existed in this part of Manhattan. I slowed to a walk. I looked aroun
cautiously—not sure exactly who I expected might stop me—an
then stepped toward the first booth. I didn't know that I was going t
do it. It was automatic. My fingers didn't need to be told what to do.

I dialed my old work number.

Morbid curiosity had gotten the better of me. The line rang three
times, but instead of clicking over to my own familiar recorded greeting, I heard Margo's voice: *Hello. You have reached the voice mailbox of Ingrid*
Yung. Please be aware that, effective immediately, Ms. Yung is no longer associ-
ated with the law firm of Parsons Valentine and Hunt, and any personal mes-
sages left on this line will not be retrieved. If you are calling with a business-related
inquiry, please dial zero for Reception, and your call will be redirected to an-
other attorney.

Only someone who knew Margo as well as I did would be able to
detect the sad little hiccup in her voice that revealed itself at the very
end of the message. Good old Margo. I missed her.

Back home, in the relative safety of my apartment, whose mortgage
I would soon not be able to afford, I tossed my newspaper and bagel
onto the polished marble counter, sank down at my kitchen table, and
held my head in both hands. My God, I was losing it, I was really losing
it. I had just pretended to be the guardian of a strange child. I had just
dialed my own voice mail.

I had the sudden, wrenching thought that I had become the kind of
person that other people felt sorry for. *Me*. Ingrid Sabrina Yung. That
was, after all, why Yoga Pants was trying to help me, right? Because
she thought I was someone who needed a job?

Well, I admonished myself, *you* do *need a job!* What, was being a nanny really so beneath me? Hadn't Rachel always said that I was great with Isabel and Jacob? Maybe, just maybe, I could do worse than to call Yoga Pants back.

In all the books and movies, wasn't that exactly what happened to career girls like me? Weren't we forever coming to some work epiphany or other, cursing out our domineering bosses once and for all, finally speaking our minds and telling them what for, then flouncing dramatically out of our midtown glass towers to discover an amazing untapped aptitude for cupcake baking, or handbag sewing, or dog walking, or some such? Isn't that how we were all expected to start over and save ourselves, if all those stories were to be believed? Either that, or meet and marry Mr. Right and hope that he had a decent place to live?

Well, I couldn't bake, for one. I'd never been big on sewing, either. And I'd recently tried what I thought was the Mr. Right route and had found myself painfully, tragically, mistaken.

Oh God. I suddenly felt very, very tired. I folded my arms and laid my head down on the table.

So *this* was what it all came down to. After all my hard work, I would not be making history after all. I would be calling Yoga Pants to be placed with a family who wanted an Asian-speaking nanny.

I sat there with my head on my kitchen table for a long, long time. I breathed in and out, steadily, listening to the muffled sounds of midday traffic drifting up from nineteen stories below, and thinking.

I was shocked by just how swiftly and completely I'd been shorn of the identifying, qualifying marks—briefcase, BlackBerry, business section of the *Times*—that had inoculated me for all of these years. I realized, with something very close to guilt, that I'd spent the better part of my life diligently accumulating, and then jealously guarding, my private trove of these Inoculating Marks. We all hoarded them— all of us Minority Darlings who had made it this far.

We collected something else, too, unbeknownst to the other colleagues we shared laughs and drinks with after work. We kept a meticulous tally of all of the slights and slurs collected over the years—each look of surprise on a new client's face upon first meeting, every hushed, broken-off conversation when we entered a room. On rare occasions, in trusted company, we aired them out, dusted them off, and tossed them around like war stories. Rolled up our sleeves and revealed them to each other, like battle scars.

Did I ever tell you about the time a woman handed me her dry cleaning as I stood behind her in line?

That's nothing. Did I tell you about the client who used the N-word on the phone before finding out I was black?

How about the time Professor Cahill asked if I'd been to Stanford on an athletic scholarship?

Please. I've been asked if both my parents are legal.

And so on.

I saw now that I'd spent the better part of my life trying to insulate myself from all kinds of hurt. And it had almost worked. All those years, it had almost become possible for me to live my day-to-day life ignoring the differences that existed between me and any other *Times*-reading, dark-suited, smartphone-toting business commuter in the city. Until now.

Making partner, I'd somehow thought, would make me whole. I would become immune to the little humiliations I had collected over all these years. But it hadn't worked. It would never work. It had been doomed from the start. I knew that now. I also knew exactly what that made me—just another dropout, just another Minority Darling who had come really, really close.

TWENTY

❦

I was curled up on the couch when the phone rang. I stirred and sat halfway up, bleary-eyed. I still didn't feel like talking to anyone. I let it ring until the machine picked up.

Hey, it's Ingrid. Leave me a message. Beep.

"Ingrid-ah," my mother's cheerful, chirpy voice came through in Mandarin—it was soothing, somehow, and my heart hurt as I thought about how much I missed my parents, how hard it was going to be to disappoint them. They'd sacrificed so much, coming here from Taipei as grad students with nothing, so many decades ago. What would it feel like for them to know that I'd had the American Dream solidly within my grasp but had let it slip from my fingers?

I strained to hear my mother's message. Her voice sounded plaintive, braver and louder than she would have sounded if she'd been calling me at work, but still tentative all the same. "Ingrid, Daddy and I haven't heard from you in a little while, and we just wanted to see if everything's all right. Give us a call when you can. I know you must be working so hard, as usual. You must be very busy at work. Love, Mom." Beep.

I had to tell them.

I threw off my blanket, picked up the phone, and dialed my parents' number. My hands were shaking badly enough that I messed up the first time and had to dial twice.

I didn't know how I was going to break this news to them, but they deserved to know the truth. They were going to be devastated. In my parents' world, it was a tragedy if the only Ivy your child got into was Cornell.

The phone rang three times before my father picked up. "Hello?" he said. He sounded cheerful, and that made my heart break just a little more.

"Hi, Dad," I said, as brightly as I could manage.

"Oh, Ingrid." I could hear him take the phone away from his ear and holler to my mom, "Yan-Mei! It's Ingrid! Hurry up! Hold on, sweetie, Mom's coming, we'll put you on the speakerphone—"

"No, wait, Dad? Actually, *don't* put me on speaker—"

There was a loud squawk, and both my parents' voices came on together. "Hello!" shouted my dad. "Hi, Ingrid!" said my mother's happy voice. "What a surprise! Only six o'clock! You don't usually call so early! Did you get to leave work early?"

Well, yes, in a manner of speaking. I nearly laughed.

"Actually," I began, "that's sort of what I was calling you guys about."

And then, without having prepared anything in advance, without having scripted how I'd do it, I just blurted it all out in a big crazy headlong crush of words. I told them—in Mandarin, so there would be no miscommunication—everything that had happened. About Marty Adler and Ted Lassiter and Hunter's horrible skit and the country club and the Diversity Committee and Dr. Rossi and Zhang Liu and the terrible meeting with the client where everything had gone horribly wrong and yes, I even told them about Murph.

I described the horrible meeting in Adler's office and admitted that I was home now—had been home for many days, in fact, thinking.

I expected that my mother would cry. She didn't. In fact, both she and my father were silent for what seemed like a very long time. When my mother finally did speak, she lapsed back into Mandarin, sounding extremely calm and practical. Matter-of-fact, even. To my surprise, she actually reminded me of Rachel.

"Well, you'll come home and get a job here, that's all there is to that," she said, with finality. Her voice softened. "Maybe you can talk to Cindy Bai or Susan Wu—maybe they know of a local lawyer here who could use a little help around the office. Just until you get back on your feet."

Help around the office? *Me,* who'd been about to become the first female Corporate partner at one of the most powerful law firms in the world? Well, hell, maybe I could, maybe I would. Maybe it had come to that.

"It's not that easy, Mom," I said. "I don't want to rush into anything. I just need to think things through right now."

There was another pause.

"It's not too late to apply to medical school," she said.

I started to laugh. And once I started, it was hard to stop. It felt great to laugh out loud.

My mother sounded annoyed. "Well, I'm just saying, you still could."

My father interrupted, "I think Ingrid's right. She just needs some time to think about things, Yan-Mei."

My heart swelled. *Good old Dad.*

Then my mother said quietly, "You could come back home, Ingrid. Start over. There are lots of nice places for young people to live in Maryland and Virginia. I'll help you look."

I didn't *want* to live in a nice place. I wanted to be in Manhattan.

"I'm sure," my mother continued, "in a different city, no one will even care that you'd been on some bad project with some mean, bad boss at some company up in New York. Maybe they won't even know of this Valentine company. Maybe no one will even have heard of it."

I sighed. "They'll have heard of it, Mom, believe me. They'll all have heard of it."

After a pause, I said, "I'm sorry. I wish I didn't have to tell you all of this. I wish my news were better."

My mother sighed, too. "Ingrid-ah." She paused, and I could tell she was trying to bring herself to say something difficult. "Your father and I were always so worried about you with that job, living in that lonely apartment, not eating proper meals, working so late every night and coming home by yourself at three in the morning. Maybe"—she hesitated—"maybe this is a blessing in disguise. Please come home. All you need is some time, to try to figure out what will make you happy."

I sat there pressing the receiver to my ear, stunned. All along, I'd thought that my parents weren't equipped to hear about when my life turned bad. When in fact, maybe all they'd wanted was for me to be *happy*.

"Your mother and I raised a smart girl," my dad said. "You'll figure out a way. I'm not worried."

All of this time, I thought I'd been busily protecting my parents. When it turned out perhaps they hadn't needed much protecting at all. But maybe *I* had.

"Promise me you'll at least think about coming home," my mother said. "Maybe in the fall. Things always seem to look so much brighter in the fall. Remember you used to tell me that?"

I smiled into the receiver. "Yes," I said softly.

After we said good-bye, I sat there for a minute longer, thinking about what my mother had said.

The fall had always been my favorite season. There was just something I loved about that sharp autumnal crackle in the air, which I still associated with new lunchboxes and the delicious whiff of spiral notebooks and Magic Markers. I loved going back-to-school shopping with my mom for new sweaters and skirts at Sears and Penney's. Fresh starts, in other words. Fall felt like a fresh start. One could go away over the summer and come back a totally reinvented self.

Anything seemed possible.

TWENTY-ONE

I t wasn't until three evenings later that I finally felt calm enough—
and brave enough—to listen to all the phone messages that had
been piling up ever since I'd left Parsons Valentine. When I felt good
and ready, I poured myself a glass of red wine, wrapped myself in an
old flannel blanket, pressed PLAY on the machine, and curled up onto
the couch to listen. I leaned my head all the way back and closed my
eyes.

"Ingrid, sweetie." Rachel's voice was strained. "Are you okay? I just
heard about what happened at work. Call me." Beep.

"Hi, it's me again," said Rachel. "Where are you, Ingrid? Are you
okay? Haven't heard from you in a few days, are you still eating? Let me
know if you want me to come over. Just give me a call to let me know
you're all right, okay? Doesn't matter how late." Beep.

"Ingrid?" It was Margo, speaking in soft tones, and I knew she was
at work, trying not to be overheard. "Honey, I heard what happened.
We're all in shock. We just can't believe it. You deserve it more than
anyone. Let me know if there's anything I can do for you, honey."
Beep.

"Ingrid. It's Tyler. Listen, I have no idea what happened, and no one will tell me anything. I can't believe it, Ingrid. You're the one person everyone thought really deserved it. This is total bullshit. Anyway, I just wanted to say I'm worried about you. Call me when you're feeling up to it. I just hope you're okay, sweetie." Beep.

A moment later: "Yung, it's me." Murph's low, warm voice filled my living room.

I sat up, sloshing red wine into my lap and onto the couch.

"I know you probably hate me, but I just wanted to tell you that . . . that I'm really sorry about everything that happened." He paused. "I mean about the partnership vote, and . . ." He trailed off. "And about us, too. I'm really, really sorry. I know I screwed up." He paused again and sighed. I could tell he was trying hard to sound plaintive and pathetic. "And I hope, in some way, I mean, I know it's a lot to ask of you, but I hope that in some small way, at some time down the road, you might even come to forgive me." A final pause. Then, "So, that's all I really wanted to say, Ingrid. Call me sometime, if you want. I mean, I hope you will. Bye."

How dare he?

I leapt off the couch. I stood there in the middle of my living room, about to scream. I screwed my eyes so tightly shut I saw angry spirals of red. How *dare* he call here, invading my home, sounding so calm, so collected, so reasonable? In what parallel universe would any of those things Murph had said to me—all those horrible, painful things that he'd screamed at me in his apartment—ever be, in any way, *forgivable*?

I looked down. The red wine I'd spilled was seeping into the fabric of my beautiful, impractical, celery-colored couch. I rushed to the kitchen, ran a couple of white dish towels under the cold water, and dashed back to the living room, where I daubed and then scrubbed the fabric. No matter what I did, the ruby color wouldn't come up. All I succeeded in doing was further spreading the stain around.

Fuck. I give up. I really just give up.

I stalked into the kitchen, balled up the ruined dish towels, and hurled them into the sink. I stood there, bracing myself against the smooth polished countertop, and closed my eyes, pressing the heels of both hands hard against them, trying to make the angry spirals of red go away. I opened my eyes. I took a few deep, soothing breaths.

In, out.

In, then out.

Again.

Breathe.

Calm.

Okay.

I leaned forward and rested both elbows heavily on the cool marble surface. As usual, my kitchen was spotless. When you never cooked, your kitchen remained clean. My gaze fell upon the only thing that was cluttering up the countertop—the *Wall Street Journal* that I'd picked up three days ago, lying inches from my left elbow. As I glanced at the newsprint, one of the headlines that I'd only skimmed earlier at the Bagel Boat now leapt out at me in sharp relief:

CONGRESS IN PARTISAN STANDOFF
ON DRILLING REFORM

I bolted straight up. I grabbed the paper and flattened it out on the counter. I opened it to the page with the full news article and read:

BY DEBRA M. FINNEGAN

Democrats in the House and Senate plan to introduce new legislation in the coming months that will dramatically increase offshore drilling safety requirements and remove caps on corporate liability for catastrophic oil spills, sources on Capitol Hill say.

HELEN WAN

Environmental groups, labor unions, and advocacy groups
for workers and small businesses disproportionately affected by
last year's BP oil spill in the Gulf of Mexico have expressed
frustration over Congress's slow legislative response to that
disaster. Democrats facing the upcoming election year are attempting to woo back their traditional voter base by proposing
a new reform bill that will take a harder line on offshore drilling safety.

Key changes in the new bill include the elimination of liability limits for private companies involved in offshore drilling ac-
cidents, new regulatory standards for offshore rigs, and mandatory
OSHA and environmental safety upgrades for owners and op-
erators of such drilling platforms.

Although Republicans are expected to oppose the new bill,
which could prove costly for large oil conglomerates, experts
now say that if a bloc of lawmakers can agree on adjustments to
the bill to ensure that smaller oil companies will not be disproportionately affected, the reform package has a chance to pass
with a slim majority. "We know we're in the very early stages yet,"
said Rep. Kathryn McAlister (D-CA), newest member of the
House Energy and Commerce Committee, "but we're confident
that we will prevail."

When I'd finished the article, I read it again. And then again. *Thank
you, Debra M. Finnegan.* I closed my eyes, summoning everything I could
remember from Professor Gunderson's Legal Ethics and Professional
Responsibility class so many years ago.

Before I lost my nerve, I picked up my cell phone. I still had the
number programmed in, after having called it so many times over the
past two months, but my hands were shaking so badly now that I had to
hit the button twice.

Finally, I heard ringing on the other end. Once, twice, three times.

"Slugger," said the gruff but warm voice on the other end of the line. "Well, well. To what do I owe this nice surprise?"

TWENTY-TWO

༄

The intercom buzzed in my front hall. I looked up, bleary-eyed, annoyed at the interruption. I'd been up all night, sitting at my kitchen table, working feverishly on my laptop, creating spreadsheets and budgets and lists, typing in all the scribbled notes and strategies I'd begun jotting down following the forty-five-minute phone conversation Lassiter and I had had last night.

The intercom buzzed again.

I thought about pretending I wasn't home, but Dennis knew everything. I sighed, glancing at the clock on my cable box. *Who* showed up unannounced at ten thirty on a Saturday morning? Honestly, it was uncivilized. I was in a camisole and pajama bottoms. I hadn't brushed my teeth. I set down my sixth cup of coffee and padded into the hall, pulling on an old cardigan as I went. "Hello?" I said warily into the intercom. I was half-expecting an eviction call any day now.

"Hey, Ingrid. There's someone here to see you," said Dennis. "Okay to send him up?"

"I'm not expecting anyone," I said. "Can you find out who it is?"

I heard a muffling noise and Dennis saying to someone in the background, "She says she's not expecting you. What's the name?" A silence, then a mumbling.

Dennis came back on the line. "His name's Justin Keating."

Unbelievable. What was he here to do, gloat?

"Please tell him to go away," I said. "I don't want to see anyone right now."

More muffled voices. Dennis sounded adamant, but the mumbling persisted.

Dennis sighed into the receiver. "The kid says it's really important. Says it'll only take a few minutes."

Three minutes later, Justin rang my doorbell.

I opened the door a crack, without undoing the chain. "Well," I said. "This is quite a surprise, Justin. What do you want?"

Justin looked around nervously. He was wearing jeans and a gray hoodie. His hands were shoved in his pockets, as usual, but today he wasn't smirking. He looked stressed out.

"Can I come in?"

I sighed, then undid the chain and opened the door wider.

He stepped inside and looked around cautiously.

I closed the door and then turned around to look at him, folding my arms across my chest. "Okay. So now you're in. What do you want?"

He looked surprised. "Did you not get my e-mail?" he asked.

I exhaled impatiently. "Justin, the firm took back my BlackBerry. I no longer even *have* a Parsons Valentine e-mail account."

He shook his head. "I know. That's why I had to ask Margo for your Gmail address."

"I haven't been checking *any* e-mail, Justin. I've been taking a much-needed break." I looked him square in the eye. "Why'd you need to get in touch with me so badly?"

"I have something to show you." He reached inside his jacket and produced some kind of long computer printout, handing it to me.

"What's this supposed to be?" I said, not reaching for it.

"Just read it," he insisted, giving it a shake.

I sighed. I took the piece of paper from him and smoothed it out. It was a log from the Parsons Valentine mainframe servers. A running table showed dates, times, usernames, hardware IDs, document numbers, and computer workstation locations.

"So?"

"Down here." Justin pointed.

Two lines on the printout had been highlighted. I peered closely at them. It had a document number, Doc 235986, version 12, next to my username, *isyung,* and the time, 11:44 P.M. The line directly underneath said Doc 235986, version 12, next to the username, *jdmurphy,* and the time, 12:08 A.M.

I looked up at Justin, amazed.

"Where'd you get this?"

He looked at me and shrugged. "The servers record every single time anyone accesses any document. This shows that Murph went into the SunCorp term sheet after we both went home that night. And we didn't proof it again when we printed it out the next morning."

"But I already tried looking up the doc history myself, and I didn't see anyone else's usernames on the document except ours."

He shook his head. "When you look it up at your own workstation, it only shows you who accessed it the normal way on one of the firm's computers. It doesn't show who may have accessed it remotely, checked out a copy, then checked it back in. But the servers record *everything.*"

I stared at the log in amazement. "How do you know all this, Justin?"

"Eh. No big deal. I majored in comp sci. Some buddies and I are actually trying to launch a tech start-up, but my dad made me get a 'real job' in the meantime. That's how I ended up at the firm."

"I didn't know you were a comp sci major."

He shrugged. "You never asked."

I looked at him. "No, I guess I didn't."

"Anyway, IT prints out the server logs every week, and then they just leave them out in the bin to be recycled. This wasn't hard to find."

"But how'd you even know to look for anything like this?" I asked, still clutching the printout like I didn't quite believe it existed, like it could still flutter away if I blinked.

"I saw Murph there late that night. So I kind of had a hunch. Especially after I saw you and Murph together, and then everything that happened. *You* know."

"Justin. I could kiss you."

He smiled. "You don't have to," he said quietly. He turned toward the door, preparing to leave.

"Justin," I said again.

"Yeah?" He looked over at me. His hands were still bunched in the pockets of his hoodie, and his shoulders were all hunched up, as if he were cold. He looked so young, standing there at that moment, much younger, in fact, than his twenty-three years.

"I was just wondering, I mean, I'm curious . . ." I stopped and began again. "I'm just wondering why you're doing this for me. I was always— kind of hard on you."

He paused and thought for a moment. "I don't know," he said, shrugging. "I guess maybe because you never seemed to care who my dad was. You weren't just pretending to like me because of him." He looked at me and smirked, and some of the old slyness crept back into his face.

"You were the only lawyer at the firm who treated me like crap, just like I was any other paralegal."

TWENTY-THREE

⚬

Monday morning, I paid my cab driver, thanked him, and then, on a whim, tipped him more, much more, than I could really afford. "Hey, thanks," he said, and twisted around in the driver's seat to look at me.

I said, "Wish me luck, will you?"

"Don't know what you need it for, but good luck, miss."

I stepped out onto the sidewalk. The cab peeled away with a screech and nosed back into the stream of Madison Avenue traffic. I stared after it for a moment. No turning back now.

I reached into my handbag and put on my big, dark Audrey Hepburn–style sunglasses, the ones I imagined lent a certain aura of mystery. I lifted my chin, tilted my head way back, and stared up at the familiar fifty-story building, its flags rippling above the entrance, its bronze corporate sculpture out front, its landscaped terrace up top, the blue sky and a few wisps of white cloud perfectly framing my view of the glittering silver tower. I was nervous—of course I was—but I also felt better than I had in weeks. It felt terrific to be in heels again, to hear them clicking confidently along beneath me on the sidewalk, to have someplace I needed to be. I was wearing my favorite killer black crepe suit with a classic georgette blouse, diamond stud earrings, and lady-like alligator pumps. I was wearing a black pencil skirt, and feeling unapologetic about it.

I drew myself up to my full height—all five feet three inches of me—took several deep breaths, and walked into the building. For one fleeting moment, I felt like I could simply blend back into the crowd of scrubbed, powdered and groomed, immaculately jacketed-and-tied Parsons Valentine foot soldiers spinning in through those revolving glass doors.

But far too much had happened for that.

I clicked across the marble lobby, as I had done on thousands of other mornings just like this one, past the imposing mahogany-paneled walls, past the elegantly backlit corporate art exhibit—this month, a series of Walker Evans Depression-era photographs on loan from the Whitney—right up to the granite reception desk bearing the large burnished gold letters that spelled out PARSONS VALENTINE & HUNT LLP.

Ricardo was on duty.

He grinned upon seeing me, but it quickly faded as he remembered the last time I'd been here, being frog-marched out of the building by a uniformed guard. Ricardo glanced around quickly before saying in a low voice, "Ingrid. It's really good to see you."

"It's great to see you, RC. How've you been?"

"Fine, fine." He looked around again. "But the question is, how've *you* been?"

"You know what? I've been all right."

"That's good. I'm glad to know that." He darted another look around, then asked, "So, what are you doing here?"

I looked at the huge round clock above the reception desk. It was almost ten forty-five. At this point in the morning everyone would already be settled in at their desks upstairs. For the moment, Ricardo and I were alone.

"RC," I said, "I need to ask you for a big favor. I need you to let me up to see Marty Adler."

He hesitated. Then he reached into a desk drawer in front of him and quickly slid a blue plastic keycard across the granite counter at me. "Anyone asks, somebody dropped that near the elevators, got it?"

"Got it." I smiled. "Thanks, RC. I knew I could count on you."

I made my way over to the last bank of elevators and pressed the button for thirty-seven. The ascent was smooth and swift, the quiet *swoosh* oddly calming as we climbed higher and higher up from street level.

I was jolted back to reality by a warning *ding.* The car stopped on Adler's floor, and I stepped out.

Luckily, no one happened to be walking by, and I dashed over to the interior glass doors, slid the keycard into the panel, and pulled as the green light clicked on. I really hoped Adler would be in his office. The way I figured it, I'd have four or five seconds to convince him to see me before he picked up the house security phone.

Feeling a weird rush of adrenaline, I surged down the hall. I rounded the corner and ran smack into Sharon, Adler's secretary, who'd been balancing a foam coffee cup that was now upended on the floor, the hot black liquid seeping into the carpet. She cursed under her breath, then looked up at me. "How on earth did you get in here?" she asked in a nasty voice. "You know I'm going to have to call Security—"

"You do that," I said, before striding to Marty Adler's office and letting myself in.

He was alone, sitting at his desk with his Starbucks, his *Wall Street Journal,* and his blueberry muffin. The bright midmorning sunlight streamed in behind him, illuminating his head and shoulders, almost like a halo.

"Ingrid." He jumped up.

"Marty, before you say anything, please just hear me out," I said.

He backed away from me in slow, careful steps. He actually held both palms up, as if I were a masked gunman.

"Listen, Marty," I said, my voice strong and clear and steady. "*Murph* accessed the SunCorp term sheet, the night before our meeting. He went in and deliberately made those errors in my document so I'd be humiliated in front of you and Lassiter. And I can prove it to you."

Adler had backed all the way up against the window, and now he stood there, both hands gripping the ledge behind him, as if for ballast. He had a deeply pained expression on his face.

Sharon poked her head into the room, smelling of coffee, and glared at me. "I'm so sorry, Mr. Adler, I don't know how she got in here. I'll call Security right now and tell them to—"

"Wait just a minute, Sharon," Adler said, holding a palm up at her, but keeping his eyes trained closely on me. "Will you please just give us a minute?"

Sharon glared at me again before backing out of the room, pulling the door closed behind her.

I exhaled the deep breath I had been holding. "Thank you, Marty."

He shook his head fiercely. "Don't thank me, Ingrid. What the hell's this *proof* you're talking about? These are very serious accusations. I find it hard to believe that Jeff Murphy would do anything of the sort."

I removed the server log from my handbag and handed it to him.

Adler looked at me suspiciously, then put on his bifocals and scanned the page.

He took his glasses off and handed the printout back to me. "I'm sorry, Ingrid. But I'm not sure how I can conclude that one of our attorneys actually accessed a document with the intention of *sabotaging* one of our own client's pending deals. There are a hundred legitimate reasons Murph might have needed to look at that document." He crossed his arms across his chest, shaking his head slowly. "Just what would you have me believe—that Murph went out of his way to sabotage you?

To sabotage *us*? Why in the world would he ever take such a stupid risk? It doesn't make sense."

He shook his head again, with more conviction. "No, no, I'm sorry, Ingrid, but I'm afraid we came to the only reasonable conclusion there was to make."

This took me aback. I had to pause a moment to think what to say next. Truthfully, I had been counting on Adler giving me more of the benefit of the doubt. That Adler might actually not believe me, that he would not even be willing to *listen* to what I had to tell him, after everything I'd done for him and sacrificed for this firm, was unbearable. It hurt to realize, finally, that the pool of goodwill these partners had for me was always going to be shallower than the ones they harbored for Murph and Hunter, and others who reminded them of their own sons and brothers and selves.

Adler said, "I don't see the need to call for Security if you leave without a fuss, Ingrid, but you do need to leave. Right now."

A current of rage overwhelmed me. It was amazing how much braver you got when you had nothing left to lose.

"No," I said hoarsely. "You don't seem to understand, Marty. *I am not leaving here without clearing my name.*"

Adler said nothing. We stared stonily at each other.

Finally I said, "If you don't believe me, you can call Justin Keating in here and he'll tell you himself."

That seemed to get his attention. Adler narrowed his eyes at me. "Donald Keating's kid? What the hell does *he* have to do with any of this?"

"Justin's the one who found out Murph did this," I said. "Justin's the one who told *me*."

"Oh, for fuck's sake." Adler let out a heavy sigh. He turned his back on me, faced the vast picture window, and stood there shaking his head for what seemed like a long time. I crossed my arms and waited. Finally he stalked back over to his desk and gave his green leather swivel chair an angry spin. He glared at me. He buzzed his intercom. "Sharon, get Justin Keating in here. Yes, *now*."

Justin answered immediately. It was as if he'd been waiting for Adler's call.

Fifteen minutes later, Murph knocked a shave-and-a-haircut as he poked his head around the door. "You wanted to see me, Marty?" he asked as he poked his head around the corner of Adler's office door—it was the exact same way he'd entered *my* office about a thousand times during our years together, working side by side as colleagues at this firm.

"Yes." Adler rose somberly from his desk. "Get in here, please, Jeffrey."

Hearing his full first name, Murph laughed. "Whoa. *Jeffrey,* huh. Nobody ever called me that except my mom if I'd been playing ball in the—" He took a few steps into the room and then stopped short as I stood from Adler's couch.

The look on his face was priceless.

"Hey, Murph. Surprised to see me?" I asked.

He recovered fast. "Ingrid. Hey," he said, managing to sound almost normal. He looked questioningly from me to Adler and then at Justin, who shifted uncomfortably in the chair across from me. "What are you doing here?"

Adler sighed. "Murph, I've just heard some very disturbing revelations, and—"

"Revelations?" Murph laughed again, but I could hear the nervousness in it. "What are you talking about?"

Adler cleared his throat. "It would *appear*," he said, "that we have located a log that shows you accessed the SunCorp term sheet the night before our pre-close meeting with the clients. Now. My question to you is, why would this log say that?"

"I have no idea," said Murph.

Adler gestured toward the coffee table.

Murph shot me a look. He picked up the printout, then screwed up his forehead in a convincing approximation of bafflement. "What is this? What does it have to do with me?"

"Read it," Adler commanded.

The room was silent as Murph scanned the log.

"Check out the date and time, Murph. You purposely sabotaged the SunCorp document so I'd look bad at the meeting with Marty and the client. And we all know it."

He looked over at Adler, who glanced away.

Murph gave a desperate, wild laugh. "I don't know what the hell you're trying to prove here, Ingrid. If you're insinuating that I would deliberately forge a client document, you're even crazier and more emotional than we all thought!" He looked hopefully in Adler's direction.

Adler looked back at me. He seemed to be sizing me up, trying to decide something for himself. Murph took advantage of Adler's uncertainty to pounce on me.

"I have absolutely no idea what you're talking about, Ingrid," he hissed, rattling the printout at me.

Justin cleared his throat. He said, very quietly but clearly, "I saw you, man. It was really late, and I saw you waiting for us to finish working on the term sheet, log out, and leave for the night. That's what made me think it might have been you."

Adler was looking intently at Justin; something seemed to solidify in his expression. He turned back to Murph. "Well?"

Panic flickered in Murph's eyes, but his expression quickly reverted to outrage and disbelief. He cursed softly under his breath. Then he turned back to Adler, who was kneading his forehead between thumb and forefinger.

"Marty, listen to me," said Murph. He was struggling to keep his voice level. "You don't actually believe this, do you? You're telling me you're going to believe what this—this fucking *kid,* who's been here *three months,* has to say over what *I'm* telling you? I swear I have no idea what he's up to with this, Marty."

Adler sighed. "Justin has no reason to make any of this up."

Murph let out a caustic laugh. "How do you know that?" he spat out. "For all we know, she's been sleeping with *him,* too, along with half the firm!"

Justin's face flushed, from either anger or embarrassment, I couldn't tell.

"Now that's *enough,*" boomed Adler.

I was so angry I was actually shaking. I couldn't believe I'd been taken in by Murph's act. I'd been more than taken in. I'd been swallowed whole.

Justin spoke up again, in a louder and steadier voice. "I saw you, man."

Murph turned and looked at Justin incredulously. He opened and closed his mouth, and his bottom lip was trembling.

Adler sighed. "Murph, I'm afraid I'll have to speak to the rest of the Management Committee about this matter. You know that. And you know what that means, don't you."

Game over. I had rightly gambled that when it came down to Marty Adler having to side with either Justin or Murph, Murph didn't have a chance. Just as I hadn't stood a chance against Murph on my word alone, neither of us had stood a chance against Hunter. In the hierarchy of influence at Parsons Valentine, everything was relative.

Adler actually looked sad as he continued, "Murph, I think it's best if you take the rest of today off while we investigate this matter. If you leave quietly right now, without making a scene, there'll be absolutely no need for me to get Security involved."

"Whoa, whoa, whoa. *Security?*" Murph erupted. "This is bullshit!"

"Murph, please," Adler said. "Let's try to be reasonable and fair here. Let's not make this any more difficult than it has to be."

"Fair?" Murph whirled around and pointed at me. "*Fair?* You think I didn't see what was going on? You think I didn't know that Hunter was in and Ingrid was next?" He barked out another laugh. "She's a woman, *and* a minority. I didn't stand a goddamn chance. You think that's fuck-ing *fair?*"

"You're not leaving me with any choice here, Murph," Adler said, picking up the phone. "Yes, I need two officers from Security up here right away, please."

Murph paced around the room, ranting under his breath. Justin, Adler, and I stared at him. None of us moved.

Finally Murph turned and stared at me, shaking his head, those green eyes flashing in anger and disbelief, lips peeled back in a snarl. "Who the hell do you think you are?"

I looked at him straight on. And I was sad to find that there was utterly nothing left of the Murph I thought I knew. We were strangers to each other.

"I know exactly who I am." I added, more softly, "It's you I'd worry about."

Adler beckoned to the two beefy security guards who'd appeared in his doorway and tilted his head toward Murph. "I'd be grateful if you would please escort this gentleman from the building."

Murph shot me one last cutting look before jerking his arm away from the security guard who'd tried to take his elbow. "You can bet your ass you'll be hearing from my employment lawyer, Marty," he tossed back at Adler as the two guards steered him out of the office and down the hall.

As soon as Murph was out of sight, Adler walked silently to the door and closed it. He sighed and turned back around to me. "Ingrid," he said solemnly.

I drew up my shoulders and flashed Marty Adler a magnanimous smile. I breathed in luxuriously. I had waited for this moment. I was prepared to be gracious. I would take the high road. I was going to accept the firm's apology. It was going to be fun to see Adler grovel a bit.

"Ingrid," Adler repeated.

I waited.

"It occurs to me that the firm is now going to need someone to close the SunCorp deal as the acquisition moves into its next stage. Of course, in light of the circumstances, I think we'll be able to reinstate you immediately to your old associate position."

That was it? After everything that had happened, that was all he had to say? No apology, no *we're sorry we ever doubted you*? No *how can you ever forgive us?* No getting down on his knees and groveling at all?

Well, once again, and for the very last time, I had overestimated them. This time, though, it was okay. It made me feel better about what I was going to do next.

I smiled sweetly. "Oh, *thank* you, Marty."

Justin whipped his head around, looking incredulously at me.

"But," I continued, "I don't think you're going to need anyone to handle SunCorp anymore after all."

Adler laughed. "What are you talking about? Of course we do. First we've got to file ASAP for Hart-Scott-Rodino, then after we finally *get* regulatory approval, it'll be time for us to prepare the next round of—"

"It's definitely time for *someone* to file for regulatory approval," I agreed, then said, slowly shaking my head, "but it's not going to be Parsons Valentine."

"What in the world are you talking about, Ingrid?" Marty Adler whipped his little round glasses off his face and blinked angrily at me.

"I'm just saying," I replied, in a perfectly cool and calm voice, "that

I understand SunCorp has decided to take its legal business somewhere else.

"You see," I continued, opening my handbag and passing him the *Wall Street Journal* clipping, "Ted Lassiter was very appreciative when I let him know about the potential offshore drilling reforms that are going to be voted on shortly in both houses of Congress. If the bill passes, the current seventy-five-million-dollar cap on liability for off-shore oil spills goes away. Private companies are going to be on the hook for *everything*. And you know what that means, right?"

Marty Adler continued to blink furiously at me, wordlessly opening and closing his mouth, like a hooked fish.

"It means that would trigger the MAC clause. And that might very well mean having to pay the breakup fee. And since that's set at five percent of the purchase price . . ."

Adler looked heavenward, frantically doing the math.

". . . that would mean a hefty forty-nine-million-dollar fee to back out of the deal. Ted Lassiter was *extremely* grateful for my advising him of all this. And even more surprised that his current counsel hadn't mentioned a thing about it."

Adler started to sputter. "You poached *SunCorp*? You ungrateful little—"

"Ungrateful?" I cocked my head to one side and smiled. "I like to think of it as *my* little breakup fee from the firm. I'm walking away, Marty."

"Don't make me laugh," Adler scoffed. "I'm going to have you dis-barred so fast your head'll spin. Have you forgotten about a pesky little thing called the New York Rules of Professional Conduct? Using a client's confidential information after you've left the employ of your for-mer firm is—"

"Perfectly legal," I finished. "Not to go all Perry Mason on your ass, Marty, but let me refer you to Rule 1.9(c)(1), which provides that a lawyer who has formerly represented a client may not thereafter use the client's confidential information *to the disadvantage* of the former client. I think even you would have to agree—and I *know* Ted Lassiter certainly does—that it was to his distinct advantage for me to warn him about a potential forty-nine-million-dollar breakup fee. Not only that, but I didn't have to use any confidential information. I know that print media's supposed to be a dying beast and all, but I don't believe that a *Wall Street Journal* article qualifies as confidential information just yet."

Adler's face was bright red. He slammed a fist down on his desk, hard. He was making ineffectual little spitting sounds. Finally he closed his eyes for a beat. When he opened them a moment later, he said in a tight, strained voice, "Ingrid, let's . . . let's neither of us do anything rash. Let's just both take a moment to calm down here. I think I speak for the entire partnership when I say that, under the circumstances, we would be very willing to reconsider your partnership bid immediately, instead of deferring you any longer. Just come back to the firm. You can keep SunCorp here with us. *You* will be the relationship partner on it, I promise. *You'll* get all the credit for keeping them here."

"How thoughtful of you, Marty." I picked up my handbag and went to the door. "But I wouldn't come back to this firm if you made me managing partner."

As I turned my back on Marty Adler, I looked over at Justin and widened my eyes at him. *Thank you.* Justin was grinning at me in open admiration as he followed me out the door.

TWENTY-FOUR

❧

Murph was quietly let go the next day. Since the firm could not officially establish an unethical motivation for Murph accessing the document, his employment lawyer managed to negotiate a settlement whereby the firm agreed to give him a generally positive reference, and both parties agreed to a perpetual confidentiality and nondisparagement clause. With a decent reference from Parsons Valentine & Hunt LLP, Murph could start over at another firm, no problem—perhaps even as Of Counsel or a lateral partner. He was going to be fine. The Murphs of the world would always be fine.

But, as I was finally learning, so would I.

I had worked too hard for too long, and was too good at my job, to give up on my end goal—that is, not to pass Go and collect that final Inoculating Mark. It might have been naive to think that becoming the first minority woman partner at an esteemed international firm would make me immune to the subtle forms of racism and sexism that still enraged me—that success would thicken my skin—but I've never been able to give up on an ideal very easily.

I realized that, ultimately, someone had to try. Someone's always got to be the first one to do anything, after all. And I was never going to win as long as I continued to play by other people's rules. Instead, more of us needed to get into the business of making them up for ourselves.

The day after my story got reported in the *Wall Street Journal*—along with the business section of the *Times,* the *New York Law Journal,* Salon, Slate, Gawker, even a wittily observed "Talk of the Town" item in the following week's *New Yorker*—that is to say, the day I got my reputation back, the job offers began pouring in. And once they began to flow, they did not stop. By the end of that week alone, I had offers from nine other huge corporate firms in the city—every single one of Parsons Valentine's top competitors, along with calls from both *Fortune* and *Forbes,* who wanted to know whether I was granting interviews.

It was, of course, a very smart move for Parsons Valentine's competitors to make me an offer. An astonishingly easy PR win for one lucky firm—just by giving me a job, they'd get automatic credit for being the enlightened, twenty-first-century-thinking firm that took in the very darlingest of all the Minority Darlings, at the same time adding a talented young lawyer to their ranks. It had never been in question how hard I was going to work. Or, ultimately, that my work was of "partnership caliber."

Tyler Robinson called to congratulate me on all the job offers. I congratulated him back. Tyler had given notice the week after I was fired. The timing made it look like a protest on my behalf, but what had really happened was that an in-house job offer had materialized for him at last, and Tyler was now general counsel of a successful investment fund.

The only offer of employment I even considered for a moment, though, came a few days after my public acquittal. I got home, flushed and sweaty, from a morning run in Central Park—a new habit I'd had time to cultivate since leaving the firm—to find Dennis handing me a lush arrangement of a dozen red roses. "These just arrived for you," he said. "Secret admirer?"

I plucked the tiny cream envelope from among the blooms and read it right there in the lobby.

Slugger:

Heard you've recently become a free agent. How about coming to play on our team? I still want the right lawyer running this, as you were all along. Just say the word.

—Ted

I smiled at Dennis. "Not so secret, actually," I said.

I went straight upstairs to my apartment and called Ted Lassiter.

"I'm flattered, Ted, really I am. And yes, I'd still be delighted to close the Binney deal for you and SunCorp. But here's the thing—I don't think I'm ready to go back to working for somebody else."

"This will be different," he said. "It won't be like it was at the firm."

I hesitated. I thought about what Murph had said, about why Adler had wanted me at the SunCorp beauty pageant in the first place. "Tell me something," I said.

"Anything."

"Why didn't you ever say anything to me about SunCorp's minority vendor requirements? I know about them, okay?" I said. "I'm over it. It's okay to talk about them."

"I'd be happy to talk about them, if I knew what the hell they were," said Lassiter.

"You mean your board of directors never passed a rule? That your outside law firm's got to have at least one woman or one minority lawyer working on your deal?"

Lassiter laughed. "If they had, I'd sure as hell hear about it. Look, the only rule we've got about who SunCorp does and does not hire is that we need the best lawyer out there running our deals. Period. And as far as I'm concerned, that's you."

It was the nicest thing anyone had ever said to me. I exhaled the breath that, until then, I didn't even know I was holding.

"Now," Lassiter said. "Are you sure you won't consider coming on in-house at SunCorp? We're looking at plenty more deals coming up in the near term. Big ones. Mark Traynor could really use a terrific deputy general counsel like you."

But I had a much better idea.

TWENTY-FIVE

⟡

The law offices of Ingrid Yung PLLC officially opened for business that October. SunCorp still keeps me busy, as do all the other clients who began to buzz around one by one—shyly at first, circling warily like seventh graders at a dance, then approaching in a steadier, more confident stream, as CEOs and their general counsels began to realize that they actually recognized some of the companies on my client list, and that these other companies were getting cited and praised for being so "forward-thinking" in their selection of outside counsel.

To be sure, the *Fortune* magazine story certainly helped. The article ran with a big glossy photo of me standing by the windows with sunlight streaming into my new corner office, under the title "The Mouse That Roared: One 'Yung' Woman Takes On the Old Boys Club"—a headline that was great for business.

Also luckily for me, Margo took all of two seconds to accept the job I offered her. She then cheerfully scouted out my new office space, ordered our business cards, and set up appointments with website and logo designers and a publicist. I adore our new office—it is a lovely, light-filled, warm and inviting corner box in the sky. And yes, it has a view of the park.

I had warned Margo there would likely be a pay cut compared to Parsons Valentine, but she said she didn't care. Turns out, there wasn't a pay cut at all—it was just criminal what assistants were earning over at Parsons Valentine. No wonder they could afford to pay the lawyers so much. Margo is now my executive assistant instead of my secretary—a simple and civilized change in nomenclature that the other attorneys at my firm have adopted, too.

The other attorneys I'm talking about here are Dave Cavender, who handles our corporate tax matters (and who, now that he has more flexible hours, has been pursuing stand-up comedy on the weekends, and building up a bit of a following); Sofia Mateo, a brilliant lateral securities partner from Stratton and Thornwell, who read the *Fortune* story and called me up that same afternoon to pitch herself for a job; and our associates, Andrea Carr, Cameron Alexander, and Jason Steinberg, who all forwarded me their résumés the very same morning that my job posting went live on Above the Law, even though all three of them had already started working at Parsons Valentine.

When Andrea Carr showed up for her interview, I asked her why she would want to quit an established, known quantity like Parsons Valentine to launch her career at a start-up like mine, and she told me without blinking that she wanted to help make history, that was why. I hired her on the spot.

You might not be surprised to learn that it's much harder heading up my own law firm, but it's also the ride of my life. I love being my own boss, making up my own rules as I go along, never having to question whether I am liked, or *well liked*. It's hard work, of course. There's a lot more pressure to bring in clients, and I am, as it turns out, as Murph had tried to warn me in his own special way, *always thinking about business development.*

There are plenty of ways, obviously, in which we can't compete with the Parsons Valentines of the world. We don't have a fancy cafeteria, unlimited expense accounts, or an in-house gym. We don't take black town cars when the subway gets us where we need to go perfectly well. I can't afford a lavish summer associate program, or an R&R suite with showers and cots. (I tell my associates that the real "R&R suite" is your own apartment. If it is two in the morning, by all means, *go home already!*) Our office pantry is tiny, and I keep meaning to buy us a new coffeemaker, as the old one kind of sucks.

Having my own firm is both liberating and terrifying in equal parts.

But it's also encouraging to be surrounded by a bunch of smart, hardworking lawyers who come to work every day looking happier than I ever saw them before, who are more productive and engaged in the hours that we're actually at work because we aren't insulting each other's intelligence having to account for what we are doing every second of the day. That's right; I have dispensed with billable hours. We bill our clients by the type of transaction they want us to handle, and the results we get. This means that there is no incentive for Andrea, Cameron, or Jason to surf the Web at their desks until midnight every night, trying to rack up billable hours. It was a system that always struck me as ridiculous.

I have a casual dress policy on Fridays, but not on the other four days of the week. I *am* still running a business here, after all.

"Any messages, Margo?" I stopped by her desk on my way back from lunch.

"Your mom called," she said. "Call her back. And here's your afternoon mail." She handed me a stack of journals, letters, and bills. I leaned against the ledge and sorted through the letters quickly. A request to be on a panel titled "M&A Transactions in the 21st Century," a speaking invitation to a symposium called "Kicking In the Door: Women Leaders in the Law," and a solicitation to sponsor a table at the

Asian American Legal Defense and Education Fund's Lunar New Year Gala. I handed them all back to Margo, nodding. "Check out the dates, but yes to all three."

I walked into my office, bumped the door closed with my hip, sank into my comfy desk chair, and swiveled around to face out the window. It was a gorgeous early fall day in Central Park.

"Hello?"

"Hey, Mom."

"Ingrid-ah?"

"Yes, it's me!"

She still wasn't used to this; *me* actually calling *her* in the middle of a weekday. Now that I set my own hours and schedule, it had gotten a little easier.

"Are you still coming down to visit me and Dad this weekend?"

"Yep. I'm taking Amtrak. I'll get in around noon on Saturday."

"Good." She sounded happy. "That's all I wanted to know."

"Wait, that's it?" I said, glancing at the clock. "I still have a few minutes before my two o'clock. Nothing else you wanted to chat about?"

"Not much is new here. We'll chat when you get here." Then she asked, "How's your friend Rachel doing?"

"Rachel's fine, Mom, as always." Actually, Rachel was better than fine. She had just gone back to work, three days a week, at Proskauer. So far, so good. Now that she was back in midtown on a regular basis, we met for lunch every other Tuesday.

"That's good." I could hear my mother's car keys jangling in the background. "Ingrid-ah, I have to go now. I'm meeting Auntie Wu for lunch. I'll call you later, okay?"

"Okay," I said.

"Okay, we'll see you Saturday." My mother clicked off.

It was kind of nice, not always being the one who had to rush off the phone first.

Margo buzzed my intercom. "Ready for your two o'clock? She's here, a few minutes early."

My two o'clock appointment was with a young woman named Grace Chen, who was interviewing for a first-year associate position with my firm. She'd already met with Dave, Cameron, and Andrea last week, and they'd given her a unanimous thumbs-up. I scanned the neatly formatted résumé lying on my desk.

Name: Grace Xiao-Li Chen. College: Stanford University, summa cum laude, English and Economics. Law School: Harvard University, Order of the Coif; *Harvard Law Review,* Notes Editor; Harvard Law Women, President. Hobbies: Modern Dance, Italian Renaissance Architecture, Slam Poetry. Languages: Fluent in French and Italian; Conversationally Proficient in Mandarin Chinese.

Wow. Sometimes, as I was reviewing one or another of these kids' résumés, I felt that there was no way I would have gotten into law school had I been applying now.

I threw open my door and leaned my head out. Margo was standing just outside my door, leaning against her ledge, chatting with a radiant young woman. She was pretty, with shiny shoulder-length black hair and bright, confident eyes. Her smile was heartbreakingly earnest.

"Hi there," I said, extending my hand, smiling, and looking directly into her eyes. "You must be Grace. I'm Ingrid. Welcome. Let's talk in my office."

I was grateful that I wouldn't have to pretend to ignore her, or anyone else, ever again.

That afternoon, Cameron Alexander knocked on my office door. "Sorry to bug. Got a second?"

"Sure." I waved her in. I have a liberal open-door policy at my firm.

Cameron perched on one of the plush sage-colored armchairs opposite my desk.

"Just *one* sec, I'm about to send this off," I told her, my eyes glued to my computer screen. I was finalizing a subscription and shareholders agreement. It was the kind of simple document I'd normally leave to one of my associates, but Justin Keating's tech start-up had just gotten an impressive round of angel financing, and I'd agreed to look at their deal as a personal favor.

"There." I clicked SEND and turned my full attention to Cameron. "What's up?"

She grinned. "So I saw Grace leaving in the elevator bank earlier. What'd you think? She's pretty amazing, right?"

"Pretty amazing," I agreed. "We're still bringing back a couple of others next week, though."

Cameron nodded. "I know. We still have a ton of great résumés coming in. You know that we're the new destination firm for Harvard's Office of Career Counseling, right? I heard they're telling the top students to just apply directly. I think it's because it makes the career counseling staff feel less guilty, or something."

I laughed and knocked on the table. "Let's hope it stays that way."

Cameron cleared her throat and tucked a loose strand of golden hair back behind her ear. "So. Um, Andrea, Jason, and I have sort of been thinking . . ."

I froze. "Yes?" What, were they asking for a raise? More days off? Were they all sick of our little lab experiment already, and going back to the safety of a juggernaut like Parsons Valentine?

"We were thinking that it's time we had a firm outing. All the other firms do it. You know, take a day off and spend it somewhere fun. Just the seven of us. While the weather's still good."

Was that all? I was so happy in my relief that I laughed. I leaned back in my swivel chair and gave myself a little scoot off my desk, gliding gently toward the windows. I raised my arms and laced my fingers together behind my head. "Look. I'm fine with you guys taking a day off, you know that, but I think you also know that the Oak Hollow Country Club just really isn't my style."

She gave a vehement shake of her head. "Who said anything about a country club? Are you kidding? None of us would want it to be there. But what about someplace completely different? Someplace that's the total *opposite* of Oak Hollow."

I laughed. "What, like Coney Island?"

Her eyes lit up. "Exactly."

Andrea stopped just outside my door, her arms loaded with files. "What's this about Coney Island?"

"We will be holding our first annual Yung and Associates official firm outing at Coney Island," I informed her. "You're all cordially invited."

Andrea grinned. "Seriously? No forced golf, squash, or tennis? We don't have to eat a catered chicken puck at a white-tablecloth dinner?"

"No forced golf! No chicken pucks!" I confirmed.

Andrea and Cameron high-fived each other in the air.

We had 100 percent attendance at the Yung & Associates firm outing. Actually, more than 100 percent, if you counted Tim Hollister, who came along as my date.

Yes, *that* Tim Hollister. I'd bumped into him a month ago at a Corporate Legal Ethics CLE at the New York City Bar, and he'd stopped me on the way out. "Ingrid, it's great to see you," he'd said. "I hear your new firm's going really well. That's terrific." I remember scanning his face for any signs of a smirk. I couldn't find anything amiss.

I admit to being a little cautious, both because Tim's still a partner at Parsons Valentine and because I hadn't really dated anyone since the whole debacle with Murph, but Tim seemed genuinely happy for me. We made plans for coffee the next week, and then lunch the week after that, which lasted for three hours, and led to dinner the following week. Which lasted til the wee hours of the morning. So we shall see.

As we all meandered along the boardwalk, Tim and I polishing off a funnel cake between us, Cameron and Jason suddenly stopped short, looking up ahead.

"Oh, it's *on*," Jason said.

Cameron nodded. "It is *so* on."

I looked. They were staring straight ahead at the Cyclone.

Cameron and Jason insisted on waiting three extra rounds just so they could get the first car of the roller coaster. But when it was finally their turn to ride in front, and the train came roaring with a loud *clackety-clack* into the rickety old station, the two of them stepped aside and motioned for me and Tim to get in the front car.

"Seriously? You guys just waited three extra turns for the front," I said.

"Please. We insist."

"You sure?" said Tim.

The muscular, impressively tattooed ride attendant looked at the crowd waiting behind us and growled, "Yeah, yeah, they're sure. Come on. *Today*, people."

Tim grinned and grabbed my arm, and together we clambered into the front car of the Cyclone. Cameron and Jason, Margo and Sofia, and Dave and Andrea climbed into the three cars behind us.

I looked down and scrabbled at the sides of our car. "Where's the seat belt in this thing?"

The ride attendant strode over and gruffly pushed the single cross-bar down across our laps. "No seat belt required."

The train began to move. I grasped the single lap bar so hard my knuckles whitened.

As the famous old wooden coaster slowly climbed to the crest of the first hill, I snuck a sideways glance at Tim. He was smiling at me, peering down at the straight drop below and darting gleeful looks backward at the others, who were already squealing and pumping their fists in the air. I couldn't even remember the last time I'd been on a roller coaster. I used to really love them as a kid.

The rickety clicks grew louder and slower and farther between, and suddenly we were stopped, as the train balanced for one precarious moment high on top, as if bracing itself before it went down for its first drop.

Tim nudged my elbow. "Okay. Now let go."

"What?" I yelled, as we slowly nosed forward.

"*Let go!*" he yelled back. As we started to dip, and everyone behind us began to squeal, Tim lifted his arms from the crossbar and let out a loud, joyous whoop.

I slipped my hands off the crossbar and raised my arms high above my head in the precise moment that I felt the coaster pitch all the way forward. My stomach dropped, and I screamed at the top of my lungs. The wind rushed in my ears and my hair was loose and whipping across my face. I felt wildly free. I felt both young and fearless.

ACKNOWLEDGMENTS

I owe many people thanks for helping to see this book into the world.

I am so grateful to my editor, the wonderful Brenda Copeland, for giving this story a chance, and to all of the terrific people at St. Martin's Press, especially Sally Richardson, George Witte, Laura Chasen, Stephanie Hargadon, India Cooper, and Malati Chavali.

My fantastic literary agent, Josh Getzler, is responsible for the single best phone call I've ever received in my life. I'm also lucky to work with Danielle Burby and Mary Willems and everyone at HSG Agency. And thanks to Maddie Raffel, for plucking my manuscript out of the pile and insisting that Josh read it in the first place.

Thank you to Tanya Farrell and her team, who have contributed so much energy and enthusiasm.

I'm very fortunate to have a loving and supportive family: Peter, Catherine, and Linda Wan, and Steve, Kathie, and Mindy Burrell. My mom and dad had the foresight to get me a manual typewriter from Sears in the fourth grade, on which I happily banged out stories about an intrepid crime-fighting family called The Dixon Detectives. That old typewriter is still the best birthday present I've ever gotten.

Thanks to all of the friends and fellow writers who read early pages

ACKNOWLEDGMENTS

and offered wisdom, especially Maureen Brady, Susan Cain, Susan Chi, Jen Egan, Rachel Geman, Melissa Haley, Mikaela McDermott, Miriam Parker, David Rogers, Sarah Shey, and Kera Yonker.

I'm also indebted to Mindy Burrell, Shirley Chi, Ann Dolloff, Jinee Kim Ellis, Jenny Eugenio, Yuki Hirose, Natalie Krodel, Drew Patrick, John Reed, John Rudolph, Julia Rudolph, Madhu Goel Southworth, Wendy Stryker, Christine Tefft, Matt Walker, and Marissa Walsh for, over the course of many years, always asking after my novel as if it were a real thing. This simple gesture helped me more than you'll ever know.

Finally, I am grateful to my husband, Andrew Burrell, who, with patience and great kindness, ultimately coaxed this story into being. And to our son, Alex, who was not yet around during the actual writing of this book, but whose recent arrival has made the wait for publication an even happier time. Thank you, with so much love.

1. Ingrid and her best friend Rachel chose two very different paths after law school: Ingrid is poised to be the first female corporate partner at Parsons Valentine, while Rachel quit her own prestigious career years ago to stay home and raise a family. What do you think each woman thinks of the other's choices? And how does this influence their friendship?

2. At Ingrid's first meeting with client Ted Lassiter, he mistakes her for the paralegal, and assumes that Justin is the attorney. Have you ever experienced a similar scenario and how did you handle it? What do you think of Ingrid's and Marty Adler's responses to the incident?

3. Early in the novel, we learn about a childhood memory in which Ingrid's family experiences discrimination while on a trip to New York. How do you think this experience drives Ingrid's choices and identity as an adult?

4. How does being Chinese American seem to influence Ingrid's behaviors and actions at work? How has your own cultural or family upbringing affected a professional or personal choice you've made?

5. Ingrid makes a lot of assumptions about people around her: Murph, Justin, Cameron Alexander. Is this fair? Is it right for her to assume that others at the firm feel comfortable all the time in their own skin? Hasn't everyone had an "A.1. Steak Sauce moment"?

6. Was the rap parody at the firm outing handled effectively? Should the lawyers who performed the skit have been held accountable?

7. As a young Parsons Valentine lawyer, Ingrid tries to differentiate herself from Zhang Liu, the "other" Asian American associate. Why? Is this fair? Do you think Ingrid had any responsibility to Zhang Liu to act or respond differently?

8. Ingrid tries to seek out Ellen Chu Sanderson, but is rebuffed. Why? Was it fair for Ingrid to expect a different reaction? How much of an obligation do we have to "mentor" or "sponsor" those who come after us?

St. Martin's Griffin

9. Ingrid has perfected the art of "passing"—that is, seamlessly blending into the particular corporate culture at Parsons Valentine. How much has Ingrid had to "assimilate" into white male corporate culture, if at all? Is it always necessary to try to "pass" in order to achieve career success? Or is it ever possible to remain an "authentic" self while succeeding in this type of corporate environment?

10. Professor Tanaka tells Ingrid: "Sometimes, Ingrid, in the grander scheme, it behooves us to do certain things not because we *want* to, but because we are among the very few who *can*." Do you agree with this statement? Just because someone *can*, does it follow that she *must*?

11. Ingrid acknowledges that she, Rachel, and their peers are all extremely privileged women with many opportunities, but yet they have "not quite figured out how to have It All. At least not All at the Same Time." Do you agree with this statement? Is it really possible to have It All?

12. Ingrid tells Murph: "The reason you've never dated any smart, successful women before is that you can't handle it. You can't stand the idea that a woman might be better at this than you." Is she right?

13. Upon leaving the firm, Ingrid blames herself for being "duped." She says: "I had happily held out my hand and allowed myself to be led, like Hansel and Gretel, down the path, stupidly following the bread crumbs all these years, and now I had absolutely nothing to show for it. I had completely bought into the myth of a meritocracy." Do you agree that meritocracy is a myth?

14. Ingrid ultimately rejects a comfortable and cushy job offer from SunCorp and instead chooses a professional path that she finds "both liberating and terrifying in equal parts." Would you have made the same choice in her shoes?

For more reading group suggestions,
visit www.readinggroupgold.com.